HOT

A BLACK KNIGHTS INC. NOVEL

PURSUIT

JULIE ANN WALKER

sourcebooks
casablanca

Published by Sourcebooks Casablanca, an imprint of Sourcebooks, Inc.
P.O. Box 4410, Naperville, Illinois 60567-4410
(630) 961-3900
Fax: (630) 961-2168
sourcebooks.com

Printed and bound in the United States of America.
OPM 10 9 8 7 6 5 4 3 2 1

*To those who were afraid to take the leap that is love,
but did so anyway. This one's for you.*

Before you embark on a journey of revenge, dig two graves.

—Japanese proverb

Prologue

Kirkuk, Iraq
Eight Years Ago...

"WHO SENT YOU? WHAT DO YOU WANT?"

The policeman's accent made his words guttural and hard, but they were nothing compared to the granite fist that smashed into Christian Watson's nose. A geyser of blood gushed over his lips and seeped into the cut on his chin that had come courtesy of the first round of questioning.

Which had been...what? Twenty minutes ago? Two hours?

Time slowed when you were getting the sodding shit beaten out of you.

One of Christian's eyes was swollen shut. The other was split in the corner so when he opened it, the crust that had formed over the wound cracked and burned. The pain was worth it to see the fury and impotence on the policeman's face.

"My name is Christian Watson. I am a corporal in Her Majesty's Special Air Service." He rattled off his serial number before clamping his jaws shut. That was all the information the Geneva Conventions required of him. He would give no more.

Another blow landed on his cheek, making his eye feel like it would explode out of its socket. Following *that was a punch that drove deep into his gut, precisely over the spot where the bullet had gone through and through. The accompanying pain was a living thing that chewed at his intestines with hungry, needle-like teeth.*

Dizziness and nausea crashed over him. He might have retched had the chair he was tied to not toppled backward with the force of the blow. When it collided with the floor in the tiny interrogation room, the sound his skull made as it bounced off the tiles was sickening, even to his own ears.

Darkness closed in on him, a malevolent specter hovering at the edge of his vision.

For the first time since he'd opened fire at the roadblock, fear tried to take root in his heart. He could not lose consciousness. Loss of consciousness was a loss of control. Loss of control terrified him worse than any corrupt Iraqi police officer ever could.

He struggled against his restraints as his head swam sickly. Trying not to gag at the iron-rich smell of his own blood, he narrowly opened his one good eye to glare up at the policeman. His assailant wore a nasty smile. The hateful expression reminded Christian of a man from long ago. A man who had inflicted pain for the simple pleasure of it. A man who—

The space around Christian shimmered and changed, melting into a new, more terrifying whole. Suddenly he was six years old, inside his boyhood room. Gone were the scents of blood and sweat and dry wind heavy with dust. They were replaced by the smells coming from the hulking shadow looming over him: whiskey and smoke, with an underlying hint of rot.

The shadow reached for him. Massive, ham-hock hands curved into brutal, inescapable claws.

Christian whimpered, scooting backward. But there was no place to go. Nowhere to run.

"Mum!" he yelled, his voice hoarse with terror. "Mum, please!"

But she would not come. It was too late. She was too far gone. He knew she would not come.

A telltale shhhhnick *sounded as a lighter flamed to life. Orange light flickered in the darkness, licking fire into the brutal eyes of the shadowy man. Now he looked like what he was. Sadistic. Cruel. Evil incarnate.*

Christian braced himself for what would come next. Even so, the first sizzle of fiery pain shocked him with its intensity.

Tossing back his head, he screamed…

Port Isaac, Cornwall, England

"Wake up, damnit! Wake *up*!"

Christian bolted upright in bed. For a couple of confusing seconds he'd lost the plot, not knowing where he was. *When* he was. There was only darkness and the lingering memory of agony. There was only…*her*. Emily Scott. The woman who had crawled under his skin and made a home for herself there.

Tunneling up his nose was the exotic smell of her shampoo. It caused him to snap back to the here and now as if he'd been fired from a slingshot.

Buggering hell, he thought at the same time Emily said, "Holy fucking shit!"

The woman had a mouth on her that never failed to delight him. He might have smiled, had the words she'd spoken not been thick with recently disturbed sleep and something more. Something he thought might be fear.

No doubt he'd been screaming his fool head off. Which would scare the socks off of a seasoned operator, much less a pretty pipsqueak of an office manager who had somehow managed to embroil herself in a mission she had no business being part of.

Buggering hell, he thought again as remnants of the dream—correction: *dreams*—shuddered through him.

Months. That's how long it had been since he'd awoken in a pool of sweat, thrashing about as he tried to escape the ghosts of his past. He had hoped that perhaps he might have properly outdistanced them. Unfortunately, they appeared to be as keen and inescapable as ever. *The rat bastards*.

Embarrassment and shame had him running a hand over his face. The growth of his day-old whiskers rasped against the calluses on his palm.

"Hey." She shook his shoulder as if uncertain he was truly awake. "You were having a nightmare." Her Chi-Town accent emphasized the *A* in all her words, making her sound tough. Which was funny, considering she looked about as dangerous as a baby bunny.

His words were harsher than he meant them to be when he said, "No shit, Sherlock."

She drew back, taking the smell of her shampoo with her. His heart immediately hurled itself against his rib cage, as if trying to lessen the distance she'd put between them.

She huffed with exasperation, and he knew he should apologize. But the words stuck in his throat. He couldn't stomach the thought that she'd seen him like that.

So vulnerable.

So exposed.

So...*out of control*.

"You know"—she didn't attempt to disguise the venom in her voice—"a normal person would say, 'Thank you, Emily. Thank you for waking me up before I punched a hole through the bloody wall.'"

She'd donned an English accent. It was adorable. And total rubbish. She sounded more like a New Zealander than an Englishwoman.

"You're right," he admitted. "You're totally right. I'm sorry. Thank you for waking me."

His eyes had adjusted to the darkness, and he homed in on the fact that she was wearing a familiar, frayed pullover. Her brown hair was a rumpus of flyaway waves, and her face was scrubbed clean of makeup. Also—and this was a *huge* also—she wasn't wearing a bra. He was quite certain he could make out the subtle jut of her nipples through the thick fabric of her shirt.

Bloody hell. He was staring at her boobs.

Stop staring at her boobs.

Right-oh. Problem was, not staring was a tall order, considering that from the top of Emily's head to the tips of her unpainted toes, she was beautiful. Not beautiful like all those Hollywood starlets with their fake hair, medically enhanced bodies, and loads of cosmetics, but beautiful in a timeless, effortless way.

Emily's slim figure was subtly curved. She had a pert nose, big dark eyes, and a lush mouth. If he had to put a label on it, he'd say she possessed an ingenue-esque air. It tended to cause a male stampede anytime she walked into a room.

Unfortunately for him, right now she was in *his* room.

Okay. Hold the front page. Given that Emily *was* gorgeous and the cause of many a male stampede, you might ask *why* having her in his room was unfortunate, as opposed to a dream come true.

The answer was simple. Since the day he had met her, she'd made it clear she had no interest in him in *that* way. Certainly she enjoyed having him on. Taunting him. On a regular basis she took strips from his hide with the sharpness of her tongue. But when it came to nocturnal activities? Well, it was safe to say she was the equivalent of a human stop sign. *Do not pass Go. Do not collect two hundred quid.*

Masochist that he was, that made him fancy her more. As if to prove the point, his flag had already hoisted itself to half-staff. He wanted to blame his condition on those nipples. *Stop staring at her boobs!* But walking around with a half-chub was pretty much SOP when Emily was within ten meters of him.

"Do you want to talk about it?" she asked. Morning's first tender light chose that moment to filter in through the crack in the curtains. It glowed over her smooth, unblemished skin, highlighted the beauty mark high on her right cheek, and showed the sympathy in her warm eyes.

"Talk about what?"

"Your nightmare."

He snorted. "About as much as I'd fancy having my bollocks shaved with a rusty razor blade."

For a moment she was silent. Then her lips curved at the corners. "Whatever floats your boat."

A joke. She was trying to tease the tension out of him. Which might have worked, had she been anyone else.

Had she *not* had such a hypnotic smile. He was afraid if he stared at it too long, he'd fall under its spell and be helpless to do anything but its bidding.

Glancing through the slit in the curtains, he eyed the sliver of view beyond. The rising sun cast the beach in a pearlescent glow. Golden rays turned the tops of the waves in the harbor pink and silver. It was a scene from his childhood. Back when his childhood had been…if not brilliant, then at least bearable. Before it'd become a string of long, lonely days and terrifying nights.

"What time is it?" he asked, trying not to notice how his thigh touched her hip through the fabric of the quilt.

"Just past oh-six-hundred. You still have time to get more sleep."

"Not possible."

Her expression was compassionate. "Bad dreams do that to me too. I've found it helps if someone stays with me. You know, to sort of guard against the nightmare's return. Do you want me to stay with you?"

Good God, was she serious? He wanted her to stay with him more than anything. But he couldn't have her in his room, in his *bed*, without touching her. And since in the world of unwritten rules, not touching a woman unless she invited him to was bold, underlined, and all in caps, she needed to leave.

"Indeed not. I'm fine. But thank you. Thank you for checking on me. For waking me." He risked looking into her eyes and immediately knew it for the mistake it was. He was used to seeing a mischievous glint there, used to seeing derision or vexation or, hell, occasionally even grudging respect. What he was *not* used to seeing was tenderness.

Not that Emily was unkind. Quite the contrary. Beneath her tough outer shell, she had an incredibly soft underbelly. Problem was, she rarely showed *him* her softer side. Choosing instead to give him all the sharp edges she had honed while growing up in Chicago's blue-collar Bridgeport neighborhood.

She placed a hand on his thigh, and it immediately brought him out in a sweat. "If you're sure you don't—"

"I'm sure." He was quick to cut her off.

"You're good at playing the tough guy, aren't you?"

He quirked a brow, made sure his expression was all arrogance. "I haven't a need to play at it, darling."

Tossing her head back, she laughed. The sight of her exposed throat, combined with the low, husky roll of her amusement, had his flag hoisting itself to full staff.

Bloody stupid appendage!

How unfair it was that men had to do daily battle with the sex organ attached to them. Especially since that sex organ had zero brains and beastly timing.

Emily lowered her chin to regard him, that hypnotic smile still on her lips. "Let no one ever accuse you of a lack of confidence, Christian."

He considered pretending he hadn't heard her so she'd say his name again. The way she pronounced it always hit him like a shot of aged whiskey—warm, potent, and intoxicating. But instead he went with, "You say that like it's a bad thing."

"It's not. I like a confident man."

"Careful," he warned. "That sounded suspiciously like you admitted to liking me."

She shrugged. It was a delicate, unconsciously graceful gesture. "Well, I don't *dislike* you."

Heat unfurled in his belly. To distract her from the heightened color in his cheeks and the predatory gleam that had entered his eyes, he donned an expression of annoyance. "Damned with faint praise."

"Oh, it's praise you want? Well, I'm afraid you've come to the wrong woman. I'm bad at compliments."

"That's the understatement of the century." Although, truth be told, he'd heard her compliment their coworkers on many occasions. But for some reason, she was total rubbish at flinging admiration *his* way.

Which was probably why his jaw slung open when she took a deep breath and blurted, "You have really pretty eyes."

Scriiiiiitch. That sound was a needle scratching across his mental record. Had Emily Watson said he had pretty eyes? Backup. Reset. Not just pretty eyes, but *really* pretty eyes?

How odd she should think so. He'd always thought his eyes a bit…spooky. They were a strange color, somewhere between green and gold. Too light when paired with his tan skin and dark hair. Hadn't he been told as much? Hadn't his spooky eyes caused—

He crushed the memory and glanced around the room as if furtively searching for something. "Hang on a minute," he said.

"What is it? What are you looking for?"

"The white bunny. I seem to have fallen down the rabbit hole."

She swatted his arm, not attempting to be gentle. Pervy shit that he was, he liked it. Then again, how pervy was it to fancy the touch—even the abusive touch—of a woman like Emily Scott?

"See? And that's why I don't compliment you. You don't know how to take it."

"I'm sorry. You're absolutely right. Let's try this again, shall we? You think I have really pretty eyes?" He fluttered his eyelashes for effect.

She groaned and pushed up from the bed. He felt the loss of her weight, the loss of her hip against his thigh, the loss of her exotic-smelling shampoo, in a place he dared not name. "And besides," she added, "your ego is big enough without me giving it the occasional stroke."

His breath caught on the last word. It seemed to hang in the air, pounding like a heartbeat.

If she noticed his sudden tension, she gave no indication as she sauntered toward the door. Turning at the threshold, she said, "Since you're not going to get any more sleep, how about you cook breakfast for the ravenous horde, huh? I could use another hour of shut-eye."

She stretched her arms over her head and let out a mighty yawn. Her older-than-the-hills pullover inched away from the waistband of her pajama bottoms. A flash of pale, silky skin turned his mouth into a desert.

"Speaking of the ravenous horde," he said, or rather rasped, "are they still asleep? Did I wake them?"

She glanced down the hall, her dark hair falling over her shoulder in a silky curtain he longed to touch. "The lights are off in their rooms. I think I was the only one who heard. You know, since we share a wall."

Ah, yes. The shared wall.

The wall he had stared at for the last five nights while they waited for things to get sorted so they could come out from hiding and return to Chicago. The wall he might have, just maybe, pressed his ear against a time or two in the hopes of hearing her…what? Snoring? Breathing? Pleasuring herself?

He stifled a groan.

"So?" She cocked her head. "Will you?"

"Will I what?"

She frowned like his IQ had dropped fifty points in the last five seconds. Which, if he was being honest, it had. It *did*. Anytime she was in the room.

"Will you make breakfast? I know it's my turn, but—"

"Say no more." He lifted a hand. "It's done." Because even if breakfast duty was at the top of precisely no one's list, he was glad to assume the responsibility if it would get Emily out of his room. After having her so close for so long, he definitely needed some alone time with his John Thomas. "A traditional English breakfast it is," he added when she seemed to need additional reassurance.

She wrinkled her nose. "I can get on board with the sautéed mushrooms and the roasted tomato, but I've never understood beans for breakfast."

"They're good for your heart."

Even from across the dim room, he saw her eyes ignite with mischief. Emily enjoyed pushing buttons, saying things that were hysterically crass. He assumed it was because she fancied keeping the people around her off-balance. "The more you eat, the more you—"

"Good God!" he scolded before she could finish the hideous children's rhyme. "Grow up, will you?"

She drove him completely barmy. But she also made him laugh. And in his line of work…bloody hell, in his entire sodding *life*…laughter wasn't something that came easily.

"So stuffy," she complained. It was a familiar accusation.

"I'm not stuffy. I'm English, darling."

"My point exactly."

"Hurtful." He crossed his arms and thrust out his chin. If he wasn't mistaken, her eyes alighted on his bare pecs, then traveled briefly over the sleeves of black, winding tattoos that covered his arms from his shoulders to wrists.

Is that interest I see in her eyes? he wondered hopefully.

He wasn't bad to look at. He knew that. Not that he had to fight the women away with sticks or anything, but neither did he have to look very hard for a willing bed partner. Alas, whatever brief flicker of intrigue he thought he saw in her eyes disappeared before he had the chance to study it.

"Will you be happy to leave home today?" she asked, still lingering in his doorway.

"England isn't home," he assured her, his mood dropping into the loo. The good to come of *that* was that his John Thomas followed suit. So, apparently there were two cures for his flag flying at full staff. One, a swift rub and tug. Or two, talk of the country that had betrayed him. "It hasn't been for a long time."

She considered him for a moment more, then nodded and turned to knock off back to her own room. Before she disappeared down the hall, she got in a parting shot. If he had known how portentous her words would be, he might have stayed in bed with the blankets over his head. "Someday you're going to tell me what happened here."

Chapter 1

EMILY SCOTT WAS HAVING A GOOD DAY.

She'd pawned breakfast duty off on Christian. She was wearing her favorite sweatshirt, the one Paulie Konerko had signed after he helped the White Sox win the 2005 World Series. And she was on her way home. Back to the world of baseball and deep-dish pizza, towering skyscrapers and a lake so big and blue it looked like an ocean.

Add to that the fact that she would no longer have to stay cooped up in a tiny cottage with four of the most testosterone-packed males on the planet, and she'd go so far as to say her day wasn't good; it was Tony the Tiger *grrrreat*. Which was why she should have been prepared for things to start circling the drain.

Long ago, she'd discovered that good days were the ones she should worry about, since life liked to rise up and bite her on the ass when she least expected it.

Case in point: she found herself blinking in slack-jawed astonishment when two hours after she finished scarfing down Christian's delightful English breakfast—minus the baked beans, natch—he opened the front door of his uncle's cottage only to have a microphone shoved in his face.

"Are you Corporal Christian Watson?" a redheaded woman in a yellow pantsuit demanded. "Is it true you were the SAS soldier captured during the Kirkuk Police Station Incident?"

"Where have you been, Corporal Watson?" a man in a raincoat and cabbie hat demanded, holding up a digital recorder. "What have you been on about since you left Her Majesty's Special Air Service?"

Emily got a glimpse of half a dozen other people gathered on the cottage's front stoop—a honking big camera on the shoulder of one man—before Christian slammed the door shut and twisted the lock. His face was a thundercloud when he swung back into the room.

"Bloody, fecking hell," he snarled, then followed that with a string of profanity so blue it would make a sailor blush.

Why did curse words sound better coming out of his mouth? Oh, right. Because *everything* sounded better coming out of his mouth. That accent!

Turning to the trio of men behind her, Emily found their expressions mirrored her own. In a word: shock. In two words: rampant curiosity. And in three words? Well, *what the fuck?* came to mind.

"What in the ass?" Ace asked, adjusting the straps of his backpack more comfortably on his broad shoulders.

They all had backpacks stuffed with the essentials needed to flee the country—basic toiletries and a change of clothes. Usually included in their "essentials" was an array of handguns, knives, and other pointy or bangy things which, when used correctly, resulted in death. But they'd had to leave their arsenal behind during their initial attempt to hop the pond a few days prior. Since then, Emily had wondered if the men felt naked without their customary repository of combat blades and sidearms.

"I mean, seriously, what in the *ass*?" Ace repeated.

Colby "Ace" Ventura was a former U.S. Navy pilot

turned operator for Black Knights Inc., the covert government defense firm founded and privately run by none other than the president of the United States himself—now the *former* president of the United States—and staffed by some of the blackest of black-ops warriors on the planet. The firm Emily had gone to work for after she bugged out of the CIA. Although, in reality, it was probably more accurate to say the Black Knights had taken her under their wings after the fiasco with her former boss had *forced* her out of the CIA.

For the record, *she* wasn't one of the blackest of black-ops warriors. She was their office manager, having come along on this mission in a failed attempt to keep them organized, on task, and out of trouble.

"That's one way of putting it," she said. "Another way of putting it would be to steal the timeless words of Ricky Ricardo." She exaggerated her expression. "Christian…you got some 'splainin' to do."

All those hours parked in front of the television as a kid watching reruns of *I Love Lucy* while her parents were out doing who the hell knew what had paid off with a spot-on impersonation.

Unfortunately, her flippancy was wasted on Christian. "Shit," he hissed, followed by "Bloody, fecking hell."

"You said that already." She tried her best to lighten his mood. Anytime she thought of the vulnerability she'd seen in his eyes in that first second after she woke him from his nightmare, her silly, squishy, far-too-soft heart turned over. "Try something else. I like to go with *bugfucking dickmunch* or *son of a bee-stung bitch*. But I might also suggest—"

"Sod off, Emily." He glowered at her. Really, Christian

could glower like nobody's business. "Now is not the time for your scathing wit."

"No? And here I was thinking *any* time was a good time for scathing wit."

"There are bloody reporters outside."

"Yep. Saw 'em with my own two beady eyes."

This time he gifted her with a put-upon grimace. The man seemed to have a vast arsenal of sexy sneers and bone-melting scowls. And truth? She enjoyed each and every one of them.

They gave her a glimpse at the real man beneath the carefully styled hair, the designer clothes, and the expensive whatnots. The man who was down and dirty, gruff and gritty. The man a part of her couldn't wait to meet.

Only *part* of her, you might ask? Yes, only *part* of her. The wild part. The careless part. The *crazy* part that didn't have a thought in its ditzy, horny little head except *Yowza! Gimme, gimme, gimme!*

As you might imagine, that was the part she tried like hell to ignore, choosing instead to focus on the *other* part of her. The sensible part. The rational part. The practical part that didn't dare give him any more sexy ammunition to use against her already panting libido.

"What do we do now?" Ace asked.

"Back door," Angel said, already turning. Angel was a former Israeli Mossad agent turned fellow BKI badass. Emily didn't know much about him other than that he was a big ol' question mark, his past even more shadowed than Christian's.

"Right. Good idea." She hustled after him. Unfortunately, before they reached the back door, they heard the sound of voices coming from behind it.

"Trapped," she whispered, her heart kicking into overdrive. She would have liked to think the sudden uptick was a product of their increasingly alarming situation. But the truth was, it was at least partly due to Christian having come to a stop directly behind her, close enough that she could feel the blast of his body heat.

Once again, the wild, careless part of her tried to rear its ugly head. And who could blame it, considering Christian's looks were those of the high desert. Harsh. Dangerous. Stark. Like an oasis in the sand, his eyes glittered and shone.

Intensely masculine, that's what he was. Carnal. *Primal*. Six feet, three inches of big bones and hero hair and a tempting little chin dimple. The kind of guy who was attractive because he oozed confidence and testosterone and power. A breaker of hearts. A slayer of vaginas. He could get most women sweaty just by breathing.

Lucky for her, she wasn't most women.

Fine. So maybe she *was*. Because, seriously, *not* lusting after his hot bod was kind of like saying to herself, *See that fat, furry bulldog puppy? Do* not *think he's cute.* Still, whether she wanted to jump his bones was neither here nor there, since she'd learned not to mix business with pleasure. Once bitten, twice shy, baby.

"This is bad," he muttered, taking a step back. The wild, careless part of her wept while the sensible, practical part of her rejoiced.

"Worse than bad," Ace agreed.

"We need to calm down," Angel insisted in that precise way he had. Jamin "Angel" Agassi's diction was some of the best Emily had ever heard. But his voice? It was a wreck. Likely due to the fact that he'd had his vocal cords scoured after he left Israel to avoid voice-recognition software.

Talk about *ew*, not to mention *ow*.

"Right." Ace nodded. "Before we get overly excited, we need to know what we're dealing with." He lifted an inquiring brow at Christian. "Is it true? Were you the one captured during the Kirkuk Police Station Incident?"

Emily turned to study Christian's face and saw the muscle twitching beneath his right eye. As far as she could figure, it was his only tell and happened when he was really pissed or really annoyed. Which, okay, meant it happened a *lot* when she was around.

"Yes," Christian said after a five-second beat. "That would be me."

"Holy hobbling Christ on a crutch," Ace swore, running a hand through his blond hair.

"What?" Rusty Parker, a.k.a. the only civilian in the group, asked. "What was the Kirkuk Police Station Incident?"

Rusty was a former marine who had worked one summer as a CIA asset before he up and moved to England to become a charter boat captain. Emily had helped him out of a jam that summer, and they'd kept in touch ever since. When she and the other members of BKI had needed help fleeing the country the week before, after they had screwed up their mission to bring down a notorious underworld crime boss known only by the code name of Spider, Rusty had been the first person she called.

Poor guy, she thought now. She wouldn't have dragged him into this if she'd known how much trouble she was going to cause him.

"Yeah." She nodded. "I'm with Rusty. What *was* the Kirkuk Police Station Incident?"

Christian shook his head. "We've no time for this."

"Sure we do. Since our only exits are blocked by reporters, we have all the time in the world."

Christian blew out an exasperated breath that caused a whorl of hair to fall over his brow. It tried to distract Emily, but she refused to let it.

"Fine. But let's bloody well make this quick, okay?"

"We're all ears," she assured him. "Fire away."

That muscle twitched beneath his eye again. It was joined by one in his jaw. "It was near the end of the Iraq War, after major hostilities had ceased and before the incursion of ISIS into the country. I was sent in to keep an eye on a group of Iraqi policemen who were running a crime unit with rumored links to corruption and brutality in the city. My job was to gather enough evidence against them to warrant a takedown."

"Oh, I remember reading about this." Rusty narrowed his eyes in thought. "There was a shoot-out at a road-block, right?"

Christian nodded, and that dadgummed whorl snagged Emily's attention. Again.

Down, girl, she admonished her recalcitrant libido.

"Unbeknownst to me, the policemen I was tasked with surveilling had sniffed me out. I was setting off from the city to deliver a situation report to my commanding officer when I was stopped at a roadblock. At the start, I thought I could talk my way out of it, yeah? But things got quite serious quite quickly. They pulled their weapons and began shooting. I pulled mine and did the same. Took a round to the gut that put me in sad shape.

But before they managed to overwhelm me, I slotted two of the wankstains."

He said it so casually. *Before they managed to overwhelm me*. But Emily knew Christian. It must have been one hell of a fight.

"They took me 'round to the police station, where they questioned me for eight hours," he added.

Questioned. Ha! A nice way of saying he had been interrogated and likely tortured. Visions of beatings, stabbings, and oxygen deprivation bloomed in Emily's mind. It was enough to have her breakfast threatening to reverse directions.

"Is that what you were dreaming about this morning?" she asked. If the hoarse screams that had jolted her from a dead sleep were any indication, Christian's eight hours in the hands of the Iraqis had been brutal.

The look he shot her was quick and definitive, the facial equivalent of *Shut your trap*. But it was too late. Ace glanced back and forth between them, a shit-eating grin spreading across his handsome face.

"How would *you* know what he was dreaming about this morning, hmm?" Ace widened his blue eyes. "Is there something the two of you would like to tell us? Like, maybe you've finally had enough foreplay and it's time to get down to the main event?"

"Foreplay?" Emily scowled. "I don't know what the hell you're talking about."

"Oh, sure you do. All that one-upping? The verbal sparring? That's foreplay, luv."

She waved a hand through air still tinged with the smell of bacon and buttered toast. "Whatever. One-upmanship is nothing more than good, clean fun. And maybe some ego management on my part." She gifted Christian with a squinty-eyed stare, indicating his length with her hand. "I mean, you've seen him, right? The clothes. The hair. The smile. Someone has to keep him grounded."

"Rrrright." Ace nodded.

She rolled her eyes and turned to Christian. "Tell him."

Christian lifted an eyebrow that asked, *Tell him what?*

She thinned her lips and widened her eyes. Her expression said, *Tell him I'm right*.

Instead of siding with her, Christian said, "Can we please circle back 'round to the bloody subject? In case you've forgotten, there are *reporters* outside preventing us from catching our flight and getting off this sodding rock!"

Did he think their bickering was foreplay? The idea had an unwelcome trill skipping up her spine. Muscles that had no business clenching—specifically those at the tips of her breasts and between her legs—did just that.

She didn't delude herself when it came to Christian. And despite her protestations to the contrary, she *did* want him. *I mean, who wouldn't?* But he'd given no indication he felt the same. In fact, he found her *as vexing as a housefly*. His words. Not hers.

Which was fine and dandy.

It was!

After all, there was that whole "no mixing of business and pleasure" edict she was determined to live by. And even if there *wasn't*, the two of them were oil and water.

He wore designer clothes and drove a Porsche. She preferred yoga pants and sweatshirts, usually from the discount rack at Target. There was an air of mystery surrounding him, depths she dared not plumb. And she? Well, she was pretty much an open book.

"In response to my capture," Christian continued, "Ten members of the 22nd SAS Regiment along with a whole platoon of paratroopers from special forces flew in from Baghdad to retrieve me. They stormed the police station and got me out, killing three police officers on top of the two I'd taken out at the roadblock and leaving one SAS soldier…"

His voice trailed off, and the look that came over his face was one Emily hadn't seen before. *Sadness.* Not surface-level sadness, but deep, abiding, fabric-of-his-being sadness. The episode in Iraq haunted him to this day.

Her heart clenched in sympathy.

"It caused a huge international outcry, if memory serves," Ace said, picking up the thread Christian had dropped.

"The Iraqis wanted blood, revenge, recompense." Christian's voice was softer now. "Newspapers in the UK sided with them, calling the SAS trigger-happy." There was disbelief and more than a hint of derision in his face. "It didn't matter that had I been left in that police station, the Iraqis would have killed me. It didn't matter that I was under bloody direct *orders* to take any and all action necessary to avoid capture. And it didn't matter that the policemen in question were as crooked as a country lane. For all intents and purposes, the war was over. It was meant to be peacetime. We were meant to be allies. The news agencies said that because of the SAS officer who had opened fire at the roadblock, five Iraqi policemen were dead and the tentative peace between our countries was put at risk."

"They blamed you," Angel said, his dark eyes intense. As always.

Besides the vocal-cord scouring, Angel had undergone extensive plastic surgery to change his appearance. To say his surgeon had been a genius was an understatement. Angel was…well…*angelic*. So beautiful he was hard to look at.

But the surgeon hadn't been able to alter his eyes. There was a world of dark knowledge in Angel's eyes. When Emily combined that with the fact that his records had been redacted out the wazoo and she had no idea what hellish catastrophe or fuckup had caused him to leave Israel and undergo all that surgery in the first place, she had to admit he creeped her out. Just a little.

Okay, maybe a lot.

"That they did." Christian nodded. "Well, not *me* precisely. The press didn't know my name. They only knew that one of Her Majesty's Special Air Service members was the cause of the mess. And since the SAS prides itself on keeping the egg off its face, the brass were only too pleased to jump on the bandwagon. They assured the press that I, the officer responsible, would be decommissioned."

The muscle beneath his right eye was twitching again. "True to their word, two months after the incident, to throw any investigators off the trail of a man being let go so soon after, they pushed me out. I was told if I went quietly, if I didn't make a fuss, my official records would show I'd left the Service in good standing and with all due honors. No one but those with access to my classified files would ever know I was the one involved in the police station fiasco." He snorted. "I suppose it was the brass's idea of offering me an olive branch for all the good work I'd done."

Emily finally understood why he no longer thought of England as his home. He'd risked everything for his country, had nearly given his life, and when he'd needed her protection and support the most, Mother England had—

Bam! Bam! Bam! A loud fist landed on the door. The woman in the yellow pantsuit yelled, "Corporal Watson! Why did you open fire at the roadblock that day?"

"We need to get out of here, and fast," Ace muttered, glancing around the modest living area. Like any good English cottage, the place was a study in whimsy, decorated with antiques and plush, well-lived-in upholstered furniture. There was even the requisite painting of a partridge over the fireplace. "We can't afford to have our faces splashed all over the BBC."

"Like *I* can?" Christian thundered. "I'm a covert operator too, in case you've forgotten. Not to mention that my identity and involvement in Kirkuk were meant to be top secret."

"Well, I hate to break it to you, bro." Ace placed a sympathetic hand on Christian's shoulder. "But the secret's out."

"Now we concentrate on protecting our covers," Angel said.

Emily's eyes widened. "You have a plan to do that?"

Angel pointed toward the ceiling. "Create a distraction."

She glanced up, expecting to be enlightened. She wasn't. There was nothing up there but off-white paint, a silver light fixture, and a dusty cobweb in the corner.

"By doing what?" she asked. "Setting the roof on fire?"

Angel smiled. Or, at the very least, one corner of his mouth twitched. Which was as close to smiling as Angel ever came. "Be ready to run when the time is right."

Without any further discussion, he headed for the stairs. She watched him go with equal parts curiosity and incredulity.

"Am I the only one who feels like her ass is hanging in the breeze here?" she asked. "When will the time be right? How will we know?"

Christian grabbed her arm and gave it a squeeze. Okay, *what*? He *never* touched her. Not voluntarily anyway.

"Don't worry." He ducked his dimpled chin until they were eye to eye. He really did have the prettiest eyes, like molten glass, so bright and hot. "It'll be fine. I won't let anything bad happen to you."

Oh-*kay*. Well, that was just... It was just...

She was so off-balance that someone could have knocked her over with a feather. In fact, she staggered when Christian released her and jogged toward the stairs, taking them two at a time.

Oh, and on the topic of things that were pretty...

Get a load of dat ass! It was all tight and firm and covered in jeans that probably cost more than she made in a week.

Not to put too fine a point on it, but he looked *good* in those jeans. They fit him like a glove in the back *and* the front.

Before she could stop the thought in its tracks, she found herself wondering if he was a lefty or a righty when it came to what he was packing. A quick glance before he disappeared onto the second-floor landing confirmed he was a righty, and whoa, momma, what a righty he was.

How the hell had she missed that?

Oh yeah. Because she'd studiously *avoided* looking. Because once bitten, twice shy, baby. Because she didn't mix business with pleasure. She *didn't*!

"That's a good way to catch flies." Ace closed her gaping mouth by pressing a finger beneath her chin.

Chapter 2

Pendoggett, Cornwall, England

"I'M STANDING OUTSIDE A COTTAGE IN PORT ISAAC, CORNWALL, where Corporal Christian Watson is holed up with the shutters drawn and the doors locked. It is rumored Corporal Watson is the man responsible for the Kirkuk Police Station Incident."

Lawrence Michelson's boots dropped from the coffee table to the floor with a loud *thump*. His breath caught in his chest like it came with a set of hooks.

"Ben!" he shouted. "Get your smelly ass in here!"

"I'm taking a shit!" his younger brother yelled from down the hall.

"Well, pinch it off! You gotta see what's on the telly!"

Lawrence snatched the remote and thumbed up the volume. The reporter on the screen was redheaded and pretty. She tried to hide her well-padded figure beneath a yellow pantsuit, but it didn't work. On any other occasion, Lawrence would have taken a mental picture to use in private later, but considering the subject matter she was reporting on, the last thing on his mind was his cock.

"Fecking hell, Lawrence." Ben was doing up his jeans as he walked into the room. "What's so important I had to—"

"Shhh." Lawrence waved a hand, blood pounding in his ears. "Listen." He pointed to the telly.

"Corporal Watson has yet to confirm or deny these allegations," the pretty reporter continued, "but we are hoping he will pop out soon and give us a statement."

A recorded video bloomed on the screen. It showed a cheerily painted red door swinging open. A tall bloke with dark hair appeared on the threshold, where a microphone was promptly shoved in his face.

Lawrence vaguely registered that Yellow Pantsuit Chickadee yelled a question at Watson. He didn't hear what it was, however, because he was too busy memorizing the man's every feature.

Corporal Christian Watson had a stone-hewn jaw and the cheekbones to match, a hawkish nose, a five-o'clock shadow, and eerily light eyes. He struck Lawrence as the kind of bastard other men wanted to be and most women wanted to shag silly. The kind of bastard who breezed through life, unaware of the carnage he left in his wake.

The black anger Lawrence had struggled with his whole life bubbled up and filled him to the brim. He used to be able to control it. When he was younger, he'd fought and fucked, and both things seemed to quiet the turmoil inside him. But ever since his family's tragedy, *control* had become an issue. And now, looking at Watson's face, darkness crowded Lawrence's vision, and the urge to beat the living shit out of something—or *someone*—had his hands curling into tight fists.

"Stay tuned for more on this developing story," the reporter said before the video cut off. Then the screen flipped to an ad for toothpaste.

"Jesus." Ben stared at him with wide, blinking eyes. "You think it's true? You think he's the one?"

If there is a God in heaven, please let it be so.

"Let's find out, shall we?" Lawrence pushed up from the sofa, the muscles in his back twitching, the buzzing between his ears growing louder with each passing second. "It's only twenty minutes to Port Isaac. Get your sidearm."

Ben's chin drew back. "Now hold on, Lawrence. You can't mean to murder the bloke."

"I don't wanna murder him." Although that wasn't exactly true. For years he'd fantasized about killing the twat responsible for all the pain in his life. "I simply wanna talk to him."

"Then why do we need our weapons?"

"Because if we shove the business ends of our heaters in his face, he'll be more keen to tell us the truth."

"I don't know." Ben swallowed, and the sound was sticky. Then again, *cowardly* was perhaps a better word for it.

Of the three Michelson brothers, Ben had always been the anxious one, afraid of rocking the boat, of getting into trouble. Lawrence had always been the hothead, the one who *liked* to rock the boat, *looked* for trouble. And their older brother? Well, *he* had been the best of them. It was for *his* sake that Lawrence did this now. At least that's what he told himself as he walked to the coatrack by the front door and took down his cagoule.

"For fuck's sake, Ben. This is our chance. After all these years, we've a face and a name. Don't go pigeon-hearted on me now."

"If the sergeant finds out we been bringing our sidearms home, he'll put our bollocks in a vise and have our jobs."

Lawrence gritted his jaw until his back teeth squeaked.

There were times he felt he'd been born on the wrong side of the Atlantic. Unlike the Americans, who armed their police forces, the good people of England preferred their law enforcement personnel to remain weaponless pansies. And even though he and Ben had both done the extra training, passed the exams, and made it into a specialized unit that *did* allow them to carry, they were required to leave their weapons inside their ARVs—armed response vehicles—when they weren't on duty.

It was a travesty. As a constable, Lawrence felt he should bloody well be able to defend himself. And as a member of his regional firearms unit, he should certainly be trusted to take home his own damn weapon.

Which is why he did.

"What the sergeant don't know won't hurt him," he said. It was the same line he used anytime Ben got cold feet about breaking protocol.

"I don't know," Ben said again.

Lawrence loved his younger brother. He truly did. Ben was the only family he had left. But right at that moment, he would happily have pounded the sad sap's face.

"*I* know," Lawrence insisted. "Grab your coat. Grab your gun. And let's go get some answers from this bastard."

"Why can't we *all* climb over the rooftops to escape?" Emily asked.

She stood beside the lone attic window as weak spring sunlight tried to break through the rolling cloud cover outside. A storm moved quickly across the bay, headed inland with all the threatening malevolence

Mother Nature could muster. Lightning cleaved the sky, masking the sound of Angel throwing open the cranky old window. He did a quick scan of the roofline and area below.

"Because, darling, while some of us might be skilled at running stealthily across rooftops, others of us are not." Christian pulled himself through the hole in the attic floor and quickly picked his way over the uneven pieces of plywood laid haphazardly atop the joists. He handed Angel an aerosol can of something that looked like it might be deodorant.

It annoyed her to no end that he seemed not to inhabit a room so much as *fill* it. A moment ago, the place had been floor-to-ceiling boxes, plus Ace, Angel, Rusty, and her. Now, it was floor-to-ceiling *Christian*. Which struck her as particularly odd since Rusty was the one who was built like a tank.

"I'm assuming you're referring to *me*." She cut Christian a look she hoped clearly conveyed her thoughts. Which was that he'd sprouted a bunch of new assholes, and if he wasn't careful, he was in danger of becoming one *giant* asshole.

"I am," he admitted. "But besides that, it's much easier for one person to escape the prying eyes of the press than five people." When he shrugged, it was the physical equivalent of *duh*.

Deciding he was probably right, she changed the subject. "What's with the deodorant?"

"Not deodorant," Angel said. He opened his backpack to add the can to the assortment of other items he had already taken from beneath the bathroom sink.

Reading the label on the aerosol can, she begged to

differ. "Yes, it is. See?" She pointed to the big, bold letters that read: Beckham Instinct Deodorant Spray.

David Beckham was the undisputed pride of the Land of Hope and Glory. His name or mug was on just about everything.

"For our purposes," Angel clarified, "it is a bomb."

"A *bomb*!" She blinked around the dimly lit attic, dismayed to find all four men staring back at her impassively.

"The ignition for a bomb anyway," Angel added as if that made everything better.

"And what exactly do you plan to blow up?"

"A car." Angel slipped the straps of his full backpack over his shoulders.

"A car. Right." She nodded, then quickly shook her head. "Are you nuts?"

"The explosion has to be big enough to draw the reporters away from the cottage," Ace explained, proving everyone was on the same page except for her. She was convinced she hadn't even been given a copy of the damn book.

"Yes," Angel added. If she wasn't mistaken, the look on his enigmatic face *also* said *duh*.

She was getting real tired of that word. Whether it was implied or not.

"Fine. Whatever. Just…make sure the owner has insurance, if you can," she said at the same time Christian blurted, "Check for proof of insurance, mate."

Having grown up dirt poor, Emily knew what the lack of a vehicle could mean. An inability to get to work meant the loss of a job. The loss of a job meant the loss of a roof over your head, food on your table, and clothes on your back. But Christian? How did *he* know?

It occurred to her then that, even after the months they'd been living and working together, she knew hardly anything about his past, about who he was and where he'd been before joining BKI. She wasn't sure if she should be sad about that, or proud of herself. After all, getting to know him, the *real* him, would skate precariously close to mixing business with pleasure.

Still, that didn't stop her from asking, *Who are you, Christian?*

She didn't voice the question aloud. Instead, she let her eyes do the talking for her. She and Christian had been doing that a lot lately. Saying with their eyes and their expressions all the things they refused to speak aloud.

It was disconcerting. But she didn't know how to stop it, short of refusing to look at him. And considering he was two kilos of uncut *joy* to look at, she knew that wasn't going to happen anytime soon.

He lifted a dark, sleek eyebrow that asked, *Do you really want to know?*

Yes, she really did. But fear held her back. It was the fear that if she really got to know him, if she crossed over the line that tiny bit, then all the walls she'd built against him would come crumbling down.

She shook her head no.

That's what I thought, his twitching lips responded.

Angel glanced back and forth between them, trying to interpret their silent conversation. Eventually, he shrugged and threw his leg over the windowsill. In a flash he was gone, leaving the rest of them to make their way downstairs and wait for his distraction.

Emily took a seat on the sofa, her palms itching with adrenaline, her toes tapping out a nervous beat on the polished wood floor. Patience had never been one of her virtues. Neither had sitting around waiting for something portentous to happen. She prided herself on being a woman of action, a woman who took charge and—

A thought suddenly occurred, and she flicked Christian a considering look.

"What?" he demanded.

"That's why you came to work for BKI, isn't it?"

"What is?" He looked genuinely confused.

"Because you were kicked out of the SAS."

"We call it *decommissioned*."

"Same difference." She waved a hand through the air.

"To coin a ridiculously overused American phrase."

"Cut the crap."

"Another delightful American phrase."

"I'm serious."

He blew out a ragged breath and gifted her with one of his sexy, *sexy* glares.

"I would have thought it was obvious by now that your death-ray gaze doesn't work on me," she informed him. Which was sort of a lie. It *did* work on her. Just not in the way he might think.

Nothing was ever as fun as matching wits with Christian. It warmed her blood, lit her up from the inside out. Both were dangerous sensations, but she couldn't stop herself. When it came to him, she had discovered she liked playing with fire.

"Okay. Fine. *Yes*," he grumbled. "That's why I came to work for BKI. I tried working for a security firm after the SAS. I tried donating my time to teach little old ladies self-defense. I *tried* to be a civilian, but I was bloody awful at it. I've *been* bloody awful at it since the day I turned seventeen and got caught nicking a loaf of bread and a bottle of HP Sauce from the corner store and the local magistrate told me it was either a detention center or the army."

"*That's* why you joined?" Ace looked bemused. "Because it was either military service or jail time?"

Christian shrugged. "It was a common-enough tale back then. And I must admit, it was the best thing to happen to me. One month into training and I was totally army barmy. The military provided the security and consistency I never had as a child. It would have taken plastic explosives to get me out of the service in the beginning, and it nearly took plastic explosives to keep me out after Kirkuk. Then I heard about Boss."

He'd stolen a loaf of bread and a bottle of HP Sauce? The military had provided the security and consistency he hadn't had as a kid? Holy crap! Had Christian grown up poor?

Emily tried to imagine him scrawny and scruffy, with holey jeans and worn tube socks, and couldn't quite form the picture in her mind. Grown-up Christian was always so composed, so unruffled, so completely, *expensively* put together. She'd always assumed he shot out of the birth canal in a pair of Gucci chukkas.

Then again, his explanation made it startlingly clear why he'd been right there with her in demanding that Angel make sure whichever car he decided to blow up had an insured owner.

She thought she heard a rumbling noise. *Shit*. Surely

it wasn't the foundations of those walls she'd built against him. Right? *Right?*

Afraid to answer her own question, she posed one for Christian instead. "Boss? What about him?"

Frank "Boss" Knight was their esteemed leader back at Black Knights Inc.

"Our paths crossed when Boss was a SEAL," Christian said. "After I was decommissioned, I heard he'd quit the Navy to start a chopper shop." Right. Because BKI's cover was that of a custom motorcycle shop. Only the CIA and those on the very top rungs of government knew the truth of the matter. "I gave him a ring to ask him how the bloody hell he was doing the transition to being a civilian."

"Which was when he invited you across the pond to share a beer with him," Ace said.

"How'd you know that?" Christian narrowly eyed Ace.

"Because that's how he invited me."

After a beat, Christian nodded. "Yeah. He invited me. But I didn't go straightaway."

Emily couldn't help herself. Crumbling walls or not, she was hooked. She had to know the rest of the story. "Why not?"

"Doesn't matter." Christian shook his head.

Au contraire, she thought. From the look on his face, whatever had stopped him from going right away mattered quite a bit.

"What matters," he continued, "is that I *eventually* made my way to Chicago. The rest, as they say, is history."

"But now what?" she asked. "Can the press track you back to BKI? Will they—"

"Indeed not."

"How do you know? How can you be sure?"

"Because I've fallen off the grid." His was the Olympic gold of smiles. His straight white teeth upped his sexy ante by about a hundred bucks. Not to mention his mouth… Sweet heavens! He had a full lower lip that spoke of carnal appetites and a harshly defined upper lip that spoke of rigid self-control.

Not for the first time, she wondered what it would be like to kiss those diametrically opposed lips. Despite her self-imposed edict, estrogen responded to testosterone. There was nothing she could do to stop that.

"It's six years on from that flight I took across the Atlantic," he said, "and since then I've had no known address. No work history, bank accounts, assets, or debts. Boss pays me in cash. I carry fake passports and have a fake motorist's license. As far as anyone knows, I have ceased to exist. The only thing that remains of the old me is my name. And I only use that with you lot."

He spread his big hands wide. "So you see, if we can make that plane and hop back to the colonies, no one will find me. BKI will be safe. All will be well."

Would it? Emily wasn't so sure. "Except *someone* found out you were here. *Someone* found out you were part of that Kirkuk thingy, and *someone* ratted you out to the press."

Ace said the one word they were all thinking. "Spider?"

The name seemed to reverberate around the room like a tuning fork recently struck. Emily couldn't help it; she shivered.

Spider was evil incarnate. If it was awful and currently happening in the world—say, piracy, for instance, or human trafficking or illegal weapons sales—it seemed to have Spider's fingerprints all over it. Which you would think would make the man easy to find. But you would be dead wrong.

The Black Knights had been hunting Spider for months. That hunt was why the four of them were in England. Unfortunately, the closest they'd come to figuring out who Spider really was had been to find the man who laundered his money, a billionaire media mogul named Roper Morrison. Too bad finding Spider's money launderer hadn't gotten them Spider. Morrison had died before they'd had a chance to interrogate him, and the media coverage surrounding Morrison's untimely demise was one of the reasons they'd had to lie low and hole up in Christian's uncle's empty summer cottage, awaiting secret transport out of England.

"Could Spider have seen you on some CCTV footage?" Ace posited. The UK was lousy with surveillance cameras. And even though they had done their best to avoid the suckers during their time on the island, it was always possible they'd inadvertently been spied by one.

"And then what?" Christian asked. "He would have had to use facial-recognition software to identify me. Then he would have had to have someone working for him inside the bloody SAS who could get into my *classified*"—he emphasized the word—"military records. Even if all of that were possible, how could he have sorted out I was here? My uncle and I haven't spoken in years."

"Maybe it's simpler than that," Rusty said. He was perched on the arm of a delicate wingback chair. Since he was a red-haired, freckle-faced Hulk, it was like watching a rhino balance on a telephone wire.

"How do you mean?" Emily asked.

"That guy who was working security for Spider's money launderer… What was his name?"

"Steven Surry," Emily and Christian answered in unison. Hearing Christian's deep voice merge with hers made something strange happen to her stomach.

"Right." Rusty nodded. "Wasn't *he* former SAS? Could he have seen Christian at some point and recognized him? Could he have passed that information on to Spider?"

"And then what?" Emily frowned. "Spider gave Christian's identity to the press? Why would he do that? And it doesn't explain how he would know about Kirkuk."

Rusty shrugged his massive shoulders. "Maybe Spider *didn't* know about Kirkuk. Maybe he knew from Surry that Christian was former SAS. If this Spider guy is as well-connected as you all say he is, it wouldn't take him long to figure out that Christian had fallen off the map. And who better to dig up information on a dude who has fallen off the map than the press? Maybe Spider tipped off the newshounds hoping *they* would do his dirty work for him. Namely, find Christian. Total can of corn."

Rusty had been born and raised in Pittsburgh, and Emily knew from their acquaintance that *can of corn* was the way people from the Steel City said *easy as you pleasy*.

She exchanged a look with Ace and Christian. All three of them said "shit" at the same time.

Well, technically Christian said, "buggering shit." *But to coin an overused American phrase*, Emily thought, silently donning Christian's hoity-toity English accent, *same difference*.

"We need to get the hell out of Dodge," she muttered.

Christian snorted, the muscle beneath his eye going to town. "That's stating the obvi—"

BOOM!

He was cut off mid-sentence by the explosion outside.

Chapter 3

CHRISTIAN WATCHED EMILY NEARLY JUMP OUT OF HER SKIN when Angel set off the explosion. He was sorely tempted to put a hand of comfort on her arm. But touching her was torture—not to mention strictly off-limits—and he definitely didn't fancy dealing with another round of flag-at-full-staff, so instead he lifted a hand to his ear, waggled his eyebrows, and said, "Sounds like Angel is playing our song."

Emily tightened the straps on her rucksack and stood up. "You have a dark sense of humor."

"Do I?" He set off toward the back door. The sound of the reporters chattering excitedly among themselves as they rushed to investigate the ruckus was quickly drowned out by the loud, rolling rumble of thunder. The storm outside was nearly upon them. "Perhaps I do. But you live my life and see what color yours turns, yeah?"

"Doth mine ears deceive me? Or is the mighty Christian Watson feeling sorry for himself today?"

"Not sorry." He opened the shutters beside the back door a bare centimeter and scanned the steps outside. The last reporter was disappearing around the corner of the cottage. "Just stating the facts."

"Oh yeah? Well, if you're of a mind to state facts, then how about telling us why you didn't go to Chicago right away after Boss invited you to join him for a beer?"

"Certainly." He shrugged. "Directly after you tell us what made you so keen to quit the CIA."

The woman claimed to be an open book, but those particular pages of her story were redacted, paper-clipped, and superglued shut.

Her perfectly arched eyebrows slammed into a scowl. Usually, he fancied his women smiling and sated. But there was something about Emily in a pique. Her fierce expressions and sharp tongue always heated his blood.

"Do you realize you have an annoying habit of evading my questions by firing counter-questions?" When she pursed her lips again, he was forced to look away. There was too much temptation there. If he continued to stare at her, he wouldn't be able to hide the fact that he wanted to smear those lips—and the rest of her, for that matter—with butter and then lick her clean.

"Holy demented shit," Ace cursed in his usual colorful way. "I swear, you two should go see a doctor. You're both suffering from different-day, same-ol'-shititus. And it's starting to annoy the hell out of the rest of us. Now, how about it?" He looked expectantly at Christian. "We good to go, or what?"

Right-oh. Although Christian would like nothing better than to argue with Emily for the rest of the day, they were on a clock.

Tentatively, he opened the back door and poked his head outside. He was hit by the smell of salty sea air tinged with threatening rain. Without turning back, he raised a hand and wiggled two fingers, a wordless gesture for the trio behind him to get cracking.

Ace was the first to slink past Christian. He did a quick battlefield scan, looking left, right, and center, before quickly and quietly setting off down the gravel path that wound toward the bottom of the hill. The trail intersected with a road that fronted the beach. Parked on that road was an old farm truck: their target.

Angel had pointed out the vehicle before leaving the cottage. The Israeli was an expert at "appropriating conveyances." Which was a fancy way of saying he could hot-wire and filch a car quicker than most people could sign their names.

One of Angel's *many* questionable talents.

Emily and Rusty pushed past Christian and headed for the path. Christian was disconcerted to discover they were holding hands. Disconcerted and…something else. Something that felt alarmingly like that foolish tosspot known as jealousy. Which was ludicrous because (A) Rusty was gayer than a Sunday morning tea cake; (B) Rusty was simply being a gentleman, helping Emily on the steep path; (C) Rusty and Emily were old friends; and last but not least, (D) even if Rusty *wasn't* gay and *wasn't* simply being a gentleman and *wasn't* Emily's old friend, Christian had absolutely no claim on the woman.

Still, there it was. All green-eyed and snarling and making him want to chew nails. Jealousy. He was *jealous* that Rusty got to hold Emily's hand, that Rusty got to *touch* her oh-so-casually while Christian spent most of his days keeping his hands curled into fists to stop himself from doing precisely that.

Gritting his teeth, he locked the cottage. After replacing the key beneath a terra-cotta pot, he turned for the path.

He was halfway down the hill, determinedly *not* looking at Rusty and Emily, when he got the distinct urge to glance back at the cottage. Back at the place that was the symbol of his childhood when it had been relatively happy and healthy. Back at the spot he had longed for during those nights after the car accident when his mother came home too pissed to—

He shoved aside the memories, refused to look back, and quickly caught up to the couple in front of him. The day had darkened to night. Not sweetly, but more like an ugly bruise. The warmth of spring was eclipsed by the clouds, and the wind had turned cold and harsh.

In the distance, a plume of smoke drifted upward, away from the glow of the burning vehicle below. Sirens sounded, the familiar *bee-doo-bee-doo-bee* of Christian's youth. But all around them was quiet. Not a soul in sight. Everyone with a smidge of curiosity had donned their overcoats and headed toward the scene of the explosion, which was in the exact *opposite* direction of the waiting vehicle.

Angel certainly knew how to create a distraction. No question.

Christian could see the Israeli perched in the truck's driver's seat, motor running. The rest of them were near the end of the path, headed straight for the vehicle, when the sky opened up. The downpour stung like needles of dry ice and instantly drenched them to the bone.

Emily let loose with a curse that made Christian smile. Whipping open the passenger-side door, Ace quickly hopped in, scooting close to Angel. Rusty and Emily were next, piling in Keystone Cop–style. Christian realized, rather belatedly, that there was no room left for him.

While the old truck was brilliant for a quick snatch-

and-grab—no alarms and easy to hot-wire—unfortunately it wasn't built to carry a five-man crew. The bucket-style bench seat was barely big enough for the four people already stuffed into it.

He looked forlornly through the downpour at the bed of the pickup. Four rucksacks had been tossed haphazardly inside. With no small amount of displeasure, he thought, *When escaping and evading, needs must*.

Placing a foot atop the rear tire, ready to hoist himself into the back of the truck and hunker down for one of the most miserable rides of his life, he stopped when Emily poked her head out the door and demanded, "What the hell are you doing?"

Rain had plastered her hair to her skull. It dripped from her long lashes and off the center of her plump bottom lip.

Forget the butter. He didn't need it. Licking the rainwater from her would do in a pinch.

"I'm getting into the back!" he yelled over the rumble of thunder and the rattle of the raindrops atop the truck's roof.

"Don't be an idiot! You'll freeze your ass off. Get in the front. I'll sit on your lap."

The image of her cute ass snuggled tight into his crotch had his silly pecker begging, *Oh, abso-bloody-lutely*. Luckily, his mind had the right of things and was quick to interrupt with, *Oh, no sodding way in hell*.

He shook his head. "I'll be fine! It's not that far to—"

That's all he managed. She hopped from the truck and stomped toward him through gathering puddles.

"For the love of Nellie Fox," she grumbled. She was always calling on the love of some White Sox baseball player or another. Christian wouldn't know any of them from Adam. He preferred cricket and football—even though he'd lived in the States for years, he refused to call it soccer. "Stop being a damn fool, and come get in the damn truck!"

Before he could argue, she had him by the sleeve of his drenched coat and was hauling him toward the open door. He barely had time to shrug out of his rucksack and toss it into the truck's bed before she gave him a shove that was surprisingly strong, considering she probably weighed less than nine stone soaking wet.

Rusty grunted when Christian piled in beside him. Christian was far from a small man, but Rusty was even larger. They were trying to figure out how to get their shoulders to fit side by side when Emily hopped onto Christian's lap and slammed the door shut.

The loud cacophony of falling rain became a low drumming. With four big, burly men occupying the vehicle, the cold air began to heat. The smell of wet clothes and soggy leather boots quickly permeated the entire space.

"Punch it, Angel," Emily said.

The former Mossad agent didn't hesitate. He laid on the gas, and the truck puttered to life, picking up speed one cranky shift of gears at a time.

"Well, *that* went better than expected." Emily adjusted herself into a more comfortable position that, yeah, you guessed it, had her delightful derriere settling directly over Christian's crotch.

God, if you're up there, now would be a brilliant time to give me a tad bit of help! All this time Christian had spent studiously *not* touching Emily, and suddenly her ass was balanced atop his cods.

He closed his eyes and envisioned his old drill sergeant. The man had been beer-bellied, bald, and odious at dental hygiene. Not to mention that he'd had a series of unfortunate moles beside each eye, and one rather large one to the left of his nose that had sported a wiry, one-inch hair.

Keeping the vision firmly fixed in his mind, Christian began to recite the prime numbers. Given it would take more than an hour to drive from Port Isaac to Cornwall Airport at Newquay, he figured it was as good a mental exercise as any.

He had worked his way up to 1,019 when Emily began to squirm, much to the enjoyment of the very thing he was trying desperately to distract.

"Bloody hell," he gritted through clenched teeth. "This drive will be interminable if you keep up with that."

Her wet hair dripped close to his face, forcing him to breathe through his mouth lest he get a head-spinning snoot full of the exotic shampoo she used.

"Sorry," she said, still squirming. "It's just that my knees are jammed under the dashboard and— Oh!"

There was nothing for it. He had to stop that infernal wiggling, so he pulled her tight against his chest. "There. Is that better?"

For his efforts, he received a mouthful of her soggy hair. Sputtering, he pulled out the sodden strands, then gathered up her hair and swept it forward over her shoulder. His fingers inadvertently brushed the side of her face. The moment they did, he felt burned. Branded. Her skin was so soft and hot and—

Oh buggering hell.

She glanced back at him and gifted him with that

brilliant, hypnotic smile. "Yes, thanks. Much better, and—whoa! Uh, Christian?"

"It's all that blasted squirming about," he said since there was no way to disguise the length of hard flesh that prodded her bottom. It was all her fault. He was only a man, after all. "Don't take it personally."

"Don't take *what* personally?" Ace asked, craning around Rusty to look at Christian.

"The fact that he's suddenly packing a pickle in his pocket," Emily said. The woman was about as subtle as a herd of elephants.

"Only a pickle?" Ace frowned. "How very disappointing. Are we talking gherkin-sized or..." Ace left the question hanging.

Emily squirmed again, and Christian's stupid pecker sang a rousing chorus of hallelujahs. "Knock it off," he growled.

"I'm trying to determine the answer to Ace's question," she said sweetly. After one more wiggle, she told Ace, "I misspoke. It's definitely more garden-cucumber-sized."

"Oh!" Ace's eyes widened dramatically, and he turned to regard Christian with mock interest. "You don't say?"

Had Christian mentioned that Ace was *also* as gay as a Sunday tea cake?

"Can we please stop talking about my...my..." For reasons Christian couldn't explain, he was unable to spit out the word.

"Todger?" Ace supplied helpfully.

"Gentleman sausage?" Emily added, her tone full of devilment.

"Purple parsnip." Ace joined her in laughing his bloody fool ass off. "Oh, if there's one thing I can say about living in England for these last few weeks, it's that I've learned so many interesting euphemisms for a man's unit."

"And last but not least," Emily said with great enthusiasm, "Tallywhacker!"

"Haaaa!" Ace mimed wiping a tear from his eye.

"Tell me, Christian," Emily mused, "why is it you Englishmen feel the need to come up with silly names for your nether regions?"

"Because *cock* and *balls* are quite boring, darling. And if there's one thing we English loathe more than cold beer, it's tedium."

"Mmm," she hummed. It was the sweetest sound he'd ever heard. And it did nothing to dampen the enthusiasm of his…*tallywhacker*.

She didn't miss the insistent throb against her bottom, because she caught her bottom lip between her teeth and glanced back at him. One cheeky eyebrow climbed up her forehead.

"Like I said before the peanut gallery decided to get in their two cents," he informed her irritably, "don't take it personally. You're a woman with a small but rather plump bottom. I'm a red-blooded male with a sex organ that hasn't received any attention in weeks."

More like months—ever since Emily had arrived on the BKI scene—but who was counting?

"Ashy dick. That's what I call it," Ace said as Angel exited the small lane leading out of Port Isaac and merged onto a narrow country road. They would take the back roads to the airport in Newquay to avoid the myriad CCTV cameras located on the major motorways.

"I beg your pardon?" Christian blanched.

"As in, you haven't gotten it wet in—"

"Never mind." Christian was quick to cut Ace off. Was it him, or was the heater in the farm truck working overtime? Steam had formed on the window beside him. He couldn't decide if it was a drop of rainwater or a bead of sweat that slid down his temple.

"Why hasn't your…uh…*sex organ*"—Emily snorted—"gotten any attention in weeks?"

He frowned. "You're not serious."

"Sure I am."

"I've been on this bloody assignment with you lot. And before we had to hole up in my uncle's cottage, we were all living in a tiny London flat that wasn't precisely conducive to bringing home birds."

Not that he would have, even if he could have. He wasn't opposed to casual sex. Preferred it, actually. But he drew the line at sleeping with one woman while fantasizing about another. And ever since Emily had crashed into his life like a wrecking ball, he hadn't fantasized about anyone else.

"Speaking of dicks," Ace said.

"Must we circle back to that topic?" Angel piped up for the first time since they'd piled into the truck. "I would love to talk about something else. Anything else. How about we phone the pilot of the charter plane to tell him we are running a half hour late? Or how about we all simply sit here in silence? I would love that. *Lord*, how I would love that."

Every person in the truck was stunned into silence. For long moments, the only sounds in the cab were the *whir* of the tires over the blacktop and the rhythmic *whip-whop-whip-whop* of the windscreen wipers working overtime.

Naturally, Emily was the first to find her voice. "Holy hell. I think that's more words than I've heard you speak the entire time I've known you, Angel."

"That's more words than I've heard him speak the entire time *I've* known him," Ace said.

Rusty's addition to the conversation was, "I wasn't convinced he actually *knew* that many words."

Christian agreed with all of them, but he kept his mouth shut, reveling that the topic of conversation having moved on from the subject of his wedding tackle. Then Emily started squirming again.

He was about to demand she knock it off when he realized she was reaching into her jacket pocket to extract her mobile. He didn't have a chance to ask who she was ringing before her call connected and he had his answer.

"Hey, Boss," she said. "I need you to put in a call to that pilot friend of yours and tell him we're going to be thirty minutes late to the airport."

Christian couldn't hear their estimable leader's reply, but it must have been a question about what had caused the delay because Emily quickly explained. Christian squeezed his eyes shut when she got to the part about the press and his role in the Kirkuk Police Station Incident. Not that he didn't think about what had happened in Iraq—and the beastly consequences of that rescue—because he did. Far too often for peace of mind. But he wasn't used to talking about it, or hearing someone else talk about it.

I want to get home, he thought, realizing with a start that Chicago *was* home. The best home he'd ever known, filled with the best *people* he'd ever known. He hated that he'd put Emily, Ace, and Angel's covers in jeopardy, and he had *known* there were reasons beyond his past in Her Majesty's Special Air Service and his toxic familial ties that had kept him from returning to English soil. Now he was living those reasons—and dragging his coworkers with him.

"So now the question is," Emily continued, "can we use any of this to find out who Spider is? Is it possible to figure out who gave Christian's name to the press?"

Emily was quiet as Boss responded, the air whining from the vents too loud for Christian to hear anything more than the rumble of Boss's bass voice.

"Right." Emily nodded. "That's what I was hoping you'd say. Start making some calls. Shake some trees. See what rotten fruit falls out."

Indeed. Because if anyone could figure out how this cockup got started, it was the Black Knights. After years of doing the jobs too dirty or too diplomatically challenging for regular special forces or intelligence groups to take on, they had built a range of contacts the world over.

It was going to be a great tragedy when BKI finally shut its clandestine doors. Bringing down Spider was their final mission. As soon as the underworld crime lord and his vast network of criminal activity were put to bed, the Black Knights, Christian included, would all go back to being civilians.

Some of the guys at BKI were looking forward to the time when they could set aside their assault weapons and pick up their wrenches, trade in their percussion grenades for grease guns. Christian, on the other hand...not so much. Like he'd told everyone back at the cottage, he'd tried his hand at the Joe Bloggs gig. It hadn't worked for him before. He was fairly certain it wouldn't work for him now.

He'd heard a saying once that had struck a chord. It was something like, "if you keep your eyes on the battle ahead, you won't have to fight the battle behind."

That had definitely been his problem after the SAS let him go. He'd been sucked back into the life he'd had before. Fighting the battles he'd thought he'd left behind when he'd joined the army and—

His thoughts cut off when Emily ended her call and settled more comfortably against him. For a moment there, when his mind had been elsewhere, his flag had withered to half-staff. But now, with her back snuggled against his chest, her sweet-smelling hair in his face, and her ass…yeah, you guessed it, bouncing atop his cods, he was back to being locked, stocked, and fully cocked.

He let his head fall against the back window, squeezed his eyes shut, and once again began quietly reciting his primes.

Chapter 4

Rock Road, Southbound...

"JESUS, MARY, AND JOSEPH, WHAT *HAPPENED* BACK THERE?"
Ben asked as they followed far behind the rattling, green
farm truck.

They'd been tailing the vehicle for over an hour on
old country roads with high hedgerows and the occasional bucolic-looking cottage, but this was the first
time Ben had spoken. Perhaps he had been in shock. Or
perhaps he'd simply been mulling the events over for
that long.

No one would ever accuse Ben of being the sharpest
knife in the drawer. Lawrence couldn't help but think
that if it weren't for his and their older brother's influ-
ence, Ben would likely be working at the local fry shop
instead of the local police station.

Lawrence glanced over at his younger brother, not
attempting to hide the derision on his face. "Please tell
me you know a distraction when you see one."

They had barely had time to park on the seafront
road behind the reporter-clogged cottage before a great
explosion rocked the little village of Port Isaac. As a
constable, and lacking a good deal of common sense,
Ben's first instinct had been to run and investigate. But
Lawrence had stayed him with a hand and kept his eyes
glued to the cottage's garden door.

Lawrence's instincts had proved correct. Not two minutes after the initial blast, the door opened and four people made their way down the gravel path toward where Lawrence and Ben were parked. Lawrence hadn't paid three of them any mind. All his attention had been focused on Christian Watson.

He might have ducked down, had he not had the windows on his new Peugeot SUV deeply tinted. Instead, he had watched, heart thundering, blood boiling, while the foursome loaded into the truck to join a fifth.

"What are you doing?" Ben had asked, slouched low in the passenger seat despite the blacked-out windows. "Aren't you gonna go out to confront him? Isn't that why we came here?"

"You mean, aren't *we* gonna go out to confront him?" Lawrence had corrected.

That explosion had hit a nerve. Made Lawrence think he might not need to confront Watson. He might need to follow the wanker to find out what nefarious doings Watson had going. Then, once Lawrence had *confirmed* those nefarious doings, he'd be within his right to arrest the murderous tosser. Or to slot him.

Lawrence really wanted an excuse to kill the bastard. Had dreamed of it for years, in fact. A few times, those dreams had gotten him in trouble. All his unquenched rage tended to rear its ugly head when his adrenaline started pumping. He had been called on the floor twice for using excessive force on someone he'd arrested. Three times, he'd started a brawl at his local pub— always taunting his victim so that the bugger would toss the first fist and Lawrence could claim self-defense, but still.

Now, Christian Watson had fallen into his lap, and the taste of bloodlust on Lawrence's tongue was as tart and as coppery as a new penny.

Watson *was* responsible for what had happened to the Michelson family. With each furtive swivel of Watson's head or covert dart of his eyes, Lawrence's certainty—and his *fury*—had grown.

Innocent men didn't blow shit up to escape the press. They didn't move the way Watson moved. They didn't have that odd, dark knowledge in their eyes.

And speaking of Watson's eyes...

They were strange. Too light for his coloring. Made him look feral. Like a jungle cat waiting for some unsuspecting prey to stumble across his path.

The idea of finding a reason—not an excuse, a *reason*—to end the bastard was enough to have the skin on Lawrence's scalp itching with anticipation.

He could see the headline now. "Local Constable Takes Out Undesirable and Finds Justice for His Murdered Brother."

It had a certain ring to it. And even though Lawrence's older brother had talked loftily about them choosing lives of service for the guts and not the glory, Lawrence couldn't help but think there was nothing wrong with grabbing a bit of glory too. Especially if it was handed to him on a silver platter.

"You think that's what it was?" Ben asked now. "A distraction?"

Lawrence grunted. "What else would it have been?"

"Don't know." Ben shook his head.

Lawrence noticed Ben's eyes were too wide. His face too pale. "You're not getting cold feet, are you?"

"No." Ben seemed to cave in on himself. Since Ben was built like a stevedore—thanks to the good genetics their pop had passed down to all the Michelson boys—he resembled an old, worn-down mountain in the passenger seat. "I just…I just don't know what the hell we're doing, Lawrence. We had a chance to confront him, and we didn't. Now, we're ghosting him all over bloody Cornwall. *Why?*"

"Because we might catch him doing something he shouldn't be doing," Lawrence snarled. "Because if he really is the one responsible, I don't wanna confront him, I wanna make sure he *pays*. Because I bloody well *deserve* to make him pay, and so do you. Or have you forgotten?"

"I haven't forgotten." Ben's jaw sawed back and forth. "But we might have trouble making him pay. At least if he's headed where I think he's headed."

"And where's that, pray tell?"

Ben pointed out the windscreen at the sign directing motorists toward the local airport.

Buggering fuck!

"Get your weapon ready," he told Ben. "We need to hit 'em in the car park before they go inside."

―∾―

Colby "Ace" Ventura's heart pounded a mile a minute.

Not because they'd gone and blown up one car, stolen another, and were trying to get the holy fucking guacamole out of England in case the world's most deadly crime lord had somehow found them and was currently on his way to have them fitted with extra holes in their heads. That was all pretty much SOP for a man in his line of work. In fact, he'd go so far as to say it was a fairly uneventful day, all things considered.

What *was* making his heart go pitter-pat was Rusty.

Rusty, the biggest, most beautiful redhead he had ever had the pleasure of meeting. Rusty, the man he had been not-so-secretly pining for since he first set eyes on the guy five days ago. Rusty, the man who'd had an arm around his shoulders for the last hour.

It's just to give us all more space, Ace assured himself *and* his silly heart.

The latter didn't bother to listen. It kept thundering away, especially when—

Did he give me a squeeze?

It certainly *felt* like Rusty's arm had tightened. Then again, Ace could be imagining things, building sexy little sand castles in the sky. It'd been a really long time since he'd been attracted to a man. Even longer since he'd been this close to a man he was attracted to.

"Okay, I give. Why have you been mumbling under your breath this entire time?" Emily turned to glower at Christian.

"I'm reciting my prime numbers." Christian's head was pressed against the back window, as far away from Emily as he could possibly get in the cramped space.

"What the fuck for?" Bless her, the woman had a filthy mouth.

"Mental exercise."

For once, Ace was glad for the distraction Christian and Emily provided. It would take his mind off being able to feel every one of Rusty's fingertips where they pressed into his shoulder.

Did his thumb rub back and forth?

Or perhaps that small caress was simply a product of the truck's bad shocks.

Emily looked fiendish as she smirked at Christian. "You can't fool me. Your brain is as sharp as a tack."

"That was a compliment." There was genuine shock in Christian's tone. "That's two in one day. Am I dreaming? Quick, someone pinch me."

"You're not trying to get mental exercise," Emily asserted. "You're trying to distract yourself."

"From what?"

"From your ashy dick and the fact that I have a… How did you put it? 'A small but rather plump ass.'"

"First of all, I thought I made it clear you mustn't take any of that personally. And second of all, I said *bottom* not *ass*. I would never be so crass."

Ace took it back. He was no longer happy for the distraction Emily and Christian provided.

Listening to them snipe at each other made him want to reach over and knock their heads together. He knew that despite Christian's insistence to the contrary, what Christian felt for their resident office manager extraordinaire was *very* personal. The same could be said for Emily. Their feelings toward each other were written all over their faces anytime they were in the same room.

If Ace was forced to describe it, he'd say it was a dash of longing mixed with a dollop of lust sprinkled atop a near-nuclear pile of need. But to his everlasting dismay—and irritation—neither seemed willing to admit it.

Really, what the holy duck fuck was their problem?

They were both attractive. Both single. Both engaged in espionage and blacker-than-black missions. However—and this was a pretty big fracking however—for reasons he highly suspected stemmed back to trauma in their childhoods, neither of them expressed any interest in romantic relationships.

He got that. Lord, did he ever. The things a person endured in childhood often left indelible marks as an adult.

A vision of his father dragging him to that damned conversion therapist climbed out of the mental lockbox he kept it in and leered menacingly. He shoved the fucker back inside and slammed the lid shut, then imagined adding a nice big chain and a combination lock for good measure.

"Sorry I'm squashing you," Rusty said. "My shoulders and crowded conditions don't mix."

"Not a problem." Ace hoped the big man didn't hear the hoarseness in his voice.

Flipping on the stolen truck's blinker, Angel used a straightaway on the country lane to swerve around a granny in a Volkswagen puttering away at ten miles per hour under the speed limit. Since the farm truck was old and crotchety, and since the back road could use some work, the maneuver was less graceful than expected. Rusty was suddenly smashed against Ace's side. A tingle spread across Ace's collarbones, and if he wasn't mistaken, a burst of heat flew to his cheeks.

"Damn. Sorry," Rusty said again. "You okay?"

Rusty had a nice voice. All deep and sure. It hit Ace directly in his belly. Which was *not* where voices were supposed to land. They were *supposed* to land in the ears and *stay* there, damnit.

There had only been one other voice in Ace's whole life that hit him in the belly, and the fact that Rusty's did so now made him feel guilty. As if he was somehow cheating on the memory of that *other* voice.

"Fine," he said. Or more like *croaked*.

Now that lovely, terrifying heat wasn't only in his cheeks. It was everywhere. Spreading across his chest, down his arms.

He tried to blame it on the warm air coming from the vents, but knew he was fooling himself. It had nothing to do with the heater and everything to do with Rusty. Rusty and his big, strapping body. Rusty and his deep, stomach-churning voice. Rusty and his sweet smile and oddly sad eyes and…

Ace shoved his thoughts aside and lifted a hand to… what? Fan his face? Holy hobbling Christ on a crutch, talk about obvious.

Instead, he pointed the vent away from him as if that had been his intention all along. Too late, he realized that was obvious too, damnit!

Fisting his hands in his lap, he cleared his throat and tried to concentrate on something, *anything*, other than the redhead plastered along his side. It might have worked, had the people in the pickup truck offered any sort of distraction. But Christian and Emily had fallen quiet. Angel was no help. He was back to being his usual buttoned-up self. And Rusty…

Gah! Ace's mind had circled back to the very thing he was trying *not* to think about!

The seconds plodded by like hours. The air inside the truck seemed hotter, despite him having turned off his vent. And the silence… *Fracking hell, the silence!* It grated on his very last nerve because he could hear Rusty breathing, hear Rusty swallowing, hear Rusty's whiskers rasp against his rough palm when he rubbed a hand over his face.

Ace couldn't stand it a second longer. "So, Rusty," he blurted, "you never told us what brought you to England. I mean, really, how *does* a former marine from Pittsburgh end up as a charter fishing boat captain in Folkstone, UK?"

"It's a long story." Rusty shrugged.

Ace glanced at his watch, then at the sign telling him they had seven miles to go before they reached the airport. Which translated into seven more miles of silence unless he could get Rusty to fill it. Since seven more miles of silence would feel like an eternity, he figured he'd start with something simpler. "How long were you a jarhead?"

"Eight years."

Ah, progress. "And what made you leave?"

"I got a bum knee, thanks to a bad mission over in Afghanistan that made me not so good at humping gear and squatting in foxholes. They honorably discharged me as soon as my contract came up for renewal."

"Was that difficult? I mean, assuming you wanted to stay in the Corps?"

Again, Rusty shrugged and remained frustratingly silent. *It's like pulling teeth*, Ace thought.

"And afterward? Is that when you moved to England?"

Rusty shook his head, his eyes zeroed in on the road ahead, but unless Ace was mistaken, Rusty wasn't really seeing it. He seemed to have turned in on himself. "I ended up going back to Pittsburgh to work for my pop at U.S. Steel. But I..." Rusty's jaw hardened. "I wasn't happy there."

"No? Why not?"

"Lot of good ol' boys I didn't fit in with 'cause I'm…" Rusty made a rolling motion with his big paw.

"I think the word you're looking for is *gay*."

"Yeah." Rusty hitched one mammoth shoulder. "And then there was my dad's crew, the white-collar boys. But I didn't fit in with them either 'cause I'm more brawn than brains."

"I wouldn't say that."

"You don't know me so well." Rusty chuckled, but it sounded fake, and within a second, his face fell flat. "But the long and short of it is, when my grandfather died and left his house in Folkstone and his charter fishing business to my mom, I jumped at the chance to make a fresh start. To try something new."

Ace couldn't put his finger on it, but there was something about Rusty's story that didn't gel. "And your folks? They were okay with you moving half a world away?"

Ace wouldn't have thought it possible, but Rusty's jaw hardened further. "Not really. But I had to. I needed… um…well, I guess I needed space."

Call it intuition or a sixth sense, but suddenly Ace knew what Rusty wasn't saying. His heart sank. "Your folks don't know you're gay, do they?"

For a redhead, Rusty's skin was incredibly tan—*all those hours spent on an open deck, no doubt*—but Ace still spotted his blush.

"It'd kill my mom if she knew," Rusty said. "She's a devout Christian. Some might even call her a bible-beater. And my dad, well…let's just say he's made it clear my whole life what he thinks of *fuckin' fairies*."

The way Rusty spat out the words, Ace knew Rusty

was quoting directly from his old man. Hadn't Ace heard similar nastiness from his *own* father?

His mental lockbox rattled around, threatening to disgorge its contents once again. "You want some advice?" he asked Rusty.

"Not really."

Ace gave him some anyway. "Rip off the bandage. Even if your folks are hurt, hell, even if they say they never want to see you again, at least you won't be living a lie."

A muscle ticked a sharp rhythm in Rusty's cheek. "Easier said than done."

"Like most things," Ace insisted. But a final hitch of those shoulders told him Rusty wasn't buying it.

Too bad, he mused. *I thought maybe we could—*

He squashed the thought before he could finish it. He'd been down that road before. He refused to go down it again. And besides, his heart belonged to another. Always had. Always would.

Still, it'd been nice to fantasize. Just for a while.

Angel followed the signs directing them to the private hangar at the airport, and they eventually found their way to a meandering access road that would take them there.

Ace had always appreciated private air travel. Since the über-rich and famous, or those folks with bull's-eyes on their backs, tended to get around that way, it meant private jet hangars were discreet. Discriminating. Exactly what a quintet of covert operators needed. Or rather a trio of covert operators, one mouthy office manager, and one poor, unsuspecting former-marine-turned-civilian.

Passing through the gate of a chain-link fence, they

pulled into a small parking lot. Since theirs wasn't a commercial flight, there was no need for gung-ho security measures. The thought being, if someone wanted to hijack or bring down their own plane, well...so what? It's not like they'd be taking innocent civilians with them.

With the rain still coming down in sheets, it wasn't until they were piling out of the truck and wiping it down for fingerprints—leaving behind easy evidence was a no no, and of course there was Rusty's identity to protect—that Ace noticed the black SUV swinging in to park three spots down. He didn't give it a second thought. Figured it was a pilot or a mechanic or even an air traffic controller. That was until he saw two men hop from the vehicle and lift sidearms.

The driver yelled in a thick English accent, "Put your bloody hands in the air!"

Chapter 5

Cornwall Airport Newquay...

EMILY BARELY HAD TIME TO BLINK, MUCH LESS REACT, WHEN the two men hopped from the car brandishing big, black handguns.

The same could not be said for Christian.

No sooner had the man in the SUV shouted his order for them to reach for the sky than Christian grabbed her wrist and yanked her behind him. He took a half step back, pinning her between his big body and the farm truck.

The rain was biting, and the metal of the truck was cold, but Christian's back and legs provided surprising warmth. They helped ease the chattering of her teeth. Alas, nothing could stop the runaway beat of her heart. Blood pounded like a snare drum in her ears, then crashed like cymbals.

She prided herself on her bravery. How many times had she stood up to the playground bully? Or cursed out the preppy girls who'd teased her about her clothes or her ratty shoes or the fact that her mother was on her third husband in four years? But there was a vast difference between mouthy kids from the South Side and the two men pointing really scary weapons in her direction.

So close, was all she could think. They had been so close to making a clean getaway.

"You!" The man who had barked the order to put their hands in the air spoke again. "Come 'round to this side of the truck so I can see you!"

Emily glanced over her shoulder to see Angel nod. Just an infinitesimal jerk of his chin. His advance was slow and calculated, not a hitch in his step that would cause their assailants to get antsy as he joined the rest of them on the passenger side.

When she dared peek from behind Christian's broad back, she blinked away the icy water sluicing down her face and saw all the men in her group were mirroring Christian's stance. Muscled legs slightly spread. Big hands raised in the air, but only lifted to shoulder level.

None of them would put their hands any higher unless ordered, because all of them knew it was the work of an instant to drop their hands, should the opportunity arise for them to make a move to disarm their assailants. People who actually put their hands all the way over their heads, arms extended, were fools who hadn't been through months of CQC training and then spent years putting that training into practice.

Even Rusty, who'd waved buh-bye to the marines over four years ago, hadn't forgotten the lessons he'd learned about close quarters combat.

"Who are you?" Christian demanded, his voice competing with the roar of the rain against the corrugated roof of the private jet hangar. Rivers of water poured from the gutters, the tin channels unable to keep up with the rate of the deluge. "What do you want?"

"*I'm* asking the questions here, Watson!" the man yelled.

Emily would not have thought it possible for

Christian's muscles to clench any harder. But suddenly he was wound as tight as the yarn inside a baseball.

Their assailants, whoever they were, knew who he was. And it wasn't like Emily's day had been a rainbow sandwich before, but she got the feeling it had just gotten a whole hell of a lot worse.

"How do you know me?" Christian's low tone said he'd like nothing better than to reach down the men's throats and start pulling their bones out of their mouths one by one.

"What did I just say?" the man shouted.

Obviously, he was the one in charge. Big and burly, with a flat nose and a Neanderthal brow ridge, he reminded Emily of a barroom brawler. And yet there was something in his eyes that assured her he was more than that. Some scary knowledge or odd certainty.

Or maybe that's simply rage, she thought, trying with little to no success to blink the rain from her eyelashes. She didn't remember ever being this wet in her whole sorry life. Rain had filled her hiking boots until it felt like she was standing in buckets of water. The leggings she usually found so comfortable clung to her like a sopping wet second skin.

She felt Christian struggling to hold his tongue, struggling not to tell Neanderthal to take his handgun, shove it straight up his ass, and pull the trigger. All of the Knights, but Christian in particular, disliked taking orders from anyone who didn't have the title "president" or "general" in front of his name.

She didn't know what possessed her. She snuck a hand under the hem of Christian's coat, beneath his sweater, and laid her fingers against the hot skin of his lower back. Then she rubbed. Gently. Soothingly. If she wasn't mistaken, Christian shivered. But there was no way to know if it was because of her touch or because her fingers were ice cold.

"Tell the woman to step out from behind you!" Neanderthal shouted.

The woman. Not Emily. Not Miss Scott. So whoever they were—Spider's men?—they only knew Christian.

"Go bugger yourself!" was Christian's quick response. *See* what she meant about being bad at taking orders?

"You sorry sonofabitch!" Neanderthal yelled. Peeking from beneath Christian's raised arm, Emily saw spittle fly from Neanderthal's mouth and mix with the pouring rain. "Do you fancy dying?"

He took a step closer to the group, and Emily didn't miss the change in the men with her. They hadn't moved. Hadn't batted a lash. But suddenly they reminded her of a nest of vipers, poised and ready to strike.

"What I fancy is for the woman to stay precisely where she is," Christian murmured, but somehow his voice cut through the clamor of the rain. "Whatever you want, whatever you came here to do, you can do it with her back there."

"You're not the one calling the bloody shots here!"

Yep. Rage. That's definitely rage I see in his eyes.

The fool took another step closer to the group. But he quickly realized his mistake when the atmosphere around them turned electric. You could almost *taste* the tension and anticipation in the air. He quickly back-pedaled toward the SUV before yelling to his companion. "Ben! Come 'round to this side! I need you next to me!"

Aha. So Neanderthal's cohort was named Ben.

Apprehension detonated at the base of Emily's brain. If Neanderthal let a name slip, it meant she and the BKI boys were dealing with one of three possibilities. One, Neanderthal was an idiot. Two, Neanderthal had never done anything like this before. Or three, Neanderthal didn't worry about slinging around names because he planned to kill them all.

None of those scenarios made her very warm and fuzzy.

Christian must have felt the same. The muscles beneath her fingertips went rock hard. He was readying himself to make a move. Any move. All he needed was an opening.

Ben, who had been aiming at the group over the steaming hood of the SUV, slowly skirted the front of the vehicle. His black work boots splashed through puddles. His jeans were soaked clean through and hung low on his waist.

He looked a lot like Neanderthal. So much so that Emily decided they had to be brothers. But where Neanderthal appeared resolved to do whatever it was they'd come to do, *Ben* looked uncertain. His dark eyes were too wide. The big-knuckled hand on his weapon was too shaky.

Once Ben was in a better position, Neanderthal turned his attention back to Christian. "What are you up to, Watson? What did you blow up back in Port Isaac?"

"A car," Angel answered for Christian. There was no hesitation in Angel's voice. No inflection. Just those two words.

Emily's eyes pinged to the Israeli and noted that he wore the same unreadable expression he always did, despite the rivulets of icy water sluicing down his too-handsome face. She wondered if he'd look like that even if a nuclear bomb was about to fall on their heads.

"To distract the reporters, eh?" Neanderthal's thick lips quirked in a knowing smirk. "So you could sneak out the garden door, catch a plane, and leave the country?"

"Yes." Again it was Angel who answered. Maybe because he feared what calamity might spill out of Christian's mouth if Christian was left to do the job.

"And go where?" Neanderthal demanded. "To do what?"

"None of your business," Christian said.

See? Calamity.

She pinched him, but he ignored her warning. Instead, he leaned harder against her, wedging her more tightly against the pickup truck.

"I was hopin' you'd give me a reason to shoot you," Neanderthal lifted his weapon. Rain dripped in a steady stream from the barrel, and the yawning black hole at the end of it was aimed between Christian's eyes.

Emily flinched.

Christian didn't.

"I thought I needed to hear you say it," Neanderthal continued. "I thought I needed to *know* you were responsible for what happened. But I don't. All I really need to know is whether or not you're a fucking asshole." His accent made *fucking* sound more like *fooking*, and he smashed some of his words together so much, and left the hard consonant sounds off the ends of others, that Emily had a tough time understanding him. "And I have my answer."

"Hang on a second," Ben said, but Neanderthal was

already squinting one eye. Emily was sure she saw the muscles in his thick finger tighten on the trigger.

She didn't think.

She simply acted.

"Wait!" she yelled, squirming from behind Christian and dodging his hands when he tried to grab her. She stepped in front of him and raised her chin, projecting confidence and daring Neanderthal even though her insides were swirling around like the dark-gray storm clouds overhead. "If you want to kill him, you'll have to go through me."

Wow! Her voice didn't even shake. When she had time to look back on this moment—if she *lived* to look back on this moment—she was going to be quite proud of herself.

"Sodding hell, Emily!" Christian hissed at the same time a bolt of lightning sizzled overhead. It was accompanied by a deafening crash of thunder that made Ben flinch.

That's all the distraction Angel needed. The Israeli looked like a James Bond/Bruce Lee badass mofo when he bounded forward two steps and knocked Ben's weapon from his hands. A split second later, he executed a textbook roundhouse kick that swept Ben's legs out from under him.

Before Ben even hit the wet surface of the lot with a loud grunt, Neanderthal was bellowing his outrage.

Emily hardly heard it. She was too focused on Ben's gun. It had landed in an oily-looking puddle not two feet from her. Heart pounding, she went for it. All instincts and no rational thought.

Unfortunately, that landed her in a heap of trouble.

Reaching for the handgun, her fingertips had barely brushed the metal when a terrible pain ignited in her scalp. She screamed in surprise when Neanderthal yanked her up by her sodden hair. A second later, the cold kiss of his gun barrel landed on her temple, and the hand in her hair snaked around her throat. Neanderthal's fingers dug into her skin until she could feel the warning pinch of his stubby nails.

"You stupid cunt," he hissed. Then, "No! Not one more step, you sorry sonofabitch!"

When Emily dared glance from the corner of her eye, she saw Christian crouched in a fighter's stance. He wore a grimace of epic proportions, and even though his eyes were icy green, they seemed to burn with fire when he caught and held her stare through the deluge. That fire banked a second later as he straightened and turned his attention to Neanderthal.

"Let the woman go." Even though his expression had gone from *sudden death* to *cold calculation*, his voice still sounded harsh and rough, like flames crackling over dried flesh.

Neanderthal ignored him. "Damnit, Ben! Get back to your bloody feet, and get your weapon!"

I'm sorry, Emily said with her eyes when Christian flicked her another glance through the driving rain. She had ruined their chance to turn the tables on the caveman brothers.

We'll discuss it later, the muscle twitching in his solid jaw told her.

I hope we have *a later*.

Don't worry about that. His jaw hardened to granite. *We will*.

She blew out a steadying breath, desperately praying he was right. *Trusting* him to be right.

Ben pushed to his feet with a groan. After a quick shake of his head, he glanced at the puddle near Emily's feet. Every eye in the group followed Ben's down to the stranded weapon, and the electricity in the air didn't have anything to do with the storm.

Emily wasn't a great shot—which maybe she should have considered before going for Ben's handgun—but she had worked with the Black Knights long enough to recognize the make and model of the piece.

A Glock 17. Meaning it had seventeen rounds in its clip. Plenty to do the job of killing every one of them.

Ben hesitated, which infuriated Neanderthal all the more. "For fuck's sake, Ben! Do it! Hurry!"

Emily winced. The sound of Neanderthal's voice so near her eardrum threatened to blow the sucker. It let out a warning buzz.

Ben's legs were shaky. His eyes darted around the mass of hulking, angry men—well, everyone looked angry except for Angel. *He* looked the same as he had this morning at the breakfast table.

She tried to catch his gaze to convey how sorry she was that she'd fucked up his super awesome disarming of Ben, but he refused to look at her. Instead, he kept his pitch-black eyes focused on Ben, who was in the process of limping toward his lost weapon through the driving rain and deepening puddles.

"You had better think twice about hurting her," Christian said, water sluicing from his face and making his harsh features appear even harsher.

"That's a tall order," Ace piped up for the first time,

the deluge having darkened his blond locks to brown. "He looks like he'd have a hard time thinking once, much less *twice*."

What the hell? Now *Ace* had joined Christian in his death wish? *Calamity times two!*

Christian wore a wolf's smile. It was all teeth and promised the spilling of blood. "Who are you working for?" he asked Neanderthal. "Spider?"

"Shut up!" Neanderthal bellowed, shoving the barrel of his weapon more tightly against Emily's head.

Closing her eyes, she tried not to grimace, not to broadcast her pain. The BKI boys needed to concentrate on the situation, not her. She'd already made one mistake. She refused to make another.

With her eyes shut, her other senses heightened. She could smell Neanderthal's cheap cologne trying to mask the scent of old sweat. Feel his harried breath. Sense the rapid tattoo of his heart against her back. He was scared, not as sure of himself as he pretended to be.

A subtle *clack* told her Ben had palmed the Glock. She blinked open her eyes in time to watch pandemonium unfold.

The back door of the hangar burst open, and a man in black pants and a white shirt shouted, "Hello! You must be Boss's friends, and I—"

Ben, with an itchy trigger finger and an even itchier case of self-control, swung on the newcomer and fired.

The *boom* of the Glock was obscene, despite having to compete with the roar of the rain. Even worse was the look of shock on the newcomer's face when the round ripped through his chest.

"You *bastard!*" Christian bellowed, taking a step

toward Neanderthal at the same time Angel took a step toward Ben.

"Uh-uh!" Neanderthal yelled, shoving the barrel of his weapon so hard against Emily's temple that her head tipped sideways, water running horizontally across her face. She couldn't help herself. She cried out in pain. "Unless you fancy this woman's blood on your hands, you'll stop right there!"

"What do you *want*?" Christian shouted, veins standing out on either side of his neck. The look in his eyes as he blinked the raindrops from his lashes was like nothing Emily had ever seen.

There he was. The man she had always known was buried beneath that refined exterior. The warrior. The soldier. The down and dirty. The nitty-gritty.

He was beautiful in his fierceness. Terrifying in his rage.

"Jesus, Mary, and Joseph!" Ben screamed. "I killed him! I bloody well killed him!"

"Shut up!" Neanderthal yelled.

Ben didn't shut up. "We hafta get outta here!" His voice broke like a pubescent boy's.

Neanderthal didn't seem to hear him. Just continued to stare daggers at Christian. Christian stared cleavers right back.

Keeping his weapon trained on the group, his arm shaking violently, Ben ran over to Neanderthal. "Please." His eyes rolled with hysteria, water droplets beading up in his bushy eyebrows. "Please, Brother. I killed that man. Please. You gotta get me outta here."

Emily felt Neanderthal shudder with fury. He wanted to kill Christian. She could *feel* his need for it. It battled with his need to save Ben.

"Please!" Ben used his free hand to grab the sleeve of Neanderthal's jacket and give it a hard shake. "Please, get me outta here! You wanna lose another brother, for Christ's sake?"

That seemed to snap Neanderthal out of it.

Emily felt the pressure on her throat ease a split second before Neanderthal planted a hand in the middle of her back and gave her a hard shove toward Christian.

Stumbling into the arms waiting for her, she didn't pretend not to need Christian's strong, warm embrace.

"This isn't over!" Neanderthal yelled as he backed toward the SUV. "We know who you are now!"

Christian didn't respond. None of them did.

Three seconds later, Ben and Neanderthal were inside the SUV and fishtailing their way out of the parking lot.

Emily blew out a ragged breath. But any reprieve was short-lived because the sound of boots splashing through the rain puddles reminded her of the man in the black slacks and white shirt. The dead man. She'd seen the blood bloom on his chest like a sickly red rose, watched his eyes roll back in his head, and had known in that instant that he was a goner.

Damnit. *Damnit!*

She pushed from Christian's arms, but couldn't stand to lose contact with him completely. She felt dazed, confused, like someone had glued wool around the inside curve of her skull. She was an office manager, for crying out loud. Not an operator. She'd never had so much as a stapler pressed against her temple, much less a semi-auto. And she'd *never* witnessed a man being murdered. Considering all that, she wasn't too proud to admit she needed Christian's support.

Threading her fingers through his much larger ones, she turned and raced with him toward the trio already huddled around the fallen figure.

She didn't get farther than five steps before Christian tugged her to a sudden stop.

"What?" She glanced up at him through the downpour. "We need to go—"

"Why, Emily?" The muscle beneath his eye was going mad. His jaw was working to beat the band.

"Huh?" She blinked away the rain, only to have more cling to her lashes. "What do you mean? Why what?"

"Why did you do it?" His voice was quiet. His eyes were not. "Why did you step in front of me?"

"Because I thought he was about to fucking kill you, you big dummy! I thought—"

She didn't manage more than that. Her face was suddenly caught between Christian's big, warm hands. His touch was gentle despite the strength of his fingers and the rough calluses on his palms. Then, in an instant, her lips were sealed tight against his.

She blinked, shocked as shit, going cross-eyed trying to look at him, trying to determine what the hell was going on. Christian was kissing her?

Then his hot tongue pushed against the seam of her lips. Sweet baby Jesus, Christian was *kissing* her!

Chapter 6

WHAT WAS HE DOING?

What the bloody hell was he *doing*?

Emily didn't realize it, but all her acts of caring, her selfless moments of kindness—from waking him from his nightmare to pulling him into the cab of the pickup truck—had torn open his chest, ripped out his heart, and served it up on a platter.

Then, when she had stepped in front of him, ready to take a bullet that was bloody well meant for him, he had stopped pretending that what he felt for her was lust mixed with a heavy dose of vexation. Stopped pretending that he wasn't completely arse over teakettle about everything she did, everything she said. Each smile. Each laugh. Each witty quip.

In that moment, he had known. Heart. On. A. Platter.

All she had to do was take it.

Unfortunately, *he* was the one taking.

Taking a kiss she hadn't granted. Taking a taste she didn't return. Taking advantage of a beastly situation.

Had he lost his mind? Had he forgotten the unwritten rule? The one that was bold, underlined, and all in caps?

Not to mention he'd lost control of himself, of the moment. He blamed it on the memory of Emily in that bastard's grip. The sight of her there—a pistol to her head, her eyes wide with fear but her jaw gritted tight because she refused to give in to it—was forever tattooed onto the backs of his eyelids. He knew he'd see it when he closed his eyes at night.

It took effort, but he ripped his mouth away from Emily's and dropped his hands. Curling his fingers into fists, he locked his jaw until his molars begged for mercy.

"Whaaa?" She blinked up at him through the rain.

"Sorry," he ground out. The word was guttural. Hard. "I shouldn't have…" He shook his head, water flying from the ends of his hair. "Just…sorry, okay?"

Her mouth opened in a bewildered little *O*. That mouth that tasted like mint toothpaste with a lingering hint of buttered toast. His favorite flavor used to be Welsh cakes, but now it was Emily. Emily and her mint toothpaste with lingering hints of buttered toast.

"That won't happen again," he assured her before grabbing her hand and towing her toward the others.

He had thought for sure the man in the black pants and the white shirt was dead. Ben's shot looked as if it had drilled the bloke directly in the heart. Which meant Christian felt like a total prat for stopping to ask Emily why she had stepped in front of him—for stopping to *kiss* her—when they arrived in time to hear the decidedly *alive* man whisper his name. "Philippe Dubois."

"You're Boss's friend," Ace said, applying pressure to Philippe's wound. "You're the former Armée de L'Air commandant."

"*Oui. C'est moi*," Philippe managed, water dripping from his chin and earlobes. He wasn't wheezing. That was good. Meant the bullet hadn't collapsed his lung.

"Don't try to talk, Philippe," Ace told him. "Rusty, call airport security."

Christian was already pulling his mobile from his soaking hip pocket. The rain had let up. No longer a deluge, it was now more of a steady drip. "We don't need security. We need an ambulance. This man needs to go to hospital."

He dialed 999 without hesitation and waited for his call to connect. Dropping his free hand back to his side, he was startled when Emily grabbed it, threading her fingers through his. They felt dainty, delicate. And freezing wet. He desperately wanted to kiss them warmer, kiss them dry.

Glancing at her, he blinked the water from his lashes but couldn't stop the questions in his eyes. *So you forgive me? For taking without asking? For kissing you when you've given me no indication you were interested?*

Before she could answer, an operator's voice sounded in his ear, all efficient and bored. After explaining the nature of Philippe's wound and what had happened in the vaguest of terms, he gave the operator their location. When she asked for his name, he growled, "That's not what's bloody important. What's bloody important is a man's been shot and needs help. Hurry!" He abruptly hung up. "Help is on the way," he announced.

Philippe's white shirt was soaked with blood despite the pressure Ace applied.

"Damnit," Christian growled, looking around for something to stanch the bleeding. *Nothing else for it*, he decided, dropping Emily's hand—he really, truly hated doing that—and shrugging out of his coat. Next came his sweater. He tossed both pieces of clothing to her.

His white cotton undershirt was wet and sticking to his skin, but it would have to do. Pulling it over his head, he twisted it, wringing out as much water as he could, before handing it to Ace. "Here. Use this."

Ace took the wadded shirt, tucked it beneath Philippe's button-down, and pressed it to the wound. The Frenchman grimaced, but nodded that he was okay when Ace asked after him.

Christian's lungs were on fire, his heart black at the senselessness of it all.

Ben and his douche canoe brother had obviously come looking for Christian. To off him? It had certainly looked that way. But instead, they had nearly offed an innocent bystander.

He wanted to hop in that silly farm truck, take off after them, and then...what? Strangle them with his bare hands? Because he sure as fecking dog shit didn't have any weapons. They'd left those behind, not wanting to get caught with them while fleeing the country.

"We need to go." Angel stood from his crouch beside Philippe.

"Go?" Ace glared up at him, flinching at the raindrops landing on his cheeks and brow. "Are you crazy? We have to stay here until help arrives."

"No." To someone less observant, Angel's expression would look cold, calculating. But Christian saw the subtle twitch of Angel's jaw, the brief flicker of regret in his black-on-black eyes. "We cannot be here when help arrives. Too many questions. Too many people."

"We're already bumfucked," Ace insisted. "Surely everything was caught on the security cameras."

Everyone looked around, squinting up through the rain at the corners of the hangar and the lampposts across the small access road. Well, everyone except for

Emily. When Christian glanced over at her, he saw her eyes raking over his naked torso. He felt their path like a set of soft, searching hands.

Or maybe she was simply shocked by the sight of his tattoos in the light of day. Most times he went out of his way to hide them, wearing long sleeves even in the summer.

"No cameras," Philippe managed. He looked like the quintessential Frenchman. Thin, crooked nose. Neatly trimmed mustache. Severe lips that had gone white around the edges with pain. "Politicians and…celebrities fly from here, *oui*? Is why I choose this place, *n'est ce pas*? If you go now, your covers remain intact."

"Right." Rusty nodded, the ends of his curly red hair shedding water droplets across his already soaked shoulders. "And then there's the small matter of the truck. Someone could have reported it stolen by now. If we wait around for the authorities, we—"

"I'm *not* leaving a dying man!" Ace thundered.

"*Non*." Philippe shook his wet head, chuckling dryly. "Not dying. Bullet went through and through. I will survive. But you must go."

As much as Christian hated to say it: "He's right. We'd best be off." The rain was still loud enough against the corrugated roof of the hangar that anyone inside would have difficulty hearing what was going on outside. But it might not be long before someone came to investigate what had become of Philippe.

"Go." Philippe shoved at Ace's shoulder. Then he grabbed Christian's undershirt and took over applying pressure to his wound. "I will tell the *gendarmerie* nothing. Say I lost consciousness and did not see what happened or who shot me."

"I hate everything about this," Ace grumbled.

"We all do, mate." Christian clapped a wet hand on his soggy shoulder.

For a long moment, they stared down at Philippe, none of them wanting to leave a man behind. All of them knowing it was the only way.

Emily was the one to break the silence. "Christian," she whispered, her voice hoarse, her big, brown eyes seeming to take up her whole face. Water had made her eyelashes ink-black and spiky. "Your clothes."

She held out his sodden sweater. He'd pulled it over his head when the distant cry of sirens sounded.

"Fuck!" Ace cursed. His tortured expression said he was torn between saving himself and staying to make sure the Frenchman made it.

"Go!" Philippe insisted again, sucking the rainwater from his lower lip. "Come back tomorrow. Same place. Same time. My partner will take you to Chicago." He made the last sound more like *Shy-cago*. "I owe Boss a favor, *oui*? When you get home"—he panted heavily, the pain etching lines in his face—"Tell him…tell him we are even."

"Thank you, Philippe." Emily chewed her lip. Christian couldn't tell if it was rain or tears that gathered in her eyes.

"*Je t'en prie*," Philippe said, a ghost of a smile on his lips. "Anything for you, *ma belle*."

"Come!" Angel yelled, already running for the truck. "We must go!"

Angel never raised his voice, so the force of his command had them all racing after him.

They were in the truck, the old engine sputtering to

life, when the rain stopped as quickly as it had begun. Like a giant fist in the sky had suddenly switched off the faucet.

A delicate tremor shook Emily's thin frame. Christian pulled her firmly against his chest. Taking his coat from her frozen hands, he draped it over her, creating a wet cocoon.

Angel stomped on the gas, and Christian turned around as they skidded out of the parking lot. Behind them, Philippe, their chance of getting out of England, quickly disappeared from view. In front of them? A giant set of unknowns.

Who was Douche Canoe? Who was Ben? Were they Spider's men?

Christian knew the answers to none of those questions. The only thing he was certain of was that he was holding Emily in his arms, and this time he wasn't counting the seconds until he was forced to let her go. This time, there were no prime numbers. This time, he reveled that the incomparable Emily Scott was precisely where he'd always wanted her to be.

—⁓—

Saint Columb County Road…

"Oh shit! Oh *shit!*" Ben shrieked. "I can't believe I killed him!"

Fury had a red film falling in front of Lawrence's eyes when he whipped his SUV behind a billboard advert of some prick in a cowboy hat hawking Milkybars. The placement of the signage seemed ridiculous since they were on a narrow service road that couldn't see more than a handful of cars even on its best day. Nosing his vehicle into the bushes, Lawrence winced at the screech of branches against the paint.

*Goddamn Ben! God*damn *Ben!* Not only had Lawrence's cockup of a brother shot a man in cold blood—a man who *wasn't* Christian Watson—but now Lawrence's brand-new Peugeot was taking a beating because of the appearance of Ben's latent homicidal tendencies.

Slamming his SUV into Park, Lawrence turned on his younger brother. "You sodding *wanker*!" he roared. "Why did you have to go and shoot that bastard?"

Instead of answering, Ben glanced around, his eyes rolling wildly. "What are you *doing*?" His face was a dark shade of red. Ben had a vein that ran up the center of his forehead like a garden snake. When he got mad or scared, it grew to the size of an anaconda. "We don't need to *hide*! We need to get the feck out of here!"

"And go *where*?" Lawrence gripped the steering wheel until his knuckles turned white. "You wanna hop a flight and flee the country? And then what? Live on what money?"

"Jesus." Ben rubbed a shaking hand over his face. "I'm buggered. I'm well and truly buggered."

"Yeah, mate," Lawrence agreed. "And you've buggered me as well. You're a murderer, and I'm an accomplice." He posed his initial question again. "Why did you hafta go and shoot him?"

"Didn't mean to. Was an accident." Ben looked like a wild Scottish pony ready to bolt. "I was nervous. Didn't expect you to act like you were gonna slot Watson."

It hadn't been an act.

In that moment, fury—and the memory of their

older brother—had outweighed all of Lawrence's rational thoughts. That Watson had been standing there, so defiant, so arrogant, when the eldest Michelson brother *couldn't* because he was rotting six feet underground—not to mention what had happened *after* the Michelsons had covered his casket in dirt—had struck Lawrence as the ultimate injustice. He had been determined to balance the scales. An eye for an eye, and damn the consequences.

He hadn't snapped out of his bloodthirsty trance until he heard Ben's weapon bark and turned to see some wanker in a white shirt go down like a sack of potatoes.

"And those blokes…" Ben shuddered. "Did you see how quickly they moved? That whole time I thought we were seconds away from having them waylay us and turn our own weapons against us. When I heard that door open and that guy shout…" He swallowed. "Instinct took over. I protected my six and took a shot before I had time to think."

"And a helluva shot it was."

"You say that like it's a good thing."

"Not good that you've screwed us over, but good that all those hours at the firing range paid off."

Ben laughed, but it wasn't a happy sound. "I guess they did, didn't they?"

"Yeah." Lawrence shook his head in wonder. Of all the things for his twat of a little brother to excel at. Too bad it'd landed them in a world of trouble. "But now we gotta figure out what we're gonna do."

"I could say it was self-defense."

Lawrence snorted. "With five witnesses who will claim the contrary? Not sure any jury will believe you, Brother."

Ben shook his head. It caused a curl of hair to flop over his left eyebrow, reminding Lawrence of when Ben was a boy with big eyes and a penchant for lying in their back garden to watch the butterflies flit around their mother's rosebushes. The two eldest Michelson boys had always been sword fighting with sticks or playing at being soldiers by hiding in the bushes and ambushing their fat tabby cat, but Ben had been the gentle soul. The dreamer.

All the anger drained from Lawrence in that moment. He knew without a doubt that he would do whatever it took to save Ben's sorry hide. He hadn't been there for his older brother. He would make up for that by being there for his younger one.

"But wait…" The fire of an idea sparked in Ben's eyes. "We could say we went to Port Isaac to confront Watson about our brother after we saw the news program. And then we could say we heard the explosion and saw Watson and his mates acting suspicious. And *then* we could say we decided to follow 'em to see what they were on about. We could say that when we saw they were about to hop a flight and flee the country, we thought it was our duty as constables to stop them and ask them some questions. We can say one of 'em attacked me, and in the confusion, I fired a wild shot and accidentally slotted that bloke. It's close enough to the truth to be believable."

Ben looked altogether pleased with himself. But the merits of his argument flew out the window when the sound of an engine reached Lawrence's ear and a flash of green caught his eye.

The old truck.

Watson and his friends were loaded inside and flying

down the access road like the hounds of hell were baying at their heels. They were fleeing the scene. They were fleeing the bloody scene!

Suddenly, the solution to all Lawrence's problems presented itself.

He shoved his Peugeot into gear and slowly backed from behind the billboard, careful to wait until the farm truck was too far ahead to see his maneuver. Once he could barely keep sight of the vehicle, he stomped on the gas in pursuit.

"What the hell?" Ben blinked in astonishment.

"Your idea 'bout how to handle things is good." Lawrence gave his brother only half a mind. He was too busy getting details sorted. "But I have one better."

"What's that?" To say Ben's tone was leery would be an understatement.

"We kill 'em all. Get rid of the witnesses."

"Oh Jesus." Ben turned as white as a ghost.

"Best leave him outta this one, little brother." The fire of upcoming battle burned through Lawrence's veins. Watson would pay. Watson and all those with him would *bloody well pay*! Lawrence had already lost his family because of that fecking tosser. He refused to lose his freedom too. "Today, we do the devil's work."

"Who the hell *were* those guys?" Emily demanded.

She was shaking. But she wasn't sure if it was because she was soaking wet. Because she'd recently been oh-so-lucky to have her head introduced to the business end of a loaded weapon. Or because Christian had kissed her, and as a result, her whole world had gone wonky.

Surely it wasn't that third thing. In the universe of kisses, his hadn't been all that groundbreaking. In fact, she'd barely had time to react when he'd pulled back, looked at her like she'd kneed him in the gnads, and then swore it would never happen again.

Of course, she couldn't deny his lips had been hot and dominant. Truth was, she couldn't recall ever being kissed like that before. It was part possession, part concession. All need.

So, yeah. Okay. Maybe in the universe of kisses, his *had* been pretty groundbreaking. And if he'd given her a damn second to get over her shock, she could have sunk in and enjoyed his oral onslaught while simultaneously conducting one of her own.

A voice in her head piped up, reminding her of what had happened the last time she'd decided to throw caution to the wind and knock boots with a coworker. It was interrupted by Christian saying, "All we know for certain is that they're brothers."

"And likely Spider's men," Angel added.

Christian's tone was skeptical when he said, "Perhaps. But when I brought up Spider, neither of them flinched. And what did that one say? Something about *me* being responsible?"

"Maybe they're just good actors," Ace suggested. "And all of that about you being responsible could be because they're blaming you for what happened last week. For being part of the team that took down Spider's money launderer."

"Perhaps," Christian said again.

"So what the flippin' freak are we supposed to do now?" Emily asked. "And, Angel, why are you going the wrong way? Shouldn't we be headed back in the direction we came?"

"The authorities will come that way. So we go this way," Angel said.

"Right." She nodded. "And hope this road doesn't dead end and screw us over royally."

"It doesn't dead end. It turns into a proper provincial lane about a mile ahead, meanders through the countryside for another three miles, and then splits into a Y," Christian said. "If we go right once we're there, we'll be on our way toward the motorway. If we go left, we'll end up at Trenor Manor."

Emily frowned back at him. "First of all, how did you know all that? You a walking GPS or something? And second of all, what's Trenor Manor?"

"When I was a boy, my parents used to bring me 'round this way after visiting my uncle in Port Isaac. As for Trenor Manor, it's an old Elizabethan manor house. It's been kept up by the National Trust for years. They used to give tours a few hours each day."

"The motorway it is," Ace said determinedly.

"But first we need to exchange this vehicle for another. If the truck has not been reported stolen yet, it soon will be," Angel added in that stiff, overly formal way he had of speaking. Emily knew it was an affectation. Angel was careful with slang, contractions, accent, anything that would give anyone an idea where he was originally from. "The local police will start looking for it by combing through CCTV footage," he continued. "The last thing we want is to be spotted in this thing."

"And then what?" she asked. "Do we rent a motel room and lie low?"

"Too risky." Ace shook his head. "We don't want some front-desk clerk to hear from the local news that a pilot was shot at the airport. He or she might decide that the five soaking wet people who checked into Room 8B seem suspicious and call the local five-o."

"Right," Rusty agreed. "Better to stay off the grid. I say we find some field or derelict underpass to park under, then stay put and do our best impression of a can of sardines until tomorrow."

The thought of spending the rest of the day and all night wedged into the stolen truck out in the middle of nowhere—with nothing to eat, nothing to drink, nowhere to wash up or change into dry clothes—had Emily's top lip curling in distaste. Not that she expected room service or silk sheets when running for her life, but still...

She suddenly wished she'd eaten a few more slices of bacon for breakfast. And maybe said *yes* for once to a helping of baked beans.

Had she remembered to restock the granola bars in her backpack?

Christian checked the time on his big, black diver's watch. "I might have a better idea." He tugged his phone from his hip pocket and brought up his mobile web browser.

"What are you thinking?" Emily asked, wiggling into a more comfortable position.

Christian wasn't exactly a contender for the title of Most Comfortable Lap. He was far too solid. Too hot. Even the freezing rainwater soaking her clothes wasn't enough to combat the sheer magnitude of the heat coming off him.

Glancing over her shoulder, she expected an answer to her question. But instead, she discovered herself on the receiving end of the most sexually aggressive, completely carnal, totally *hungry* looks she'd ever seen.

Her breath sawed out of her so fast it almost hurt. Then the look on his face was gone, and she was left wondering if she'd imagined it in the first place.

She convinced herself that *of course* she had. Given her poor performance when he lip-locked her, there was no way he was considering a repeat. Which, okay, yeah, that made her pride prick up. She was overcome by the oddest urge to grab his ears and lay a doozy on him. You know, just to prove she could.

"I'm thinking there's a way we can avoid the motorway, avoid being crammed into a motel room or this truck, and instead each have our own bed tonight," he said, and she found her eyes glued to the dimple in his chin. She'd always wanted to press a finger into it.

"Color me intrigued," she said.

"Trenor Manor is in the middle of nowhere. It's nestled back in a thick wood. And according to the website"—he pointed to the screen on his phone—"the house should be empty of sightseers in ten minutes. If things are still run as they were twenty-five years ago, the caretaker will lock up and set off soon after. We could break in and stay until the place opens up at oh-nine-hundred tomorrow."

A manor house set back in a thick wood? Emily got the oddest impression that she was poised to enter a fairy tale. Would the clock and teapot come alive? Would she find herself dancing around in a yellow ball gown?

Beneath Christian's smooth facade definitely lurked a beast. Trouble was, no amount of makeup or hair product would ever turn her into Beauty. She had none of the soft curves or cushiony flesh that men seemed to go *goo-goo-gah-gah* over. Well, except for maybe her ass. Any extra weight she carried seemed to end up there. But even if you took her out of her leggings and sweatshirt and slapped on some lip gloss and mascara, the most she could hope for was passably pretty.

"It could work." Ace's expression was contemplative. "As long as we could get in and disarm the alarm system. I mean, this place has to have an alarm system, right?"

"Hi." Emily waved to Ace. Then she pointed to Angel. "Have you met Angel? I don't think he's met an alarm system he can't disarm."

"Thanks for the vote of confidence." Angel took his eye off the road to glance into the rearview mirror. If she hadn't been watching him, she might have missed the slight narrowing of his eyes.

"What?" She tried to glance through the back window, only to be met with one of Christian's perfected scowls.

Obviously she *had* imagined that carnal, hungry look on his face earlier. Because now his fierce green eyes held a familiar irritation that raised her hackles.

She tried her best to ignore it and instead focus on the situation at hand. "What do you see back there, Angel?" she asked. Then thought, *Oh, screw it*. It wasn't in her nature to back down from confrontation. "And also, Christian, why are you trying to fry my eyebrows off my face with your laser-beam eyes?"

"You're squirming. *Again*," he muttered through a clenched jaw.

"So?" Then she felt the ungentle prod of his erection. "Oh." She bit her lip, trying not to laugh. "Sorry."

But she wasn't *really* sorry. After that kiss, and certainly after he'd given her that disgusted look and promised it would never happen again, her ego could use the boost. Plus, it might be enough to stop her from kissing the holy Moses out of him.

You know, just to prove she could.

"We might have company," Angel said. "There's been a vehicle behind us for a while. Too far back to make out the color or model, but…"

He let the sentence dangle when they came to the Y in the road. Emily glanced right. Nothing but pasture, rolling hills, and the great, gray ribbon of the A39 in the far distance. To the left was more of the undulating Cornish countryside. But further along she could see where the open farmland snuggled up to the deep green of a forest.

"I suggest we wait here for a bit," Angel said. "See what we see."

And so that's exactly what they did. They waited. In silence. Until Emily couldn't hear anything except Christian's deep breathing. Until she couldn't see anything but the arm he'd wrapped loosely around her waist. Until she couldn't feel anything but the heat of him all along her back.

Until she thought she'd go flippin' crazy.

When she opened her mouth to say—she wasn't sure what, anything to distract herself from everything that was Christian—Angel pointed at the rearview mirror. "There. See that?"

They all leaned toward the rearview mirror, but the vehicle behind them had already headed downhill, sinking out of sight.

"Could be nothing," Ace suggested.

"Could be the authorities," Angel disagreed.

"Could be those asshats from the airport," was Rusty's addition.

Emily hated to be left out, so she added, "Could be the authorities *looking* for the asshats from the airport."

But after another minute of silence, another minute of waiting, it appeared whoever had been behind them had turned off onto another road. The vehicle's running lights never reappeared in the rearview mirror.

A hard puff of air blasted from Ace's lips. "Holy Noah with his balls out. I will be *so* happy when we ditch this island. I've had just about all the fun in England I can stand."

"Hear, hear," Emily concurred.

Apparently satisfied that their tail wasn't, in fact, a tail, Angel turned the farm truck left, heading for the woods that loomed in the distance. As the line of trees drew nearer, Emily was left with an odd sense of misgiving. Or perhaps it was a premonition.

Something important would go down at the manor house. She didn't know what it would be.

Then again, maybe her imagination was running away with her. Hadn't she envisioned herself in a yellow ball gown not five minutes ago?

Chapter 7

THE UNNAMED ROAD LEADING THROUGH THE WOOD TO THE manor house was just as Christian remembered: gravel, full of potholes, and as country as a thatched roof. Small rocks lined the edges. Beyond them was a forest of towering trees. And beneath the trees were the first purple blooms of bluebells.

Soon the forest floor would be covered with the delicate harbingers of spring. But in late March, only the most intrepid and impatient flowers pushed through the black, leaf-strewn soil to make their presence known.

A feeling of familiarity was soon replaced by something else. Something a tad wistful and melancholy. It was what happened to remorse after a number of years. It turned into a soft, sooty kind of sadness.

Emily proved she was a witch or a mind reader, or both, because she glanced over her shoulder and said, "So, we hid out in your uncle's summer cottage for five days, and now we're about to hide out in a manor house that your parents apparently took you to as a kid. Yet, in all the time I've known you, you've never talked about family. Not your folks. Certainly not an uncle. And in all the time we've been in England, you haven't tried to contact any of them."

A couple of seconds ticked by. When Emily pursed her lips, Christian felt a muscle twitch under his left eye. "Pardon? Was there a question in there?"

She rolled her eyes. "The question is, what gives? Where are your folks? Where is this mysterious uncle? And why haven't you gone to see any of them since you've been back here?"

Before he could answer, Angel hit a pothole. The truck lurched sideways, forcing Emily to loop an arm around Christian's shoulders or else risk being tossed headfirst across the laps of the other three men in the vehicle. Suddenly her face was disturbingly close, her nose a mere inch from Christian's.

He could see the gold flecks in her irises, the slight irregularity in the roundness of the small beauty mark high on her cheek. His mind immediately went somewhere it shouldn't. When he exhaled, damn if his breath didn't shudder out of him.

"My parents are dead," he whispered, and wondered if she really did suck in a lungful of air when his breath feathered over her lips or if he was simply imagining it. "And I haven't gone 'round to see my uncle because we've not spoken in over twenty-five years."

Emily shook her head, her eyes suddenly sad, saying without words, *I'm so sorry.* Aloud, she said, "I shouldn't have brought it up."

He shrugged, still slightly breathless at how near she was. If he leaned forward the tiniest bit he could... No. *No!* Had he learned nothing from the airport's car park? He'd have to be blind, deaf, and dumber than a turnip not to realize she hadn't kissed him back.

"I can be too nosy sometimes," she said, keeping her voice low, making the conversation feel intimate even though there was no way everyone in the truck wasn't listening in.

The quirk of his mouth said, *Sometimes? How about* all *the time.*

"Fine." She chuckled. "I'm too nosy *all* the time. Which means you won't be surprised that not five seconds after admitting it, I'm asking you what happened twenty-five years ago to make you lose touch with your uncle."

He could have prevaricated. He didn't fancy talking about his past. But given his recent revelations—you know, the bit about him being arse over teakettle for her?—and despite her out-and-out rejection of him back at the airport, he wanted her to *know* him.

"My dad died," he whispered. "Afterward, Uncle David didn't fancy having anything to do with me or my mum."

She cocked her head, a frown drawing her eyebrows together. "That's kind of an asshole move, don't you think?"

"Not really. Considering it was my mum's fault Dad died in the first place."

He watched the emotions flicker through Emily's eyes. There was shock. Sadness. Followed by something that made him grit his teeth because it looked dangerously close to pity.

He could take loads when it came to Emily. Her teasing. Her taunting. Ruddy hell, even the fact their kiss had proved she really *didn't* fancy him. At least not *that* way. But one thing he couldn't take was her pity. Or anyone else's, come to think of it. Because only wretched, pathetic things were to be pitied, and he hadn't pulled himself out of the gutter by his bootstraps to allow anyone ever to see him as a wretched, pathetic thing again.

When he didn't carry on or explain, she lifted her brow, a question in her eyes. *And?*

And what? his pursed lips answered her.

She dropped the silent eye-conversation and decided to go with the real deal. "You can't seriously think to leave us hanging on that hook. You have to give us more."

Us. That was suddenly the sticking point.

No matter how intimate their conversation might *feel*, the truth was it wasn't intimate at all. Christian wanted *Emily* to know him, not every Tom, Dick, and Harry within earshot. Or Rusty, Ace, and Angel, as the case may be.

"I haven't got to do anything except for die and pay taxes," he told her.

She narrowed her eyes. "Stop trying to Christian Watson your way out of this thing."

"Am I meant to know what that means?"

"You know." She made a rolling motion with her hand. "You change the subject, or clam up, or turn the tables and start grilling me so I forget what I asked you."

Before he could respond, Angel yanked the truck a hard right and took them over the rocks lining the road with teeth-clacking speed.

"What the—" Emily grabbed the dashboard with one hand and a fistful of Christian's hair with the other.

"Hell!" Ace finished for her.

"Company," was all Angel said as he maneuvered the old farm truck around trees like a rally car driver on an obstacle course.

He drove them down into a small depression, soggy leaves squishing under the tires. Christian's cods took a beating, thanks to the rough ride and Emily's ass.

Then Angel stomped on the brake. The farm truck skidded to a stop, and the Israeli immediately switched off the engine.

All was quiet except for the *tick-tick* of the cooling motor and the *drip-drop* of the water that fell from the wet trees to land atop the truck's roof.

"Leave the roots if you will, darling." Christian grabbed Emily's wrist. He could feel the rapid thrum of her heartbeat beneath the soft heat of her skin.

"Huh?" She blinked at him. "Oh!" She released his hair, then ran her fingers through it. He didn't know if she was trying to get it back into place, or if she was trying to soothe the sting of her fisted fingers. All he knew was that he wanted her to carry on touching him for…well…*forever*.

Sod it all.

"The people you thought were behind us before?" Ace asked, craning his head, trying to see above the shallow ravine to the road beyond.

"No." Angel shook his head. "This car is coming from the direction of the manor house."

Christian's chin jerked. He saw Emily's do the same. "How could you tell?" he asked. "We were 'round a bend."

"I saw a piece of gravel hit a tree up ahead. Likely kicked up by a tire."

Emily made a face. "You *saw* that? My God, who *are* you?"

Angel turned to her, one corner of his mouth quirked. It was the Angel equivalent of an ear-to-ear smile. "I'm Batman."

Emily's pretty mouth slung open, and she turned to blink at Christian in astonishment. "Did he just make a joke?" She squinted at Angel. "I didn't know he knew *how* to make jokes."

"I didn't know he watched movies," Ace added.

Rusty got in his two pence. "Maybe he doesn't. Maybe he reads comic books."

That had them *all* turning to squint at Angel.

"What?" Angel demanded. "Why are you all staring at me like I have two heads?"

"We're trying to imagine you with a Marvel in hand," Ace said.

"I think Batman is a DC Comics character," Rusty corrected.

"I *watch* movies," Angel insisted. Christian was surprised to see a look of pique flash across the Israeli's face before he once more donned his impenetrable mask. "What? Do you think I crawled out from under a rock?"

"Maybe not a *rock*..." Ace let the sentence dangle.

Since Angel's history was a big, black hole, and since he'd been taking solo missions since signing on with BKI, the Chicago compound was often rife with speculation. The most commonly asked questions were: Who is he really? Where is he really? What the hell is he up to really?

Angel shook his head. Then he jerked his chin toward the window. "Look there."

They all rubbernecked a peek over the lip of the depression and saw a late-model sedan fly by them on the gravel road. A woman with snow-white hair pulled back in a severe bun was at the wheel. By the certain way she roared down the winding road—Christian might go so far as to say the *reckless* way—there was no doubt she was familiar with her surroundings.

The caretaker has left the building!

"How much farther to the manor house?" Angel asked.

"One mile, give or take," Christian told him.

"Then this is as good a place as any to leave the truck."

"What?" Emily looked around. "Why leave it here?"

Given how bravely she'd faced down the Wankstain Brothers, it was difficult for Christian to remember that she wasn't an operator. She had all the grit of one. All the fire in her eyes and steel in her spine. But she didn't have the training the rest of them did, or the knowledge that had come through endless missions in countless different countries.

"This is a stolen vehicle," he explained, reaching for the door handle, "and if it's been reported stolen, we daren't have it anywhere near us. Also, even if it *hasn't* been reported stolen, we still don't want there to be any evidence of our presence at the manor house. Who knows if the local constable does patrols out this way? Best to leave the truck here. Out of sight."

"Right." Emily nodded, sliding off Christian's lap to follow the others who were already piling out of the truck.

Christian remained where he was for a couple of seconds. For one thing, his right leg was asleep. For another, he needed a tad bit of time to battle the odd sense of bereftness that Emily's sudden departure caused.

When he finally exited the pickup truck and grabbed his rucksack from the bed, it was to find Emily frowning and gnawing her lower lip. "What's wrong?" he asked.

She looked around at the dripping forest, then back at the gravel road. "This truck could sit out here for weeks before it's found."

His frown asked, *Yeah, so?*

Her pursed lips said without words, *So whoever owns it no doubt needs it*.

See? She tried to act all tough and take-no-guff. But she couldn't hide her soft underbelly. Emily cared. Even about people she didn't know and would likely never meet.

He glanced around. Everyone was busy shrugging into their packs. Everyone except Angel, that is.

The former Mossad agent was wiping down the inside of the truck again. He seemed to do that by rote, which was odd considering the man didn't even *have* fingerprints. They'd been burned off him at the same time he'd undergone extensive plastic surgery and had his vocal cords scoured.

When Christian turned back to Emily, it was to find her still eyeing the truck, still gnawing that delectable lower lip and driving him to distraction. He desperately wanted to tell her they could move the farm truck to a more visible area. But that wouldn't be thinking with his brain. That would be thinking with the decidedly less intelligent organ beating behind his breastbone.

Laying a reassuring hand on her arm, he could feel the delicateness of her bones even through the puffy fabric of her damp coat. It reminded him how Head Honcho Wankstain had manhandled her and made him entertain a brief fantasy of cutting the bastard's bollocks off. "When we make it back to Chicago tomorrow night," he said, "you can call in an anonymous tip. How does that sound?"

Her expression went from *I hate everything about this* to *sunshine and rainbows*. In fact, the smile she sent him was huge and toothy and so damn hypnotic he had to look away.

"Everyone ready?" Angel slammed the driver's side door with his elbow. When he was met with a series of nods, he grabbed his rucksack and slung it over his shoulder. "All right then." He headed in the direction of the manor house.

Ace and Rusty fell into step behind him, leaving Christian and Emily to bring up the rear.

"Ladies first." Christian waved a hand.

"Age before beauty," she countered, that mischievous glint he loved so well winking at him from her dark eyes.

"I'm hardly *that* much older than you." He turned to trail after the others because he knew better than to fight her.

Emily could be frustratingly stubborn when it came to him. A few times he'd wondered if perhaps, just perhaps, and despite her protestations to the contrary, it was because she had a bit of a thing for him. But that kiss had proved otherwise. She might as well have had a combination lock on her lips for all the encouragement she'd given him.

Heat flew to his face at the memory, and he thanked his lucky stars she'd taken pity on him and hadn't brought it up since. In fact, she seemed perfectly pleased to pretend it had never happened.

Good. Great. Brilliant.

He was pleased too. He *was*. She'd let him down in the gentlest way possible, and even if it'd caused a rather large fissure to snake across his heart, at least the bloody organ wasn't broken.

He could keep Emily in his life as a coworker, might he even be so bold as to say…a *friend*? And that would be enough.

He *swore* to himself it would be enough.

"How would you know how old I am?" she asked, dragging his mind back to the conversation. "You been reading my file?"

He knew he'd hit a nerve because her South Side accent had thickened. It was her defense mechanism. When someone or something got too close, she turned up the volume on her blue-collar Bridgeport 'hood girl.

"Indeed not." He shook his head, determined to fall back into their familiar routine of taunting and slagging...or *teasing* as the Yanks liked to call it. Because even if that wasn't all he wanted from her, at least it was something. "But the fact that it would bother you if I did piques my interest. For a woman who claims to have no secrets, you sure are prickly as a hedgehog about certain aspects of your past."

"There you go, trying to Christian Watson your way out of answering the question by pulling a conversational about-face."

"Touché," he allowed. Then he told her, "You celebrated a birthday three months ago, and I overheard you telling one of the women back at BKI that you could no longer get away with making silly mistakes. That it was one thing to cock things up in your twenties. You could blame it on youth. But once you hit thirty, being young and inexperienced didn't hold any water."

"Eavesdropper," she accused.

"Loud talker," he fired back.

Glancing over his shoulder, he found her head down. She was watching her footing over the uneven, leaf-strewn ground, and her damp hair created dark, wavy curtains that hid her face from him. The forest held the earthy aromas of moist soil and wet moss. But even so, he was almost certain he could detect the slightest hint of her shampoo.

Without glancing up, she said, "But you're still two years older than I am, so my statement holds. Age before beauty."

"Fine." He blew out an overly dramatic breath as he returned his attention to the path. "I'm old, and you're bcautiful."

He heard her boots stumble to a stop behind him. When he frowned over his shoulder, the look of astonishment that wallpapered her face brought him to an immediate halt. "What? I just let you win. Why are you staring at me like I've sprouted a second set of twig and berries from my forehead?"

"You think I'm beautiful?" The last word winged up an octave.

His brow pinched. "Of course I do. Any heterosexual red-blooded man would."

Emily shook her head. "I'm too skinny. I don't know how to put on makeup. I barely have any boobs."

"Are you serious? Or are you fishing for compliments?" How could she not know how truly lovely she was? The woman had occasion to look in a damn mirror.

"I don't even *own* a set of high heels." She set her jaw at a mulish angle. "My preferred mode of dress involves hair ties and sweatshirts. I am the most *un*glamorous woman I know."

Okay. Apparently she really *didn't* know how lovely she was. It was the bloody damnedest thing.

"Glamour doesn't have anything to do with beauty, darling. As for your breasts…" He allowed his gaze to travel over her chest, even though he couldn't see past her puffy coat. Warmth stole into his blood, making him glance off into the distance. "Most men would say they've no use for more than a mouthful."

Speaking of mouths, when he turned back, it was to find hers slung open. Deciding he'd said more than he should, he set off after the others. After a couple of seconds, he heard Emily's hiking boots crunching atop the wet leaves behind him.

"On the subject of secrets…" she said, even though they were well past that stage in the conversation. "Don't think I've forgotten that you still owe us an explanation for why you didn't join Boss in Chicago right away. Plus, that bit about your folks requires further clarification, and you know it."

"And *now* who's Christian Watsoning her way 'round the subject?" He purred the words, but there was steel woven into his tone.

Chapter 8

"WHICH WAY DID THEY GO?" BEN GLANCED RIGHT, THEN left at the Y in the road.

"You're asking me?" Lawrence growled incredulously. "*You* were the one who was meant to keep watch on 'em while I was driving."

"I *was*!" Ben shot back. "But we waited too long in the valley between those hills, and I lost sight of 'em."

"And whose fault was that? You said they were parked and that we needed to hold steady to make sure they hadn't spotted us."

"They *were* parked. And for a bloody long time too!"

Red once more tried to crowd Lawrence's vision, but he blinked it away. He couldn't let his anger consume him. He had to keep sight of the goal, which was saving Ben's sorry hide, saving his own sorry hide, and finally balancing the scales of justice for his family. "Damnit, Ben! We're not meant to be fighting about this. We're not each other's enemy. *They're* the enemy."

"Why?" Ben shook his head perplexedly. "Because *maybe* Christian Watson was the stupid prat who got our brother killed? We don't even know for sure if—"

"We *know*," Lawrence insisted, his fingers tapping impatiently on the steering wheel. Time was of the essence. And this conversation was wasting precious amounts of it.

"*No*. We *don't*," Ben insisted, the vein pulsing in his forehead.

Lawrence's little brother could be infuriatingly stubborn when he wanted to be. Lawrence recalled the time when Ben was eight years old and had gotten fed up with his older brothers always picking on him. To solve the problem, Ben had pitched a tent in the back garden and *lived* there for two whole months. It was only once winter set in and their mother feared her baby boy would die of hypothermia that she finally, with great crocodile tears in her eyes, convinced him to move back into the house.

"We *don't* know if Watson is guilty," Ben continued. "We *suspect*. That's a different thing entirely. As for the others? They're innocent. I think we needa slow down and rethink this—"

"*Innocent?*" Lawrence spat incredulously. "Would *innocent* people set off an explosion in a tiny seaside village? Would *innocent* people take the back roads to a private airport hangar when the motorway would have been twice as fast? Would *innocent* people knock off from the scene of a crime? For Christ's sake, Ben. *Think* about it. They set off the explosion to escape the press. They took the back roads to avoid the CCTV cameras. They knocked off from the scene at the airport because they don't wanna speak to the authorities. They. Are. *Not*. Innocent. They are bad people doing bad things. And even if it wasn't our job to take scum like 'em off the streets, remember that doing 'em in is the only way we're getting out of this without being thrown in the clink."

"Speaking of cameras," Ben said, "who's to say what happened at the airport wasn't recorded, huh? We could've been caught on tape—"

"No." Lawrence didn't let him finish. He could almost *hear* the second hand of an imaginary clock *tick-tocking* in his ear. "There weren't any cameras."

"How can you know that?" Ben's face had turned candy-apple red.

Lawrence was meant to be the hotheaded one, so it irked him to have to be coolheaded now. "Remember that stabbing six months back? The one where two airplane mechanics got into a row in the car park over a woman, and one came away from the scuffle with a screwdriver lodged in his eye?"

Ben frowned. "The charges on the screwdriver stabber were dropped, weren't they?"

"Indeed." Lawrence nodded emphatically. "Because the stabber insisted the victim accidentally ran into the screwdriver when he went on the attack. And since there were no cameras or recordings to prove the stabber wrong, he walked away scot-free."

"That was here?" Ben shook his head. "I mean, back at the private hangar?"

"The very same. So as long as we play our cards right, we can get outta this."

"But *killing* 'em all, Lawrence? That's going too far."

Lawrence begged to differ. "Why? They're obviously mixed up in some bad shit. How do we know they're not murderers themselves? That explosion back at Port Isaac? It was ruddy *huge*. I'd be surprised if there weren't casualties. And besides, slotting 'em all not only saves our hides, but it also gets justice for our family. Haven't we always talked about making the one responsible pay?"

"Yeah...but..." When Ben swallowed, his throat sounded sticky. "How will we explain five dead bodies?"

A slow grin spread across Lawrence's face. Ben blanched and backed away as if Lawrence had spiders crawling between his teeth. "We won't have to explain anything. Old Man Murphy is pouring a foundation for his new barn tomorrow night. We'll simply go in late and dump the bodies in the concrete before it dries. Then pour more over the top of 'em and even it all out. No one will ever know."

Lawrence had never fancied their neighbor. The stodgy old farmer had always looked at Lawrence out of the sides of his eyes, like he didn't trust Lawrence, like he sensed something was *off* with Lawrence. But now the grumpy, gray-haired fart would come in handy.

"You've watched too many gangster movies," Ben accused.

"And learned from the best of 'em."

"But what about the dead man at the airport?"

"See, the beauty of this plan is that we won't have to explain *anything* as long as we take care of the witnesses."

"But my weapon is in the ballistics database. Once they pull the slug from him, they'll—

"We've access to the database. We'll go in and swap out your information so no one's the wiser. Don't you see? If we do everything just like I say, no one will ever know we were at that airport." Ben opened his mouth, which compelled Lawrence to play his trump card. "And before you try to throw another spanner in the works, remember our parents. Remember what happened to 'em."

"Jesus," Ben breathed, shaking his head.

"I already told you to leave him outta this." Lawrence flipped on his blinker. "And we're going left here."

"Why?" Ben looked around confusedly.

"Because they did their best to avoid the CCTV cameras before, and I'd bet my left bollock they'll do their best to avoid 'em now."

Ben eyed the GPS display on the console of Lawrence's SUV. "But there's nothing this way," he insisted as the hedgerows grew on either side of them. "It's a drafty old manor house that's been kept up by the National Trust."

"Then a drafty old manor house is our destination." Lawrence stomped on the gas as a sense of fate grew inside him. This day, this *moment* was what he'd been waiting years for. It was his destiny, when he put right all the wrongs done to his family.

Trenor Manor…

Emily mimicked the men by taking cover behind the mossy trunk of a tree near the edge of the clearing that surrounded the old estate house.

Her heart hammered. Not because she was scared they might be seen or because the mile trek through the woods had been all that arduous, but because she was still reeling from the fact that Christian thought she was beautiful.

Not cute. Not kinda, sorta pretty. But *beautiful*.

To recap: he'd popped a boner every time she climbed into his lap. He'd kissed her without warning—*holy duck balls had he ever!* And he'd admitted to thinking she was beautiful.

And guess what that means, boys and girls? she thought a little desperately. *That means I'm in serious trouble.*

It was one thing to withstand his savage good looks, his smooth British charm, and his panty-melting accent when she thought he didn't like her. *Haters gonna hate, and all that jazz.* It was another thing entirely to withstand it when she was getting the impression that the exact opposite might be true.

How would she ever be able to look at him, talk to him, *work* with him knowing that he wanted to, in the parlance of their time, introduce his boy part to her girl part?

Then again, she could be making a mountain out of a molehill. There *had* been that look on his face after he kissed her. And then there was the itty-bitty, not-so-insignificant fact that he hadn't brought it up since.

Not a word.

Not a gesture.

Not even a silent eye-convo.

So perhaps, like he'd said, his erection didn't have a thing to do with her. And perhaps that kiss had been nothing but a knee-jerk reaction in the heat of the moment—something he immediately regretted. And perhaps him saying she was beautiful was simply a matter of semantics, like… Did he think spotted puppies and babies were beautiful?

Glancing two trees over, she tried to catch Christian's eye. She wanted to ask him, *So, you want to do me or what?* Unfortunately, he couldn't feel her eyes tapping him on the back. Or else he was ignoring them. Which left her with no recourse but to sigh and turn her attention toward what seemed to hold his. Namely, the manor house.

Large by American standards, but likely somewhat

small in a British nobleman's estimation, it was two stories of weathered gray stone. Its deeply pitched, gray slate roof sported six chimneys, and its leaded-glass windows were a web of diamond-shaped patterns that caught the weak sunlight straining through the brooding cloud cover overhead. The front lawn was well kept with bushes shaped into fanciful creatures. And two timeworn rock lions guarded the gravel footpath leading up to the gabled front door.

Like most historic homes in England, the manor house looked like something straight out of a fairy tale. Again, Emily was hit with the image of herself twirling around in a frilly yellow dress. Of course, the image was ruined when she let her mind's eye travel down the length of her imaginary gown to her weathered hiking boots. She hadn't been kidding when she said she didn't own a pair of heels.

"Brilliant. Looks like we're good to go," Christian whispered. "Let's fan out. Check the security system. Emily, you and Angel go 'round to the right. Ace and Rusty, you two head left. I'll see to the front, and then we'll all meet in the back garden, yeah?"

It didn't escape Emily's notice that Christian had paired her with Angel. If he was lusting after her hot bod—she couldn't resist a mental snort—he would want to keep her with him, right? Right. So she *had* been making a mountain out of molehill.

When Christian finally turned to look at her, she gave him a smile, trying to make it look friendly, all calm and serene. You know, the total opposite of what she was feeling. Her expression must not have been very convincing, however, because Christian frowned at her.

His pretty green eyes asked, *What the bloody hell did I do this time?*

Instead of answering, she dropped his gaze and walked over to Angel. "All right, partner," she whispered. "In the timeless words of Larry the Cable Guy, let's *git-r-done*."

Angel cast her a hooded glance. "Am I supposed to know who that is?"

She shrugged. "Figured I'd take a chance. You *did* whip out that Batman quote earlier. Thought maybe you were getting hip to American pop culture, yo."

He snorted before quietly sliding from behind the tree.

She followed in his footsteps, ignoring the urge to creep after him on tiptoe with her arms drawn up and her hands curved into claws like some sort of cartoon character. Especially since Angel walked with an easy, almost lazy confidence. He was all *nothing to see here, folks. Just out for a stroll*.

Of course, there was a catch. He wasn't making any sound. His footsteps didn't scuffle over the grass. There was no hitch in his breath when they paraded down the slight embankment toward the manor's front lawn. Which, conversely, drew her attention to her *own* labored breaths, to the sound of her own hiking boot snapping a rogue twig in two.

"Damnit," she hissed.

Angel sent her a look.

She wasn't sure what *kind* of look. His face was as impassive as ever, so she was forced to whisper, "What?"

"Act natural," he said. His gravelly voice barely carried through the windless air.

"Right. And what's natural about skulking around a five-hundred-year-old house looking for weaknesses in its security system?"

One corner of his lips twitched. "Everything. Just another day on the job."

"For *you* maybe."

Thirty seconds later, they were around the side of the house. Angel scanned the exterior, his eyes alighting on the windows, skimming over the roofline, scrutinizing the perimeter.

Since she didn't know what the hell she was supposed to be looking for, she contented herself with a close-up examination of the manor. The gray stone of its exterior looked thick and substantial, but there were places where lichen and moss had taken root, lending whole sections a fuzzy, greenish hue. The vast two-story wall—speckled with eight windows, four on each level—was an imposing sight, seeming to reach up into the sulking clouds. And the grass around the manor stopped a good six feet from the foundation, as if it dare not intrude upon the stately grandeur of the place, leaving that task to a bed of mulch and a row of well-tended rosebushes.

All in all, it was quite a house. A throwback to an era when things were built to last and landowners ruled the roost.

As an American, Emily was impressed by the sheer gravity of a structure that had seen armies rise and fall, watched rulers come and go, and withstood the ravages of five centuries of wind and rain and chaos.

"Come." Angel distracted her from her inspection.

"What's the verdict?" she whispered, following him around to the back of the house.

She was shocked to discover that unlike other historic homes she'd seen during her short sojourn in England, this one didn't boast a vast back garden. The English seemed to really get off on bushes and shrubbery. Instead, there was a simple rock patio running along the back of the manor. Beyond it, the forest hulked, tall and dark and slightly foreboding. Emily thought it whispered of mysteries, at least to anyone who cared to listen.

Whoever had built the place had obviously valued privacy over opulence. Or maybe it was a simple matter of neglect over the generations. Perhaps the original owner's descendants had grown too poor or too indifferent to keep up the grounds, and so had let the trees reclaim the land.

"No cameras," Angel said. "No motion detectors. No floodlights. Only sensors on the doors and windows. Very elementary. Easy to disarm."

"Just another day on the job?"

His dark eyes glinted. "Exactly."

"Christian will be glad to hear that. I think he was looking forward to staying here tonight. You know, a walk down memory lane or whatever."

"And you are happy to make Christian happy, no?"

She stopped in her tracks, frowning at Angel. "No. Well, yes. I mean, I want *everyone* to be happy. What's wrong with that?"

Angel shrugged. "Nothing. I thought perhaps after what happened…" He let the sentence dangle.

"What do you mean after what happened?" Her nerves jangled with alarm. "What happened?"

"I saw him kiss you."

Right. Damn. So there was *that*.

"Didn't mean anything." She waved a dismissive hand. "It was a heat-of-the-moment thing and— Shit on a stick!"

Her boot slipped on the damp grass, and she plowed headlong into Angel. He would have caught her easily, except that he'd been in the process of turning, so she'd caught him off-balance. They were a tangle of pinwheeling arms and legs as they each tried to regain their footing.

No use. *Timber!*

Angel grunted when she landed atop him, her forehead smacking his chin. For a second, she was too dazed to move. Stars flashed in front of her eyes.

Pushing up onto her knees, she rubbed her abused noggin. "You have the hardest chin in the world," she accused. "What's that thing made of anyway?"

"I could say the same for your *head*." Angel massaged his stubble-dusted chin.

"Am I interrupting something?" The sound of Christian's low voice swirled inside Emily's ears. He was leaning against the corner of the manor house. "Should I turn 'round and give you two a minute?"

Blinking in confusion, she realized she was straddling Angel and that one of his big hands was curled unconsciously around her thigh. A split second later, she was scrambling to her feet.

"It's not what it looks like," she blurted, then immediately furrowed her brow.

What the…? Why the hell did she say that?

Christian didn't say a word, but his eyes were filled with… What was that? Dismissal?

She felt cut off at the knees and wondered how she

was going to get around on bloody stumps for the rest of the day.

When Angel pushed off the ground, brushing grass clippings from his back and legs, Christian shoved away from the corner of the house and started toward them. He moved with the easy grace that came courtesy of good genes, honed muscles, and no small amount of masculine virility.

"It's a simple system," he said, stopping in front of them. "We can disarm it, no problem." He directed his statement to Angel, but his eyes flicked briefly to Emily.

She sucked in a startled breath at the coolness she saw there. No, not coolness. *Coldness*. He reminded her of an ice sculpture. So hard. So glossy. If she squinted, would she see her own reflection on his surface?

"Th-that's what Angel just said." Why was her voice shaking?

"Ah." That single word seemed to say more than most people managed in ten paragraphs. "I guess if Angel said it, it must be true."

Okay, so… What. The. Actual. *Fuck?* Why was he suddenly and inexplicably pissed at her?

Chapter 9

"You want me to do that?" Angel asked when Christian fished his lock-picking set from his rucksack.

"I can bloody well pick a lock," he managed through gritted teeth. "Get ready to disarm the alarm once I open the door."

For a moment, Angel was quiet. Then he said softly, his voice raspier than usual, "It was an accident, you know."

"What was?" Christian inserted the tension wrench into the bottom of the keyhole and slid the pick in beside it. Now it was a simple matter of sliding and jiggling until all the pins in the lock fell into place.

Civilians took such comfort in locks. If they had any idea how easy one was to pick, they wouldn't sleep so well at night.

"Emily slipped and took me with her," Angel said. "We landed in a tangle."

Christian glanced over his shoulder, glad to see that Emily, Ace, and Rusty had walked toward the small gravel car park. They were keeping an eye on the narrow country lane, making sure no one happened upon them. It wouldn't do to be caught red-handed picking the lock. Not much they could say to talk their way out of *that*.

"No skin off my nose," Christian told Angel, turning back to concentrate on his task.

"Really?" There was no mistaking the skepticism in Angel's voice. "You could have fooled me."

Christian sighed and glared up at Angel. "What the devil are you on about?"

"You and Emily."

"There *is* no me and Emily."

"Really?" One of Angel's dark eyebrows arched. "You could have fooled me."

"You're repeating yourself."

"If there is no you and Emily, then what was that kiss in the hangar's parking lot about?"

"Like Emily told you"—if Christian gritted his teeth any harder, his molars might explode—"it didn't mean a thing. Heat of the moment." Her words scraped across his brain like fingernails down a chalkboard.

"So"—Angel nodded—"*that* is what this is all about."

"What *what* is all about?"

"You turning into Oscar the Grouch. You heard Emily say that. Then you came around the corner and saw us on the ground. But like I said, it was an accident."

Christian sighed and let his head hang between his shoulders. Angel was right. Seeing Emily on top of the handsome bastard *had* made Christian want to box Angel's ears until his head rattled.

Lifting his chin, Christian did his teammate the courtesy of looking him in the eye when he said, "Sorry. Didn't mean to take any of it out on you."

"Understandable." Angel gave a Gallic shrug. "Probably would have reacted the same way if the woman I loved was on top of another man."

A startled breath wheezed from Christian's chest. "Love?" The word barely had enough oomph to make it past his lips. It was one thing to admit to himself that he was sweet on Emily. Another thing altogether to admit it to someone else. "I wouldn't call it love."

"No?"

"Maybe the opposite." *Liar, liar, drawers on fire!*

"Hate?" Angel scoffed. "Let me be the first to tell you, the opposite of love is not hate. The opposite of love is indifference, which is one thing you do *not* feel for Emily."

"Fine." Christian punctuated the word with a terse downward jerk of his chin. "So it's not hate. It's annoyance." Then he figured he'd better sprinkle some truth into his pack of lies if he had any hope of throwing Angel off the scent. "And an unhealthy amount of lust."

"What's the holdup?" Emily called to them. Her arms were crossed against the damp and cold, and the mother of all scowls scrunched up her pretty face. "Christian, if you're having trouble with the lock, let Angel do it."

Let Angel do it. Right-oh. Because Angel was sooooo accomplished, sooooo bloody brilliant at everything.

Bugger it all. There was that green-eyed monster again.

Christian turned back to the lock and gave it his full attention. Two seconds later, the pins fell into place and the front door swung open on squeaky hinges. The alarm let out a series of warning chirps that reminded Christian of the many times in his misguided youth when he'd smashed through the window of the corner store or the local Tesco to filch some food after his mother had squandered their government support check at the pub.

Angel wasted no time jogging inside. After a quick three-sixty spin, the former Mossad agent spotted the alarm keypad on the wall. Pulling off the casing, he did some quick work with the wires. Five seconds later, the alarm blipped off.

Christian could admit, if only to himself, that Angel *was* bloody good at the cloak-and-dagger stuff. Emphasis on the *dagger*.

Standing, Christian turned toward the car park and waved for the others to come inside. Rusty was the first to breeze past him in the open doorway. The redheaded giant whistled at the interior of the manor house.

Ace followed Rusty inside, mimicking Rusty's whistle. But given that Ace's eyes were glued to Rusty's ass, Christian was quite certain the flyboy's appreciation had less to do with the house and more to do with the marine-cum-fisherman.

Emily was the last one through the door. Before she stepped all the way inside, however, she flattened a hand on Christian's belly.

"Good idea about this place." She flicked a quick glance around the marble-floored entry with its small wooden desk, pamphlets that gave a brief history and site map of the property, and wood-paneled walls. "This is *much* better than a moldy motel room or spending the next twenty-four hours cooped up in the truck."

Thoughts. He should be having those. Words. He should be speaking them. But the second she touched him, a bolt of lightning blazed down his spine, shooting electricity into all his nerves, making speech or thought impossible.

"That was a compliment, Christian." She snatched her hand away. The skin on his stomach throbbed in an exact outline of her handprint. "You're supposed to say 'thank you,' or 'no worries,' or anything besides trying to glower me into the ground. And just FYI, I know we're good at having wordless conversations, but I don't speak glare-ish. So if you got somethin' you wanna say to me, you're gonna hafta spit it out."

Ah. And *there* was the blue-collar Bridgeport 'hood girl in all her bad grammar glory. Why he should find her so adorable was anyone's guess.

"I haven't anything to say." That was a lie. He had a million things he wanted to say to her. A million more things he wanted to ask her. Like, *why* did she always bust his bollocks? And *why* was she so quick to scurry off Angel when she saw him standing at the corner? But he knew better than to rip open his chest and expose his heart. She might eat the bloody thing whole.

He lifted an eyebrow that asked, *So? Was there anything else?*

Her mouth thinned into a straight line that called him *the most exasperating man alive.*

He tilted his head, his grin saying, *What else is new?*

Emily threw frustrated hands in the air and turned to march deeper into the house.

"Make yourselves familiar with your surroundings now," he called to the others, who were already fanning out to inspect the place, "while the sun is still up and we can see what's what."

After sundown, they daren't turn on the lights. That was a surefire way to bring unwanted attention to themselves. And since the manor house was tucked way back in the wood, no streetlamps for miles, it was going to get quite dark.

"You remember which way to the bathroom?" Emily glanced at Christian over her shoulder.

Her unbound hair was a curtain of drying waves against her slender back. An image blazed to life in his brain of how it would feel to wrap a length of her hair around his wrist so he could pull her head back and hold her still while his lips and tongue marauded over the tender flesh of her neck.

"Down the hall on the left." He was shocked at the breathless sound of his voice.

"Thank you." Her smile was so syrupy he was tempted to look around for a stack of pancakes.

Sodding hell. He was cocking things up. Why couldn't he act normal around her?

Oh, right. Because now he knew what it was to hold her in his arms, to kiss her sweet lips, to…*love* her. Normal had pretty much gone the way of the dinosaurs.

———

Lawrence pulled his vehicle to the side of the gravel road and shoved it into Park.

"What are you on about now?" Ben demanded. "The manor house is a quarter mile up the way."

"And if they're holed up there," Lawrence said, "we don't wanna alert them to our presence."

"Oh." Ben nodded. "Right." When he swallowed, his Adam's apple bounced nervously.

Lawrence leveled a steely-eyed look at his younger brother. "Are you up for this? Tell me now if you're not, 'cause you'll slow me down and create a distraction I don't need."

"No." Ben swallowed again. "I mean, yeah. I'm up for it. You're right. It's the only way to set everything right. But, Lawrence… Brother, I gotta tell you, I don't like it."

"You don't gotta like it, Ben. You just gotta do it."

Ben firmed his jaw and pushed himself from the SUV. Lawrence followed him out, gun in hand.

"How you wanna do this?" Ben asked, heading toward the tree line next to the road.

"We sneak up to the place and see what's what." Lawrence's heart beat with an eager rhythm. When he sucked in a breath, the air felt stingingly crisp and cool. It flooded his lungs and hardened his resolve.

This was right. What they were about to do was *right*. He knew it. He *felt* it.

Neither of them spoke as they trudged through the dripping forest toward the manor house, their booted feet kicking up the smell of wet leaves and dark, fertile soil.

Lawrence imagined what his life would have been like had Christian Watson not buggered it all by starting that ruckus at the Iraqi roadblock. His brother would be alive. His parents would be alive. And maybe he wouldn't feel the need to hurt people. Maybe he wouldn't have so much hatred in his heart that it required an occasional outlet and—

"It's up ahead," Ben whispered, pulling Lawrence from his thoughts.

He motioned for Ben to keep going and stayed tight to his brother's flank. Once they reached the edge of the forest, they positioned themselves behind neighboring trees. Lawrence narrowed his eyes as he took in the great gray manor house and the recently cut front lawn.

His eyes skimmed over the bushes trimmed to look like flying horses and dragons, slipped past the rock lions, and landed on the gravel car park. The *empty* gravel car park. A hard stone of bitterness and self-disgust settled in his chest.

He'd chosen wrong. He'd thought Watson and his mates would avoid the CCTV cameras, but obviously they—

"They're not here," Ben breathed.

Lawrence couldn't tell if his little brother sounded annoyed or relieved. Either emotion cheesed Lawrence off, since what Ben *should* be feeling was fear. And fury. And a bone-deep frustration that they wouldn't be spilling the blood of their enemies this day!

"I can bloody well see that, Ben. I got eyes."

"So what you wanna do now?"

What did he want to do now? What did *he* want to do now? Well, he wanted to fit his little brother with some cement galoshes, sail him out to the middle of the Celtic Sea, and feed him to the fecking fishes! If it weren't for Ben, Lawrence wouldn't be *in* this mess and—

No. *No*. He forced himself to take a deep breath. Forced down the anger that was always so near his surface. Ben was family, and the Michelsons stuck together. Plus, maybe Ben was right. Maybe Lawrence *had* watched too many gangster movies.

"We go with your original plan," he said decisively, turning back into the forest as his mind raced through the possible stumbling blocks in their new path. "And we hope like hell it holds up to scrutiny."

Trudging alongside him, Ben glanced at his watch. "But it's been too long. The body at the airport musta been discovered by now. How in sodding hell are we gonna explain why we fled the scene? And what are we gonna say when someone asks why we waited over an hour to call in what happened?"

"Easy," Lawrence said. "We were chasing the perpe-trators all over Cornwall." Again, it was close enough to the truth to be believable. "And we couldn't call it in 'cause your mobile is broken."

"But that doesn't explain why we wouldn't have used *yours*."

"I forgot mine at home in my hurry to leave the house to confront Watson." Lawrence smiled. It wasn't the way he'd wanted to play things. But if he and Ben kept their story straight, they might come up smelling like roses.

"Is that true?" Ben lifted a brow and hopped over a fallen log.

"It is." Lawrence had never been so pleased to forget his phone in his life. "We say we chased them and lost them, and only after that did we stop to make the call."

"Okay." Ben nodded. "Okay, it could work."

"It *will* work," Lawrence insisted as they broke through the cover of the forest and headed toward the parked SUV. "We just gotta stick to the story. And it'd probably be better if we call it in to our own unit. They'll be more likely to take our words at face value." After all, hadn't his unit turned a blind eye the few times some sack-of-shit pub patron had accused Lawrence of being the one to start a fight?

"Right," Ben said, opening the passenger door and hopping inside.

Lawrence was behind the wheel a second later, crank-ing over the engine and hanging a u-ey. They hadn't made it far, maybe a half mile or so, before a flash of green caught his eye. He stomped on the brakes so hard that the SUV fishtailed down the road.

Ben gripped the dashboard. "What in hell?"

Lawrence shifted the Peugeot into reverse and backed up slowly, squinting through the trees, searching for—

"There!" He pointed, stepping on the brakes a second time.

"There *what*?" A deep scowl wrinkled Ben's brow.

"*There*." Lawrence shook his finger in the direction of the truck. It was parked in a depression. The only thing visible was a portion of its roof. He wasn't sure how he had seen it. He hadn't been looking. It had just jumped out at him.

Fate…

The word drifted through his mind once again.

"Oh Jesus," Ben breathed when he saw what Lawrence was pointing at. "You think they're in there?" Ben's hand was suddenly on the butt of the gun protruding from his waistband.

"No." Lawrence shook his head. "I think they're inside the manor house." He quickly pulled the SUV to the side of the road. "It's back to plan B."

Chapter 10

Colby "Ace" Ventura had a gaze that could be unnervingly intent.

Rusty Parker felt the power of it when he walked into the large upstairs library. With its wall of windows, the library was lighter than any other room of the house. Which meant when Ace turned to look at him hovering in the doorway, there was no escaping the force of those ocean blues.

Oh, how Ace had sighed after Rusty admitted he hadn't told his parents he was gay. It had been a gusty sound. Full of censure.

The bitter, acidic taste of self-loathing splashed from the back of Rusty's throat. On the heels of that rushed a tide of indignation.

How dare Ace judge him for how he chose to live his own damn life?

Like many men of his size, men who hadn't had to prove themselves because nobody messed with them, Rusty was usually slow to anger. Yet, right at that moment, he felt the burn of it in his chest like a hot ember.

"This is really something, isn't it? The only other place I've seen with this many books is the Harold Washington Library in the South Loop back home." Ace turned in a slow circle to take in the mahogany bookshelves that lined the room from floor to ceiling. The only vertical space that wasn't covered with books was the wall with the windows. In the place of books—and everywhere there wasn't a window—there were paintings hung frame-to-frame. Most of the artwork was portraiture, but there were a few landscapes and still lifes thrown in for interest.

Oriental rugs covered the parquet floor, and leather furniture made up three distinct seating areas. A massive wooden desk sat at the far end of the library, and Rusty couldn't help but wonder if, over the centuries, the owners of the house had collected the books because they wanted to read them or because they wanted to impress people into thinking they were smarter than they actually were.

Little of A, little of B, he finally decided.

"I mean," Ace continued, "don't you just love it? I feel like I need a smoking jacket, a pipe, and a monocle."

"Never been much of a book reader myself," Rusty said.

Ace tilted his head, his mouth twitching. Rusty didn't know if Ace was about to frown or smile, and tried really hard not to notice how the weak afternoon light turned Ace's blond hair into a fiery halo around his face. Ace might not have the nickname, but the man could appear damned angelic, given the right circumstances.

"Why do you do that?" Ace asked.

"What?"

"Play the dumb jock card?"

Rusty's heart hitched. Then it felt like it started beating backward. "Working with the hand I've been dealt, I guess."

There was that sigh again. So full of censure.

Rusty clenched his hands into fists. "Why do *you* do *that*?"

Ace's chin, that chin that looked like it belonged on a Greek statue, jerked back. "I'm sorry. I don't know what you mean."

"Judge people."

"I don't judge people." Look in the dictionary, and next to the word *insulted* would be a picture of Ace's tan, blond-haired mug.

"Yeah." Rusty nodded vigorously. "You do." Now that he was going, he couldn't stop. "You think I'm weak or spineless or plain ol' stupid for not being out and proud." Not only were his fists clenched, but the muscles across his shoulders were too. "But not everyone needs to air their dirty laundry for the world to see."

"I didn't judge you. Not until right this minute when I found out you think of your sexual orientation as *dirty laundry*." Ace emphasized the last two words.

Heat flew to Rusty's face. "Stop trying to use my words against me, damnit!"

"They're your words. If they can be used against you, it's your own fault."

Rusty was gripped by an overwhelming desire to punch something. He considered making that something the blond-haired god standing in the middle of the room. Instead, he said through clenched teeth, "And now who's treating who like a dumb jock?"

Ace's color heightened. His fierce blue eyes traveled over Rusty's face, past his beard-stubbled jaw, and landed on his lips. "I wasn't judging you back in the truck. I'm not judging you now. I'm just...*disappointed*, I guess is the right word."

"Which is a nicer way of saying the same damn thing," Rusty snapped. "Disappointed in me because I don't have the balls to come out to my folks. Disappointed that I've chosen to keep that part of my life a secret because I *love* them and I don't want to hurt them. Disappointed that I'd choose their happiness over my own. No matter which word you want to use, it's still judgment."

"No." Ace jerked his chin side to side. "Disappointed because I thought maybe there was something happening between us. Disappointed because I was excited by the prospect. Disappointed because that bit of whimsy went buh-bye the minute you told me you're closeted."

The steel went out of Rusty's spine at the same time all the air left his lungs. "You thought something was happening between us?" Who had shoved a glob of glue down his throat? The words were so sticky they barely came out as a whisper. "Why does me being in the closet change that?"

"It just does." Ace glanced over Rusty's shoulder. "Did you pick out which room will be yours tonight, Emily? Dibs on the blue one. It has a bed with gauzy curtains. I've always wanted to sleep in one of those."

Rusty watched Emily shove past him and was hard-pressed not to yank her back into the hall and then shut the door in her face. He and Ace needed to finish their conversation, *damnit*. He felt… No…he *knew* Ace had been about to reveal something important.

Of course, he could never be so rude to Emily. Not only had she been the one to rally support from the CIA for him when he'd been pinned down in enemy territory with no friendly evacs in sight that summer he'd spent working as an asset, but she'd made sure to keep in touch with him over the years. Emails, the occasional phone call… Emily took to heart that old proverb that once you saved someone's life, you were forever responsible for it.

"The blue room's all yours," she told Ace, walking wide-eyed into the center of the library. "I laid my claim on the yellow one. It looks over the back patio and has some funky, sparkly art on one wall. But that's neither here nor there, because get a load of this place!" She spun in a circle and started humming a song that was vaguely familiar.

She had changed into a pair of leggings and one of her many oversized sweatshirts. Both seemed to have survived the storm relatively unscathed inside her backpack.

"It's a ceramic mural," Rusty said, still battling his annoyance at her interruption.

"Huh?" Emily stopped spinning to scrunch up her nose at him.

"The funky, sparkly art on the wall in the yellow bedroom. It's a ceramic mural." He pushed away from the doorframe, walked to the seating arrangement on the left side of the room, and collapsed into a leather chair. Its springs whined under his weight.

When Emily blinked at him, he expounded. "There are three types of murals. Painted, ceramic, and tile. Painted is self-explanatory. So is tile, which is basically a painting on tiles that are then affixed to the floor or wall. What's in the yellow bedroom is a ceramic mural. Meaning it's a picture that's been made up of mosaic pieces of mirrors, tiles, and ceramics. In my opinion, ceramic murals are the most interesting kinds of murals."

"Said the man who claims to be all brawn and no brain," Ace muttered, and Rusty shot him a scathing look.

"Yeah, that's right. I know something about art and decor. Does it *get* any gayer than that? You should be patting me on the back."

Ace snorted. "Sorry to say, but knowing the difference between shag and berber or a Pollock and a Picasso doesn't make you a card-carrying member of GLAAD."

Emily glanced back and forth between them, a line appearing between her eyebrows. "Did I miss something?"

"Nothing." Ace waved a hand and started toward the door. "Where's the bathroom you used, anyway? The only two I've clocked on my tour have signs saying they don't work."

After Emily gave him directions, Ace left the room. Emily's gaze immediately fell on Rusty.

"What?" he demanded as she ambled over and plunked down on the leather sofa.

"What was that all about?"

"What do you mean?"

"I mean all the sarcasm about brawns and brains combined with the veiled eye threats. I left my Rusty-Ace handbook in my other pants. So out with it. What's going on between you two?"

"Nothing." That was the whole fucking problem.

"I don't believe it," she scoffed. "I think he likes you. And in my opinion, you'd be crazy not to buy a ticket on that ride."

"Sorry to say, but that ship has sailed."

She scrunched up her nose again. "We're mixing metaphors. I'm getting confused."

"Doesn't matter. It's nothing. Drop it, okay?"

He could tell she wanted to press the issue but didn't. *Bless her*. Instead she sighed and said, "Sorry I dragged you into this, Rusty."

"You didn't drag me anywhere. You called, gave me the lowdown, and I volunteered to help. Remember?"

"Yeah, but I thought you'd give us a quick boat ride across the Channel after we outed Morrison as Spider's money launderer, and that would be that. I didn't think we'd end up here." She waved a hand to indicate the opulent room.

"You mean hiding out in a big, drafty house after having spent a week hiding out in a dinky seaside cottage?"

She laughed. "That and the fact that since we can't be certain Spider didn't catch *all* our likenesses on some CCTV camera, you have to come with us back to the States and put your business and your whole flippin' *life* on hold."

It had been decided that it wouldn't be safe for Rusty to return to his house in Folkstone or his charter fishing business in Dover until the Black Knights could identify Spider and either kill him or hand him over to the authorities, who would hopefully find him a moldy eight-by-ten in which to finish out his days.

"My life was already on hold," he muttered.

"What's that supposed to mean?"

"Nothing. Forget it."

"Why are you suddenly being enigmatic?" She frowned. "Too much time around Christian and Angel? Have they rubbed off on you? What happened to the straight-shootin' Midwesterner I've grown to know and love?"

"Straight-shootin'?" He scoffed. "You heard me tell Ace I'm not *out*." He made air quotes.

She shrugged. "I mean, I don't really get *why* you don't tell people you're gay. It's nothing to be ashamed of, and fuck anyone who thinks it is, even if they *are* related to you. Then again"—she made a face—"I'm probably not the best person to be handing out advice when it comes to familial relationships. I might as well have been raised by a pack of wolves."

For a moment, they both lapsed into silence. Then Emily spread her hands. "I guess the bottom line is this: It's your life. Live it however you damn well please."

"*Thank you*," he said, still fuming over Ace and his holier-than-thou, gay-by-birth-fabulous-by-choice, proud-to-be-out-and-you-should-be-too judgmental self. "Try telling that to your fair-haired flyboy coworker. He seems to think I'm doing something wrong."

She sighed. "I think that has more to do with *him* than you."

"What's that supposed to mean? What do you know?"

She hitched a slim shoulder. "That's a conversation for you and Ace."

The fact that she had interrupted what he assumed was going to be that very conversation was something Rusty decided to keep to himself.

"But before we got off on this tangent, I was apologizing for getting you into this," she said. "And before you start to argue again, I *did* get you into this. You wouldn't be here if it weren't for me."

Rusty happened to *like* the tangent, especially since it promised to shine some light on Ace's behavior. But he knew a conversational stalemate when he saw one.

The look on Emily's face on that subject screamed two words: *dead end*!

"You shoulder too much responsibility, dollface," he told her. "Which makes you worry too much. It's not your job to make sure everyone and everything is A-okay all the time."

She chuckled. "Yeah, see? That's where you're wrong. I'm the office manager. *Manager* being the key word there. Making sure everyone and everything is A-okay is part of the job description."

Rusty regarded her for a few seconds. "I hope they realize what they have in you."

"And what's that?"

"Generosity of spirit. Consideration. *Caring*. In their line of work, that's hard to come by. Caring too much means hurting too much if and when things go sideways and someone gets injured. Or worse, gets dead."

The word was enough to make her blanch, but she feigned bravado. "I don't know who you're talking about. Generous? Considerate? *Psshh*. More like mouthy and nosy and pushy."

It occurred to Rusty, not for the first time, that Emily had a strange habit of trying to convince herself and everyone around her that she was something she wasn't. Something harder, meaner. Something decidedly *un*-Emily.

"You're like a Cadbury Crème Egg," he told her.

She rolled her eyes. "This should be good."

"Hard on the outside, but soft and sweet on the inside."

"Dude, you are cuckoo for Cocoa Puffs. And how did this conversation get turned on me? Weren't we talking about you and how badly I've fucked up your life?"

The fact that Rusty was beginning to realize he didn't

really *have* a life, at least not the one he wanted, made him grit his jaw. "Nope." He enunciated the word so the *P* really popped.

"Hmm." She frowned. "That's strange. Because I could have sworn we were."

For a long time, she watched him. No, not watched him. *Looked* at him. Like she was trying to peer inside his soul. He shifted uncomfortably and sent a silent thanks skyward when she eventually shrugged and turned her attention to the room. Once again, she began to hum that vaguely familiar tune.

"What *is* that?" he asked. "I recognize it, but I can't figure out from where."

She waggled her eyebrows. "It's the theme to *Beauty and the Beast*."

Rusty smiled and flicked a glance around the massive library. "Do you think Mrs. Potts and Chip will come to life?"

"I'm hoping." Emily rubbed her hands together. "I've been envisioning myself in a yellow ball gown all afternoon."

Rusty laughed. Some of the tension caused by Ace's censure leaked out of him. Emily had that effect on people. Oh sure, she was quick to boss and pester. But she was also quick to accept and encourage. It made her easy to be around.

"Fine. You can be Belle," he told her. "But then which one of us gets to be Beast?"

"Christian, of course. He's the surliest, most irritable of all of you."

"Ha! You *make* him surly and irritable."

"*Moi?*" She feigned innocence. "What do *I* do?"

"Tease him. Incessantly."

She twisted her lips. "I can't help it. He gets under my skin, and that bugs me. I'm beginning to think he'll bug me for as long as I live. And then probably after I'm dead too, because the damned can do that."

Rusty fought another smile and lost the battle. "Is that what you tell yourself?"

"And if what you say is true, that I tease him incessantly," she said, ignoring his question, "then it's for his own good. He's too poised. Too collected. Too…" She waved a hand, searching for the right word. "Unaffected. Someone needs to ruffle his feathers."

"You've decided that someone should be you?"

"Who else has the balls to do it? All that perfection, not to mention that stuffy English arrogance, keeps everyone else at bay."

"Hmm."

Emily thrust out her chin. "*Hmm?* What's that supposed to mean?"

Since Rusty had already had all the confrontation he could stand for one day, he didn't answer. Instead, he pushed up from the sofa and extended his hand. "Belle? Care to dance?"

"You're changing the subject," she accused.

"Quick on the uptake, aren't you?" He started singing. "*Tale as old as time.*"

Emily threw back her head and laughed before accepting his hand and jumping to her feet. "*True as it can be!*" she sang in a lovely alto.

Together they belted out the third line as Rusty pulled her into a waltz that might have gone fairly well had she not fought him for the lead.

"Damnit," he grumbled as she really gave her all to the chorus. "I'm the man. I'm supposed to direct this dance."

To prove his point, he spun her around and dipped her low. Which is when something in the doorway snagged his attention. That something turned out to be Christian. And the look on the man's face made Rusty want to reach up and pat his hair. You know, to put out the fire Christian's laser-beam eyes had started there.

"Speak of the devil," Rusty whispered in Emily's ear as he pulled her to a stand. "Or would that be, speak of the Beast?"

Chapter 11

EMILY'S SMILE FELL THE INSTANT SHE TURNED AND SAW the man, the myth, the legend himself leaning against the doorjamb. Christian's booted feet were crossed at the ankle, his strong arms folded, and his eyes were like the sky before a tornado strike. Green. Ominous. *Threatening*.

And there it is. That patented scowl.

Rusty took one look at Christian's face and said, "I, uh, I think I'll go look to see if I have any dry clothes." She felt the breeze of his departure when he exited the room. *The cowardly weenus!*

After he disappeared, she returned Christian's glower. "What did I tell you?" She planted her hands on her hips. "I don't speak glare-ish."

"How can you bloody well brush it off like that?" His accent was low and smooth. Hearing it had everything inside her going liquid and heavy.

"Brush what off?" Oh, for the love of Adam Eaton. What had happened to her voice? It didn't sound like her own. It was far too breathless.

"That kiss. *The* kiss."

Ho-kay. So they *were* going to talk about it.

"I wasn't brushing it off. It's just…what's there to say, you know?" She tried to make her shrug look casual.

"Indeed not." He shook his head. "Why don't you explain it to me."

She spread her hands. "It was the heat of the moment. And like you said, you haven't gotten a little strange in a long time. Your adrenaline was high. I'd just placed myself in front of what might have been a bullet meant for you. It stands to reason you were grateful, overcome, and you'd have lip-locked anyone in that moment."

She tried to read his thoughts in his eyes, but he was being irritatingly stingy with them. Finally, he said, "You really believe that?"

"Should I not? You're the one who looked like you'd gotten your nuts caught in a vise after you kissed me. And if memory serves, you're *also* the one who apologized and promised it wouldn't happen again."

His eyes traveled over her face, past the curve of her cheek, alighting on her lips, which throbbed and opened as if his gaze were a physical touch. Then his scrutiny dipped lower, skimming down her chest and over the subtle slope of her breasts.

She wasn't mistaken. His nostrils flared. The hands curled loosely around his biceps clenched. Then he met her gaze head-on, and suddenly she felt filled with a delicious secret she had no business knowing.

"Do you *fancy* it happening again?" he asked.

There was a strange buzzing in her ears. Had someone opened a window and let a bee into the room? "Better question is, do *you* fancy it happening again?"

"I asked you first, Emily."

"I asked you second, Christian." She was never one to be outdone.

He grunted, his expression telegraphing annoyance. "For once, would it be possible for us to carry on a conversation that didn't sink to the level of six-year-olds?"

Tall order. The man brought out her baser self. She was all emotion and impulse with him.

"*Maybe* I'd want it to happen again," she admitted. Hell, *why* was she admitting this? Oh yeah. With him, she liked playing with fire. "If only to prove that I have far more skill than that poor showing in the parking lot. You caught me off guard. I didn't have time to demonstrate my oral expertise. And I'm not the kind of woman who likes the thought of not—"

Her words died in her throat. She tried to resuscitate them, but his decidedly wicked smile obliterated any hope she had of getting the conversation back on track.

He made everything so much worse when he pushed away from the doorframe and walked toward her. It took every ounce of willpower she possessed to hold her ground. It was like being stalked by a sleek, dark panther. There was danger in every one of his muscles. Her instincts yelled for her to run.

When he stopped in front of her, she had to tilt her chin up to look at him. It was either that or stumble back, which her pride refused to let her do. She pasted on an expression she hoped was full of bravado. Her quirked brow silently asked, *What's up?*

His hitched chin answered, *You tell me*.

But she couldn't tell him anything. Because she couldn't think straight. Not with him so close. Not with that whorl of hair falling over his brow. Not with the scent of him—all warm wool, earthy aftershave, and that indefinable aroma that was healthy man—filling her head and making her dizzy.

So slowly she could feel every crashing beat of her heart against her breastbone, he cupped her jaw and feathered his thumb over her bottom lip. Lightning crackled beneath her skin at the point of contact. Every muscle in her body forgot what it was made for and loosened. She stumbled toward him, grabbing his biceps for balance.

He had removed his coat, but still wore his silk sweater. The fabric was mostly dry, thanks in large part to his immense body heat, and it fit him like a glove.

As ZZ Top liked to say, *Every girl's crazy 'bout a sharp-dressed man*.

Since she'd been born and raised in one of Chicago's many working-class neighborhoods—where men usually wore work boots, hard hats, and coveralls—Emily figured she was more susceptible than most to the visual feast of a well-heeled gentleman. It was as if she'd spent her life looking at chickens, and suddenly she was faced with the stunning beauty of a peacock.

Of their own accord, her eyes flitted to his mouth. He had the kind of lips that managed to look hard and soft at the same time. The kind of lips that scattered thoughts and obliterated resolve.

Her voice was husky when she said, "So what happened to 'That won't happen again'?" She imitated his accent. Or at least she *tried* to. She could never get it just right.

"Never let it be said that I'm the sort of bloke who doesn't give a woman a fair shake. Here's your chance to show me your oral expertise, darling." The word *darling* sounded more like *dahling*.

"Hit me with your best shot," he added when she didn't make a move. Simply stood there gaping up at him like an addlepated nitwit.

"You stole that line from Pat Benatar," she accused. But really she was stalling, and they both knew it. "And someone once told me that a girl worth kissing isn't easily kissed."

"You think there's anything easy when it comes to the two of us?"

"No." The word was a breathy exhale.

His eyelids lowered to half-mast, but the look in his eyes was anything but lazy. It was hot. Hungry. Full of things she couldn't have and therefore shouldn't contemplate. The same look she'd caught a brief glimpse of in the truck.

So she *hadn't* been imagining things. Her blood heated and raced through her veins at the realization.

She expected him to slam his mouth over the top of hers like before. But, no. Oh no. He took his time. He used the callused pad of his thumb on her bottom lip. Rubbed. Rubbed. *Rubbed*.

Her eyes fell to that tempting indent in his chin. She couldn't help herself; she reached up and pressed her finger to it. His skin was warm, his beard stubble scratchy.

"I've always wanted to do that," she whispered.

"Then you should have." He used his thumb to open her mouth. Then slowly, so damn slowly, he bent toward her.

His warm breath feathered over her lips. It still held the faintest lingering hints of the buttered croissants with strawberry jam he'd eaten that morning.

Yes, he'd cooked a full English breakfast for the rest of them. But he'd satisfied himself with croissants because the man had a sweet tooth. Given the choice between sugar or protein, he chose sugar every time.

"If you fancy me stopping," he murmured, so close she could see the rings of gold circling his pupils, "now is the time to tell me."

Her voice was gone. All she could manage was a shake of her head.

What was she doing? What the hell *was she doing?*

He smiled. A flash of white teeth before his lips claimed hers with a gentle pressure that allowed her to settle in and get the feel of him.

She'd been right. His lips *were* soft and hard. The skin like velvet. The insistence like steel.

He nibbled on her lower lip, sucked it into his mouth so that her toes curled. Then he angled his head and fit his lips more securely over hers, his tongue a demand as it sought entry to her mouth. She didn't hesitate, even though she knew she probably should. She opened to him, and he wasted no time sweeping inside.

Sweet Jesus! The man could *kiss*! It was like he took the act as seriously as he took everything else in his life. There was such precision. Such expertise. Such…*control*.

Her kneecaps disappeared. She figured she should put some serious effort toward finding them, but she couldn't think much beyond the heat of his mouth on hers, his tongue inside. Tasting. Delving. Mapping and… *Shit!*

It was happening again. She was so overcome by the fact that Christian Watson was kissing her that she was standing there like a boneless, brainless moron. Which would never do. Especially since she'd just been talking big about her oral expertise.

He may have started the kiss, but she was damn well determined to finish it, to *show* him she wasn't all talk and no action.

Her hands got lost in his hair as she went up on tiptoe and pressed herself against him. Her nipples had tightened into painful points, and she couldn't decide if the pressure of his chest hurt or helped. She only knew she wanted to get closer. Sink deeper into his heat. His solidity. His *maleness*.

Catching his tongue between her teeth, she sucked, giving him an idea of what it would be like if she had another of his body parts in her mouth. He must've had a good imagination because the noise he made in the back of his throat was so guttural and raw that her womb clenched.

She suspected she could be in the middle of pruning the bushes or doing her taxes, and if he made that sound, she'd be close to coming on the spot.

She didn't know how long they stayed there. There was no concept of time. No end to her. No beginning to him. Just a mishmash of teeth and lips and tongues.

She kissed him until she ran out of breath.

Then she kissed him some more.

All the while, that voice in her head screamed obscenities, called her every dirty name in the book. But her body had already switched sides, her uterus yelling that it wanted to have all his babies and pleading with that voice to give up and come to the Dark Side too.

No. No. *No!*

Sanity reasserted itself, and Emily ripped her mouth from his, stepping back on legs that were almost too shaky to hold her. She dropped her head, shielding her face with her hair. She couldn't let him see how much he affected her. How much she *wanted* him.

"I th-think that's enough of a demonstration of my

p-prowess," she stuttered, wiping a hand over her tingling lips. She wasn't sure if she was trying to rub the taste of him away or rub it in.

He dragged in a heavy breath, then seemed to have to force it back out when he was done with it. She glanced at his face to find his gaze hot, heavy, and colored with frustration. He looked ready to blow up or implode. Like a beautiful, dark star.

"I want you, Emily," he blurted.

Never accuse the man of beating around the bush. And the way he said her name made her feel like he was caressing her body with his strong, heavy hands. Which he *had* been, right before she remembered he was persona non grata and stepped out of his trance-inducing embrace.

"I think you want me too," he added.

The sound of her heart's furious pace was thunder in her ears. "B-but you don't like me. You always pick fights with me."

A muscle ticked beneath his eye. "Who picks fights with whom?"

Whom? *Whom?* Did people actually use that word?

Still, he had a point. Since day one, she'd given him shit at every turn. Partly because it was fun. Partly because she loved it when he glowered at her so menacingly. Partly because, like she insisted to everyone else, *someone* had to keep his ego in check. But mostly because it was a way of engaging with him, of flirting and teasing and provoking him with their clothes *on*.

"Whatever." She rolled her eyes. "Chicken or egg. The point is, I irritate you to no end. In fact, if memory serves, you said I was as vexing as a housefly."

"You *are* as vexing as a housefly. I like it."

Oh, he had to stop saying things like that!

"Which brings me around to something *else* you said," she added, rushing ahead.

"And what was that?"

"That it's been a really long time since you've been laid. And that your…" Her eyes drifted down to the fly of his jeans. Oh jeez. *That* was a mistake. She ripped her gaze back to his face. "Your…uh…"—she swallowed and motioned toward his package—"didn't have anything to do with *me*."

"I lied."

Ho-kay. She had to sit down. It was either that or fall down. She wanted to blame her sudden dizziness on skipping lunch, but it had everything to do with Christian and the words coming out of his mouth.

How her legs carried her the ten feet to the sofa, she would never know. But she thanked her lucky stars they did. *Screw grace*. She didn't attempt any as she collapsed onto the cushions, grimacing when the leather couch squeaked in affront.

After a brief hesitation, Christian settled into the chair across from her like all big, sturdy men did. Slowly. Confidently. Stretching his long legs out in front of him and crossing them at the ankles.

After a beat, when it became obvious she wasn't going to be the one to get the ball rolling again, his mouth twisted wryly. "Record this day for posterity. I've rendered Emily Scott speechless."

His self-satisfied smirk was just the kick in the pants she needed. "Why did you lie?"

"Pride." He said the word without hesitation. "I didn't

think you felt the same for me, so I figured it was better if I kept how I felt about you on the DL."

"Don't try to use 'hood-rat lingo. Just sounds silly." Here he was giving her all kinds of truths, and she was lying through her teeth. Because honestly, that smooth baritone paired with that delicious accent sounded good, like an invitation to sin, no matter which words he used.

"I'll have you remember I've been living and working in Chicago for years now," he said. "And given the shop"—that's how they referred to BKI headquarters—"isn't located in the nicest part of town, I think I've earned the right to adopt the lexicon."

"The shop is on the North Side. Which, as you know, doesn't count as *the 'hood*." She made the quote marks with her fingers.

"Fine." He blew out an exasperated breath. "I didn't think you felt the same, so I figured it was better if I kept how I felt about you to myself. There. Is that better?"

"You *didn't* think I felt the same? Past tense? What changed your mind? Not that kiss." She hooked her thumb over her shoulder to indicate the spot where they'd almost eaten each other alive. Goose bumps peppered her skin at the memory. "For all you know, that was just me putting on a show, proving I got chops when it comes to the ol' tongue tango."

His lips twitched like he wanted to smile, but for some reason, he refused to. "Anyone ever tell you that you have a decidedly singular way with words?"

"Thanks to my South Side raising, yo." She beat a fist against her chest and pursed her mouth into a duck face worthy of a selfie. "Ever watched an episode of *Shameless?* That pretty much sums it up."

"I thought *Shameless* was set in the Back of the Yards neighborhood. Aren't you from Bridgeport?"

She lifted a shoulder. "Different zip, same attitude. And you're doing it again. Christian Watsoning your way out of answering my question."

"Stop using my name as a verb."

"Stop skirting the issue. What changed your mind? What made you think I want you?"

He regarded her for so long she began to think he was refusing to answer. Then he said, "I was thinking about how you were so quick to scramble off Angel when I came 'round the corner of the manor earlier. I was thinking about how you were so quick to tell me that finding the two of you in a tangle wasn't what I thought it was. I was thinking that you wouldn't have done either of those things unless you didn't fancy me getting the wrong impression. And then I was thinking... Why *wouldn't* she fancy me getting the wrong impression? Why would she care what I thought?"

"And the answer you hit on was that I *wanted* you? That's a pretty big assumption. Ever considered seeing a plastic surgeon to have your ego downsized?"

The stare he fixed on her was so hard, so sharp, that she imagined herself pinned to a corkboard like a butterfly.

"Am I wrong?" Challenge gleamed in his distracting, too-pretty eyes.

She considered lying. A lie was so much easier than the truth. But she couldn't bring herself to do it. Maybe because she respected him too much. Maybe because he was putting himself out there, and she couldn't bear the thought of trampling all over him. Whatever the reason, she heard herself say, "No. You aren't wrong.

But it doesn't change anything. To use one of your phrases, *that*"—once again, she arced a thumb over her shoulder—"won't happen again."

His eyes went from blazing fire to green ice. "Why not?"

"Because I don't mix business with pleasure. Ever."

Chapter 12

"WHAT A LOAD OF COBBLERS," CHRISTIAN BLURTED.

He was still reeling from the intensity of that kiss. Bloody *hell*, was he still reeling. And he would have fancied nothing better than to pull her off that settee and straight onto his lap to repeat the endeavor, but for reasons he felt forced to cry foul on, she was bound and determined to throw a wrench in the works.

She didn't mix business with pleasure? Ha! Since when?

Her pale-pink lips flattened. "There you go again. Using phrases I don't understand."

"It means bullshit. Rubbish. I know for a fact that you had something going with your boss back when you worked for the CIA."

Her chin jerked back so fast he was surprised she didn't give herself whiplash. "You *have* been reading my file!" she accused.

"No." He shook his head. "Again, I overheard you talking to one of the women at BKI. You intimated that an ill-fated romantic relationship with your boss was the reason you quit the Company."

"Eavesdropper!" she accused.

"Loud talker!" he shot back, leaning forward in his chair.

He realized he was seconds away from jumping on top of her. Whether to punish her for the lie or simply because she was never so tempting as when her hackles were raised, he wasn't sure. But since he prided himself on being a man of control, and since there was that itty-bitty rule about not touching a woman unless he was invited, he forced himself to sit back. There was nothing he could do to unclench his fists from the chair's armrests, however.

"Why did you lie just now?" he demanded.

"I didn't lie."

"Abso-bloody-lutely you did."

"No, I didn't."

Sweet Fanny Adams, they were doing it again.

"Then explain how you can tell one person that you quit the CIA because of a dalliance with your boss and then claim to me that you never mix business with pleasure. One of them is a lie."

"Nope. They aren't mutually exclusive."

"How so?"

Emily's jaw set at an obstinate angle, telling him without words that she was finished with the conversation.

Bugger it all!

Then an idea occurred, and a cool blanket of calmness wrapped around him, banking the fire of his frustration.

If there was one thing that could win out over Emily's stubbornness, it was her curiosity. The woman's nosy nature got the better of her every time.

"I'll make you a deal," he said. "I'll tell you one truth if, in return, you tell me one as well."

She shook her head. He ignored the way a lock of her hair came to rest over her breast, the end lovingly curled around the tip as if to frame her unseen nipple. "But I don't want to know just *one* of your truths," she said.

"I want to know *all* of them, you big smelly onion. For months, I've been dying to peel away your layers and see what's underneath."

See? Curious as a cat. And if she was keen to get to know more about him, that had to mean she cared, yeah? Or at the very least *wanted* him? But despite the fact that earlier he had been champing at the bit to tell her his tale, to let her get to know the real him, sanity had returned and suddenly the thought of whipping open his emotional raincoat and exposing himself filled him with dread.

What if she didn't like what she saw? What if the real him—warts and scars and dodgy psyche and all—sent her running for the hills? He wasn't sure he would survive that kind of rejection.

Not from her.

"Two," he grumbled, feeling the tension in the muscle beneath his eye. Only Emily would think to negotiate at a time like this. "I'll give you two truths."

"Three." She was quick to come back. "I want *three* truths."

He grimaced. "This is turning into a terrible deal."

"Something tells me you wouldn't recognize a *good* deal if it crawled up your pant leg and bit you on the pecker. Three little truths. That's all I'm asking."

He experienced a jolt when she mentioned the words *bite* and *pecker* in the same sentence. His perverted mind immediately conjured up an image of *her* down on her knees, her soft mouth wrapped around… He shoved the vision aside.

And *little*? He knew beyond a shadow of a doubt that the three truths she'd asked for would be anything but little. She didn't want to know what his favorite color was—pink, like her cheeks—or what side of the bed he slept on—whichever side of the bed she didn't want. She wanted to know *him*. To unearth the dark, disturbing things from his past that had formed him into the man he was today.

"Fine." He stuck out his hand. "You win. Three truths. But I get to ask my questions first."

When she reached to shake on the deal, he pulled her off the sofa and into his lap. She squeaked her surprise.

"What are you doing?" She squirmed to be let go.

"You got what you wanted. Three truths. It's only fair I get what *I* want too. Which is you on my lap." If he was going to open the lid on his dark past and expose her to all its shadows, he needed to keep hold of her while he did it. Whether to ground her in the present or to keep himself grounded there, he wasn't sure. "Now, stop wiggling," he scolded. "Unless…" He made certain his grin was lecherous. "You fancy wiggling a tad to the left. That would be quite fine, and I—"

She shoved a finger over his lips. When he kissed it, she was quick to scowl and yank it away. She tried to act nonchalant about it, but he caught her rubbing at the spot where his lips had been. He could see the goose bumps on her arms, and a deep sense of satisfaction gripped him.

"Your jeans are wet," she accused.

"Not that wet," he countered. In fact, they were mostly dry.

"Fine. But I would've thought you'd had enough of me sitting on your lap after the truck ride." She looked petulant and flustered and quite pretty with her long hair having dried into soft, beachy waves. It was shiny and mink brown. But he knew when the sunlight hit it just right, he would see scattered strands of deep auburn and burnished gold.

"Quite the contrary," he told her. "I found I rather enjoyed it. Now I'm hooked."

"Humph." She crossed her arms.

He was tempted to kiss the frown right off her lips. Then kiss his way back to her ear so he could whisper dirty things to her before he made way down to her neck so he could suck on—

"That fecking bastard bruised you," he growled. There were four discolored circles on the side of her slim throat where lead Wankstain Brother had throttled her.

"It's nothing." She waved a dismissive hand. "It doesn't even hurt."

It might not hurt, but that didn't stop Christian from imagining tearing out the asshole's jugular—*with his teeth*—for daring to lay hands on her. In fact, he got so lost in the fantasy he didn't realize how much time had passed until Emily said, "Well? Are we gonna do this thing or not? I ain't got all day."

Right. The truths. And she'd whipped out her 'hood-girl grammar, which revealed how nervous she was about what he might ask.

Brilliant. He *wanted* her nervous. He didn't want to be the only one.

"Truth number one," he began, "why did you say you don't mix business with pleasure when you do…when you *have*?"

"It wasn't a lie," she insisted, still wearing a mulish expression that made him snuggle her closer despite her protests. After a couple of seconds, she gave up and leaned against him, all soft weight and sweet-smelling shampoo. "If you recall, I didn't say I'd *never* mixed business with pleasure. I just said I *don't* mix them. As in currently."

That didn't bode well for him, did it? Something hard and sharp settled inside his chest. "Why? What happened between you and your boss?"

"He fell in love with me."

The way she said the words was how someone else might say, *The sun darkened, the moon turned to blood, and the Four Horsemen of the Apocalypse appeared on the horizon.*

The hard thing that had settled in his chest turned out to be a vise. It clamped around his heart. "He fell in love with you? Is that such a bad thing?"

"*Yes!*" she huffed exasperatedly, looking at him like the answer was obvious. "Because it ruined *everything* when I didn't love him back. When I *couldn't* love him back. And believe me, I tried. Richard Neely was smart and handsome and about the sweetest thing ever."

If it was difficult seeing Emily holding hands or dancing in the arms of Rusty, a man who had no more sexual interest in her than he would in a kumquat, then it was absolutely agonizing imagining her in the arms of a man she thought of as smart and handsome and sweet. A man who had loved her and had no doubt *made* love to her on many occasions.

"He had these cute dimples," she continued. "And on Sunday mornings he would bring me breakfast in bed and then—"

"Oh, go on then." Christian clapped a hand over her

mouth. "Spare me the details." Green had edged into his vision, and he was afraid if she continued, he might hulk out and start tearing books from the shelves in a jealous rage.

"He did anything and everything I ever asked," she said when he dropped his hand. "He never argued with me. He always gave me anything I wanted."

As opposed to Christian, who *always* argued with her.

"But…" She shook her head. "I didn't love him. Not the way he wanted to be loved or deserved to be loved. And it caused huge problems at work when it all fell apart. He didn't understand *why* I didn't love him, and I couldn't explain it in a way he accepted. So his adoration turned to anger. His love to hate. It got to where he couldn't stand to be in the same room with me."

Her expression was resigned and more than a bit sad. "As you can imagine, that made working in the same office more than a little difficult. He tried to get me a transfer. He really did." She shrugged. "But there were no positions available. So I took pity on him and quit."

That's Emily for you, Christian thought. *Tough and tenacious on the outside. Selfless and sweet on the inside.*

Of course she would sacrifice herself for her former lover. She'd been up for taking a bullet for Christian, and until today they'd barely even *touched*.

"And that's when you made the decision never to mix business with pleasure again?" He watched her closely.

"Exactly. I *loved* my job with the CIA. Thought I'd never find work like that again. Then, Boss offered me the gig at BKI. And holy shit! I love working there just as much. Maybe more. I will *not* fuck it up. I will *not* put myself in a position to have to start over. Not again."

For a long time, Christian remained quiet, arranging his thoughts, trying to come up with a good way to assure her that her past held no sway over her present. She hadn't loved this Richard Neely bloke? So what? That didn't mean she couldn't fall in love with *Christian*. That didn't mean she shouldn't give the two of *them* a fighting chance.

"You said you couldn't explain to Neely in a way that he would accept the reason why you didn't love him," he said. "How about trying to explain it to me."

"Nope." She shook her head. "You've had your three truths."

He blinked. "I beg your pardon. I've only—"

"Think about it," she interrupted. "You asked why I lied, and I told you. You asked what happened between me and my boss, and I told you." She ticked off his questions on her fingers. "And you asked why Richard falling in love with me was a bad thing, and I told you." Her grin was decidedly wicked when she finished with, "That's three, bucko. Now, it's my turn."

The muscle beneath his eye, not to mention the one in his jaw, went properly crazy. "You fight dirty," he accused.

"And don't you forget it." Her grin was positively impish.

Emily was so proud of herself for the way she'd handled Christian's questioning that she was tempted to blow on her nails and rub them against her sweatshirt. But he already looked like he wanted to take a bite out of her.

Blowing on her nails and rubbing them against her shirt might be enough to push him over the edge into action. Since she'd spent five minutes convincing him she was determined to live by a tenet that made sure his mouth came nowhere near her, she kept her hands fisted firmly in her lap.

"Question number one," she said, arranging her thoughts into some semblance of order. It was more difficult than usual because she was, you know, sitting on Christian's lap. And he wasn't helping matters a damn bit by tracing slow circles over her hip with the rough pad of his thumb. Still, she managed, "You said your mother was responsible for your father's death. Explain."

He lifted a sardonic brow.

"What?" She frowned.

"I didn't hear a question in there. But I suppose I mustn't be surprised. Asking for things isn't really your forte, is it? You're better at *demanding* things. Bossy to your core."

"I've learned that if I *ask* for something, it's easy for someone to tell me *no*. Now stop Christian Watsoning."

When his brow furrowed into one of his delightfully sexy scowls, she resisted the urge to shoot a victorious fist in the air.

"Thought I told you to bugger off using my name as a verb."

"Thought I told you to bugger off changing the subject," she mimicked in his accent.

He glared at her. She glared back. Then his face softened, and his eyes drifted to her lips. The look in them said, *I want to kiss you.*

She snapped her fingers in front of his nose, forcing

his gaze back to hers. She made sure her frown replied, *Stay on topic!*

He sighed, making it sound like he was the most put-upon man in the world. Then he opened his mouth, and the story that spilled out shook the foundations of Emily's emotional walls.

"Both my folks fancied getting pissed…er…*drunk*, as you would say," he began, looking off into the middle distance as if it held all his memories. "Not every day, mind you. But on the weekends? Yeah. They blew off steam. Liked to have their mates over or go out on the town. And when they did, it was a proper piss-up, a major party. My dad was actually the worse of the two at the start. Some of my earliest memories are of my mum helping him stumble through the front door of our East End walk-up, then tossing him on the sofa and setting a dustbin beside him in case he needed to heave."

Emily frowned. She could definitely relate to having been raised by bad parents.

"One Saturday night about a month before my sixth birthday, they were at a pub with friends," he continued. Was she imagining things, or did his voice hitch? Just a little? Her heart felt that hitch all the way to its core. "Both were too plastered to drive home. But of course, of the two of them, my dad was the worse. So Mum took the keys and got behind the wheel."

Emily sensed the tension in the muscles of Christian's chest, felt his thigh tighten beneath her bottom. She was so tempted to take his face between her hands and kiss away all his pain and sorrow. So tempted to throw her hard-learned lessons right out the window and…*give in*. But instead, she clasped her hands together and squeezed her fingers tight.

"She blew through a stop sign at an intersection, and a delivery truck T-boned their Ford Fiesta." His Adam's apple bounced in the column of his tan throat. "It crashed into the passenger side of the vehicle. The docs said my dad died instantly. But my mum?" He shook his head. "She barely had a scratch. I think that actually made things worse in the end. I think she might have done better with the rest of her life had she been injured."

"What? Why?"

The questions were out of Emily's mouth before she had a chance to reel them back in. She'd used up her second truth, and she'd planned on it being something else entirely. Like, what his tattoos meant—if they meant anything—and why he'd gotten them.

The thick black patterns that inked over his muscular arms didn't jibe with the man she knew, the one who drove a fancy car and wore designer clothes. But she suspected they jibed *very* well with the man *beneath* those designer clothes. The one who was down and dirty, gruff and gritty.

"The guilt ate at her," he said. "If she'd been seriously injured, I think she would've been able to deal. But she couldn't live with getting him killed and her walking away as if nothing had happened."

So many questions buzzed through Emily's brain that she felt like she'd shoved her head in a beehive. She had to grit her teeth to keep from asking them.

And why the hell wouldn't he stop rubbing her hip? Warmth had spread from the skin beneath his hand, and now her whole body was suffused with it.

"Is she the reason you stayed in England after Boss invited you to join him at Black Knights Inc.?" she asked. The look he shot her had her lifting a brow. "What?"

"That's the second time today I've thought you were either a mind reader or else practicing witchcraft."

"Really?" The thought delighted her. "When was the first time?" Then reality sank in. Shit, that was question number three. "Never mind!" She slapped a hand over his mouth. "Don't answer that."

His eyes sparkled mischievously. He'd tried using her own technique against her, piquing her interest so she'd use up her truths.

"I'm not the only one who fights dirty," she accused.

"And don't you forget it," he parroted her words back to her. Then he placed a hot kiss in the center of her palm.

She snatched her hand away, dropping it into her lap. If he noticed that she curled her fingers, trying to hold on to the heat of his kiss, he gave no indication.

"So out with it," she demanded. "Is your mother the reason you stayed in England after Boss invited you to join him at BKI?"

"Yes." His nod was perfunctory. "After I was let go from the SAS, when I was trying to make my way as a civilian, I moved back in with Mum. After Dad died, she didn't only get soused on the weekends. She did it all day every day. Held on to the bottle like a lifeline. She was self-medicating, of course. When she was pissed, she could forget she'd been the one behind the wheel that night. But miracle of miracles, with me back home looking after her, suddenly it seemed like she was trying to pull her shit together. She stopped spending all her government support checks at the pub and instead started buying decent food for the flat. She even went 'round to the local Jobcentre offices and applied to be placed in a position."

From the tender age of six, he'd lived with a drunk mother and a dead father.

Snap. Crackle. Pop.

That wasn't Rice Krispies. That was the foundations of Emily's walls. Because she *got* it.

Her parents might not be drunks, but she knew all about addiction. Her mother and father were both addicted to love, addicted to the high it brought them. They'd sought it with single-minded determination, and their searches had, more often than not, left Emily all alone.

"Then one night, about three months after I got back, I found her in an alley," Christian continued. "She was half frozen, half dressed, and totally piss drunk. And that's when I knew."

He stopped there. Didn't say another word for a full minute, simply stared into space.

Even though she'd used up her three truths, Emily posed a question anyway. "What did you know?"

Christian turned to look at her. There was so much sadness in his eyes that her heart lurched toward him, and her arms were around his neck before she could stop them.

"That I couldn't change her," he said, his voice deep and husky. "That I couldn't help her, couldn't save her. And she was too far gone to have any hope of saving herself. So, I trundled her off to the best rehab facility in the country the next morning. It cost all my savings to get her in a six-month program. Then I bought a one-way ticket to America. Got on that plane with nothing but a change of clothes in my rucksack and a paltry roll of pounds secured by an elastic band."

Emily desperately wanted to know what had become of his mother, if she had ever sobered up, how she'd died. But she'd already pushed her luck and gotten one more truth than he'd agreed to give her. So she bit back the questions poised on the tip of her tongue and said simply, "I'm so sorry, Christian."

Although *sorry* didn't come close to describing what she was feeling for him in that moment. She wasn't sure there were words in the English language that could do her emotions justice.

Then, because he *had* given her one more truth than he'd agreed to, and because her emotions were running high and she felt she should do *something*, she decided to answer the last question he had posed. After all, turnabout was fair play. She prided herself on being an equitable woman.

"I can't imagine what it was like to lose a father so early in life," she said, playing with the ends of his hair where it brushed the back of his warm neck. "Or to know what it was to grow up with an alcoholic mother. But like you, I'm sort of the collateral damage of my childhood."

His dark eyebrows slashed into a vee. "What do you mean?"

"You asked me to explain to you what I couldn't explain to Richard. Why I couldn't fall in love with him." Part of her mind was on the ugly truth she was about to reveal; the other part was distracted by the feel of his hair between her fingertips. It was so soft. Strange for a man who in all other respects was the epitome of hardness. Hard body. Hard head. Hard…ahem. "I'm willing to give it a try."

The look he sent her was guarded.

"But I want to make another deal with you," she said.

"I'm listening."

"I want you to let me go back over to the sofa." His pretty green eyes narrowed. "What I'm about to tell you is important, and I need to be able to concentrate to get it right. To *explain* it right. I can't concentrate when we're like"—she motioned between them—"*this*."

One corner of his mouth twitched. "Why not?"

Her pursed lips told him *you know why* without having to say the words.

Indulge me, his twinkling eyes answered.

She blew out a windy breath. "You're *distracting*, okay? You're all…" She waved a hand to indicate his entire form. "And it's distracting."

Not to mention destructive. As in, sitting on his lap, his arms around her, her arms around *him*—when had that last thing happened exactly?—was destroying her emotional fortifications, ripping them apart brick by brick until it was hard to remember *why* she was so determined to keep him at arm's length.

"You *do* want me." A satisfied grin kicked up the corners of his mouth. That mouth that she now knew from experience was magic. If she was a witch, then he was definitely a warlock. A sexy, tattooed English warlock.

She clucked her tongue. "Ah, ah, ah. Your arrogance is showing again."

"Admit it," he demanded.

"Okay, I admit it. You, sir, are arrogant." Devilment had her fighting a grin.

"Admit that you want me, woman. I'm not letting you go until you do."

"Fine." Her frustration had her raising her hands and letting them fall back into her lap. "I want you. What red-blooded heterosexual woman wouldn't? You've got that whole unholy trifecta thing going for you."

"Unholy trifecta?" He looked genuinely confused.

"Tall, dark, and handsome," she explained, touching his chin dimple. She couldn't get enough of it. "Plus, there's the accent."

"I'm not the one with an accent, darling. *You're* the one with an accent."

"Whatever. The point is that it doesn't matter that I want you; I can't have you. And I'll try to explain why if you'll let me go back over to the *damn sofa*!"

She clamped her mouth shut, heat flooding her cheeks when she realized he'd gotten under her skin and made her lose her shit. *Again.* He had an unnatural knack for it.

"Fine." He opened his arms, letting them come to rest on the arms of the chair. "You win. Your freedom for an explanation. Although, in truth, I'm hardly sure this is a better deal than the last one."

That Emily should feel so bereft without his strong arms around her, without that thumb drawing maddening circles on her hip, was completely absurd. Which was why she scrambled off his lap and flounced over to the sofa. She didn't want him to see the truth of her feelings on her face.

Only after she had settled into the corner, drawing her feet up onto the cushion and hugging her knees to her chest, did she dare look at him. "Like I said earlier," she grumbled. "You wouldn't know a good deal if it—"

"I'm warning you, Emily." His expression was so fierce, so focused that she found herself fighting for breath. "If you mention the words *bite* and *pecker* in the same sentence again, I can't be held responsible for what I'll do. Likely *bite* you and then try to use my *p*—"

"*Okay!*" She screwed her eyes shut and covered her ears. It felt as if someone had tossed a bucket of scalding water over her head. "I get it!"

When she blinked open her eyes, it was to find him reclined back in the chair, a smug half smile plastered over his irritatingly attractive face.

Chapter 13

MARK THAT ROUND A WIN FOR WATSON, CHRISTIAN THOUGHT, watching Emily struggle to organize her thoughts and ignore their most recent—and smashingly heated—exchange.

He *liked* that she was having difficulty getting herself situated. He *liked* that he could knock her off-balance. And he liked most of all that she'd admitted to wanting him. If it wouldn't have made the others in the manor house come running to investigate, he would have howled his triumph at the ceiling.

"Are you quite finished gloating?" she demanded, shooting darling little eye-daggers at him.

"Almost." He indulged in a deep, satisfied sigh.

"You are the most infuriating man. Has anyone ever told you that?"

"Yes." He nodded. "*You*. On many occasions."

"Well, the truth can never be overstated." She hugged her knees tighter to her chest and tried to scowl him into some sort of submission.

He widened his smile and gave her earlier words back to her. "Are we gonna do this thing or not? I ain't got all day."

She looked like she was sucking on a lemon. "That's a terrible impersonation of me."

"What's good for the goose is good for the gander."

"Are you saying *I* do a bad impersonation of *you*?"

"You sound like a Kiwi, darling. With a tad bit of Australian and Scottish and maybe some Welsh thrown in for fun and confusion."

"Humph." She looked offended. It was delightful.

"Now," he said, leaning forward and resting his elbows on his knees. With his hands clasped together, he turned serious. "Tell me why you didn't love this Richard bloke."

Because he wasn't you, Christian. He imagined those words tumbling out of her mouth and felt light as air. Which is probably why the landing hurt so much when her answer had him hurtling back to earth.

"Because I can't love anyone. Not romantically, anyway."

For a long time he stared at her, trying to make sense of her words. "So you're saying, what? You're like…a Vulcan or something?"

"You've been hanging around Ozzie too much," she accused.

Ozzie, computer-hacker genius and all-around tech guru at Black Knights Inc., was also a true-blue Trekkie. The man had more *Star Trek* T-shirts than Christian had pairs of socks. And Christian had *many* pairs of socks.

"Stop trying to change the subject," he warned.

She twisted her lips. "But I thought you just said what's good for the goose is good for the gander?"

"Emily…"

She blew out a windy breath. "Fine. *No*, I'm not a Vulcan. I have feelings. Lots of feelings. Around you, those feelings tend to oscillate between annoyance and lust, which, if you must know, is altogether crazy-making. And stop it!" She pointed at his face. "Stop with the self-satisfied smiles every time I admit to having a thing for your hot bod!"

He tried to wipe the grin from his face and failed.

She rolled her eyes. "But when it comes to love—romantic love, long-lasting love—I'm defective. It runs in my family. Now, whether that's due to nature or nurture, or a mix of both, is anyone's guess. I'm just saying it's a fact, proven over three generations."

She tilted her head. "Ever read *It Ends with Us* by Colleen Hoover?" She didn't wait for his response. "No. Of course not. When do you have time to read?"

He didn't. Not really. Except for the occasional car magazine while in the loo.

"Well, anyway…" She blazed ahead. "It's this really sad yet really empowering tale of a woman who comes from an abusive household and then finds herself married to a man she deeply loves but who also turns out to be abusive.

"In the end, she decides to stop giving her husband any second chances, to stop waiting for him to change, and instead to leave him and break the cycle of abuse. It ends with *her*. And like her, I'm determined to break the cycle of looking for love in all the wrong places, the cycle of marriage and divorce and marriage and divorce. I want to have kids someday. And I don't want them to get fucked over by me the way I got fucked over by my parents. It ends with *me*."

She really hadn't been having him on when she'd said she couldn't explain why she couldn't fall in love with Neely. Christian actually found himself feeling sorry for the man. Because, *sweet Fanny Adams*, Emily was usually good at getting to the point. But he'd listened to her try to explain herself for at least two minutes, and he was more confused *now* than before she started.

He sat back in the chair. Opened his mouth, then closed it again when he realized he didn't know what to ask or where to begin to try to unravel the convoluted strings of her explanation. Finally, he settled on, "Tell me more about this defect that runs in your family. You said three generations, yeah? What does that mean?"

"Right." She nodded and dropped her feet to the floor. Leaning forward, she said, "It all starts with my grandparents. Not my mother's parents. I never met them. They died before I was born. It's my father's parents I'm talking about, Grandpa Joe and Grandma Ivy. Between the two of them, they have eleven marriages. Six for my grandpa and five for my grandma. Although, they'll probably be tied soon at six and six. Grandma Ivy called me last month to tell me she's in the middle of divorce proceedings from her fifth husband because she's fallen in love. *Again*." Emily made a face. "This time it's with one of the men who attends physical therapy with her at the retirement home."

"How old is your grandmother?" he asked.

"Eighty-three."

"Wow. Impressive."

"What's impressive?" Emily frowned. "That she's lived to be eighty-three or that she's racked up five-going-on-six marriages in that time? Because believe me, Grandma Ivy is cute, but she's no Elizabeth Taylor."

A glimmer of understanding sparked to life. "So that's your grandparents," he said. "Which I assume is the first generation. Tell me about your parents, the second generation."

"Okay." She dipped her chin. "So my folks got married when they were both nineteen. They had me a year later. And two years after that, they got divorced. My mother has since proceeded to marry and divorce *six* other men over the span of my lifetime. Right now, she's single. But she keeps texting me pictures of this oily-looking used-car salesman from south Florida, so I expect I'll be receiving a wedding invitation in the mail any day now. And if she thinks I'm going to another online registry to buy her another damn blender, she's got another think coming."

Her face was mutinous. Christian wasn't sure she'd ever looked more lovable. Except for perhaps when she'd woken him from his nightmare with an expression of concern. Or maybe when she'd stepped in front of him to stop a bullet, her piquant chin thrust up in defiance. Then again, there was the time… *Oh, sod it all!* Fact was, Emily *always* looked lovable.

"And then there's my father," she continued, blowing out a resigned breath. "He's on marriage number four. Which, given my family's track record, puts him at the back of the pack. But not if you take into account the number of women who've lived with him over the years."

Christian was almost afraid to ask. "How many?"

"Twelve." She flashed the number on her fingers. "Some have lasted a couple of months. Two have lasted a couple of years. None have outlasted my mother, who managed to tie him down for a whole *three* years."

"That's loads of upheaval for a kid." Christian imagined the men and women, the *strangers*, who must've passed in and out of Emily's life.

A stranger his mother had dragged home soon after his father's death was the reason he… No. He pushed the memory away and hoped to God Emily had never suffered at the hands of one of her parents' lovers the way he had suffered at the hands of—

He couldn't say the man's name. Not even in the privacy of his own mind.

"It wasn't upheaval so much as neglect," Emily said. "My folks were always so busy chasing that shiny, new person who would make them feel young again, or excited about life again. And it's easy to ditch one spouse and move on to another when you're dirt poor and the divvying up of property isn't an issue. For the most part, they simply ignored me. I was an inconvenience that they shuffled back and forth between them on the whim of the day."

An image of Emily, small and alone, scratched knees, and big, dark eyes taking up her whole face bloomed to life in Christian's mind. If only they hadn't been separated by a sea. If only they'd grown up in the same city, on the same block, they might have been able to give each other the comfort and security they had so desperately needed and longed for as children.

"I'm sorry, Emily." The words seemed small and inadequate compared to the sadness he felt for that little dark-eyed girl who'd only wanted what all little girls wanted: to be loved and cherished.

Nothing for you to be sorry about, her sad eyes told him. "It could have been worse," she said aloud. "You know that because it *was* worse for you."

When it came to childhood trauma, Christian wasn't one for splitting hairs. The young psyche experienced hurt, uncertainty, and fear without really categorizing it. But that was a conversation for another day.

"And you?" he asked. "The third generation? As far as I know, you haven't a string of ex-husbands trailing behind you."

Emily's mouth twisted into a moue of disgust. "I was gonna be different. I was gonna show 'em all that it *was* possible for a Scott to find a true love and make it stick. Ain't nothin' but mind over matter, you know?"

Once more, she'd donned her South Side 'hood-rat persona, wrapping the guise around herself like a suit of armor.

"I was careful all through high school, all through college. I never did what my friends did and told some hot jock that I loved him. I held those words dear. Told myself I was only gonna say 'em to one man. The one man I knew I'd spend the rest of my life with."

When Christian swallowed, his throat felt sticky. What sorry wankstain had shoved a wad of peanut butter down his gullet? "Did you…say them to Neely?"

Her laugh was bitter. "See, that's the thing. I *wanted* to. When I first met him, I thought he hung the moon and stars. He was so smart and so handsome and so—"

"We've been through this already," Christian cut her off. If he had to sit and listen to her sing Neely's praises one more time, he might blow his bloody top. "He was amazing. I get it."

"He *was*," she insisted, making Christian grit his teeth. "He pampered me with gifts and attention, all the things I never got as a kid. And at first I ate it up with a spoon. There were so many times I *wanted* to tell him I loved him, but I didn't. I held back because…it was too soon, or it wasn't the right moment, or whatever. But then, about six months into the relationship, all his gifts and attention stopped making me feel loved and started making me feel sort of, well…*suffocated*."

She closed her eyes and shook her head. "It wasn't flowers every once in a while; it was flowers every week. For no reason. I think he wanted me to squeal and jump and clap my hands like I was as delighted by the twentieth bouquet as I had been by the first. When I didn't, he got his feelings hurt. But maybe he *should* have, right? Because he was being so thoughtful, and there I was…"

She waved a hand. "But it wasn't just that. There were the date nights. Which turned out to be *every* night. It was exhausting. We both worked hard, and most times I'd get off a ten-hour shift and want to go home, put on my ratty sweatpants, and eat Cheetos while binge-watching Netflix. *That* hurt his feelings too. He didn't understand why I'd ever choose that over a romantic meal with him."

She picked at one of the buttons on the tufted arm of the sofa. "He texted me constantly, even when we were in the same room. And if I didn't call him the minute I walked in the door to tell him I'd made it home from work, he'd pout and send me on a guilt trip. It all became too much. And those bright, sparkly feelings I had for him turned to dust."

She looked up, held Christian's gaze, and finished with, "Just like my parents. Just like my grandparents."

"Emily, you're not like—"

"But I am, don't you see?" she interrupted. "I'm *exactly* like them. If there was one man on the face of the planet I should have fallen in love with, it was Richard. And I *did* fall in love with him. At least I think I did there for a little bit. In the beginning. But because I'm a Scott, it didn't stick."

Christian had his own ideas about what had happened. "It sounds like this guy was needy and controlling, maybe even downright overbearing. And you're an independent woman. It's no wonder you began to feel suffocated."

"Of course you'd say that," she scoffed. "You're trying to get me to throw caution to the wind and do the horizontal mambo with you."

Christian snorted. The things she said delighted him nearly as often as they made him fancy taking her over his knee and paddling her sweet ass. "That may be true. About the…uh…horizontal mambo. But it doesn't change the fact that I think Neely was all wrong for you, and I'm hardly surprised you kicked him to the curb. What bothers me is that your relationship with *him* has made you determined not to give a relationship with *me* a go."

When her face blanched of color, he quickly added. "Not that it's a relationship I'm after." *Liar, liar!* a voice singsonged inside his head. "Ruddy hell, I haven't the first clue how to be a boyfriend. I even hate the word. It's juvenile sounding. I'm hardly a boy." And he didn't just want to be her *friend*. He wanted to be her *everything*. Her every thought. Her every smile. Her every witty quip. Suddenly, he understood how Richard Neely had felt. A woman like Emily turned a bloke into a possessive prat. "I'm a man. A hard man. A difficult man. An uncompromising man. And I haven't got it in me to change."

She smirked. "You say all that like you're telling me something I don't already know."

He went on as if she hadn't spoken. "So the difference between me and Neely is he wanted to be your everything. He wanted forever. Which meant that when things between the two of you came to an end, he was devastated. But I've no need to be your boyfriend. I've no need for forever."

Liar, liar! that vexing voice sang again. The buggering shit needed to shut its gob.

"So when things between *us* end, it'll be easy. We'll go back to being coworkers and acquaintances. No harm, no foul," he finished.

What are you doing? What are you doing?

Well, the voice hadn't shut up, but at least it was on to a new refrain.

Truth was, Christian wasn't sure *what* he was doing. He only knew that Emily would put the kibosh on any chance of something happening between them if she thought it might hurt him in the long run or affect her position within BKI. So he was lying through his teeth to convince her neither of those things would happen.

Perhaps it was arrogance…bloody hell, in the end he might look back and realize it was flat-out *stupidity*… but he couldn't help but think that if he could only get close to Emily, if he could convince her to share her body with him, then eventually she would also share her heart and soul.

He didn't believe for a split second that she was anything like her parents or grandparents. Emily was one of the most caring, most loyal, most *determined* people he had ever met. When and if she ever decided to take on a man for the rest of her life—*Please, God, let it be me!*—she would be a smashing success at it.

The trick would be convincing her to give it a go in the first place. And he figured the first step toward accomplishing that goal would be to convince her to let him into her bed.

"I'm speaking of scratching our itch, Emily. Finding pleasure in each other's bodies and leaving it at that. I'm speaking of keeping it casual," he lied.

"People say that, but they always have trouble keeping it casual." She told the truth.

"I won't."

She eyed him for a long moment. Then, "You *really* don't want anything more from me than a quick slap-and-tickle?"

"No, I daresay I don't. And we *must* work on your euphemisms, woman."

"Says the man who unrepentantly admits he comes from a land with about a bazillion colorful terms for dick and balls."

He hardened his stare, his eyes demanding, *Stop stalling. What will it be, Emily? Yea or nay?*

When she swallowed and nodded, everything inside him grew still. Her eyes held an invitation to which he RSVP'd by pushing up from the chair and joining her on the sofa.

Her breath caught when he cupped her face, rubbing a thumb over her mouth because, ruddy hell, it begged for attention when it wasn't being kissed.

"Come then, Emily." He dropped his voice so his words were a bare growl. "Let me show you why God made beautiful women and well-hung Englishmen."

—⁓—

Christian's words fell like sexy-as-hell anvils and crushed the argument poised on the tip of Emily's tongue. His mouth smiled, but his eyes didn't. In fact, she'd go so far as to say his gaze was downright predatory.

A million reasons why what he was proposing was a terrible idea tumbled through her head. But none of them outweighed his offer.

Maybe because she *wanted* him more than she'd ever wanted another man. Or maybe it was simply because her self-destruct button was bigger than most people's and she had this annoying habit of pushing it. Regardless of the reason, she found herself saying two words that were likely to come back to haunt her. "Okay, Christian."

Victory blazed in his eyes, making his irises shoot green fire. Then he was kissing her.

No. Wait. Calling it a kiss was misleading. It was so much more than a mere kiss. It was a claiming. A warning. A dark promise of unspeakable pleasures to come.

She had just twined her arms around his neck, ready to settle in and get the show on the road—once she made a decision she didn't see the point in dillydallying—when the sound of someone clearing his throat came from the open doorway.

Christian broke the seal of their lips enough to bark, "Go away!"

Emily chuckled at the fierceness of his tone.

"I hate to interrupt," Angel said.

"Then *don't*!" Christian snarled.

"But Rusty and Ace are tearing into each other

downstairs, and I think Emily should intercede before they kill one another."

Christian let his forehead fall against Emily's. "To be continued?"

"You betcha" was what she told him, but she had a sneaking suspicion that if she had time to think about what she'd agreed to, she might waffle on her decision.

Christian sat back, taking his lovely mouth, sweet-smelling breath, and delicious heat with him. He dropped his hands from her face, and her cheeks stung at the cool kiss of the air.

"What in the world could Rusty and Ace have to fight about?" He turned to Angel.

By way of answer, Angel simply shrugged.

"I think—" Emily had to clear her throat. Passion had thickened it, making her words no more than a hoarse whisper. "I think it has something to do with Ace being out of the closet and Rusty being *in*," she managed. "It's caused tension."

Christian frowned at her before posing a question to Angel. "And what, precisely, is *Emily* meant to do about that?"

Again Angel shrugged. This time he added a set of splayed hands to the gesture.

Christian sighed and stood from the sofa. Emily took the opportunity to suck in a deep breath and will some feeling back into her limbs. Christian's kiss had caused all her blood to rush to her core. It was still tingling.

When he glanced down at her, he caught the look on her face and smiled. Or smirked rather. As if he knew the effect he had on her.

The arrogant SOB.

When she stood, she hoped he couldn't tell how rubbery her legs were. His ego was big enough as it was.

"Not that I think it's any of our business, but let's go stop the bloodshed, shall we?" He offered his hand.

She hesitated to take it. Number one, because Angel was watching, a spark of curiosity in his hell-black eyes. And number two, fuck buddies didn't hold hands. Fuck buddies just…well…*you know*.

"No use closing the barn door after the horse has bolted, Emily." Christian tilted his head toward Angel. "He's caught us kissing. *Twice*."

"Right." She took his hand, doing her best to ignore the *zing* she felt when his rough palm rubbed against her much softer one. "It's casual," she told Angel. "We're keeping it casual."

Instead of answering, Angel simply raised a brow. Which infuriated her. Because that cocked brow said *whatever you have to tell yourself* louder than words ever could.

"Are you going to announce that to everyone we meet?" Christian asked as they walked past the mahogany end table parked beside the chair where he had previously sat. With her. In. His. *Lap*.

"I think it's best to disabuse our coworkers of any ideas to the contrary, don't you? Put everything out there so there's no confusion. I mean, living and working with them day in and day out will mean they're hip to what's happening. No keeping *that* cat in the bag. But they might not be hip to what we're *thinking*, and then they might assume…um…things." It was only when she ran out of steam that she realized she'd said all that without taking a breath.

One corner of Christian's mouth twitched.

"Wind her up, and watch her go," Angel said. "I think you make her nervous, Christian."

"He doesn't make me *nervous*," she lied. Oh, he made her so nervous. "He makes me annoyed. And horny." She figured a dose of honesty was a good way to cover up her untruths. "Which is a seriously unfortunate mix and one of the many reasons—*hundreds* of reasons actually—why we're keeping it casual. Like I said." Her hard stare said, *Tell him, Christian.*

"Mmm," he hummed noncommittally.

She opened her mouth to demand exactly how she was supposed to take that *mmm* when she tripped over the edge of the rug.

Christian was there to catch her, strong hands wrapping around her arms. "Careful," he whispered. "You'll have to remember to watch your step after one of my kisses has turned your kneecaps to Jell-O."

She glared at him. Partly because he was right. Partly because it embarrassed her that he was right. But mostly because she'd had about all she could take of his smug, arrogant, self-satisfied—

"I know because *I* have to concentrate extra hard not to melt into a puddle after one of *your* kisses."

Her pique leaked out of her faster than water through a sieve. When he said things like that she…*felt* things she had absolutely no business feeling. Soft, bright, sparkly things.

"Now that you two have agreed to bump uglies," Angel grumbled in his sandpapery voice, "you are going to get on my last nerve. I can already tell."

"Bump uglies?" Emily was grateful for the distraction

from Christian's blistering gaze and from all those soft, bright, sparkly feelings. "I've already had to get on Christian for trying to sound 'hood-ratty. Don't make me do the same with you. Both of your accents make slang sound ridonkulous."

And besides, she had the sneaking suspicion that what Christian was packing in his pants was anything but ugly. That she was poised to find out—and soon—had her knees loosening again.

"For some reason," Christian said as he retook her hand and resumed their journey across the room, "she thinks she has the right to claim ownership of all slang and pop culture references."

His smile and the humor twinkling in his eyes threatened to infect her with something truly dangerous. A good mood. Because like good days, good moods were usually the precursor to life rising up to bite her on the ass.

"You know what?" she said. "I think I like it better when neither of you is talking."

Christian turned to her then, the heat in his eyes asking, *Would you rather I was using my mouth for something else?*

She swallowed, unable to answer back, even with her eyes.

Angel glanced back and forth between them and made a face. "Yes. My last nerve. Mark it as official."

She frowned at him. "No, it is *not* official. Because we're not going to get all lovey-dovey like everyone else back at BKI." Most of Emily's coworkers were married, engaged, or otherwise coupled up. Love was definitely in the air in Chicago. So much so that sometimes

walking around the shop and seeing so many pairs
making googly eyes at each other had her fighting the
urge to gag. Of course, other times she could admit how
nice it was. How terribly refreshing it was to see couples
that lasted. "We're keeping it *casual*." She stressed the
word to Angel. "Nothing sickening or annoying about
us. Spread the word."

Chapter 14

"I DO *NOT* HAVE A HOLIER-THAN-THOU ATTITUDE ABOUT MY sexuality *or* my life!" Ace roared.

That Rusty Parker had the unmitigated gall to accuse him of being judgmental not once, but *twice*, was bad enough. That the man had actually sought him out, herded him into one of the bedrooms, then slammed the door and proceeded to rip him a new asshole, advancing on him the entire time until now they were nose to nose, was even worse.

Especially since Rusty was so very large. So very impressive. So very...*sweet* smelling. No cologne or aftershave, just healthy male mixed with the great outdoors. It was almost enough to make Ace lose track of his end of the conversation.

"Yes, you *do*!" Rusty growled. "You think 'cause *you* got no problem with everyone in the world knowing what happens in your bedroom, that everyone else ought to be the same! And if they aren't the same, then they should feel ashamed!"

"It's not like I'm videotaping my sexcapades and posting them on the Internet! I simply don't hide the fact that I'm attracted to men. I work in the shadows, but I *live* in the light. That doesn't make me holier-than-thou; that makes me honest!"

"So now you're calling me *dishonest*?"

"Oh, for..." Ace spun away, pressing the heel of

his hand to his head. His heart pounded with anger and excitement, and he decided it was best if he focused on the first and ignored the second. "I'm not calling you anything. You can live your life however you see fit."

"Thank you. I will." Rusty was breathing hard. He looked absolutely glorious. All hulking shoulders and heaving chest.

Damn him! Ace had to look away. "But I have to tell you," he continued, his teeth clenched so hard his molars made a sound similar to a rusty blade caught in a garbage disposal, "it's a hard row to hoe. Not only for you, but for whomever you might one day fall in love with. Believe me. I've been there."

And he wasn't going back. Not ever. He made sure that fact was plastered across his face when he met Rusty's hostile gaze.

Rusty swallowed and stood straighter. For a moment, only silence passed between them. And that hostility? Ace watched it slowly disappear. Eventually Rusty asked, his voice low and soft, "Who was he?"

Grief sliced into Ace as hard and as sharp as a knife's edge.

Who was he?

Only the most beautiful man Ace had ever seen. Only the bravest man he had ever met. Only the man who had given his all to his country and who had tried, truly tried, to give his all to Ace.

Only the love of Ace's life.

"Glen Brogan." He said the name like a prayer. "A pilot. A major in the air force."

"What happened between you two?" There was curiosity in Rusty's hazel eyes.

"He died." The two words stuck in Ace's throat like they were covered in superglue. "And I couldn't be there."

"I'm sorry." The apology sounded so sincere it made Ace want to forget what a douchewad Rusty had been not two minutes ago.

Ugh. He really was a sad sack. A sucker for a macho, macho man.

"Was it Don't Ask/Don't Tell? Is that why you couldn't be there?" Rusty asked, referring to the now-defunct U.S. policy on gays, lesbians, and bisexuals serving in the military. Under DA/DT, they had not been allowed to reveal their sexual status—and weren't allowed to be asked about it either. Basically, the policy had turned any sort of sexuality besides heterosexuality into a dirty little secret.

"That was part of it," Ace admitted. "Another part of it was his family. They didn't know, and he couldn't bring himself to tell them."

And oh, how they had argued! Ace hadn't spent most of his teen years standing up to his narrow-minded father, preachers who promised damnation, and head-shrinkers who tried conversion therapy only to become a closeted adult. He had fought too hard to be who he was. To be *accepted* for who he was. To accept *himself* for who he was.

But he had loved Glen with all his heart. And when he hadn't been allowed into that hospital room in those last hours…

He swallowed, opened the lid on his mental lockbox, and shoved the heartrending memory back inside.

"How did he die?" Rusty's deep voice was quiet. "I mean, I don't want to pry or anything, but—"

"Of course you do," Ace countered. "But that's okay. I don't mind telling you." Well, actually he did. It *hurt* to talk about Glen. But if it could help Rusty reassess his situation, then maybe it would be worth it.

Taking a deep breath, he said, "He was shot down over Afghanistan in 2011. He managed to survive the crash. Managed to survive ten days of Taliban torture before a SEAL Team was sent in to get him. But he didn't survive his rescue. At least, he didn't survive for long *after* his rescue."

Ace closed his eyes, the memory of the phone call he'd received still as clear in his mind as if it'd happened yesterday. Gina, Glen's sister, had phoned to tell him Glen had been rescued. Ace had muffled his tears of joy at the news. But those tears of joy had soon turned to tears of anguish when Gina had gone on to say that Glen had been taken to Ramstein Air Base in Germany, and that he wasn't expected to live. Gina had said she thought Ace would want to know since he and Glen were "best friends."

Ace had hopped the first military transport he could find. And he'd made it to Ramstein in time, but—

"Was he injured in the attempt?" Rusty broke into his thoughts, and Ace blinked open his eyes.

Rusty and Glen couldn't be more physically different. Where Glen had been short and lean, Rusty was tall and bulky. Where Glen had been dark-haired and tawny skinned, Rusty had a mop of auburn hair and too many freckles to count. But they were both exceedingly *gentle* men. Both quick to defend. Both willing to volunteer their help to whomever needed it.

Too bad both of them refused to accept who they were.

"The Taliban shot him in the stomach when they heard the SEALs coming." Ace grimaced at the pain he knew Glen had suffered in his final days. "He survived for nearly forty-eight hours. He might have survived indefinitely had he not already been weakened by the torture."

"And you couldn't go to him, even under the auspices of friendship?" There was a sheen in Rusty's eyes. Such tenderness for such a big, brutal-looking man. The only thing that softened his handsomely craggy face was a set of dimples to die for.

"Oh, I went to him all right. Just as fast as I could. And I actually got there in time. An hour before he passed, in fact. But the doctors were only allowing *family*"—Ace spat out the word like it was poison—"in the room. And since I couldn't tell anyone that Glen and I had secretly married in New Hampshire the previous fall, I wasn't family."

For a second, Ace was quiet, his mind having traveled back to that awful day. Then, before he even realized he'd opened his mouth, the last of the story poured from him. "I tried to sneak in, but some nurses caught me. I begged his family to let me see him one last time, but his mother and his sister said his final moments should be spent with family, not friends. I would have told them all to go fuck themselves, but I knew Glen wouldn't want that. He wouldn't have wanted a scene, wouldn't have wanted his family's last memory to be of me bawling my eyes out by his side and telling him how much I loved him. So I didn't get to say my goodbyes. I didn't get to hold his hand at the end. I was left to wait in the hall like an afterthought. Like a *nobody*."

"Jiminy Christmas." Rusty ran a hand through his

hair, causing the loose, bouncy curls to riot. "I'm so *sorry*, man. That's… It's awful."

"Yeah." Ace nodded. "And it's one of millions of stories like it. Lord knows I'm not the first homosexual partner to be kept out of a hospital room because in the eyes of whichever law or policy I wasn't technically family. Or the first one who didn't receive spousal death benefits. Or the first one who didn't get a damn say in funeral arrangements."

Tears of rage burned the back of his nose. It was an old wound. But it was still raw. "Glen wanted to be cremated." His voice was a bitter parody of itself. "He wanted his ashes released at thirty-five thousand feet so he could become one with the open sky he loved so much. But it didn't matter what he wanted or what I told his family he wanted. They got to decide what to do with him. Which means now he's moldering away in the family plot."

"You didn't tell his family what you were to him?" Rusty searched his eyes. "Even after he died?"

"Ha!" Ace's laugh held no humor. "How could I? He hadn't told them in life, so I couldn't ignore his wishes in death. I loved him too much, *respected* him too much for that."

For a while, nothing but silence passed between them. Then Ace sighed and said, "So now you know why I have a problem with homosexuals remaining closeted. In the end, it always causes more pain."

"For you, maybe." Rusty's jaw hardened. Those damnably tempting dimples in his cheeks deepened. "But his family… They aren't suffering more. They're probably suffering less. Their memories of Glen are untainted by—"

"Stop right there." Ace held up a hand. His sorrow

was instantly replaced by red-hot anger. "If you're about to say their memories of Glen are untainted by the fact that he was gay, then *stop right there!*" He realized he was shouting again. "There is nothing shameful or *tainted* about who or what Glen was. And his family might be able to keep their memories of him, but they are *wrong* memories. Wouldn't it have been better if they had really known him? For fuck's sake!"

Rusty shook his head, his expression something Ace could only describe as obdurate.

Desire and rage and blistering remorse mixed together and became a dangerous cocktail. Ace swallowed it whole. Let it fill him up. At least that's what he convinced himself of and the thing he blamed for what happened next.

Fisting a hand in Rusty's hair, he yanked the former marine's head down for a kiss.

The instant their lips touched, Ace was deconstructed, reduced to his most basic elements. Because Rusty's mouth was warm and soft, and his big hands grabbed Ace's shoulders. To pull him closer? To push him away? Ace wasn't sure. He simply redoubled his efforts until the sound of the door flying open on squeaky hinges had him ripping his mouth away.

"I know we're not much for privacy," he snarled, "but ever think of knocking?"

"Uh…sorry," Emily said from the doorway. Behind her stood Christian and Angel. Christian looked shocked. Angel looked impassive, as always.

"I heard shouting and thought… Never mind." Emily shook her head. "I'll just close the door and let you two get back to…uh…doing what you were doing."

"Don't bother," Ace told her, desperately trying to catch his breath. "I'm done. I've accomplished what I set out to accomplish."

"And what was that?" Rusty's voice was hoarse. Guttural. And maybe just a little bit shaky.

Good to know Ace wasn't the only one suffering the aftershocks of that explosive kiss.

"To show you what you're missing. And hoping that the loss of something like this"—he motioned back and forth between them—"might give you an idea of how much it's worth."

Christian hopped out of the way when Ace slammed through the door.

"Close your mouth, Christian," Ace snarled as he stalked by. "Or else you'll catch flies."

"Sorry." Christian snapped his mouth shut. "I'm simply…surprised is all."

Ace spun. Christian felt Angel and Emily shuffle behind him to avoid being inadvertently hit by the flaming eye arrows Ace shot his way. *The cowards!*

"What? You've never seen two men kissing before?"

"No." Christian was quick to shake his head. "It's not that. It's that I've never seen *you* kissing before. All these years you've been playing the part of a monk. I only thought…" *You'd decided to eschew all romantic entanglements after your husband died.*

He daren't say that last part aloud. He'd learned the subject of Ace's husband was strictly off-limits. Ace turned green and clammed up anytime the man's name was mentioned.

"What?" Ace advanced on him until there were only a few feet separating them. "What did you think?"

Any other time, Christian would have risen to the challenge in Ace's eyes. He wasn't one to back down from a fight. But he knew the flyboy's frustration didn't have anything to do with him. It had everything to do with the redheaded colossus standing slack-jawed in the room behind them. Christian just happened to be in the wrong place at the wrong time.

Well, that, and he couldn't seem to say the right thing to bring Ace's boil down to a simmer.

Then it hit him. Ace was boiling. Colby "Ace" Ventura was actually *boiling*!

Christian fought a smile. Not to put too fine a point on it, but Ace was a *good* man. A caring man. A loyal man. Sure, he liked to bust his teammates' bollocks, and he had a bothersome habit of stealing Christian's perfectly toasted bagels out of the oven when Christian wasn't looking. But when push came to shove, there was no denying one simple fact: Ace was *nice*. And for too many years he'd shut himself off, holding on to his remorse, never letting anyone get close enough to light a fire under his ass. But to Christian's delight, it looked like Rusty was just the guy to stoke the flames.

"I was thinking it's about bloody time you let someone in," Christian said.

Once again, that seemed to be the exact *wrong* thing to say.

"I'm not letting him in!" Ace pointed an accusatory finger at Rusty. "Because despite every battle the LGBTQ community has fought over the years, he refuses to be *out*! Now, if you'll excuse me. I'm going to go punch something. If I can find anything that isn't five hundred years old and worth a bazillion dollars, that is."

When Ace turned on his heel, Angel popped out from behind Christian's back and blurted, "Christian and Emily have decided to do the deed. But they insist on keeping it casual."

Ace stopped in his tracks, his back still to them.

Emily punched Angel in the shoulder. Then she punched Christian too.

"*Ow!*" he complained. "Why are you hitting me? *I'm* not the one who said it."

"And why are you hitting *me*?" Angel demanded, what passed as a scowl shadowing his face. "I thought you *wanted* me to spread the word."

"Learn to pick your moment, man!" Emily tossed her hands in the air. "Jeez!"

Ace glanced over his shoulder. Some of the heat was gone from his eyes. "Is it true?"

"Is what true?" Christian countered. "That Emily and I have decided to give the ol' rumpy-pump a go?" He found himself battling the sophomoric urge to scream *hell yeah* before slapping high fives with everyone in the room. "Yes. It's true. It's also true that we're keeping it casual. Emily wants that made clear. It's the only way she's agree to mix business with…*pleasure*." He stressed the word and waggled his eyebrows at Emily.

"Oh, for the love of Shoeless Joe Jackson!" she sputtered. The slash of pink in her cheeks made her look fresh and young—and heightened the appeal of her already enticing little beauty mark.

"Good." Ace nodded. "It's about time." Then he

trudged down the hall and disappeared around the corner, presumably to find something to hit.

"And with that"—Angel dusted off his hands—"my job here is done. Time for me to head out while there is still light to see by. I can find food for tonight and a car to appropriate for tomorrow."

Right. They must do that, mustn't they?

As much as Christian wanted to take Emily's hand and yank her up those stairs so he could have his way with her, he couldn't forget the mission came first. Always. Right now, their mission was to do whatever it took to get the hell out of England.

"There's a sheep farm about a mile east," he said. He'd seen it on the map of the area he'd pulled up on his mobile after checking for the business hours at the manor house. "I should think it'll have food *and* transportation. I'll come 'round with you to scout it out."

"I'll come too," Rusty volunteered, heading in their direction. He still looked a little shaken and a whole lot peeved by Ace's kiss.

"No." Angel shook his head. "I prefer to work alone."

Christian crossed his arms. "No shit, Sherlock. But we'll come nonetheless."

"No."

That was it. The one word. It was so Angel-like.

"Fine." Christian shrugged. He didn't like shirking his duty, but he wasn't going to embarrass himself by standing there and squabbling. Besides, filching some food and getting a bead on a vehicle didn't really require three people. Or even two, for that matter.

Not only that, but letting Angel go it alone had the added benefit of affording Christian the opportunity to yank Emily up those stairs so he could have his way with her. "Good luck then," he said. "I'll keep my mobile on. If you run into trouble, text me."

Angel nodded, spun on his heel, and was 'round the corner and off to do decidedly Angel-y things a minute later.

"So." Christian turned to smile down at Emily, anticipation tightening his belly.

"So." She bit her lip.

"Uh." Rusty ran a hand over his jaw. "I think I'll just…" He didn't finish the sentence, simply shut the door in their faces.

"Shall we?" Christian offered Emily a hand.

She scowled down at it like it was covered in horse hockey. "Seriously? That's it? I mean, I know we're keeping this casual and all that jazz, but a gal could still use a little romance."

"It's romance the lady fancies?" Christian's smile stretched across his face. The anticipation in his belly had turned to ravenous hunger. "Then it's romance she shall have."

Without warning, he bent and scooped her into his arms. Yelping, Emily swatted at his chest, but he was undeterred as he traipsed down the hall to the staircase and took the steps two at a time.

Chapter 15

EMILY WAS BREATHLESS BY THE TIME CHRISTIAN KICKED THE door shut on the yellow bedroom. Strange, because *she* wasn't the one who'd run up the stairs.

Then again, Christian had stolen her breath the first time they were introduced, and he'd been stealing her breath on a daily basis ever since. Something as innocuous as seeing him playing catch in BKI's back courtyard with little Franklin, the son of one of their coworkers, or polishing his weapon so it shone as fresh and crisp as the clothes he had tailored to fit him like a glove was enough to have her stopping in her tracks, grabbing the nearest solid surface, and searching for the air that had deserted her lungs.

So, yeah, being in his arms, being carried up a flight of stairs like a heroine in a romance novel, was *certainly* enough to have her fighting for oxygen.

When he set her on her feet, caging her between his big body and the door—his hands flat on either side of her head, his eyes promising naughty delights and unspeakable intimacies—emotions exploded inside her. They shot up a mushroom cloud that made it impossible to swallow.

There was fear.

There was uncertainty.

There were second thoughts.

Of course, there was desire.

It was all too much. She fell back on the familiar and teased him. "Oooh, what a display of testosterone! Where do you keep it all?"

"Ninety-liter drums in a storage unit back in Chicago."

She blinked and sputtered. "Did you just make a joke?"

"Mmm." He leaned forward to brush a finger across her chin, his brilliant-green eyes glued to her lips with laser-like focus.

That's all it took for the fear and uncertainty and second thoughts and desire to reassert themselves. To swirl around inside her in an amorphous blob that throbbed like a beating heart.

"Christian?" His name was out of her mouth before she realized she wanted to say it.

"Yes, Emily?"

"A-are you sure about th-this?" She hated the vulnerability those halting words revealed. She wanted to project toughness, but in that moment she didn't know how. The look he gave her was so hot, so hungry, that her knees began to shake.

Damn mutinous things! She was going to have to have a talk with them. Too often recently they'd been failing her when she needed them most.

I am abso-bloody-lutely sure, his expression assured her. Aloud, he said, "I want you." Those three simple words sounded as sweet the second time as they had the first.

Would they sound as sweet the hundredth time? Or the thousandth time? Or the millionth time?

Whoa, Nelly! That kind of thinking was totally crazypants. There wouldn't *be* a hundredth time, much less a thousandth time or a millionth time. This was going to be casual. And that meant it was going to be over quickly. A few slam-bam-thank-you-ma'ams, and he'd grow tired of her.

Why that thought should bother her was a mystery she dared not explore.

"And you want me," he continued, such arrogance, such confidence in his tone as he lifted her hair away from her shoulder and grazed the callused pad of his thumb over a bruise on her neck. Her skin was so sensitive that his touch burned like fire. "So stop overthinking things. And simply"—he leaned close, putting his mouth next to her ear—"give in to me. Give in to this. You know you want to."

His hot breath swirled inside the shell of her ear, making her toes curl.

"Promise me," she whispered. "Promise me you won't fall in love."

Slowly, languorously, he pulled back to study her from beneath hooded lids that did nothing to hide the predatory light in his eyes. "I won't fall in love," he swore, and even though she knew she should breathe a sigh of relief, it felt more like her lungs were squeezed in a tight fist. "Can you say the same?"

Could she? A sliver of doubt appeared where none had been before. She caught her bottom lip between her teeth, and his gaze snagged on the move. He rumbled, deep in his chest. It was the sound a hungry lion might make.

Dear, sweet baby Jesus, he was so unspeakably sexy, and he was going to kiss her. She saw his intent. Waited impatiently for the feel of those diametrically opposed lips, for the press of that insistent, uncompromising tongue. But one second stretched to two. Two quickly became ten.

"Christian?" There it was again. His name ripped from her lips without her consent.

Answer me, Emily, his eyes said. *Can you say the same?*

She nodded jerkily. "You know I can. I explained it to you." Why did that suddenly sound like a lie?

"Then there's something you should know before we do this."

Oh Lord, she thought. *Here it comes*. This was the part where he confessed to having a bad case of genital warts, or to only liking anal sex, or to wanting to wear her panties on his head while they were doing it.

"I can be…*demanding* in the bedroom," he said, and she released a breath she hadn't realized she'd been holding.

"Oh-kay?" She'd meant it to be a statement. It came out as a question. "Meaning…what? You give instructions or—"

"I like to be in control," he told her, still hovering close. Still looking at her like kissing her was the only thing he could think of doing, and holding back was stretching his willpower to the breaking point.

"And what does *that* mean?" Visions of the red room of pain, of whips and chains and spikes and ball gags circled around inside her head and splashed a cold glass of water on her ardor.

She knew a lot of women found that whole Fifty Shades thing sexy. But she preferred her pleasure to come with a side of *more* pleasure. Pain was for gym workouts and mornings after too much booze, thank you very much.

"It means that, yes, sometimes I give instructions. But it also means that I like to have a woman at my mercy."

Her chin jerked back until her head butted against the door. "Okay, bucko. Time to stop beating around the bush and shoot me the straight skinny. Are you saying you wanna whip me? Gag me? Put clamps on my nipples and drag me around by my—"

He silenced her with a kiss that was as short as it was cyc-crossingly hot.

"None of that," he whispered against her lips. "You don't mix business with pleasure. I don't mix pleasure with pain."

"Well, thank God for that."

"But I do fancy a bit of bondage," he said, and it felt like a hot, hard knot tightened inside her womb. "I like to tie a woman up. It turns me on knowing she is helpless to withstand the pleasure I give her."

"Oh-kay." This time it *was* a statement.

"I'm hardly saying I need to do it every time. But sometimes, it's all I want, yeah? Will you be okay with that?" He ducked his chin, forcing her to meet his eyes. "Some women don't enjoy feeling that vulnerable. They aren't keen on giving up control. They don't trust enough to—"

"I'm fine with it," she said. Or rather *panted*.

She had never been tied up before, but she'd fantasized about it plenty. In fact, it was her *favorite* fantasy.

In her job and in her life, it always fell on *her* to take care of things, to be in charge and make sure everything ran smoothly. The thought of letting someone *else* shoulder the burden and take the lead, the thought of… *letting go* was incredibly freeing. And incredibly *erotic*.

A smile slowly stretched his delectable mouth. "You're certain?"

"Stop talking now." She fisted a hand in his hair and pulled him down for a kiss.

He didn't resist, taking possession of her lips in a way that had goose bumps breaking out over every inch of her skin. Cupping her face, he angled her head this way and that until she was dizzy with the suction of his mouth, with the soft, slow dip and retreat of his skilled tongue.

When her treacherous knees started shaking again, threatening to stop doing their damn job, he seemed to know. He palmed the back of her thigh and hooked her leg around his waist. And then…

Oh, and then she lost her flippin' mind because he rubbed himself against her. Christian Watson rubbed his *dick* against her. And it was hard. And it was big. And it made heat and moisture slick her panties.

The friction was so good. Better than good, in fact. It was totally amazeballs. And if he kept it up, she would c—

He grabbed her other leg, hooking it around his waist before spinning her away from the door. She thought he was walking them toward the bed, which was why she was so confused when he set her on her feet beside one of the windows. She grumbled her displeasure when he stopped kissing her. That is, until she saw his intent.

He reached for the chenille rope that held one side of the velvet, buttercup-yellow curtains back.

"Provisions," he said after he'd untied the length of rope and shoved it into the back pocket of his jeans.

To her utter dismay, a giggle of delight burbled from the back of her throat. An actual *giggle*. For Pete's sake, she was *not* a woman who giggled.

Christian lifted a brow, studying her. "You *like* the thought of being tied up, don't you?"

"Maybe" was all she allowed, clearing her throat because she was almost certain she felt another idiotic giggle threatening, and she refused to give in to it.

"I think this agreement of ours might work out perfectly." He untied the other side of the curtains and stuffed that length of rope in his back pocket as well. His accent made the word *perfectly* sound more like *puhfectly*.

"Now." He looked her up and down, fingering the hem of her sweatshirt. "Let's be rid of this, shall we?"

Her eyebrows drew together. "But…uh…what about those?" She motioned to the lengths of chenille in his pockets.

"I've found it's easier to undress women *before* tying them up."

"Would you please stop talking about other women?" She scowled at him.

First it was *some women* don't like feeling that vulnerable. Then it was *some women* don't like giving up control. Now it was easier to undress *women* before tying them up. If he used the term one more time, she might be tempted to take those ropes and hog-tie *him*. But not to do dirty things to him. Rather, to smack him around until he promised to forget every single woman who'd come before her.

Uh-oh. Oh no. That's dangerous thinking.

"Jealous, darling?" That infuriating self-satisfied smile was back in place.

"Oh, shut up." She whipped her sweatshirt over her head and tossed it to the floor.

Huzzah! She pumped an imaginary fist when, instead

of saying something arrogant or smug, he made a breathless noise—it sounded sort of like *unhhh*. Then he swallowed so hard his Adam's apple *clicked* in his throat.

His eyes landed on her pale-pink bra, traveled slowly over the lace of the cups, and settled on the little red rose sewn between them. His eyes settled on the *rose*. Not her boobs. The *rose*. *Damn*.

Suddenly, whipping off her sweatshirt didn't seem like such a good idea. Even though the weak afternoon sun was beginning to sink toward the west, there was still enough light to show him that, true to her word, she didn't have much in the way of boobs. On her good days, the most she could hope to fill was a B cup.

Self-conscious, she crossed her arms over her chest.

"Don't." His voice was like gravel crunching under tank tracks. Pulling her arms away, he fingered the little red rose like he couldn't help himself. "I think you're the most beautiful woman in the world."

"*Psshh*," she scoffed, but then immediately sobered because the look in his eyes said he was telling the truth.

"May I?" He trailed his fingers over the gentle slope of her breast before slipping them beneath one thin, silk strap.

A nod was the only answer she was capable of giving him. Her voice had ceased working the instant the tips of his fingers grazed her skin.

Slowly, like he was unwrapping a delicate gift, he pulled the strap off her shoulder. The second strap soon followed. When he reached behind her for her bra's clasp, she ducked her chin, not wanting to see his face when he realized how little she had to offer. Her bra was one of those push-up things. It lifted and plumped and gave the illusion of a fullness she didn't truly possess.

A finger slipped beneath her chin, forcing her to meet his heated gaze. "Stop trying to hide from me, Emily. Never hide from me."

Her nostrils flared when, with a snap of his fingers, her bra was undone. Oh, for heaven's sake, he was good at that. *The scoundrel!*

Then all thought leaked out of her ears because he was kissing her. Like kissing the holy *hell* out of her! In fact, his kiss was so deep, so thorough, so completely panty-slicking that she didn't notice he'd pulled off her bra until he broke the suction of their mouths and took a step back.

Her first instinct was to cover her breasts. But instead she gritted her teeth, thrust up her chin, and watched his eyes drift over her. His study was so intense it almost felt like a physical touch. And when his gaze fell on her nipples, she sucked in a breath, shocked to feel her areolas tighten, squeezing the centers into tight, painful buds.

"Beautiful," he murmured. "So soft and round and topped by the sweetest pink nipples I've ever seen."

Okay, so if there was one nice thing she could say about her boobs, it was that her small areolas, which were barely bigger than her nipples, gave her girls the appearance of heft. And looking at him looking at her with so much hunger, with so much *wonderment*, she began to feel a confidence she'd never had before.

Christian didn't look at her and see small tits. He looked at her and saw tits. He was such a *guy*. And she couldn't be happier for it.

Not asking permission this time, he cupped her left breast. His palm felt hot and rough when he plumped her high. The pad of his thumb was deliciously abrasive when it feathered over her distended nipple.

Oh, for the love of Robin Ventura. There went her knees again.

She reached for the windowsill to steady herself. But her hand slipped off the edge, causing her to stumble and glance over her shoulder to locate the recalcitrant sucker. No sooner had she steadied herself—not only thanks to the windowsill but to Christian's warm hand curling around her hip—then movement outside snagged her attention.

"*Eep!*" she squeaked and grabbed the curtains to cover her breasts.

Oh great. Not only had Christian turned her into a woman who giggled, he'd also turned her into a woman who *eeped*. What came next? Flowers in her hair? Frilly dresses? *Jeez!*

"What?" Christian came up behind her. "What is it? What did you see?"

"Uh…Angel," she said. "I saw him heading into the trees."

"You're certain it was Angel?" His hand on her hip, the feel of his cock pressed into the groove of her ass combined with his voice so near her ear to have her on the verge of losing her balance. Again.

"Of course. Who else would it be?" She stepped away from him before she melted into a foolish Emily puddle on the ground.

"Perhaps I should go investigate. I could—"

"It was Angel," she assured him with a frown.

"But just to be safe—"

"Ugh," she grumped. "You are so clam-jamming me right now, man."

"I beg your pardon." He actually looked affronted. It was sort of cute. "What does *that* mean?"

"You know." She rolled her hand. "Like cock-blocking, except for girls."

A snort escaped him, and she could tell he was biting the inside of his cheek. "Such a way with words." He shook his head, then nodded. "Right then." He whipped the curtains away from her chest.

She *eeped* again. Which made it official. She was an *eeper*.

"Let's pick up where we left off, shall we?" He bent and scooped her into his arms. And damned if she didn't giggle. "I was about to toss you on the bed and get you starkers."

"Starkers?"

"Naked, darling."

"Oh, then by all means." She waved a lofty hand toward the big four-poster bed with its cream and canary quilt and fat, fluffy pillows.

That's right, Lawrence thought with a lip-curl of disgust. *Go ahead and shag that skinny bird while you can, mate. It'll be the last fuck you ever get.*

He and Ben had stuck to the tree line and skirted 'round to the back of the manor house. Lawrence had made the mistake of stepping forward to get a better look at the movement he saw in the window when suddenly he'd been presented with a view of sweet little titties. Luckily, the dark-haired woman hadn't seen him before he slipped back into the shadows of the forest.

"Too skinny for my taste," Ben muttered, still watching the window.

"Skinny, fat, short, tall." Lawrence shrugged. "As long as she's got a pair of suckable nipples and a wet cunny, I'm in."

Ben snorted. "He always said you lacked discerning tastes."

"Who?" Lawrence asked. "Our esteemed brother?"

"Yeah." Ben nodded.

"He was one to talk." Lawrence chuckled. "You remember that time we were in London celebrating his acceptance into SAS training and he left the pub with that totty in six-inch heels?"

"The one who looked like she mighta had an Adam's apple?"

"He ever tell you what happened after he went back to her hotel room?"

Ben shook his head.

"Me neither." Lawrence grinned. "Which is funny 'cause you know how much he liked to brag about his conquests."

"Quiet as a church mouse the next morning, wasn't he?" Ben asked.

Instead of answering, Lawrence burst into laughter. He covered his mouth with his hand and shook his head, watching Ben's eyes twinkle in the gloom of the forest. But his humor died a quick death, because almost immediately he was reminded that their brother was gone and they'd been placed in this impossible situation because of the man who was currently warm and cozy and dipping his wick into some pretty, dark-haired chickadee.

Rage instantly replaced his amusement. A bitter curse

took the place of the laughter on his lips. "We'll wait 'til late before making our move," he said, his mind spinning through scenarios and latching on to the one that might possibly work.

"And then what?" Ben asked, all the playfulness gone from his voice. "If we do 'em in the house, there'll be evidence. Blood everywhere."

"We won't do 'em in the house. We'll get 'em to come *outta* the house."

Ben glanced at him, trepidation in his eyes. He still wasn't totally with the program.

Well, get *with it, little brother,* Lawrence thought. *It's the only way.*

"How do you propose we do that?" Ben asked.

"The woman." Lawrence smiled, some of his humor returning. Only it wasn't the warm humor of a fond memory. It was the cold humor of forthcoming revenge. "We simply hafta get the woman."

And then he laid out his plan.

Chapter 16

EMILY'S BROWN HAIR FANNED OUT ON THE QUILT WHEN Christian tossed her on the bed. She bounced, her pretty little breasts jiggling delightfully. The sight had his dick throbbing so hard he had to reach down and give it a tug to soothe it.

"Hey!" She came up on her elbows, her legs dangling over the edge of the bed. "What's the big idea?"

"Told you I meant to toss you on the bed before taking your clothes off. Never say I'm not a man of my word."

"Oh. Right." She nodded, avidly watching him position himself between her spread legs. "You *did* say that, didn't you?"

When her attention pinged down to his cock, he realized he was still stroking himself. "You want some help with that?" The look in her dark eyes was positively *devilish*.

"Yes." He slipped his thumbs beneath the elastic waistband of her leggings. "I most certainly do." When she reached for him, he caught her delicate wrist. "But not yet. First, I have other things to attend to."

"Oooh. I *do* like the sound of that."

He grinned at her, lying there with a smiling face and smoky eyes, so open, so honest. So completely uninhibited. Apparently, Emily approached sex the way she approached life, with vigor, candor, and unabashed eagerness. It made his silly heart sing and his even sillier cock pulse with anticipation.

This will be jolly good fun, he thought. Then he realized that, no matter how often she vexed him or teased him or provoked him, when it came down to it, she was fun. Being around her—trading insults or barbs or kisses or quiet moments in the kitchen before she'd had her first cup of coffee and he'd had his first cup of tea—was fun.

He hadn't had much fun in his life.

Perhaps that's why he'd fallen so hard for her. She gave him something he hadn't realized he'd been missing and didn't know he'd always yearned for.

"The first time I make you come," he told her, pulling her leggings over her flaring hips and down her silky thighs, "it's going to be with my fingers."

She flopped back on the bed, crossing her arms beneath her head. Her breasts pointed impertinently toward the ceiling, making his mouth water.

"Mmm," she hummed. "Tell me more."

"The second time I make you come"—he bent to work loose the laces of her hiking boots so he could slip them off her feet—"it will be with my mouth."

He saw her brow pucker as he was pulling off her second sock. "What?" he asked, loving that she was lying there, letting him have his way with her, offering no help and no protest.

Tough, tenacious, take-no-guff Emily Scott was allowing herself to be vulnerable, allowing *him* the control he craved. It spoke more eloquently of her strength and confidence than anything else ever could.

"I've never been able to come from oral sex," she admitted, and the thought of another man with his head between her legs, with his mouth on her, made Christian grit his teeth. "I'm not sure why. Maybe it's me. Or maybe I've never been with someone who was any good at it."

"I'm good at it," he promised, whipping her leggings off and tossing them over his shoulder. Now she was naked except for her panties.

God love her, they were pink cotton. Simple yet charming. Unadorned but still somehow gorgeous.

Just like the woman who wears them, he thought.

"And you *are* a man of your word," she said, watching him from beneath hooded lids.

"Indeed." He reached for her panties.

The small smile she wore disappeared when he slowly, gently ran a finger along the waistband. To his delight, goose bumps rose across her flat belly.

"And now," he said, "for the pièce de résistance. You ready?"

Her chest rose and fell in quick breaths as she jerkily nodded.

Expectation flashed through his blood until his veins throbbed as he carefully peeled her panties away and flung them over his shoulder to join her leggings and socks. He sucked in a startled breath when she lowered her legs and he saw that she was…

Shaved.

Smooth as could be. Pink and plump and glistening with desire.

Ding! Ding! Ding! It was like he was one of Pavlov's ruddy dogs, salivating at the dinner bell.

"Sodding hell," he groaned, once again reaching down to soothe the ache in his cock. "You're bloody gorgeous, Emily."

She released a shuddering breath and blushed. *All over*.

He wanted nothing more than to fall to his knees, bury his head between her legs, and taste. But he didn't want to shock her with the intensity of his hunger. And besides, this time, their first time together, she deserved finesse. She deserved soft kisses and sweet caresses. She deserved to have every part of her body tended to.

Which he would do.

Starting now.

"What about you?" she asked, dodging his lips when he crawled into bed beside her and tried to claim her mouth.

Impatient, he asked, "What about me?" Now that the moment had arrived, he was keen to move things along. His cock was pulsing so hard he wasn't entirely sure it wouldn't go off in his sodding trousers.

"Aren't you going to get naked?"

"In time," he promised. "But first"—he trailed a finger over her delicate collarbone, watching her breasts quiver gently in response—"I want to have you like this, naked, vulnerable, at my mercy while I remain clothed. It's a turn-on." And also, if he was starkers, she would be able to touch him. If she touched him, he would almost *certainly* go off before he was meant to. He'd wanted her too damned much for too damned long.

"You're kinda kinky, aren't you?" Her eyes twinkled.

"Let's find out, shall we?"

He didn't wait for her reply, simply claimed her mouth in a kiss he meant to keep slow and sweet. He wanted to give her an idea of *his* oral expertise, but slow and sweet quickly became hot and hungry. He lost all control when it came to her. Jolly good thing was, she seemed to suffer the same affliction. In no time, they were eating at each other like starving creatures.

Long minutes flew by while their tongues dipped and parried, tasted and tangoed. And all the while, from the corner of his eye, her pretty breasts beckoned. Small, soft mounds of flesh topped by tiny pink nipples that reminded him of candy.

When he could no longer resist their lure, he caught one silky globe in his hand, rubbed his thumb over the tip to make certain it was nice and hard, and then dipped his head to suck it into his mouth.

Emily buried her hands in his hair, pulling him close. When he flicked the turgid little nub with his tongue, she hissed and arched into him. Then she encouraged him by telling him to "keep going" and "suck harder."

He proved that he was as good at taking orders as he was at giving them by doing precisely as she asked. When she cried out his name, he felt like a god. All-powerful, indestructible. *Bulletproof.*

His skin felt alive for the first time because she touched it.

He could feel every individual strand of his hair because she grasped it.

He could taste every unique note of her skin because it was *her* skin.

Emily…

The woman of his dreams. The woman of his desires. The woman he loved.

Releasing her nipple, he pulled back and smiled at the glistening point. It was ruby red and fully engorged. Being a fair-minded man, he immediately tended to her other breast.

Only when both had been thoroughly loved, and
when Emily was mewling and squeezing her thighs
together to try to alleviate the ache his attention to her
nipples had created, did he reclaim her greedy mouth
and slowly slide his hand down her flat stomach, past
her softly jutting hip bones, to cup her mound.

Soft…so soft he wanted to weep.

Swollen…so swollen his cock jumped behind his
zipper.

Wet…so wet he couldn't stop himself from sliding
his fingers inside her folds to find her distended clitoris.

He was going too fast. He had wanted to go slow, to
touch and taste every inch of her before finally bringing
her to the inescapable heights of ecstasy. But he was too
greedy. Too anxious to please her, to give her the release
her writhing body and breathy sighs begged of him.

Rubbing the bud at the top of her sex, he swallowed
her whimpers and smiled when her hands left his hair
to grip his shoulders. Her nails dug into his muscles as
she mindlessly, wordlessly encouraged more from him.

Oh, he would give her more. He would give her
everything.

"I'm going to put my fingers inside you," he whispered against her kiss-swollen lips. "Open your pretty
legs for me."

Her eyes opened a fraction, and he could see her pupils
had dilated to the size of pie plates. She was ready. She
was close. And she didn't hesitate to follow his command, spreading her thighs wide as she planted desperate, biting kisses across his chin.

Thrilling at her quick acquiescence, he softly, delib-
erately slid not one but *two* fingers inside her. He wanted

her to feel full, feel stretched and satisfied and pushed to her limit right from the get-go.

He got his wish.

She turned her face into him and bit the spot where his neck met his shoulder, crying out at the pressure and the pleasure. Her body pulled his fingers deeper, eager and wanton.

Oh, ruddy hell. She was tight. And slick. And so unbearably silky. A man's greatest fantasy come to life, burning hot in his arms. No. Not hot. *Volcanic.*

"Please," she begged when he slowly pumped, testing her boundaries, feeling her delicate muscles contract as he curled his fingers upward, sliding the rough pads of his fingertips against the nerve-rich patch of flesh on the roof of her channel.

She'd released his shoulder. Now it was her lower lip that was caught between her teeth.

"Shhh." He covered her mouth and soothed that delectable lip with his tongue. "I'll take you where you want to go. Hold on to me. Ride it out. That's it."

Her hips bucked in counter-rhythm to his hand. She was mindless now, seeking pleasure with an uninhibited abandon that delighted him and pushed him too close to the edge.

He had to swivel his hips away from her. It was either that or go off early like a horny teenager in the back seat of a car. Every time she bucked, her thigh brushed against him, and the friction was building to dizzying heights. Pressing his cock hard into the mattress, both to ease the ache and stave off his brain-melting need to orgasm, he continued to work her body faster, harder.

Ripples. He felt them start in the muscles deep inside,

a telltale sign. Pulling back, he wanted to watch her face the first time she came. And then she was. Coming, that is. Flying apart in his arms. Flinging herself headfirst off the cliffs of pleasure. And it was the most amazing, most brilliant thing he had ever seen.

Gone. His rational mind.

Gone. His sense of control.

Gone. His heart.

She stole the first two when she threw her head back and screamed his name. As for the third? Well, that was already hers.

Emily was boneless, senseless, *sightless*.

Oh, wait. She could still see. Her eyes had simply squeezed tight against an ecstasy unlike any she had ever known.

As the last shudders of release quivered through her, she cracked open her eyelids to find Christian staring down at her, that self-satisfied grin firmly in place. This time, it didn't irritate her so much. Probably because this time she was pretty damn satisfied too.

Talk about an orgasm for the record books. She had no idea how long it had lasted. Ten minutes? An hour? It had felt like forever.

He *was* a warlock. She was absolutely convinced of it, because there was undeniable magic in his hands.

Multiple times, when she had thought she was on the downhill slide of bliss, he had done something with his fingers, pressed, rubbed, pumped, and she had been back at the pinnacle. Coming and coming and coming some more.

"How was that?" he asked, pressing a soft, hot kiss on her lips.

She snorted. "You *know* how it was, you scoundrel. I think I made it obvious."

"Well, there were a few signs. You panting 'yes, yes, *yes*!' over and over was one of them. Screaming my name was another. You're quite loud, Emily."

She tilted her head against the quilt. "You thought maybe I wouldn't be? Hi." She waved. Wow. Her arm felt like it weighed a hundred pounds. "I'm Emily Scott, office manager and renowned loudmouth."

"Hello, Emily Scott." He caught her lips in another mind-blowing kiss. "I'm Christian Watson. The man who is going to make you come again."

As if to prove his point, he pumped his fingers inside her.

"Oh God, no." She shook her head, squeezing her thighs around his gently marauding hand. "I can't. I'm so sensitive."

He stilled his fingers before slowly, carefully sliding out of her. Despite her tenderness, her body clutched at him, desperate to keep him inside, hating to let him go.

"Your mouth says one thing," he whispered against her lips. "But your greedy little body says another."

"My greedy little body is a traitor and an idiot," she informed him.

"Traitor?" He pulled back.

"Every time you get near me, the stupid thing flashes hot and goes all wobbly."

"Ah." He nodded. "How lovely."

"Humph. For *you* maybe, but I—"

The words strangled in her throat when Christian licked his fingers.

Heat suffused her. *Oh, no he didn't!*

Her blush deepened when, as if he were tasting ambrosia from heaven, his nostrils flared and his eyes fluttered shut. The man *was* kinky. And holy shit, apparently she loved it because her womb pulsed with renewed interest.

"You taste amazing," he said when he'd finished sucking her release from his fingers. "Salty and tangy. I want more."

Before she had time to protest, he dragged her up the bed until her head was cushioned on the pillows. Then, to her wicked heart's delight, he pulled the lengths of rope from his back pockets. The swiftness with which he secured the ends to the bedposts told her this wasn't his first rodeo.

Visions of the other times he must have done this, the other *women* he must have done it *with*, tried to invade her brain. She pushed them away with a mighty shove. She would not allow anything to intrude on the glory of being with Christian.

He *was* glorious, by the way. Straddling her hips and rising above her like a dark god. His wavy hair was a wild mass due to the careless attention of her fingers. Slashes of red stained his high, cutting cheekbones. And the muscles in his broad shoulders flexed beneath his silk sweater as he secured her wrists with the loose ends of rope.

Tied. Restrained. A supplicant to his desires.

A frisson of excitement shot through her, causing her sex to ache. Christian was right. With him, her body *was* greedy.

"Not too tight?" he asked after he'd finished securing her.

She realized she'd offered him no resistance. Instead, she had lain there all docile and pliant.

Those were two words she'd never thought to use in the same sentence with *herself*. Emily Scott was the polar *opposite* of docile or pliant. But maybe that's why this excited her so much. With Christian, she was exploring another side of her personality.

Testing the ropes, she found that while not tight—she wasn't losing circulation or anything—they were definitely secure. This was no *pretend* bondage. This was the real deal. She couldn't get out of the ropes if she tried. The only way she was getting free was if he let her. And if the fierce, focused look on his face was anything to go by, he had no intention of letting her.

"Not too tight," she assured him. Oh, for crying out loud. Was that husky, reedy-sounding thing really her voice?

"Brilliant." He pushed off the bed.

She immediately missed his heat, the overwhelming *presence* of him above her. But she forgot all about that when she saw him reach behind his head. He pulled off his sweater in that weird *guy* way, not by tugging at the hem but by grabbing the collar and whipping it over his head.

Her breath strangled in her lungs when she was presented with an unencumbered view of his naked torso for the *third* time in less than twenty-four hours. It was a banner day indeed.

Man! That thought exploded in her brain. Looking at him was like looking at the epitome of the word.

Broad, flexing shoulders. Long, strong arms covered

in thick, black tattoos. His heavy pectoral muscles were topped by the flat, brown disks of his nipples. Dark, crinkly hair grew sparsely over his chest and compressed into a thin line that trailed down his six-pack abs to disappear into the waistband of his jeans.

He watched her watching him as he bent to unlace his Italian leather boots. Then he stood, toeing out of them at the same time he unbuttoned his fly. Her eyes drank in every inch of him as it was revealed, including the glory of his red boxer briefs with the word SAXX stitched into the waistband.

Oh dear, sweet baby Jesus! Talk about a bulge.

No, not a bulge, it was a fifth appendage. There was no mistaking the length or width or plump, pulsing shape of him inside his tight briefs. Nor was there any mistaking the circle of moisture that stained the fabric near the waistband.

Her throat dried as if it'd been hit by a desert wind when she realized the wetness was for her, *caused* by her. He was weeping for want…of *her*.

Grabbing the ropes, she dug her nails into the soft chenille and held on for dear life. She knew what came next.

He took his time shucking his drawers. But when he finally stood before her, gloriously naked, she admitted the wait had been worth it. Full and engorged, his cock jutted proudly from his body. It looked even bigger, if that was possible. Then she realized why.

He was uncut.

Of course he is, silly, she scolded herself. *He's English. They don't circumcise like we do in the United States.*

She should have been prepared for the sight of his member in all its unaltered glory, but she wasn't.

Because his foreskin made him thicker, meatier, more intimidating than any man she'd ever seen.

On top of that, his thighs were huge and muscular, dusted with crinkly man hair, and she could just glimpse the dimple in one side of his firm ass. To put it mildly, Christian Watson was one big, unrepentantly masculine specimen.

Come and get me, big boy!

She tugged at the ropes, suddenly needing to be free. Her fingers itched to touch him.

"You tied me up before I got the chance to touch you," she accused him.

"That was the point, darling." He crawled over her. "I've wanted you too much for too long. If you touched me, I'd pop off in your hands in thirty seconds flat."

The thought of feeling his thick, steely shaft jerking with release in her hand made her nipples tighten and the space between her legs contract.

"You say that like it's a bad thing," she panted when he settled himself between her thighs, allowing his shaft to nestle against the slick welcome of her channel as his chest pressed into the soft pillows of her breasts.

They each hissed at first contact. He was so hard, so hot.

Rub herself against him like a cat... That's what she wanted to do. She must've unconsciously started because he shook his head. "Ah, ah. None of that or you'll have me going off against your belly."

"Again," she said breathlessly, "you say that like it's a bad thing."

"Stop wiggling, Emily. I'll move off you if you don't."

The thought of him taking all that hardness and heat

and delicious man hair away had her dutifully stilling beneath him, a pout on her lips.

"There's a good lass." He sucked her protruding bottom lip into the heat of his mouth.

She would have slapped him upside the head for being an arrogant, high-handed tyrant if her hands weren't tied. And if she didn't secretly *like* it so much.

For long moments, they ravaged each other with lips and teeth and tongues. And only when she was panting and hanging on to the ropes with white-knuckled grips in an effort to keep from rubbing herself against him did he break the kiss and start making his way down her body.

The second time I make you come, it will be with my mouth.

His words came back to drive her wild with anticipation. She was already slick and aching and ready for another release. It was that easy with him. Five minutes of kissing, and she was on the verge of exploding like an unpinned grenade.

He latched on to her right breast, and she couldn't help herself. She gasped and arched against him. The suction of his lips was too much, the flick of his hot, raspy tongue against her nipple made her mindless to anything but pleasure.

With infinite care, he attended to her other breast before continuing his journey south. He kissed each of her ribs, dipped his tongue into the hollow of her belly button, and gently bit her protruding hip bones.

By the time he had tossed her legs over his shoulders, she was begging him not to stop, never to stop.

"You haven't got to worry about that, my darling,"

he purred, his hot breath feathering against her quivering flesh. And then... Oh, and then he put his mouth on her.

Bull's-eye!

The man needed no help locating her clitoris. He placed his lips directly over the sucker. Then he speared it with his tongue, licking, laving, flicking, and sucking until her toes curled and she pulled against her restraints so hard the bedposts groaned.

A harsh ache centered beneath his adept mouth. But it wasn't enough. No matter how she writhed or tightened her inner muscles, it wasn't enough.

She had warned him. She was obviously defective and—

Oh! My! God!

He slipped two fingers inside her, pressing upward while his tongue pressed down and flicked side to side, and suddenly she was right there. Squirming and panting and teetering on the precipice.

"Look at me, Emily," he commanded, his voice no more than a low growl. "See me make you come."

She lifted her head from the pillows and looked down to find his green eyes blazing up at her. His shoulders looked huge between her legs. His skin astonishingly tan compared to her paleness. But it was the sight of his mouth on her, ravenously feeding that sent her careening over the edge.

She lost all sense of place and time. There was only her. There was only Christian. There was only intense, inescapable pleasure.

After who knows how long, the rapturous bliss tempered to a soft, lazy sort of satisfaction. Catching her breath, she watched him place one final kiss to her core before he turned his head and sucked sweetly on the inside of one thigh, then the other.

"Y—" She tried and had to stop and clear her throat. *Holy Moses*. Had she been screaming? She couldn't remember, but her raw vocal cords seemed to indicate that she had. "Your turn?"

He crawled atop her sprawled body, a sheen of perspiration dotting his brow, the look on his face so fierce, so raw, that she shivered.

Here he was...

The man she'd always known lay inside those designer clothes and Italian shoes. Gone were his facade, his restraint, his caution. He was whittled down to his true form. And that form was all man. Hard. Powerful. Unapologetic.

Determination had replaced his charm. Passion had overcome his poise. He was now the embodiment of virility and barely leashed violence.

"Did I mention the third way I plan to make you come?" he whispered against her lips. Her legs spread wide around his lean hips. The length of him once again pressed tight to her sex.

"You didn't." She shook her head. "But I might have an idea anyway."

He smiled that heady, smug smile, then grabbed his shaft and angled it toward her opening. She wiggled against him, needing the space between them gone. Needing him *in*.

The muscle in his jaw clenched. The one beneath his eye twitched once, twice. Then she saw his stomach muscles flex. He prepared himself to take her, to impale her, to finally, *finally* give her what she'd been secretly fantasizing about for months.

Steeling herself to receive him, she blinked in astonishment, her mouth falling open when he hissed, "Shit!" and rolled off her.

"What the hell?" She scowled over at him. His mink-brown hair looked almost black against the cream backdrop of the pillowcase. One tattooed arm was thrown over his eyes.

"No condom." The two words sounded as if they'd been ripped from the depths of his chest.

"Oh!" Right. For the first time in her life, with him above her, so powerful, so fascinating and sexy, she hadn't given a thought to protection.

She'd turned into the very thing Ms. Hanoman, her seventh grade gym teacher, had warned her about.

"Saying you got 'caught up in the moment,'" Ms. Hanoman had said, standing in front of the class in her knee-length athletic shorts, a banana in one hand and a condom in the other, *"is a stupid girl's excuse for being stupid."*

Good. Great. Now Emily could add *stupid girl* to the list of things Christian had turned her into. It would go right beneath the entries for *giggler* and *eeper*. Ugh.

Her entire body ached with disappointment. Even though she had been recently satiated, she felt ridiculously empty. After so much buildup, she'd never be completely satisfied until he was inside her, filling her to the brim.

"You don't carry a condom in your wallet?" She tried not to scream with frustration.

"Don't carry a wallet. Only a fake ID and a money clip."

Sure. Made sense since he lived off the grid.

He rose up on his elbow and leaned toward her. She might be aching with disappointment, but if the pained look on his face was anything to go by, he was in absolute *agony*. Poor guy.

"I could go ask Ace or Rusty if they have one," he said.

She blushed bright red at the thought. It was one thing for everyone to know she and Christian had decided on a little bow-chick-a-wow-wow. But it was another thing entirely to go around asking for a spare love glove. Jeez.

She shook her head. "Nah. There are other ways to skin this rabbit."

His distressed expression flickered with humor. "Such as?"

"Blow job."

She might as well have said *castration* from the way he groaned and squeezed his eyes closed.

"What? Don't tell me you're the one man on the face of the planet who doesn't like having his—"

He opened his eyes and shoved a finger over her mouth. "Don't say it. If you say it again, I'll likely come."

She jerked away from his finger. "Well, isn't that the whole point?"

"I don't want to come without you."

She snorted. "Oh, cut the *ladies first* bullshit. Because if memory serves, you've already satisfied me. *Twice.* Asking for a little quid pro quo is totally acceptable at this point. I promise I won't revoke your Confirmed Gentleman card."

"I don't want to come without you."

"Has semen backed up and infected your brain?" She frowned at him. "I just said—"

He stopped her mid-sentence by claiming her mouth in a punishing kiss. She was so distracted by his thrusting tongue that she didn't realize he'd untied one of her hands until he wrapped her fingers around his hard, steely length.

Oh lord. He *felt* even bigger than he looked. So much deliciously soft skin encasing such stubborn firmness. Her fingers barely met—it was going to be *fun* seeing how foreskin changed the whole hand job dynamic. When she went to stroke, he squeezed her wrist, forcing her to stop.

"No." He growled the word against her lips. "I'll tell you when to stroke."

"But—"

"No buts, Emily. You never do as I say any other time. But here, now, you *will* obey me."

Ooooh, big, tough man in charge.

She didn't know whether to giggle or gasp. Since she was still trying to deny the fact that she'd become a giggler, she went with the second option.

"Now," he said, nipping at her lips, "open your legs for me. We need to get you warmed up again."

She could have told him she was sore, because she *was*. She could have told him she didn't need a warm-up, because she was already slick and hot and aching again. But instead she simply obeyed him, spreading her legs and moaning when his fingers gently, expertly slipped through her swollen folds and found the ultra-sensitive knot of nerves at the top of her sex.

Chapter 17

"WHAT'S THE DEAL WITH YOUR TATTOOS?"

Oh, bugger it all, Christian thought, still trying to catch his breath. *Save me from postcoital talkative women.*

He and Emily had spent ten minutes giving each other vigorous, completely kinky hand jobs that had ended with both of them coming at the same moment, and now she wanted to *talk*? About his tattoos, no less?

He reached to untie the final rope, scooped her into his arms, and hauled them both off the bed. His legs felt rubbery. His stomach quivered from the intensity of his release. And his cock, though spent, still had some life left in it, jutting impudently from his body.

"What the—" Emily began. She didn't manage more than that before he whisked the coverlet off the bed and cast it to the floor.

Surely there was a laundry somewhere in the house. The National Trust and the caretakers they employed took the job of maintaining historic residences *very* seriously. Emily and Christian were likely the first people to have slept in the big bed in nearly a century, yet the sheets and bedclothes were fresh. Before they left tomorrow, he would need to be sure he washed the evidence of his spilled desire from the quilt and then replace it.

She squealed when he tossed her back onto the bed. Arms and legs akimbo, she bounced in the most delicious way. He joined her a second later, pulling her onto his chest and tucking her head firmly beneath his chin.

When she tried to press up to look at him, he slapped her ass and growled, "Be still."

He didn't need to look at her to know she was trying to decide whether to take him to task or shiver with delight. Eventually, after a few seconds, she settled on the latter.

He smiled. One thing had become obvious. Unlike in other areas of her life, when it came to the bedroom, Emily didn't mind taking orders. In fact, she seemed to *fancy* it.

Closing his eyes, he replayed how well she'd followed his breathless instructions on how to touch him, how to spread his pre-ejaculate over his swollen head and then stroke. Soft and slow at first. Hard and fast near the end. Her palm had been so silky and hot and eager to please.

We're a brilliant match, he realized with no small measure of satisfaction.

Instead of scaring her, his need for bondage turned her on. And she was so bossy in her everyday life, it was no wonder she didn't mind letting go and allowing someone else to take charge when it came to sex.

Jolly good thing too, since he planned to tie her up and boss her around in the bedroom for the next fifty to sixty years. Quite soon she would realize that their perfectly paired sexual appetites could translate to a perfect pairing for life. And that bit about her not being able to fall in love? *Rubbish*. Slowly, day by day, stolen moment by stolen moment, he planned to prove it to her.

A sense of contentment wrapped around him. That

is until she cleared her throat and said, "So, about your tattoos…"

The last thing he wanted was memories of his dark past invading this bright, glorious moment. But the woman seemed to have latched on to the subject, and he knew how tenacious she could be once she became fixated on something. A bloody dog with a bone, that's what she was.

"What about them?" he asked reluctantly.

"Is there a story behind them?"

"Why do you ask?"

"They seem out of character. You're kinda preppy."

He snorted. *Guttersnipe, little bastard, trash*…he'd been called loads of things in his life. He'd never been called *preppy*.

"And your tattoos are the very *opposite* of preppy," she went on. "Plus, considering how many hours and how much pain you must've endured to get them, well…" She rolled her hand before letting it rest over his heart. Could she feel how the silly organ picked up its pace, as if trying to get her attention? "It's weird you don't want to show them off. In fact, you do your best to hide them."

"You're certain the CIA didn't train you to be a field agent?" He traced a slow circle on her naked hip. Her skin was so impossibly soft. Was there another woman on the planet with skin as soft as hers?

"No." He could hear the frown in her voice. "Why?"

"Because you're vexingly observant and irritatingly perceptive."

This time, when she tried to push up on her elbow, he allowed it. Her dark eyes were narrowed in affront. "Irritating?"

"What?" He lifted an eyebrow. "You thought because we're good at this"—he motioned between them—"that I'd stop finding you irritating? I will *always* find you irritating, darling. Delightfully so. You push my buttons. I fancy it. Keep doing it. And admit it, I irritate you too."

"Well, I certainly find you annoying right *now*," she huffed. "Because you're Christian Watsoning your way around the subject again."

"Must I repeatedly remind you not to use my name as a verb?"

"Must you repeatedly dodge my questions?"

He laughed. She had him there. "I got them to cover the lighter burns," he said. "I got them so that every morning when I looked in the mirror I wouldn't be reminded of what happened to me as a kid."

But, unfortunately, he'd learned the tattoos drew people's eyes. And when they looked closely, they saw the scars beneath the black ink and asked about them. He didn't like talking about his past, so he'd taken to covering his arms.

Still, when Emily said haltingly, "What…what *happened* to you?" he found himself spewing the whole sorry story.

"After my dad died, for a while my mum took up with a contemptible prat. Every night, after she'd come home from the pub pissed, he'd slither into my room to torture me by flicking on his lighter, letting it get nice and hot, and holding it against my arms."

One of her hands stole up to cover her mouth. "Oh my God, Christian. I can't even… I don't know what to say."

His shrug said, *Nothing for you to say*.

I'm sorry, her eyes told him.

Again with a shrug. This time it said, *Nothing for you to be sorry for either*.

"Did you tell your mom what was happening?"

He shook his head. "The man swore he would hurt her like he was hurting me if I told. It wasn't until about six weeks into the abuse, in a moment of sobriety, that my mum noticed the dried bloodstains on the arms of one of my shirts. She flew into a rage, kicked the guy out of the flat, and then dragged me down to the police station to file a report on the sick, twisted bastard."

"What happened? Did the police catch him? Did he go to prison?"

Again, Christian shook his head. "While we were at the station, he left town. But not before going back to our flat and nicking our telly. You would think that would have made Mum sober up. But the guilt she felt at not protecting me made her seek the oblivion of the bottle even more."

"I can't imagine it." Emily's eyes traveled over his arms, searching for the old scars beneath the heavy, midnight swipes of ink. Her voice was thick when she asked, "How could someone do that to a child?"

"What? Stay plastered all day even after realizing that being plastered had resulted in your kid getting tortured? Or sneak into a little boy's room to burn him with a lighter?"

"The lighter." As if she couldn't help herself, she pressed her fingertip into the indent in his chin. Who knew such an innocent touch could feel so intimate?

"Back then, I thought it was because he was in love with my mum, and he hated that I was a reminder of the man who'd come before him, the man *she* truly loved. But over the years I've come to realize that some people are just evil. They like inflicting pain for the simple pleasure of it. They fancy watching things weaker and smaller than themselves suffer. He was one of those people."

After Christian had been decommissioned from the SAS, he had gone looking for that evil man. Good thing he had found the sod already dead and buried, or else he likely would have quietly and bloodily put the bastard in the ground himself. It was on that day, standing next to that headstone, when he had realized he couldn't be a civilian.

He was too volatile, too barbaric. He needed an outlet for all the violence that bubbled inside him.

A sniffle had his chin jerking back. Huge pools of tears stood in Emily's eyes.

His heart broke then and there. For one thing, never in his life did he want to see such pain on the face of the woman he loved. For another thing, Emily didn't cry pretty tears. She cried like a violent storm breaking loose, and it took everything in him to hang on and weather it.

"Don't, darling," he crooned, holding her to him and rocking from side to side. "Please don't cry."

"I'm s-sorry," she sniffled, wiping away the tears that tracked down her downy cheeks. "I shouldn't be crying. It's not my tragedy or trauma. But I keep seeing you as this innocent boy with dark, unruly hair and big, bright eyes, and—"

She shook her head, unable to go on.

He didn't tell her that his big, bright eyes seemed to have been part of the problem back then. John J. Tully— There! He'd said the name, even if it was only in his mind—had liked to hiss, his breath stinking of rot from his decaying teeth, "Stop starin' at me with those spooky eyes, you daft little bastard!" as he burned a new scar on Christian's arm.

Her fingers delicately traced over his bicep, stopping when they encountered one of the puckered patches of scar tissue. Then her hand drifted lower, her fingertips finding the burn on the inside of his forearm.

Most of his scars were faint, only discernible if you knew what you were looking for. But the one on the inside of his forearm? That was a different story. The skin had been thinner there, and John Tully had been particularly brutal. That scar was hard, knotted, extra sensitive.

He hissed when she smoothed her thumb over it.

"Does it still hurt?" She blinked.

"It feels raw, like the nerves are exposed," he explained.

"Even after all these years…" She shook her head sorrowfully. "Well, maybe this will help."

Lifting his arm, she kissed the raised lump of flesh. He shivered. Not because he was cold, but because nothing in his life had ever felt so sincere…or so loving.

If she had stopped there, he might have been able to keep his shit together. But she didn't stop there. She crawled over him, straddling his legs, and proceeded to find and kiss every one of his scars.

By the time she got to the big, puckered scar on his flank, courtesy of an Iraqi policeman's bullet, he'd had about all he could take. Grabbing her shoulders, he dragged her up his body until they were nose to nose, and pretended there wasn't a bloody lump in his throat or bloody tears burning behind his eyes.

"You've got to stop that," he whispered.

"Why? Doesn't it feel good?"

"It feels good," he admitted.

But it also breaks my heart and heals it at the same time, he could have added. *And it makes me want to throw caution to the wind and tell you how much I love you, you sweet, delightful, brilliant girl.*

"Then why do I need to stop?" Her eyes pinged down to his lips. That's all it took for his mouth to water, for his lips to tingle in anticipation of one of her candied kisses.

"Because it feels *too* good. Your soft lips have made me hard again." To prove his point, he tilted his pelvis. Since she was straddling his hips, his turgid cock slid hot and hard against her delicate feminine flesh.

She moaned, screwing her eyes shut. When she opened them again, he saw a familiar glint of devilry. "Again, you say that like it's a bad thing."

He flipped her over until he was looming above her. When he pinned her hands over her head, she giggled with delight.

"When I make you come again," he swore, "it will be with my cock. Inside you. And since we've still no condoms, that means no more shenanigans. Unless, of course, you've changed your mind and are keen to have me running downstairs to ask Ace and Rusty if—"

"No!" she wailed, struggling ineffectually against his restraining hands. "I'll die of embarrassment. I swear to God. Can't we just—"

"Indeed not." He cut her off before she could put into words whatever physical delight she had in mind. If he heard her mention anything that included her mouth on his dick, he might lose the will to naysay her, and truly, he was determined to hold fast to his convictions.

All they had already done together was incredibly raw and mind-meltingly sexy. But it lacked the intimacy of joining their bodies, of rocking each other to completion as they stared into one another's eyes.

If he wanted her to fall in love with him, his first step must surely be to *make* love to her.

"Why not?" she demanded, a pout on her lips.

"I have my reasons." He loved how her eyes narrowed. Preparing himself to become the victim of her sharp tongue, he was surprised when she huffed, "Fine. Have it your way. But if we're not going to sixty-nine…" He groaned. There it was. The image of her mouth on his dick sprang to Technicolor life inside his head. "Then you have to make it up to me with another truth."

"Buggering hell." He rolled off her to toss an arm over his eyes. "You and your bloody truths. They'll be the death of me."

"I'm serious." She snuggled close to his side and tweaked his nipple.

"*Ow!*" He smacked her ass.

"*Ow!*" She tweaked his nipple harder.

And then it was on. The absolute *sexiest* wrestling match of his life. She bucked and hissed and nipped at him with her teeth until, once again, he was atop her with her wrists secured above her head. They were both blowing hard from the exertion. Both incredibly turned on. It was a vast improvement over the tears from earlier.

"Let that be a lesson to you, witchy woman." He was so tempted to kiss her lips that he had to bite the inside of his cheek. If he kissed her, they would be sixty-nine-ing so fast her head would spin.

"Oh?" She blinked up at him, all innocence and seduction. "And what lesson would that be?"

"I'm bigger than you. Stronger than you. Faster than you."

"Maybe," she allowed. There was that hypnotic grin again. "But I'm smarter. You're right back where I want you."

To prove her point, she wrapped her legs around his waist and rubbed herself against him. She was so hot, so soft and slick. His eyes crossed.

"Damnit!" He threw himself off her again. Her wicked laughter followed him across the bed when he determinedly put two feet between them.

"Okay, fine." She scooted next to him, tossed a leg across his thighs, an arm across his chest, and tucked her head beneath his chin. "We'll play by your rules, you big, hairy butthead. But if we're not going to be switching hammocks—"

"I beg your pardon?"

"You know, doing the whole over-under thing."

"You've lost me."

There was laughter in her voice when she said, "*Dukes of Hazzard?*"

"Are you speaking English?" he demanded. "Or 'Merican? Because I'm having the devil of a time figuring out what you're on about."

"Sixty-nine-ing, Sir Slow on the Uptake." The laughter in her voice turned into the real deal.

And there it was again. That image.

He groaned and once more tossed an arm over his eyes. Then he lowered it to the sheet and frowned up at the ceiling. "What does *The Dukes of Hazzard* have to do with it? You're speaking of that silly show about two cousins in the South who were always running from Mr. Pig, right?"

"Boss Hog. And, yes, that's what I'm talking about."

"Then I fail to understand the reference in the context of…" He couldn't bring himself to utter the phrase. He was already having a dreadful time not saying, *To hell with it!* and jumping her delicious bones for a vigorous bout of…*switching hammocks*.

"Remember how Sheriff Rosco P. Coltrane and his trusty basset hound Flash used to chase the Duke boys all around Hazzard County? 'This is Rosco P. Coltrane,'" she said, donning a Southern accent that was far better than her attempts at an English one, "'and I'm in hot pursuit!'"

"Right. And that has to do with what we're speaking of because…" He let the sentence dangle.

"Because that souped-up orange car the Duke boys drove was a—"

"Sixty-nine Dodge Charger," he interrupted. "Okay, I get it."

"Figured you would. Let no one ever say you don't know your cars."

Despite himself, he chuckled. "Really, darling. These euphemisms of yours…"

"Seriously? You must have forgotten that conversation in the pickup truck. Gentleman sausage, todger, tallywhacker? Any of that ringing a bell?"

"Touché," he allowed, loving that she let him pull her close. "But aren't you a bit young to have watched *The Dukes of Hazzard*?"

"Yep." She nodded, her cheek rubbing against

his chest. "Too young to have watched *The Dukes of Hazzard* or *I Love Lucy* or *Bonanza* or *Bewitched*. But considering I was a latchkey kid with no supervision and nothing to do once I got home from school every day, it's no wonder the television and all those old reruns became my friends." Before he could dwell, once again, on how wretched *both* their childhoods had been, she said, "So about this next truth."

"I suppose it was too much to hope that we'd gotten far enough off topic that you'd forgotten about that."

"Now that I'm on to your game, Christian Watsoning doesn't work on me."

He decided to give up on his demand that she stop using his name as a verb. He sighed resignedly. "Then let's have it. What truth are you on about now?"

"What happened to your mom?" His breath stuttered in his chest. "I mean, after you sent her to rehab, what happened?"

Being in the old manor house had brought back so many memories. *Good* memories. Memories of a time when both his parents had been young and full of laughter and unbroken by the horrors of life.

He could clearly remember his mum in a blue sundress standing in front of the mural on the far wall. He and his dad had been walking around the room, looking at the tiny figurines on the tables, but his mum had only stood there, studying that mural for ages, her dark hair catching and holding the fading light streaming through the windows, burning like the sun itself.

It was one of the last happy days he'd spent with her.

Chapter 18

"SHE CHECKED HERSELF OUT OF THE REHAB FACILITY AFTER a month, hitched a ride back home, collected her waiting government support checks, and took herself to the pub."

Christian's tone was frighteningly neutral. If Emily hadn't gotten to know him so well, his matter-of-fact words might have seemed harsh. But she could feel the tension in his muscles, hear the roughness in his voice.

He *hurt* for the woman who had birthed him. Hurt for her, missed her, and very likely suffered no small amount of guilt that he hadn't been enough to save her, even though the truth of the matter was, he'd done everything he could.

Emily ached for him. Always so put together. Always so stoic. Always so *in control*. But just as she'd suspected, he was as multilayered as an onion.

His surface was all poise and charm and self-assurance. But beneath that layer lay a fierce warrior, an incredibly passionate lover, a man with grit in his eye and steel in his spine. Yet, there were deeper layers still. Layers that held the loss of a father at too young an age. Layers that bore the fear and uncertainty and humiliation of living with a drunken, self-medicating mother. Layers that carried the horror and the scars of childhood abuse—she was *still* trying to wrap her head around how some sick shit could do that to a sweet, innocent boy.

Not to mention the thick layers he must have grown over the years of being a spec-ops warrior, she thought.

Crash! There they went. All those walls she'd built against him.

She supposed it had been inevitable. The minute she had agreed to go to bed with him, to stop the surface-level teasing and taunting and really get to *know* him, was the minute she'd given the go-ahead to the demolition team. But that didn't lessen the fear that rushed in to take the place of her fortifications. It was one thing to let herself be physically vulnerable to the man, another thing entirely to let herself be emotionally vulnerable to him.

Because what did that emotional vulnerability even mean?

Not for a hot minute did she think it changed her inability to have lasting love. Which was good since he'd made it clear that the last thing he was looking for was a happily ever after. But still, now that she was emotionally wide open to him, now that she thought of herself as his friend—Oh, for the love of José Abreu, *that* was an odd concept, wasn't it? Friends with the ever-annoying, always titillating Christian Watson?—he had the ability to hurt her.

What if he wanted to end things between them before she did? Or worse, what if he found someone else and fell in love? Emily could see it all so clearly, the irascible Christian Watson with his happy wife and happy life.

Truth was, she *wanted* that for him. She really did. But it would be agony having gotten to know him, having gotten to *be* with him, only to let him go when something better, something purer, something *lasting* came along.

"According to everyone who was there that night"—he dragged her from her troubling thoughts—"she had herself a proper piss-up. Downed two bottles of gin in about two hours and then stumbled home."

"Good Lord."

"The landlord found her three days later. She'd choked to death on her own vomit."

Once again, tears threatened behind Emily's eyes, but damned if she'd give in to them. This was his story, his tragedy. She wouldn't take anything away from him by wallowing in her own grief.

For a long time he was quiet. She held him close, offering what comfort she could, knowing it wasn't enough.

Finally, he said, "She was cremated. I had her remains secretly flown to Chicago. And then I sailed into the middle of Lake Michigan and let the wind and the water take what was left of her. Sometimes I wonder if I should have come back and done it here, sent her drifting down the Thames or something." If Emily looked up, she felt certain she would see his brow furrowed. "But after Dad was gone, she was never happy in England. For most of her life, this place brought her nothing but sorrow. So I thought…you know…she could never make a fresh start here while she was alive, but I could take her somewhere to give her a fresh start in death."

"I think you did the right thing. If that's what felt right, you shouldn't second-guess yourself."

"Yeah, maybe." He blew out a breath, then pointed at the far wall. "She liked that mural. Every time we came here, she would look at it and smile."

Emily ducked her chin, her gaze drifting over the wall-sized piece of art. Shards of tile, mirror, and glass made up a mosaic garden scene. There were hundreds of colorful flowers, two brightly hued butterflies, and a cheery-looking dragonfly hovering near the corner.

The instant she had walked into the room, she had been drawn to it, just like Christian's mom. She hated to think she had anything in common with a woman who could neglect her child to such an inexcusable degree, but she also liked the thought that, once upon a time, his mother had been better, been more, been good to him.

"Do you suppose it explains your need for control?" she heard herself ask.

"What? The fact that I had none as a child?"

She nodded. She'd been thinking about how much she loved it when Christian tied her up. Thinking that the reason she liked giving up control wasn't only because her job meant she always needed to be on her toes, but also because, ever since she was a young girl, she'd always been the one steering her own ship, making all the decisions because her parents hadn't been around to guide the way. Was the opposite true for him?

"Of course," he said. "I don't need to lie on a head-shrinker's sofa to know I am the way I am because I'm compensating for having no say in what I wore, how I lived, or whom my mother brought into the house when I was young."

"I thought maybe the clothes and the car had more to do with you growing up poor. You know… Now that you have some cash, you want to show the world that the kid from the East End gutter had made something of himself."

"Hardly," he scoffed. "Designer clothes can be tailored. Same for handmade Italian shoes. I *like* having control over what I put on my body. Coming up, I had to wear whatever Mum could find in the charity shops."

Made sense. And made him go up a few notches in her estimation—which she wouldn't have thought was possible since she already respected the hell out of him. Truth was, she'd misjudged him every time she'd teased him for his fussy clothes. He wasn't showing off. He was simply making up for a lot of years of neglect and chaos in a way that made him feel empowered.

"And the car?" she asked.

When he chuckled, she thought she'd never heard a more fabulous sound. "I fancy cars."

Given the seriousness and heartbreak of their conversation, she was surprised to find herself smiling.

For a long time, neither of them spoke. She hadn't realized how long until her stomach growled noisily, reminding her she'd forgotten to check her backpack for her stash of granola bars.

Easily remedied, she thought, ready to push out of bed and go in search of sustenance.

She was stopped, however, by a soft snore. Smiling, she grabbed the edge of the sheet, wrapped them both in a sweet-smelling cotton cocoon, and snuggled close to him. Food could wait. For now, she'd allow herself to enjoy lying in the mysterious and powerful and oh-so-human Christian Watson's arms.

Another snore broke the silence and had her battling laughter. He snored. He *snored*!

He wasn't so perfect after all.

Good. There was no fun in perfection.

—〜〜—

Rusty had stomped upstairs to find a book to read, anything to take his mind off the golden-haired flyboy. But none of the titles had caught his eye, so he'd sat on one of the sofas and brooded. It was only after Ace shook him awake that he realized he'd unintentionally dozed off.

"Whaaa?" he asked groggily, frowning when he blinked and saw full-on darkness had claimed the room.

Okay, so maybe it wasn't *full*-on darkness. There were a couple of those plastic night-light thingies plugged into outlets that provided *some* light. Enough to see that, sure as shit, Ace was as annoyingly handsome as ever.

The rat bastard.

And why the hell did Rusty feel like the world stopped spinning every time he looked into those ocean blues?

"What time is it?" He peered through the darkness at his watch.

"A little before twenty-three hundred. Angel's back," Ace said. "He brought food with him. Well"—his expression twisted—"if you consider a loaf of bread, a jar of peanut butter, and some strawberry jam food. I thought you might be hungry. You haven't eaten since breakfast."

"Neither have you." Rusty pushed into a seated position and realized…

Great. He'd drooled. Since there was no way to nonchalantly wipe the wet patch off his cheek, he thought *fuck it* and didn't try to be coy. Using his sleeve, he scrubbed at the drool until his skin tingled and his beard stubble protested.

"Yeah." Ace nodded. "But you're a good fifty pounds heavier than I am. You need more calories than I do."

All the anger and desire and embarrassment from earlier came back to Rusty in a flash. "So now you're calling me fat? For crying in the sink, man, enough is enough."

"You're not serious." Ace, who had been leaning toward him, straightened, crossing his arms over his chest.

"I'm dead serious. Ever since I told you about my folks, about not being out, you've been finding ways to insult me."

"In what world?" Ace's voice lifted an octave. It was too dark to be certain, but Rusty thought he saw two patches of red flood onto Ace's cheeks. "*I'm* not the one who barged into the room *you* were in, slammed the door, and then started yelling. If memory serves, that was *you*!"

Rusty opened his mouth to respond, but Ace pressed on before he could. "You're trying to make this about me, but the truth is it's all about *you*!" Ace pointed a finger at Rusty's nose, and Rusty was overcome with the intense desire to break the fucker off, or kiss it. He wasn't sure which. "It's about your shame, your fear. And it makes me so sad." Ace shook his head. "Because our people have suffered so much, have fought so hard to be accepted, to gain us the same liberties and rights and freedoms that—"

"*Our people?*" Rusty interjected, shoving to a stand.

Ace stumbled back. Rusty liked that. Liked that Ace had to look up at him. He'd never used his size against someone before, at least not someone who wasn't an enemy combatant, but he used it now, advancing on Ace, who retreated until he bumped into one of the wingback armchairs and could go no farther.

"*Our people?*" Rusty said again, or rather *shouted*.

He was usually a quiet guy, slow to anger. But something about Ace and this day was making him lose his shit. "I don't want to be part of *our* people! I just want to be *people*! No labels. No distinctions."

"Hogwash!" Ace stomped up to him until they were toe to toe.

"Excuse me?"

"That's rainbows and puppies and glittery unicorn farts! The world *labels*. You're a redhead." Ace poked him in the chest, then hooked a thumb back toward himself. "I'm a blond. You're a marine." Poke. "I'm a sailor and pilot." Thumb. "You're from PA." Poke. "I'm from So Cal." Thumb. "We're both *gay*! It's all labels. None any different from the others. So don't try to hide what's really going on with you behind that bleeding-heart *I don't want to be labeled* bullshit."

"It's none of your damn business!" Rusty's anger had grown into a fiery fury.

"But you keep *making* it my business!" Ace shot back. "You're the one who brings up the subject!"

Rusty didn't think. He *couldn't* think with Ace so close, so magnificent in his anger. He simply went with his gut and yanked Ace forward into a lip-smashing kiss.

With both hands on either side of Ace's face, he held the man still for his assault. Ace tried to shove him away, but Rusty gave no quarter. And eventually, magically, Ace stopped struggling.

What had started out as punishment quickly became pleasure. Their arms wrapped tight around each other, their mouths open and hungry. Ace tasted sweet, like cinnamon gum and sunshine. He smelled sweet too, all spicy aftershave and soap.

Rusty wanted to devour him whole. Taste and touch and *know* every inch of him and—

Ace shoved out of his embrace so fast, Rusty stumbled. When he regained his balance, chest heaving with exertion, he lifted his eyes to find Ace standing beside the chair, one hand on the back as if he needed the support, the other hand rubbing his nape.

Even in the darkness, Rusty could see that Ace's blue eyes were narrowed. "Why did you do that?"

"Kiss you?"

Ace nodded.

"Because you started a fire, and I wanted you to burn in it a little. Figured it was only fair." He shrugged his shoulders, pretending he wasn't still reeling from how quickly their passion had exploded.

For a while, Ace said nothing. Then he murmured, "But the difference between me kissing you and you kissing me is that I kissed you to prove a point to you. You kissed me to punish me."

And just like that, Rusty felt like a true shit-heel.

"Screw you for using my desire against me." Ace shook his head, his blond hair catching what little light the night-light afforded.

Even though Rusty knew it wasn't true, he heard himself yelling, "That's *exactly* what *you* did!"

"No. It's not. And the fact that you can't see the difference…" Ace didn't go on, simply let the sentence dangle.

A smarter man might have been able to offer up something in his own defense. As it was, Rusty simply curled his hands into fists and glared, a cauldron of emotion bubbling inside him.

—∿∿—

"Emily, my darling lass…"

Emily came awake in the most delicious way, with Christian leaning over her, planting sweet kisses across her collarbone.

"Wake up. Rusty and Ace are at each other's throats again." He latched on to the bone and gave it a gentle bite that sent shivers all through her.

The sound of raised male voices coming from down the hall had her groaning. "Ugh. Those two should do it already so the rest of us can have some peace and quiet."

"Mmm." He nuzzled her neck, and she tilted her head to give him better access. "I believe Ace once said the same thing to you and me."

"And see how right he was?" She speared her hands through his soft hair, loving how the thick strands curled around her fingers. "We're the epitome of peace and quiet."

He snorted and pushed up on his elbow to gaze down at her. A night-light was plugged into a socket by the door, but its glow was barely enough to see by, and in the darkness, Christian's tan skin and dark hair blended into the shadows. Only his eyes gleamed, looking feral. Hungry.

"I hate to tell you this, darling, but there is nothing peaceful or quiet about what you and I were doing in this bedroom. In fact, I'm fairly certain that at one point you screamed so loudly you made the chandelier rattle."

She bit the inside of her cheek. "*You're* one to talk. When I made you come, you threw your head back and howled. I think I heard dogs barking from three miles away."

He grinned, and that's all it took. One smile, and a wave of heat washed over her. "Cheeky wench," he said.

"I like that."

"What?"

"Being called *cheeky*. It's so much more flattering than…say…*bossy* or *impudent* or *brazen*."

"But you're all of those things too."

She gave him the evil eye.

"And I love that about you." She stilled at the l-word, her breath strangling. If he noticed, he didn't let on, simply said, "Now, shall we go put a stop to the bloodshed?"

"Maybe it's better if we let them work it out between themselves." She hoped he couldn't hear how hoarse her voice sounded. *I love that about you*. His words tumbled around inside her head, making her dizzy. But he didn't mean love like *love*, right? He meant love like *admire* or *respect* or *appreciate*. "If we hadn't interrupted them earlier, they might have already given in to each other and then they wouldn't be arguing right now."

"Perhaps." Christian shrugged. "Or perhaps they'd have torn each other to pieces."

Emily didn't like the sound of that, especially since one of her duties as BKI's office manager was to keep the peace among a bunch of big men with big personalities and even bigger egos.

"Fine," she huffed. "Let's go end the war before it turns deadly."

"Jolly good." Christian shoved up from the bed, dragging her with him. "And while you're ending the war, I'll see if either of them has a condom."

Emily had been in the process of wiggling into her

panties, but that stopped her. She frowned up at him. "I told you it's too embarrassing. We'll have to wait until—"

"It won't be embarrassing if they haven't a clue," he cut in.

"Huh?" She began searching for her bra. "What's that supposed to mean? How could they *not* know?"

"I'm going to nick their wallets while you're distracting them and see if either of them is carrying what we need."

After donning her bra, she planted her hands on her hips. "You mean, like, pickpocket them?"

It was too dark to be sure, but she thought she saw him wiggle his eyebrows. "Angel isn't the only one of us with questionable skills."

"Hmm." She pursed her lips. "Learned in SAS training or as a child?"

"You heard that bit about me having gotten caught filching bread and HP Sauce from the corner store, yeah? So, what do you think?"

"Right." She chuckled. "You and me and our misspent youths. We make quite the couple, don't we?"

She realized what she'd said when Christian didn't respond, simply stood there in nothing but his jeans, pegging her with a hard, searching stare. They weren't a *couple*. They were fuck buddies, coworkers with benefits.

Covering her misstep the best way she knew how, she bent and grabbed her sweatshirt, tugging it over her head and momentarily hiding her face from him. Once she'd brushed her hair back, she was relieved to see he was in the process of pulling on his sweater.

Careful, Em, ol' girl, she silently coached herself.

You can't say things like that, not when this thing the two of you have going is supposed to be casual.

Trouble was...it didn't *feel* casual. In fact, it felt enormous, overwhelming. Altogether terrifying.

Chapter 19

Back when Christian was twelve years old, he would have asked his Magic 8 Ball—one of the only decent Christmas presents he remembered receiving after his father died—if his plan was working. If having gotten Emily to share her body with him was bringing her closer to sharing her heart. He liked to think the answer that would have appeared in that small, round window was: *Outlook good.*

After all, she'd called them a *couple*, hadn't she? That alone was reason to hope.

Glancing over his shoulder, he saw little of her in the darkness of the hallway, only the pale glow of her skin and the whites of her eyes when she looked up at him.

"*What?*" her quirked brow asked. "Why'd you stop walking?"

Because I can't not *look at you for more than ten seconds*, he could have told her. *Because I want to kiss you so badly my heart hurts. Because I'm regretting leaving that bed for fear something might happen to make you hesitate to get back in it.* All were true. And all revealed too much of what he felt for her. Instead, he went with, "I smell peanut butter."

"That would be me." A deep, raspy voice sounded from somewhere up ahead.

Emily squeaked and was suddenly glued to Christian's

side. He fought a satisfied smile as he put an arm around her.

"Angel?" He squinted into the darkness. Unlike in the bedroom, there was no night-light in the hall to battle the gloom. "Is that you?"

"None other," Angel garbled, his mouth full of something.

As if on cue, Emily's stomach let loose with a completely unladylike grumble. "You brought food?" There was a hint of desperation in her voice.

Considering how thin Emily was, one would think she survived on lettuce and bean sprouts alone. But the truth was that the woman *ate*. She had to, considering most days she ran around the BKI shop like the Energizer Bunny, filling orders, checking mission stats, making sure their whole world operated like a well-oiled machine.

"I was able to appropriate the makings for peanut butter and jelly sandwiches from the farmer's cupboard," Angel said, still chewing.

"Oh, gimme, gimme, gimme." Emily raced past Christian toward the closed doors to the library.

Christian's eyes had adjusted to the inky darkness. He could see Angel was reclined in a spindly-legged chair beside the doors, a sandwich in one hand, two jars and a loaf of bread sitting on a small table next to him.

"I thought you were going to stop Ace and Rusty from killing each other," Christian said, following her down the hall.

"That can wait. First, food."

Christian chuckled when she grabbed the plastic knife shoved into the open jar of peanut butter and began slathering a healthy portion onto a slice of bread.

"Besides," Angel said, pushing up from the chair and cracking open the doors to the library to peer inside, "The yelling has stopped."

"What arth ay doin' now?" Emily asked around a mouthful of sandwich.

"Standing and staring at each other."

Christian took the opportunity to swipe Angel's wallet from his back pocket by stumbling into him. "Sorry," he apologized, glaring down at the rug beneath his bare feet. "I keep tripping over all these bloody carpets."

Angel eyed him curiously before turning back to the crack in the door.

Christian grinned and wiggled Angel's wallet in front of Emily's nose. Her eyes grew huge and she choked, forcing Angel to turn and helpfully pound her on the back.

Christian quickly swung away from them, opened Angel's wallet, found a ridiculous number of euros and British pounds inside, no ID, and... Aha! One condom—package slightly wrinkled but nonetheless whole. He slipped the glorious bugger into his pocket before turning back.

Emily waved Angel off with a scowl on her face. "You're not helping," she wheezed. "You're lodging the peanut butter farther down my windpipe."

"Apologies." Angel returned to the library door. He'd barely fit his eye to the crack when he hissed, "Oh shit!" and jumped backward.

Christian acted like he couldn't get out of the way fast enough, allowing Angel to plow into him, and giving himself the chance to replace the man's wallet.

"What the hell?" he sputtered, acting affronted. "You nearly sent me toppling over the railing."

The staircase terminated in front of the library doors in an intricate set of walnut newel posts and hand-turned balusters.

"Ace is coming." Angel quickly retook his place in the chair, but not before touching his back pocket and narrowing his eyes at Christian.

Christian made sure his expression was innocent as he leaned back against the banister and nodded. "Right, then. Everyone act casual and—"

Ace burst through the library door and came to a screeching halt when he saw them gathered 'round. "Oh, great," he muttered, scowling. "Nothing I like better than a bunch of eavesdroppers."

"We weren't eavesdropping," Emily assured him, shoving her partially eaten sandwich in his face. "We were enjoying dinner. Here. Eat. You'll feel better."

Ace hesitated all of a split second before snatching the sandwich and taking a huge bite. "Thank you," he said around a mouthful. Then, "I'm going to bed, and I don't want anyone to disturb me until it's time to leave this godforsaken island."

The three of them watched Ace stomp down the hall and disappear into one of the bedrooms. They all winced when the door slammed with a *bang* loud enough to make the paintings on the walls jump on their hooks.

Emily blew out a huge breath, then shrugged and reached for the knife and two more slices of bread. Angel stared after Ace, a considering frown on his face. And Christian took advantage of Ace's segue.

"Speaking of getting off this godforsaken island," he said, "any luck finding a vehicle we can nick tomorrow? You were gone quite a long time."

"First of all, we will *appropriate* a vehicle," Angel corrected.

"Sure." Christian rolled his eyes. Angel's refusal to admit that he was a dab hand at *stealing* things was rather odd, and Christian couldn't help but wonder if there was a story buried somewhere in there.

"Second of all, I was gone so long because I had to wait for the farmer and his wife to go to bed before sneaking into the kitchen to go through their cupboards."

"Indeed." Christian nodded. "Thanks for that, by the way. Emily was getting rather peckish. I don't know how much longer she would have lasted. Her stomach was grumbling so loudly it woke me from a dead sleep."

Angel eyed Emily. "It always surprises me," he mused, "how such a delicate-looking woman can be so loud."

Emily punched Angel in the arm, then turned and gave Christian a good one too.

"*Ow!*" He rubbed his abused flesh, grinning delightedly.

"As for a vehicle for tomorrow," Angel said, "the farmer and his wife have two cars, both sedans with back seats. So no more Emily on your lap."

"Oh, bad luck, that." Christian blew Emily a kiss, causing her to frown. She couldn't hold the expression for long. Soon, it melted into a secret smile that went right to his stomach and flirted rather shamelessly.

Burning a hole in his bloody pocket...that's what the condom was doing. He would have liked nothing better than to drag Emily back to the bedroom and put the thing to use, but she was in the midst of ravenously devouring her new sandwich. Not to mention there was something he needed to take care of...

"Emily," he said, "mind making me a sandwich while I throw something in the wash?"

"Sure," she said around a mouthful. "But only this once."

He frowned.

"Just 'cause we're doin' it don't mean I'm suddenly at your beck and call, ready and willing to do your bidding." Oh, how he loved it when her 'hood-girl grammar made an appearance.

"Don't get your knickers in a twist, I know you're only willing to be at my beck and call and do my bidding when I've got you tied up in bed."

"Christian!" she cried at the same time Angel said, "*That* was an over-share."

Chuckling, Christian turned back toward the mural room. It was only after he'd gone a few steps that he realized, for the first time in a long time, he was *happy*.

What a ruddy frightening prospect.

—⁓—

"Christian?" Emily whispered from the bottom of the stairs, blinking against the stygian gloom. Another nightlight was plugged into an outlet by the desk in the entryway, but the dark wooden paneling on the walls seemed to absorb what little glow it offered. "Did you get lost?"

It had been nearly twenty minutes since Christian had emerged from the yellow bedroom, the quilt bunched in his arm. With nothing more than a wiggle of his eyebrows, he'd sailed by the library doors—where she, Angel, and Rusty had been enjoying their PB&Js—and headed downstairs, having left her to blanch and turn to the two men eyeing her curiously.

"Uhhh, we just need to…um…"

Rusty had held up a hand, saying, "No explanation necessary, dollface," and she'd breathed a sigh of relief.

First Christian spouted off about her being at his beck and call and doing his bidding when he had her tied up in bed; then he had to go and parade their dirty laundry—literally—for the world to see? Had the man no shame?

Apparently not. Or maybe he was like a dog, and the whole charade had been his idea of peeing on her and marking his territory so the other two men knew she was *his*.

Pretty ridiculous, considering one of the men was gay and had *zero* interest in her sexually. And the other? Jamin "Angel" Agassi? Well, the truth was, Emily had a hard time imagining Angel letting his guard down long enough to get, you know, *naked*. In fact, she'd often wondered if he showered fully clothed and strapped with weapons. So, yeah, no need for Christian's metaphorical leg hike.

In fact, she'd been so irritated with him that she'd decided to let him make his own damn sandwich. But then Angel had finished eating and gone to bed. Rusty had followed his example two minutes later, and she'd been left with nothing to do. Which meant her mind had immediately turned to Angel's wallet and what Christian must have found inside since he hadn't attempted to pickpocket Ace or Rusty.

The thought of Christian stalking up that staircase, determination in his eyes and a condom in his pocket, had obliterated all the not-so-nice feelings she'd had toward him and instead filled her with anticipation. Not to mention a gazillion ideas of ways they could do deliciously dirty things together.

Since she figured it was in her best interest to get him fed as quickly as possible—the man was going to need his stamina for what she had planned for him—she'd tossed her hands in the air and muttered, "*Fine*. I'll make the damn sandwich."

After she'd finished, she'd waited. And *waited*.

In the dark. And the quiet. Her mind wandering back to Christian and that lovely condom. The thought of ripping open the package and sliding the latex over him had her insides melting into sticky caramel goo. That goo began to heat and bubble when her imagination went a step further—to her on her back, legs wide, and him angling his cock down, taking her slowly, his thick length stretching her as it disappeared inside—

At that point, she hadn't been able to stand it a second longer. She'd trudged downstairs, sandwich in hand, to find him.

But it was even darker down here. And quieter.

Her anticipation waned as a chill stole up her spine and the hairs on her arms lifted. She curled her bare toes against the cold marble tile and whispered again, "Christian? Did you find the washer and—"

She cut herself off when footsteps sounded behind her.

"Well, it's about damn time." She blew out a sigh of relief. "I was beginning to think you'd—" That's all she managed before a hand clamped over her mouth and cold metal kissed her temple. The sandwich fell from her nerveless fingers, hitting the tile floor with a softsounding *plop*.

"Don't move," a deep voice rumbled close to her ear.

Neanderthal. She'd recognize that accent anywhere. Not to mention the smell of him, all cheap cologne and old sweat.

His meaty hand left her mouth to snake around her throat, thick fingers pinching into skin already bruised by his first assault. With her heart trying to burst through her chest and her lungs refusing to do what they'd been made to do, she wasn't sure she'd be able to scream loud enough for anyone to hear. But damned if she wouldn't give it her best shot.

She opened her mouth. Before any sound emerged, Neanderthal whispered, "If you scream, I'll shoot the first person who comes running."

If his tone were a color, she imagined it would be bloodred. He wasn't kidding. He would kill the first person he saw. She clamped her mouth shut and turned her head slightly, *very* conscious of the pistol pressed to her temple. *Seriously? Twice in one day? Can't a gal catch a break?*

"What do you want?" she whispered.

"Right now?" He chuckled. The dry, slithering sound reminded her of worms crawling through the unseeing eye sockets of a dried-out skull. "All I want is you. Thought I was gonna hafta search the whole sodding house, but here you are. Right by the front door. Making my life easy."

Her eyes darted around the dark entryway, looking for Neanderthal Numero Dos, a.k.a. *Ben*. He was nowhere to be found. At least nowhere her straining eyes could see and—

A terrible thought suddenly occurred.

Did Ben have Christian? Is that why Christian hadn't

come back upstairs? Had Ben...*done* something to Christian?

She didn't allow herself to contemplate the possibility that Ben might have *killed* Christian, because if she did that, her psyche would shatter into a million sharp, cutting pieces. She needed her wits about her if she had any hopes of getting out of this mess.

Christian's fine, she assured herself as Neanderthal dragged her toward the front door. *He's smarter than both Neanderthal brothers put together. Tougher too. He's fine. He is. He has to be!*

"Open the door," Neanderthal commanded, his hot, wet breath swirling around her ear, making her shudder with revulsion. "Slowly. Quietly."

Her hand was shaking with fear when she did as instructed. But as soon as she opened the door, her whole body began to quake. And not only with fear. With cold too. The spring night had turned icy. Frost was forming on the grass, glinting like diamonds under the light of a half-moon.

"Now," Neanderthal said, keeping one hand around her throat and the other around the pistol kissing her head, "you're gonna walk with me down the steps and out onto the front lawn. If you try to run, I'll kill you. If you try to scream, I'll kill you. If you try to bite me or hit me or take my weapon, I'll kill you."

There it was again. That bloodred tone.

She swallowed, nodding.

"There's a good girl."

In any other situation, she would have called him on his misogynist bullshit. A man did *not* call a woman *girl* unless he wanted a hard knee to send his junk up into his throat. But considering his hissed warnings and the fact that she quite liked her head with the few holes it already sported, she kept her knee to herself and her mouth shut.

Neanderthal nudged her forward with his hip. The flagstones on the front porch were freezing beneath her bare feet. The icy bite of the breeze was even worse as it scraped along her cheeks. She tried not to wince when they made it to the gravel path, but the sharp stones stabbed into her soles. In fact, the pain became so much that she stumbled, forcing Neanderthal to release her neck and wrap an arm around her waist.

Pulling her tight against him, he lifted her off her feet and carried her until they reached the center of the path in the middle of the yard. When he lowered her, there was no mistaking his dick against the seam of her ass.

He was hard.

Gag a maggot!

"It's all your fault, you know," he whispered conversationally when he felt her disgusted shudder. "If you hadn't given me and Ben that little peep show earlier, I wouldn't be hard now."

Oh, dear sweet baby Jesus.

It hadn't been Angel she'd seen walking into the woods. It'd been Neanderthal. As he threw back his head and yelled, "All you fucks inside the manor house come out with your hands up! I have the woman, and I won't hesitate to put a bullet in her brain!" she thought with gut-wrenching anguish, *My mistake, my presumption, might have killed us all.*

Chapter 20

CHRISTIAN KNEW FEAR.

He'd lived with it most of his life. As a child, he had feared the men his mother had brought home. Feared that, even though Jessica Watson was about as nurturing as a chainsaw, she might die and leave him to fend for himself in a world that wasn't kind to skinny, funny-eyed orphans. As an adult, he had feared what he would do with his life after the SAS fed him to the wolves. Then, more recently, he'd feared what would become of him after BKI closed its clandestine doors.

However, none of that had prepared him for the tsunami of terror that crashed over him when he felt a peanut butter and jelly sandwich squish under his foot at the same time a booming voice yelled from the front lawn, "I have the woman, and I won't hesitate to put a bullet in her brain!"

His heart stopped.

His lungs ceased to draw breath.

His vision tunneled until only darkness remained.

The sheer weight of the fear threatened to take him to his knees. He might have allowed himself to succumb if the first part of Wankstain's instructions—oh, yes, he recognized that voice—had not demanded he remain on his feet.

Beat, beat, pause, he commanded his heart.

Inhale, exhale, he ordered his lungs.

Blink and focus, he instructed his eyes.

When it seemed his recalcitrant body parts were back to doing their bloody jobs, he turned toward the front door. Any other time, he might have taken a moment to consider his options, but with Emily in the man's clutches, he knew his only recourse was to *obey*.

"Holy duck fuck!" Ace snarled at the top of the stairs. Even through the darkness, Christian could see Ace was shirtless, his blond hair catching the moonlight streaming in through the windows. "Is that who I think it is?"

"None other." Christian knew that if and when the time came, he was going to end the Wankstain Brothers. "Now, do as he says."

Rusty joined Ace at the top of the stairs, and Christian didn't wait around to see if Angel had heard the shouted command. He resumed his journey toward the front door. Ten steps. That's what it would take to get to there, but it felt like ten miles. Enough time for him to file away a mounting pile of regrets and recriminations.

He should *not* have waited by the washing machine while it went through its fifteen-minute fast cycle. But he had fancied being able to head upstairs, take out Angel's condom, and use it on Emily with no distractions, no niggling thought that at some point he would need to traipse back down to the first floor and transfer the wet quilt into the dryer.

At the time, his plan had seemed capital. Now? Not so much. It meant he'd left her alone.

If he'd been by her side, he might have been able to fight off their aggressors. And, yes, he realized there wasn't much he could offer in the way of defense against a loaded gun, but still… He should have been there with her—

His thoughts cut off when he reached the door. Wasting no time, he twisted its handle and threw it open. The breeze outside was cold, biting. It matched the ice that encased his heart when he saw Emily in the same position she had been in back at the hangar's car park. Head Honcho Wankstain was at her back, his big, meaty hand around her throat, a pistol pointed at her head.

Like a black hole, the matte charcoal of the weapon seem to draw all light toward it. Christian felt his breath get sucked out of him. Felt a gravitational pull to run across the yard and…what?

It's not like Wankstain wouldn't see him coming and either plug him before he made it ten steps or else make good on his threat to put a bullet in Emily's brain. That last thought was enough to have Christian resisting the urge to fly to her side and instead hold his ground. But it didn't stop his desire to see Wankstain six feet under.

A taste for killing was like a taste for hard liquor. Once you developed it, it never went away. The most you could hope to do was control it. Christian thought he had done a brilliant job of controlling it over the years. Except for that time he'd gone in search of John J. Tully and his mouth full of rotten teeth, he had never had the urge to shed blood outside of battle.

He had that urge now. In fact, a hundred different ways he could end Wankstain's life flashed through his head in rapid-fire order. All of them were painful and properly gruesome.

"I'm sorry!" Emily called despite Wankstain growling

something, no doubt a threat, in her ear. "I was wrong earlier! It wasn't Angel I saw in the woods; it was him!"

There was such anguish in her voice. Such self-condemnation. It stabbed at Christian's heart like a carving knife, slicing the organ to pieces.

"Quite a show you put on for us too!" Wankstain shouted, his breath forming a frosty cloud in front of his face. "She's a tasty little tart, ain't she?"

Christian wanted to vomit at the thought of the men having seen Emily naked and vulnerable. And when Wankstain turned his head, pressing a wet, open-mouthed kiss on Emily's cheek, a film of red fell over Christian's vision.

"What do you want?" He didn't raise his voice. Knew it would be carried out to the front lawn by his fury alone.

"What do I *want*?" Wankstain asked. "I want all of you out here! On this lawn! *Now!* Or the woman gets it!" As if to prove his point, he shoved his pistol so hard against Emily's already bruised temple that she cried out in pain.

Before Christian knew what he was doing, he'd taken a step forward. Had Ace not come up behind him and slapped a hand on his shoulder, Vulcan neck-pinch style, he would've been off the flagstones, down the stairs, barreling toward Emily and her Cro-Magnon-looking captor, and damn the consequences to himself.

"Easy," Ace whispered, keeping hold of him. "Go easy, my man."

Christian wasn't living on the same planet as *easy*. Maybe not even in the same solar system. But some-how—he hadn't a buggering clue how—he managed to keep from losing his shit. Still, his heart beat with a terrible rhythm as he shuffled forward, following Wankstain's orders.

Thirty seconds later, he, Rusty, and Ace were all out on the lawn, shoulder to shoulder and a mere twenty feet from Emily and her captor.

I'm so sorry, her eyes pleaded.

Nothing for you to be sorry about, he wordlessly assured her with a shake of his head. *This isn't your fault*.

Wankstain glanced back and forth between them and snorted. "Aw, the way you two look at each other is so touching it makes me want to puke. Now, where's the other one?" He craned his head to glance behind Christian and the others.

Christian peeked over his shoulder at the open and empty front door. Angel was nowhere in sight. A niggle of apprehension squirmed around inside his chest.

Damnit, Angel! Where the bloody hell are you?

"Maybe he didn't hear you," he suggested, knowing full well that Angel, who slept with one eye and both ears open, hadn't missed Wankstain's initial shout. "Or maybe he means to wait and see if Spider turns up to do his own dirty work."

Christian watched Wankstain's reaction closely, narrowing his eyes when nothing registered on the man's face but confusion.

"Who the feck is Spider?" Wankstain asked. "And why do you keep bringing him up?"

Christian felt Ace shift beside him, knew the man was thinking the same thing he was. *Sodding shit. If not Spider, then what in the world is going on here?*

Needing answers and also, you know, *stalling* so that Angel could either get his daft ass out of the house or else finish doing whatever it was he was doing, Christian asked, "If you're not working for Spider, then who *are* you working for? How did you find us?"

Wankstain scoffed. "Who I work for is neither here nor there. As to how we found you, that's easy. We saw your face splashed across our telly and decided to drive to Port Isaac to have a bit of a chat with you."

One piece of the puzzle fell into place. Christian hoped to snap in another. "Which is when you saw us sneak out of the cottage and decided to follow us to the airport?"

"Right. And instead of having a bit of a chat with you like we'd planned, you lot"—Wankstain lifted his chin to include all three men—"had to go and try to be heroes, which caused an innocent bloke to get slotted."

Christian didn't correct him about the status of the pilot who had been shot. Instead, he said, "And whose fault was that? If memory serves, you and your brother were the only two who had weapons."

He was baiting the bastard, which was risky. But Angel *still* had yet to make an appearance, and Christian was determined to do everything he could to distract Wankstain from that unfortunate fact.

Fury contorted the man's face. The overgrown wonker wasn't going to win any beauty contests, even on a good day, but the hatred bubbling inside him made him downright ugly.

Wankstain kept hold of Emily, but he moved the gun from her temple and aimed it at Christian. And not that Christian ever liked looking down the black-throated barrel of a semi-auto, but he was relieved the dangerous end of the weapon was no longer in close proximity to Emily's brain.

Ace made a noise in the back of his throat, something close to the warning growl of a rabid animal. It was Christian's turn to whisper, "Easy." He couldn't have his teammate pulling an Emily and jumping in front of a bullet meant for him.

"It's *your* fault," Wankstain insisted, a muscle ticking in his slab of a jaw. "*You* started all this when you opened fire at that roadblock!"

Spittle flew from his mouth, catching the light of the moon and glistening before it joined the frost on the gravel path. Christian knew he should feel the cold, feel the bite of the icy stones beneath his bare feet. But he was numb to everything but the terrified look on Emily's face and the words tumbling out of Wankstain's mouth.

Roadblock? As in, the one in Iraq? What the actual hell? Christian didn't know this man from Adam.

"Who are you?" An icy pit formed in his stomach to match the sheet of permafrost that had grown thick around his heart. "What's your name?"

"Lawrence Michelson. Ring a bell?"

"No." Christian shook his head, hoping for that second puzzle piece and keenly aware of the two men at his side, of the woman he loved who was so close and yet so far away. "I'm afraid it doesn't."

"How 'bout *Teddy* Michelson? That jog your memory?"

"Oh sodding hell."

Snap. That was the sound of the next puzzle piece falling into place, and Christian thought he was starting to discern the whole picture. His heart broke through its icy casing and plummeted. If he dared take his eye off Lawrence's gun, he figured he'd see the organ lying on the ground at his feet.

"That's right." Lawrence nodded, his dark eyes overly bright. "You're the fecking twat that got my brother killed!"

Christian wanted to howl his frustration, his *fury*, at the sky. Instead, he held out a placating hand. "Lawrence, I'm sorry about your brother. I knew Teddy well. He was a good man. A ruddy *brilliant* soldier. But what you've been told about the Kirkuk Police Station Incident isn't the whole truth. Teddy didn't—"

"Don't you *fucking* say his name!" Lawrence snarled, more spittle flying, more hot breath crystallizing. "You don't deserve to have it pass your lying, murderous lips!"

Christian took a deep breath and tried again. "Okay," he soothed, patting the cold air in deference. "Okay. You're right. But before you do something you might regret, you need to hear what really happened in Iraq."

"I *know* what happened," Lawrence snarled. "You opened fire at a roadblock filled with Iraqi policemen. And when you got caught, my *brother* had to go in and save you!"

"I was under orders to resist capture," Christian said evenly. If Lawrence's face was the picture of rage, then Christian hoped his was the picture of calm. He got the impression he was walking a knife's edge. One wrong move, one wrong word, and Lawrence would snap and gun them all down. "I had been tasked with bringing down corrupt policemen and—"

"You're a *liar*!"

"Lawrence, please," Christian pleaded, seeing that

the man was working himself into a frenzy. Two minutes ago, when he'd thought the Michelsons were no better than Spider's henchmen, he'd wanted to send them to meet their Maker tout de suite. Now, he simply wanted them to understand. "The media never had the whole story. The SAS made a scapegoat of me when things went south and—"

"Shut *up*! Shut your lying *mouth*!" Lawrence screeched. Then he turned and yelled over his shoulder, "Ben! Go to the door and tell that last bastard to get his sodding ass out here! Tell him I'll give him thirty seconds before I start putting holes in his mates!"

A dark shadow peeled away from the gloom of the trees near the front of the manor. The massive shoulders on the shadow left no doubt it was Ben. As the younger Michelson brother skirted the lot of them and headed toward the house, Christian had a terrible realization.

"How did you find us here? Did you follow us from the airport?"

Lawrence nodded, confirming Christian's suspicions that the vehicle that had caught Angel's eye in the rearview mirror must have been the Michelsons'. So then why had the brothers waited until the middle of the night to confront Christian? And why were they insisting that everyone come out on the front lawn if all they wanted to do was talk?

The answer was obvious. Still, Christian held out a tiny sliver of hope. "So what say we have that chat now then, yeah?"

"It's too late." Lawrence's big chest heaved with emotion, his breath creating cloud after cloud in front of him.

"He's not dead," Christian insisted firmly, hoping

the Michelsons' upcoming plans hinged on that salient fact and not pure old-fashioned revenge. "The pilot your brother shot… He's not dead."

Lawrence had been looking over Christian's shoulder, watching his brother make his way across the flagstones and up the stairs toward the open front door. But *that* had his dark eyes pinging to Christian's. "He's not?"

"No. He's alive. The bullet went through and through."

For a moment, Christian thought Lawrence might call the whole thing off, lower his weapon, and slink off into the forest. But then the elder Michelson's expression hardened and what hope Christian had that this all could get sorted without bloodshed vanished.

"Doesn't matter." Lawrence shook his head. "Because you're still the reason my brother's dead. You're still the reason my mother and father are dead. And you're gonna *pay*!"

Christian bore the responsibility for Teddy Michelson's death. He might not have been the one to fire the round that had torn through Teddy's jugular—that had been the work of a corrupt Iraqi police officer—but he also had not been able to get out of the firefight at the roadblock without being caught. And that had necessitated his rescue and put Teddy and all the other soldiers of the 22nd SAS Regiment in mortal danger.

Not a day went by that Christian didn't rehash the events leading up to that roadblock, wondering if there had been some clue he had missed, something to let him know the Iraqi officers had been on to him. No matter how many times he went over it, however, he always came back to the same conclusion: Nothing. There was no way he could have known.

It was bloody infuriating. Completely demoralizing. And given the way the SAS had kicked him to the curb afterward, he sometimes wondered if it might not have been better if the Regiment had simply refused to send in a rescue team. Teddy would still be alive. But then, of course, Christian would undoubtedly be dead.

Still, did that matter in the grand scheme of things? Was his life worth more than Teddy's? Had all the good he'd done working for BKI, the countless times he'd done his part to make the world a safer place, made up for Teddy's death? Is that how the scales of the universe worked?

Christian suffered no illusion that if he asked Lawrence those questions, the man's answers would be *no*. To the Michelsons, nothing Christian had done could make up for losing their beloved brother.

"Mum and Dad were devastated by Teddy's death," Lawrence said. "Two weeks after we put Teddy in the ground, Mum stepped in front of a bus."

"Oh God," Christian whispered. Even though his heart was lying on the ground somewhere near his feet, he still felt the organ shatter.

"Dad couldn't stand the grief. Had a massive heart attack after we laid her to rest beside Teddy."

Christian screwed his eyes shut, hurting for all the damage, all the pain done to so many after the police station incident.

"I understand." He opened his eyes, determination snapping his spine straight. Glancing at Emily, he ran his eyes over her beloved face, wanting to memorize every curve, every line, every subtle texture. He would hold that memory in his mind's eye when he did what must be done. "I do. So why don't you and your brother take me into the woods and do with me what you will."

"Christian, *no*." Emily stared at him in horror.

He didn't answer her. If sacrificing himself to the Michelsons' need for vengeance would keep her and the others safe, he'd gladly do it. "The others…" He lifted a hand, indicating the two men to his left, the woman—*his* woman—in front of him. "Your quarrel isn't with them; it's with me. They're innocent in all this."

"Innocent?" Lawrence laughed, and the sound exploded over the lawn like a cannon blast. "Bollocks they are. Innocent people don't create a firebomb in a small village to escape the press. Innocent people don't take the back roads to the airport when the motorway woulda been twice as fast. Innocent people don't break into an old manor house to hide for the night."

His argument was so smooth it sounded rehearsed. Is that how Lawrence was rationalizing his plan? Had he convinced himself that Emily, Ace, Rusty, and Angel were all as culpable as Christian? A cold fingernail of dread—and inevitability—scraped up Christian's spine.

"None of you are innocent," Lawrence spat. "None of you deserve—"

He was cut off by the sound of his brother poking his head into the front door and yelling, "Hey, you! Wake up and get your stupid ass out onto the front lawn, or all your mates are gonna get it!"

Silence followed that pronouncement, and still Angel was MIA. Christian was about to try to explain away his absence when Lawrence yelled to Ben, "Never mind! Let's finish this lot, and then we'll find the last one!"

And there it was, laid out in words as plain as day. *Finish this lot.*

Panic and remorse and the need to try one last time to change the outcome this night was barreling toward at breakneck speed had Christian opening his mouth to plead with the older Michelson. But before he could say anything, Ben palmed his Glock and turned around, nodding at his older brother. And in that split second, Christian saw the angel of death appear in the dark shadows behind Ben.

No, not the angel of death. Just Angel.

"Angel, *no!*" he shouted when Angel raised his hands. Christian needed a few more minutes to try to convince Lawrence—

But it was too late. Angel grabbed Ben's jaw and gave it a hard, backward yank. The movies got loads of things wrong, but the noise a person's neck makes as it breaks wasn't one of them. The sound of Ben's vertebra snapping was as sickening as it was final. Ben Michelson was dead before his body hit the ground.

"*Noooo!*" Lawrence roared, flinging Emily away from him and swinging his weapon toward Angel, a murderous gleam shining in his eyes.

It was done. There would be no quarter given to the Michelsons this night.

Christian had enough time to see that Emily was okay—she'd stumbled but had managed to stay on her feet—before he lunged. He made it a step before Lawrence's pistol barked, the sound oddly amplified by the cold stillness of the night.

Pain burned through his arm, but he ignored the sizzle, still barreling toward Lawrence, sensing Ace and

Rusty hot on his heels. He took an additional three steps before jumping and tackling Lawrence to the ground.

Lawrence roared his fury when Christian landed on him and was quick to get one hand on Lawrence's wrist, the one holding the gun. Christian curled his other hand into a fist that he used to smash Lawrence's nose. *Bam! Crunch!* Blood gushed over Lawrence's face.

Christian knew his knuckles would hurt later—bone meeting bone was never fun—but right then he felt nothing but determination. He had to disarm Lawrence. And fast. With his brother dead, Lawrence was beyond reason.

Christian's punch would have knocked out most men and dazed many others. But Lawrence was built like a rhino, and mindless with rage to boot. He seemed to shake off the blow as if it was nothing, and before Christian knew it, a hard punch landed against his ribs. Lawrence's meaty fist felt like a pile driver. Christian's rib cage *creaked* in warning. Another one of those punches, and he'd be in a world of pain.

They rolled and spat and kicked and snarled, fighting for control of the weapon. The smell of Lawrence, body odor thinly disguised by harsh-smelling cologne, surrounded Christian in a toxic cloud until finally, he was able to bring down his elbow on the crook of Lawrence's arm. As he'd hoped, the move momentarily paralyzed a nerve, causing the Glock 17 to slip from Lawrence's grip.

Christian palmed the weapon, rolled off Lawrence, and stood. His chest worked like a bellows from the effort. Adrenaline left a sharp, tangy taste on his tongue.

Aiming down at Lawrence, he curled his finger around a trigger that was warm and worn smooth.

"Don't move!" he commanded when Lawrence pushed to his feet.

Either Lawrence didn't hear him or else didn't care. The brute wiped a hand beneath his nose, smearing blood across his cheek, and then turned on his heel.

For a second, Christian thought Lawrence was going to flee the scene—and even though it would be hell on all their covers, he would have let him go. Then Christian realized Lawrence had no thought of leaving, because he reached for a sheath on his waistband and came away with a tactical fighting knife that sported a matte-black blade. The fool was determined to fight to the death, taking as many of them with him as he could.

"Stop!" Christian bellowed, giving Lawrence one last chance. Hoping beyond hope the man would realize he was outgunned and outnumbered.

No such luck. Lawrence roared his mindless outrage and sprinted toward Emily.

That's all it took. There was no hesitation, no second-guessing as Christian aimed and fired. The *boom* of the Glock as it belched up a round sounded profane. The round entered the back of Lawrence's skull, and a plume of pink and red mist exploded from the front of his head.

Christian could tell by Emily's expression of shock and horror that Lawrence's face was gone. She took a step back, a hand going over her mouth.

Lawrence's body wobbled once. Twice. Then crumpled to the ground.

Shit. *Shit!* If only Lawrence had listened to reason.

"Are you okay?" Christian demanded of Emily, still blowing hard and trying like hell not to stare at the man he'd just sent to meet his Maker.

The second she nodded, he allowed himself to succumb to the weight of his regret. He fell to his knees, and Lawrence's weapon dropped from his nerveless fingers. Glancing over his shoulder, he saw Angel casually shove Ben's weapon into the waistband of his jeans before stepping over the body.

Two men dead in ten seconds. Just that easy.

He had been right the first time. It *had* been the angel of death that had appeared behind Ben. But if Angel deserved that designation, then surely Christian did too.

"Damnit!" His anguish felt like a hard, sharp nail lodged in his throat. No, not a nail. A railroad spike. "*Damnit!*"

"They came here to kill us," Ace said quietly, putting a hand on Christian's shoulder.

"At first I thought they were covering their tracks, taking out the witnesses who saw Ben shoot that pilot," Rusty said. "But then there was that look on Lawrence's face when you told him the pilot was still alive."

Yes. Christian remembered it well. It was the moment he had gotten his first inkling of just how gruesomely this night would end.

"He was crazy," Ace said. "You could see it in his eyes. All he wanted was blood, revenge for something that wasn't even your fault."

"But it was my fault, don't you see?" That railroad spike twisted in Christian's throat. "If not for my failed mission, their brother would still be alive. Same for their mother and father."

"Christian, you can't—" Ace began, but Christian tuned him out.

He glanced numbly at his arm, blinking at the deep furrow Lawrence's bullet had cut through the fabric of his sweater. The ragged edges glistened with his blood, but the round had only grazed him.

That didn't seem right, did it? Two men were dead and he was only grazed?

His mind immediately hit on his mother, on the regret and the self-condemnation that had slowly eaten her from the inside out. Strange that besides their dark hair and the subtle dimple in their chins *that* would be the thing they had in common and—

"Christian?"

He looked up to see Emily standing beside him. So beautiful and sweet with her dark eyes and wild, wind-blown hair. She knelt in front of him and took his face in her hands. It was only when the cool kiss of her soft palms landed on his cheeks that he felt the wetness there. Was he crying?

"You are *not* to blame for any of this. You hear me?"

He tried to look away, but she gave his head a shake, forcing his eyes back to hers.

"There are a lot of people at fault here. The SAS. Lawrence and Ben. But not you. *You* didn't do anything wrong. So don't get sad. Get *mad*! *I* am!" Despite the cold, her face was mottled red. "I'm so fucking *mad* on your behalf!"

And though he would not have thought it possible, he felt a somber smile tug at his lips. Dear, sweet, *ferocious* Emily. A tigress. *His* tigress.

A part of him knew she was right, knew the words she spoke were the truth. But another part of him figured he was a tad bit right too. At least some of it had to rest on his shoulders.

"Emily..." Her name was an invocation, a prayer.

Once and for all, she proved she was a mind reader and pulled him into her arms. She claimed his mouth in a kiss that tried to heal all the things that were broken and hurting inside him. Lithe arms crushed him to her, because she was Emily and she knew he needed her strength in this moment of doubt and despair.

He thought he heard a phone ring, but the tornado of emotions swirling inside him and tossing sharp, painful debris at his head made it impossible to concentrate. It wasn't until he felt a heavy hand on his shoulder that reality—and a bit of sanity—returned.

"I hate to do this," Ace said, "but I have Boss on the line. He has good news. At least, I think it's good news."

Christian regretfully released Emily's lips. But he didn't release *her*. No. He needed to keep hold of her.

"Seems Philippe's partner was able to get here earlier than planned." Ace held the phone against his chest. "She's waiting at the airport and wants to know when we can get there so she can submit a takeoff time to air traffic control."

Christian glanced around at the carnage, at the... *death*. Such senseless death.

"Right-oh." He nodded, wanting nothing more than to leave merry ol' England behind. Once again, the place had proved the undoing of him. "Let's get the bloody hell off this sodding island, shall we?"

Chapter 21

36,000 feet over the Atlantic...

EMILY GLANCED DOWN THE AISLE OF THE SWANKY PRIVATE jet at the lavatory door. Still closed. Which meant Christian was still inside tending his wound.

She had asked if he needed any help, but he had waved her off, looking so tired and defeated that her squishy, far-too-tender heart had *ached* for him.

Nothing that had happened during the last twenty-four hours was his fault. But Christian being Christian, all noble and principled and self-sacrificing—when the big, dumb dope had told Lawrence Michelson to take him into the woods, she'd nearly had a heart attack—was determined to shoulder at least *some* of the blame for the brothers' deaths.

Ridiculous, since it'd been *Angel* who'd offed one of them.

Wondering if the former Mossad agent was suffering any aftereffects from the night, she glanced over to find him reclined back in a plush armchair. He was fast asleep. Like, seriously. His face was as still as a picture. His arms were folded over his chest. And he was so ethereally beautiful that she was reminded of all the vampires that'd taken over television since that whole Twilight thing went gangbusters.

Nope. No guilt or regret there.

"I can feel you watching me." Angel's deep, scratchy voice made her jump. Okay, so obviously he *wasn't* asleep. That was even spookier. "And I know what you think."

"Oh yeah?" she asked, even though he had yet to open his eyes or turn toward her. "And what do I think?"

"That I should feel remorse for snapping Ben's neck. But you know as well as I do that the Michelson brothers had come to kill us all. I waited until I was certain of that before I made my move."

"I know that."

He cracked an eye open, pinning her with it. "Do you?"

"*Yes*." She nodded.

"Good." He closed his eye and turned back into the undead.

Emily made a face and glanced around to see if either Rusty or Ace had something to add to the conversation. But Rusty was stretched out on the comfy leather sofa bolted into the fuselage in front of Emily's seat. One big arm was across his flat stomach, the other tossed over his head. He pretended to sleep. But, occasionally, he would glance over at Ace, a look of confusion and longing contorting his handsome face.

For his part, Ace was kicked back in the seat behind Angel's, going through a stack of magazines like he was determined to read every damn article. Considering the one he was perusing now was titled "Cuticle Care and the Art of Flawless Nails," Emily figured his magazine fascination had more to do with avoiding conversation with Rusty than anything else.

Okay, so obviously they had nothing to add. Which was good, she supposed. She wasn't all hyped to rehash the horror of the night. And, honestly, she wished the two of them would find some common ground and stop—

Her thoughts were cut off by the sound of the lavatory door opening. Turning, she saw Christian exit the bathroom. A stark white bandage showed through the hole in the arm of his sweater—that was *another* thing that'd nearly given her a heart attack: when Lawrence had pulled his trigger and she'd seen Christian in the way of the bullet. But Christian didn't join her now. Instead, he pushed aside the curtain at the back of the plane, the one separating the sleeping compartment from the main cabin, and disappeared behind it.

Chewing her bottom lip, she debated whether to follow him. Back at the manor house, he hadn't wanted her anywhere but at his side.

Together, the two of them had replaced the quilt on the bed and helped Angel remove any trace that any of them had been inside the manor house. Together, they'd watched Angel reset the alarm while Ace and Rusty dumped the Michelsons' weapons into a nearby pond. They wanted to leave as little evidence behind as possible that could paint a picture of what had happened to the brothers. Together, they'd climbed into the farm truck for the ride to the airport. Since it was still dark, and since they were working against a deadline, they had chosen to take their chances with the truck as opposed to stealing another vehicle.

Together, they'd wiped the truck free of fingerprints after Angel parked it behind a billboard close to the private jet hangar. And together, hand in hand, in fact, they'd said hello to Brigitte—pronounced *Brigeet*, Philippe's partner and their pilot—and then loaded onto the private jet, breathing sighs of relief once they were airborne and officially leaving England behind.

But maybe now Christian wanted to be alone. Maybe now he needed time with his thoughts and—

Fuck that. What he needed was *her*. And who cared if going to him was crossing their coworker-with-benefits/ fuck buddies line. Because it certainly didn't cross their friends-with-benefits line. And she'd come to realize that more than anything else, Christian was her friend.

She opened her backpack, searching for a granola bar she might have left and— Aha! She pulled one out and saw it was a little squished, but no matter. It would still taste great. Dark chocolate, nuts, and sea salt were a delicious combo any way you sliced it. She shoved the bar in her pocket.

She'd just pushed up from her seat when Angel spoke again. "Tell Christian the next time he wants to borrow a condom, all he has to do is ask."

Her cheeks heated. "I, uh, I told him I'd be too embarrassed if he did that."

"Nothing embarrassing about practicing safe sex," Ace muttered.

"Oh, *now* you decide to join the conversation?"

Ace blinked at her in confusion.

"Never mind." She turned her back on the three men, heading toward the rear of the plane.

"Christian?" She pulled the curtain aside to find him sitting on the end of the narrow bed, his elbows on his knees, his face in his hands. "Is there anything I can do to help?"

He didn't say anything, simply nodded his head and grabbed her wrist. Dragging her next to him on the narrow bed, he pressed her down into the mattress, then turned to spoon her. With his big body wrapped around her, he whispered into her hair, "Just lie here with me. I want to hold you for a while."

So that's what she did. She lay with him, feeling his solid heartbeat against her back, hearing him breathe, caressing the arm tucked securely around her waist, and reveling in the warmth of his skin. After a while, she pulled the granola bar from her pocket and reached back to wiggle it in front of his face. "You need to eat."

She felt him shake his head. "Not hungry."

"*Eat.*" She wiggled the bar again. "That's not a request."

His put-upon sigh gusted against the back of her hair, but he grabbed the granola bar and rolled onto his back. "You're bossy," he accused.

"I prefer the term *strong-willed*." She turned onto her side to face him. Going up on her elbow, she cupped her chin in her hand and watched him tear open the wrapper. "Does that intimidate you?"

"What?" He took a giant bite, and the smell of chocolate and nuts filled the small space. "That you're strong-willed?"

She nodded.

"Please." He made a face as he chewed. "Strong-willed women intimidate boys. They *excite* men."

"Good answer."

He wiggled his eyebrows. But too soon his expression sobered, turned haunted.

"I meant what I said earlier," she murmured. "None of what happened tonight was your fault."

She'd drill it into his head if she had to. Tell him

over and over until he finally believed it and the hurt left his eyes.

She couldn't bear that look. It hit her right in the ol' love muscle and made her far too aware of all those bright, sparkly feelings. *Dangerous* feelings. *Deceitful* feelings because, sure, right now they seemed like they'd always be with her, but she knew from experience how quickly they faded.

"You were fearless tonight," she told him. "And fair. And above all else, *brave*."

He scoffed. "There are loads of things you can say about what it means to kill a man. Brave isn't one of them."

"Do you always suffer…um…" She wrinkled her nose. "I guess the word is *remorse*…afterward?"

"Killing should never rest easy on anyone's shoulders."

Her mind drifted back to Angel, unrepentant and on his way to a good night's sleep. "Agreed. But that doesn't answer my question."

"No." He shook his head, chewing and swallowing. "I don't generally regret it. Perhaps because anytime I've ever taken a life it was to protect my fellow soldiers or teammates."

"Which is exactly what happened tonight."

"Perhaps," he allowed.

"*No*." She scowled at him. The only lights in the sleeping cubby were on the floor. A whole line of them on either side of the cabin led the way to the nearest exit. But they gave off enough glow to cast his face in shadows, making his high cheekbones, his broad forehead, and his wide jaw seem that much more impressive. "Not *perhaps*. Certainly. Positively. Without a doubt. You did everything you could to reason with Lawrence, and you did the *only* thing you could when he came after me with that knife."

"I just keep thinking there had to have been another way. With four of us, could we have somehow subdued him?"

"You mean before or after he'd gutted me?" She lifted a brow.

A hint of a smile pulled at his lips. She wanted to turn it into a *full* smile. "You're right. I know you're right. But perhaps—"

"And there's that word again," she interrupted him. "How about I make you a deal?"

He groaned around a mouthful of granola bar. "Another one?"

"You'll like this one. I promise."

"I have my doubts."

"You cut the word *perhaps* from your vocabulary for this conversation, and instead repeat the phrase *None of what happened tonight was my fault* ten times—and *mean it*—and I'll give you another truth. Anything you want to ask me, I'll answer and—"

Before she could get in another word, he was already repeating the phrase. She quietly counted until he got to the eighth recitation, then interrupted him. "Now, look me in the eye when you say it these last two times." She donned her best schoolmarm stare. "Because I'll know if you really believe it. I'll see it in your eyes."

"Don't you mean my *pretty* eyes?" He fluttered his lashes. Jeez, they were ridiculously thick.

She chuckled at the memory of that morning.

Wow. *Really*? It'd been less than twenty-four hours

since she'd told him he had pretty eyes? She felt she'd aged ten years between then and now.

"Yes. I mean your *pretty* eyes. Now"—she waved a hand—"go for it. Give it your all."

"None of what happened tonight was my fault. There. Happy now?"

"Perhaps."

"Hey!" He frowned. "I thought we were cutting that from our vocabularies for this conversation."

"No." She shook her head. "I said *you* needed to cut it from *your* vocabulary. I didn't say anything about myself. You should pay more attention."

"Right-oh." He wadded up the empty granola bar wrapper and shoved it into his pocket. Then, he pulled the neck of her sweatshirt aside so he could kiss her collarbone. Chills erupted under his lips and spread out from there. "I promise to pay vast amounts of attention to this spot here." He moved his lips to her throat. "And this spot here." Now his lips were on her earlobe. "And this spot here."

After standing barefoot on the front lawn of the manor house, with the cold air trying to cut her to the bone, she'd wondered if she'd ever get warm again. She shouldn't have worried. One kiss from Christian, one sexy word spoken in that low baritone with that accent, and she was on fire.

"I would very much like you to continue exactly what you're doing," she said breathlessly, "*after* you repeat the phrase one last time." She shoved at his shoulders, experiencing a secret thrill when she barely budged him.

Had she mentioned that underneath that perfect hair and those perfect clothes was a tough, tattooed brute?

He pulled back, his eyes brightened by hunger. She

still couldn't quite believe that *she* could do that to him. She of the barely B cups and inexhaustible supply of ratty sweatshirts.

For a second, she thought he was going to rapid-fire repeat the phrase, just to get it over with so he could go back to seducing her—and really, had that been the case, she wouldn't have protested—but then his expression turned serious, and that muscle beneath his eye gave a twitch.

"None of what happened tonight was my fault." His accent made the last word sound more like *folt*.

"That's right." She searched his eyes. "That's one hundred percent right."

He flopped back on the bed, blowing out a gusty sigh. "But that doesn't make me feel any better about it. Three brothers…" He shook his head. "Gone because—"

"Because your country didn't support you and instead let you be the fall guy for something terrible," she interrupted him.

"But I still feel like a wretch because…"

He didn't carry on, simply heaved another sigh.

"Because what?" she prompted, poking him in the ribs with one finger.

"Because I *am* responsible for not knowing the Iraqi police officers had ferreted out my mission. If I'd known, I could have—"

"Stop it." She held up a hand. "Stop right there, or I'll put my foot so far up your ass I'll knock out your teeth. Number one, I'm sure there was no way you could have known your cover had been blown."

"How can you be sure?"

"Because you're *you*, you big, dumb dope. You are

the most detail-oriented guy I know. You're irritatingly meticulous. Not to mention *thorough*."

"And number two?"

"Number two, if you start shouldering the blame for everything that happened after Iraq, you'll never stop. Tell me, are you responsible for the plaque buildup in Mr. Michelson's heart? Are you responsible for the bus driver who didn't stomp on the brakes hard enough or soon enough to avoid hitting Mrs. Michelson? Are you responsible for Ben shooting Philippe? Are you responsible for Lawrence's craziness and his unwillingness to listen to reason?"

She could see him pondering her questions and got her mad on. "In case you're wondering, the answer to all of those questions is *no*. And if you contemplate for one more second that it might be *yes*, then I hate to have to be the one to tell you, Crazy Train, but this ain't your station."

"I only wish I'd had more time to talk him down." Christian shook his head. "I'll always wonder if I might have been able to—"

She cut him off. "You wouldn't have. Lawrence Michelson was dead set on killing us."

She didn't tell him about Lawrence's boner, or how it had flexed and pulsed against her bottom when Lawrence had stopped pointing his weapon at *her* head and had instead started pointing it at Christian's. The thought of killing Christian had excited Lawrence. *Sexually*. Gross with a capital *G*.

"So let's do this one more time, huh?" she continued. "Let's get rid of all that shit in your head and clear out the stink. Repeat the phrase."

"You have *such* a way with words."

"So you've said. Now do it."

"Bossy," he accused.

"Strong-willed," she corrected.

"Fine." Another sigh. "None of what happened tonight was my fault."

This time when he said it, she didn't hear a silent *but* tacked onto the end of the phrase. She nodded with satisfaction.

"Now, about that truth," he said.

"Ugh. I was kinda hoping you'd forget about that."

He tilted his head against the fluffy pillow on the bed—there were definitely some perks to flying in a private jet. "Why does the thought of me asking you another truth make you nervous?"

"How d'ya know it does?"

"Because you've slipped into your 'hood-girl grammar and your Chicago accent is extra thick."

She narrowed her eyes. "Anyone ever tell you it's a nut-punch-worthy offense to refer to a grown woman as a *girl*?"

"Duly noted. Anyone ever tell you that you're bloody brilliant at trying to Christian Watson your way out of answering a question?"

Damnit. He had her there. "I thought we agreed to stop using your name as a verb."

"How do you plan to have children?"

All the air left her lungs in one long, gusty exhale. "Who says I wanna have kids?"

"You did. You said, and I quote, 'I want to have kids someday. And I don't want them to get fucked over by me the way I got fucked over by my parents.'"

She had said that, hadn't she? Word for word. *See?* Detail-oriented.

"What have I told you about trying to mimic an American accent?" she grumbled.

"Stall much?" He quirked a brow.

"Damnit! Get out of my head!"

"Turnabout is fair play, darling. Feels like you've been in my head all day."

He wasn't going to let it go. She could tell. And she *had* made a deal with him.

"I'm looking into artificial insemination," she admitted. "Boss has asked me to stay on as the office manager once BKI goes civilian. It's like I've finally found the home I've always longed for, so I'm ready to start building the life I've always longed for. And *that* means two kids, hopefully about two years apart. I *hated* being an only child. It was so lonely. *Is* so lonely. Well, *you* know. And, wow. I'm sort of rambling on like a prison letter, aren't I?"

He pushed up onto his elbow and cocked his beard-stubbled chin. Without fail, he shaved every morning. And without fail, by evening he was rocking a sexy-as-hell five-o'clock shadow.

Before she realized her intent, she'd touched the tip of her finger to his chin dimple. He ducked, kissing her hand before saying, "You've thought about this a lot, haven't you?"

She nodded. "And the cherry on top of this awesome two-kid sundae is that I'll have all the Black Knights Inc. guys around—you included, if you decide to stay on after we go aboveboard—to be positive male role models. It'll be perfect."

Except, for the first time ever, a dark smudge appeared on the surface of her perfect plan. When an image of a little girl with bright-green eyes and a dimple in her chin flared to life inside her head, Emily quickly snuffed it out.

For a long time, Christian said nothing, simply searched her face. She expected some sort of debate. One of the many arguments she'd heard before. *A child needs a father. Raising children alone is incredibly difficult. If you* do *happen to find someone you want to spend the rest of your life with, they might not want to be saddled with two kids who aren't theirs*. Yada yada yada, bullshit, go fuck yourself.

He said none of this, however. Instead, he completely obliterated her by saying, "I think you'll make an excellent mother."

"Well, *that* might be the sweetest thing anyone has ever said to me." She had to swallow past the lump in her throat. "You are *such* an overachiever."

He smiled—a real, full smile—and damned if it wasn't an arrow through her soul. She realized that haunted look was gone from his eyes. No doubt he would never look back on this day or what happened in Iraq with anything resembling indifference. But perhaps, just maybe, she'd helped him see there was nothing for him to be ashamed of, nothing he could have done differently. He'd *saved her life*. Lawrence would have slit her open from her throat to her thighs if Christian hadn't pulled the trigger when he did.

"Now…" She leaned forward to nip at his delectable bottom lip. She was so thrown by his last statement that she had to distract herself. Those bright, sparkly feelings? Well, they were bursting all over the place like the fireworks over Navy Pier on the Fourth of July. And if she'd thought she was emotionally vulnerable to him before, it didn't compare to how exposed she felt now. "You've been set straight on today's events, you've been fed, we're on a bed, so what do you say we put that condom you stole from Angel to good use?"

Chapter 22

Vixen…

That was the look Emily was going for as she bit her bottom lip and waggled her eyebrows. But Christian saw the uncertainty in her eyes.

He'd really thrown her for a loop when he told her he thought she'd make an excellent mother. And even though it'd gutted him to hear her say she planned to become artificially inseminated, especially since he could quite easily imagine a little girl with his eyes—they were better suited for a girl—his chin dimple, and Emily's dark, wavy hair, he couldn't deny the truth of his statement.

She *would* make an excellent mother. She'd be strict yet kind. Consistent yet open to the occasional bending of the rules. And most importantly, she would be absolutely ferocious in her love for her children. She would stand against the world for them, lay down her life for them, make bloody well certain they never went a day without knowing they were her everything.

She would be the mother she never had. She would be the mother *he* never had.

If he hadn't already loved her with every fiber of his being, imagining her as a mother would have sent him falling ass over tits. And it *killed* him that she wanted *him* to be a part of her children's lives, that she thought him worthy of the honor.

It also gave him hope that eventually, with time, she'd come to realize she didn't need a sperm donor. All she needed was him.

"Christian?" There was a question in her eyes. He'd been silent too long. "If you're not up for it, I underst—"

He caught her sweet mouth in a kiss meant not only to silent her words, but also her thoughts. Not up for it? Was she mad?

As always happened anytime their lips touched, he was completely overwhelmed by her. Pressing her into the mattress, he cupped her face and kissed her with everything he had. Trying to convey everything he could not say aloud with the caress of his lips, the stroke of his tongue.

When he finally pulled away, they were both fighting for air. "Not up for it, eh?" He quirked a brow, grabbed her hand, and guided it down to the strain of his cock against the fly of his jeans. "Darling, since the first time I saw you walk through the doors of BKI, I've been up for it."

She caught her bottom lip between her teeth and grinned up at him. Then she curled her delicate fingers around his cock and squeezed. It was enough to have his eyes crossing. A groan rumbled from the back of his throat.

"We have to be quiet," he instructed, pinning her with a knowing look.

"I can be quiet."

"Mmm," he said skeptically. The woman was a wildcat in the throes of passion. She screamed her pleasure at the top of her lungs.

"I can," she insisted, her chest rising and falling with breaths quickened by anticipation.

She continued to stroke him. Which would never do.

Two more minutes of attention from her busy, talented hand, and he'd go off in his drawers.

Grabbing her wrist, he forced her fingers free of him. His silly cock wept at the loss of friction, but he silently promised the silly bugger the reward would be worth the wait.

"I'm going to take your clothes off now, Emily," he told her, not recognizing his own voice. It had dropped three octaves, going low and growly with desire. Not waiting for her acquiescence—the hungry, eager look in her eyes was all the agreement he needed—he whipped her sweatshirt over her head.

Delighted, he watched as her hair spilled out and spread across the stark white pillow. Even in the dim light of the sleeping cabin, it shined with silky health. Usually, she kept it secured in a ponytail or a sloppy bun atop her head. But when she let it down…heaven help him.

Picking up a lock, he held it to his nose and inhaled that sweet, exotic scent that was uniquely her. He didn't know why he confessed what he did then. It simply slipped out of him. "I've been using your shampoo in the shower."

She was pressing a finger into the dimple in his chin, but that had her feathering her fingers through his hair. "You have? I *thought* that bottle was getting empty faster than usual."

"But I haven't been washing my hair with it."

"No?" Her brow puckered. "Then what have you been doing with… *Oh!*"

A dark blush stole onto her cheeks, and he couldn't help his wicked grin. "If I live to be a thousand years old, the smell of your shampoo will make me hard."

"Kinky." She giggled, her breaths coming faster. She *fancied* the thought of him lathering up his hands and having a wank.

"You haven't seen anything yet," he promised, claiming her mouth in another kiss as he undid her bra and slipped it from her shoulders.

Pulling back, he eyed the treasures he'd uncovered. "Ah, Emily. You have the prettiest pink nipples in the whole world. I can't get enough of them."

He bent to take one tender peak into his mouth, enchanted when it furled tighter. She hissed, her hands stabbing into his hair to hold him to her. When he tongued the turgid little nub, she moaned his name, turning to throw a leg over his hip so she could grind herself against his hardness.

"I have a confession too," she whispered when he kissed his way to her other breast.

"What's that, darling?" He closed his mouth over her neglected nipple and caressed it the way she liked. Slowly, with the flat of his tongue.

"I poured a drop of your cologne onto a washcloth," she said, panting. "And then laid it beside me in bed while I used my vibrator."

That had him releasing her nipple. It made a *popping* sound when it slid past the suction of his lips. "You touched yourself and thought of me?"

A sultry grin tilted her lips. "You aren't the only one who's been up for it since the minute I walked through BKI's doors."

He groaned, letting his head fall against her naked shoulder. The thought of her lying in bed, pleasuring herself...

Dear God.

"I want you to introduce me to your vibrator once we're home." He lifted his chin to catch her stare. "I need to know what I'm up against. Take the measure of my competition."

"Believe me"—she reached between them to stroke him again—"there's no comparison. You've got it beat by a mile."

He let her have her way for as long as he could stand it, maybe ten seconds, before he grabbed her wrist and pulled her hand away. Finding her other wrist, he manacled them in one hand and pressed them into the pillow above her head.

"I can't have you touching me." He reached for his belt, quickly undoing it and pulling it from the loops. "I'm too close to the edge already."

"But—"

"No buts." He cut her off, circling his belt around her wrists and cinching it tight.

She pouted prettily, but he could see the excitement in her eyes.

"Now, keep your hands above your head," he instructed, scooting down the bed to attack the laces on her boots. They dropped to the floor within seconds of each other—*thunk, thunk*—and then her socks, leggings, and panties joined them in a heap.

"Please," she begged quietly, writhing on the bed, gloriously, unabashedly naked. "Christian, I don't want to go slow."

"I hear you, darling," he assured her. They'd taken care of foreplay back at the manor. Joining their bodies together now was as necessary as breathing.

Reaching over his head, he pulled off his sweater. Toeing out of his boots, he undid the buttons on his fly and then shucked his drawers and jeans all in one go. His socks joined the pile of clothes on the floor as he knelt on the edge of the bed, grabbed her knees, and spread her legs wide.

She was pink and plump and so deliciously bare that his cock jerked and a hot drop of pre-ejaculate slipped over his swollen head. She saw it and dropped her hands to touch.

"Ah, ah," he scolded, grabbing the loose end of his belt the second before her fingers found him. He lowered himself atop her, pulling her arms back above her head. His heart thudded with joy and impatience. "No touching."

"But I *want* to touch." Her breath was hot and sweet, still smelling of peanut butter and jelly as it feathered over his lips.

"Later," he promised her, loving the feel of her thighs beside his hips. Loving the feel of her soft breasts cushioning his chest. Loving *her*.

He claimed her mouth in a harsh, thorough kiss as he ripped open the condom he'd slid from the pocket of his jeans. Fisting the latex down his length, he felt his stomach muscles contract at the delicious friction. He was close. Too close.

Emily wasn't helping matters by mewling and writhing and returning his kiss with so much enthusiasm that the control in which he took so much pride threatened to shatter.

Breaking the sweet, suctioned seal of their mouths, he pressed up on his elbows and stared down into her passion-glazed eyes. That he could turn the indomitable Emily Scott into a soft, pliant thing filled with want made him ridiculously satisfied and maybe a touch smug.

"Are you ready?" He framed her pretty face with his hands.

"I've been ready," she panted. "Told you that."

"Let's make sure, shall we?"

Reaching between them, he slid two fingers down her silken cleft to find that, indeed, she was slick and swollen and prepared to receive him. When he thumbed over her distended clitoris, she moaned. Pushing one finger deep inside, he was pleased to feel her body suck and grab at him.

Yes. She was most definitely ready.

Gently sliding out his finger, he shushed her when she grumbled her displeasure. "Patience, darling. I've got what you need."

Grabbing the base of his aching cock, he angled it toward her waiting entrance. Then he paused, drawing out the moment, building the anticipation for the instant he would finally, once and for all, claim the woman he loved…

Emily held her breath as Christian pushed slowly, so inexorably slowly inside her.

Had she mentioned he was a rather *large* man? Girthy. Meaty. Each inch into her tightness was a struggle to gain. His jaw was locked down so hard it looked like it could take a hit from a wrecking ball and come out the winner.

"Relax," he grunted. He'd barely made an inch or two of headway.

She nodded, but relaxing was impossible when he was looming above her like a dark angel. When he was pressing into her inch by thick, glorious, *preposterous* inch.

She was stretched tight. Pleasure unlike anything she had experience before bordered on pain.

This'll never work! she thought frantically, her fingers curling around the trailing end of his belt, her nails biting into the leather.

Growling his frustration, he lowered his head and engulfed her nipple in the heat of his mouth. She'd had her chin tipped down, watching the place where they were joined, but that had her head falling back against the pillow, her eyes fluttering shut.

He had the most wicked, wanton inferno of a mouth. It sucked. It laved. It nipped until she was squirming against him, trying to take him deeper, to force him farther so that he would fill the aching, hollow place inside her.

"Be still," he growled around her nipple.

And he thought *she* was bossy?

"Can't," she panted, lifting her legs and pressing her feet into his ass, urging him forward.

Releasing her breast, he cradled her face between his big, callused hands. He looked at her so tenderly. That tenderness was only slightly overshadowed by the frustration that had the muscle ticking beneath his left eye. "You have to relax."

She shook her head against the pillow. "Can't do that either. Please, Christian. Please just—"

He shushed her, taking a few shallow strokes,

swiveling his hips to help soothe straining muscles. Then he shoved forward in one long, glorious glide. When she felt the hot weight of his testicles press against the curve of her ass, she knew he was seated to the hilt.

She cried out in pleasure, in pain, and he placed a hand over her mouth, holding still inside her, so desperately large, so hopelessly hard. She could feel the pulse of him, the beat of his heart echoing in the steely column of flesh filling her to the brim.

She'd done it. She'd taken him. It was heaven. It was hell. It hurt so good.

Only when he'd assured himself that her loud mouth was under control—she hoped to God the noise from the jet engines had drowned out her shout—did he remove his hand and replace it with his lips.

For long minutes, he didn't move, simply allowed her to get used to having him inside her, to let her clenched muscles relax. He smoothed out every wrinkle, touched places she'd never been touched. And eventually, slowly, all her discomfort was overtaken by need.

The need for movement.

The need for friction.

The need for something to assuage the deep, throbbing tension coiled so tightly inside.

"Oh, Christian," she breathed against his mouth, arching her hips into him. "I need—"

She didn't have to say more. He knew what she needed and began to move. It was a subtle retreat that had his hot, hard cock strafing nerves that cried out with joy and then screamed for more, more, *more*!

As he slowly rocked forward, the tip of him pressing forcefully against the entrance to her womb, he lifted his head and held her gaze. Possession glinted in his eyes. A promise of pleasures yet to come.

"Quiet," he warned as he set a rhythm. Slow at first. Testing her. Stretching her. Exciting flesh that gripped him with greedy abandon.

There was no air to breathe. She didn't care. All she cared about was the man above her. The man inside her. She wanted...she *needed* to touch him. To hold him. Without a doubt, this was the hottest sex she'd ever had. But it also felt undeniably intimate. Which scared her a little. And excited her a lot.

"Please untie my hands." The plea was out of her mouth before she realized she'd meant to say it. "I want to touch you."

Reaching up with one hand, he undid the buckle and tossed his belt aside.

Free from her restraints, she traced the hard bulge of his shoulders, let her fingers trail down the groove his back muscles created of his spine, and stopped at the hard, puckered scar on his back where the round he'd taken to the gut during the shoot-out at the Iraqi road-block had gone through his body.

When she lightly followed its dimension with her fingertips, he trembled and stopped moving above her. Instead, he dropped his lips to her neck to place a hot, openmouthed kiss against her pulse point.

He'd suffered so much in his life. Too much. And yet it hadn't broken him or hardened him. Through it all, he had managed to stay tough yet tender, strong yet sweet.

Yes, *sweet*. Because as surly and grumpy and gruff as he could be, the truth was he'd never treated her with anything less than gentleness. No matter how she'd teased him or wheedled him, he'd never made her feel disrespected or dismissed.

All those bright, sparkly feelings coalesced and fused inside her. She felt the *boom* of their atomic explosion deep in her chest. Tears pricked traitorously behind her eyes.

It was too much. *He* was too much.

"Emily," he whispered, pushing up on his forearms. His bright eyes cut though the gloom of the sleeping compartment like laser beams, and the white of the bandage against his black tattoos stood out in fierce contrast. "I—"

He cut himself off.

"What?" she prompted, turning to kiss the scar on the inside of his forearm, hoping her lips eased the pain that had stayed with him all these years.

He groaned, his eyelids fluttering shut. When he opened them again, she saw something she didn't recognize, some strange emotion shining back at her. "Nothing," he whispered, shaking his head.

She would have pressed him further, but she was too preoccupied with the need for him to move. He *had* to start moving again. Nothing had ever felt so delicious as when he was moving above her, within her.

He claimed her mouth in a kiss that turned her thoughts formless. They became nothing more than golden, glorious blobs that pulsed like drumbeats. And then… Oh, and then he began to thrust again. Slow at first. Then building the momentum.

His tongue surged into her mouth in rhythm to the beat of his body. Her hands curled around the hard, firm globes of his ass as his hips pistoned in long, purposeful jabs that pushed her pleasure ever higher.

Cries built in the back of her throat and were caught in the heat of his mouth. She grabbed his shoulders, her nails biting into his tough, tattooed flesh, and held on for dear life. He grunted her name over and over again, his voice guttural, barely human, and in complete contrast to his usual cultured, controlled words.

And then it happened. He grabbed her knee, pulling her leg up high against his flank, changing the angle of his thrusts. The pull and push of his rigid flesh became too much. Her sheath tightened as her heart swelled.

No, no, no. Not her heart. It couldn't be her heart. It had to be—

He shortened his strokes, quickened his hips, and shocked her into taking the plunge. Suddenly, she was weightless and falling, pleasure unlike anything she had ever known exploding through her in a series of bright, incandescent blasts.

Her first contraction triggered his release. His back bowed, straining, he locked himself inside her, and the pulse of him drove her orgasm to new heights. She must've screamed his name, because he put his hand over her mouth. He was definitely yelling her name, so she slapped *her* hand over *his* mouth. Locked together, they stroked and strove to wring the last ounce of pleasure from each other's bodies.

Eventually, they collapsed in a heap. For long moments all they could do was try to catch their breath as the wonder and glory of what they'd done hit Emily. Being with Christian was unlike anything she'd ever known. It was profound. Intense.

After what seemed like hours, he pressed a tender

kiss to the bruise on her temple, still so hard and large inside her.

Cupping her face, he used his thumb to tilt up her chin. For a second, he simply held her wondering gaze. Then he whispered the three words she never wanted to hear from him. "I love you."

Everything inside her that had been hot and gooey froze into a solid block of ice.

I'm the world's biggest fool.

That single thought circled 'round and 'round in Christian's head as Emily pushed at his shoulders, demanding, "Damnit, Christian! Get off me!"

With reluctance, he rolled onto his side. Slipping from the heat and tight comfort of her body was agony. Knowing this first time he was with her might very well be the last time was even worse.

Why had he said that?

Oh right. Because what they'd done together was unlike anything he'd ever experienced. It hadn't only been shagging. It'd been love. They'd made *love*. *He'd* made love for the first time in his life, and it'd been radiant, soul touching. He was changed for it. And he'd thought...

He'd thought she was too. He'd been sure he'd seen love shining up at him from her dark, slumberous eyes. Sure he'd tasted it in the hungry sweetness of her kisses. Sure he'd felt it in the way she touched him, lovingly smoothing her fingers and lips over all his scars, and then holding him like she never wanted to let them go. Like she was trying to crawl inside him to become part of him once and for all. Like she'd allowed *him* to crawl inside her, to make a place for himself in her heart.

I'm the world's biggest fool.

She shoved into a seated position, glaring down at him. Her hair was a rumpus of crazy waves, her skin still flushed pink with exertion and passion.

"Please tell me that was a knee-jerk reaction." Her breath sawed from her, causing her chest to rise and fall, guaranteeing his eyes remained glued to her pretty breasts. "Tell me that you say that to all the women you sleep with because…because…I don't know *why* you'd say that, but—"

"I've never said it to anyone else," he interrupted her. He could have lied, he supposed. He could have grabbed on to the lifeline she'd tossed him and pretended that what he'd said meant nothing. Perhaps if he were a smarter man he would have.

Take it back, she begged with her eyes.

I can't, he silently told her with a shake of his head.

There was so much anguish in her voice when she whispered, "You promised," that something hard and sharp settled in the center of his chest.

He hadn't meant to hurt her. He *never* wanted to hurt her.

"You made me promise I wouldn't *fall* in love with you, but it was too late. I was already *in* love with you, so technically I—"

"Seriously?" She cut him off, reaching for her clothes. "You're going to play the semantics game with me now?"

"Emily, please listen to me." He laid a hand against the smooth, narrow line of her back.

"No." She batted his fingers away and shrugged into her bra. Her panties came next as he curled his hands into fists so tight his blunt nails cut into the skin of his palms.

After she pulled on her leggings and sweatshirt, she turned to him. Her eyes ran over his face, his chest, and lower.

"For the love of Alexei Ramirez, cover that thing up." She tossed his sweater over his hips, effectively covering his cock. He was still mostly hard. Even though he'd experienced one of the most—no, it'd been *the* most devastating orgasm of his life—he hadn't had enough. He would never have enough. Not when it came to her. "It's distracting as hell," she finished.

"Emily, please let me explain." He dutifully held his sweater over his dick.

"Right. Yes." She nodded a little frantically. "Please explain to me *when* exactly you did all this falling in love. Was it when you were telling me I was as vexing as a housefly? Was it when I woke you from your nightmare? Was it when I was sitting on your lap in the truck? *When?*"

He shrugged. "There wasn't a specific look or a certain touch or a definite place or moment. By the time I realized what'd happened, I was already ass over teakettle."

He was digging himself in deeper. He knew it. Yet, he couldn't stop.

"How could you do this to me?" She covered her face with her hands. "How could you let me put my job on the line when you knew—"

"Emily." He cut her off, pulling one hand away from her face. "I would *never* put your job on the line. I would *never* jeopardize what you've found, the *family* you've found at BKI. If you don't feel the same about me, then I—"

"I *don't*," she swore a bit too forcefully.

Those two words were hatchet strikes to his heart, but at the same time, he couldn't help but think, *The lady doth protest too much*.

"Fine," he told her. "That's fine. Forget I said it then. We'll simply carry on as we are, and when—"

"Are you *crazy*?" she shouted, and he flicked a furtive glance at the curtain, wondering how much of this conversation his teammates and Rusty were overhearing. "We can't *carry on as we are*!" She mimicked his accent. Badly, as usual. "We have to stop everything!"

"If that's your wish."

She pulled at her hair. "No, you big idiot! That's *not* my wish! My *wish* is that you'd never opened your mouth so we could keep doing…" She made a rolling motion with her hand toward the bed. "Because it was just about the greatest thing ever. No!" She pointed at his face. "Wipe away that smug smile right this minute because…because…" She threw her hands in the air. "Because you've ruined *everything*!"

And with that, she grabbed her boots, tossed aside the curtain, and stomped out of the sleeping compartment.

Christian flung himself back against the mattress with a sigh. *I'm the world's biggest fool*. It was his new mantra.

He should have kept his sodding mouth shut. He should have stuck with the plan to seduce her night after night, to love her day after day, until eventually she realized she loved him too. And she *did* love him.

He hadn't imagined their connection, hadn't imagined the look in her eyes or the way she held him. She was simply scared. Scared to take the leap. Scared to give in. Scared because growing up she'd had nothing but bloody *awful* examples of what romantic love was meant to be.

So, right-oh. It was a setback for sure. He'd lost this battle, but he was determined to win the war.

A plan began to take shape. A *new* plan. Before long, he was smiling…

Chapter 23

Black Knights Inc.
Chicago, Illinois
One month later...

EMILY HAD A HEADACHE PULSING BEHIND HER EYES. INSTEAD of Advil, she planned to kick it in the teeth with some good old-fashioned whiskey.

It'd been almost four weeks since they'd returned from England, and in all that time, they hadn't been able to determine *who* had given Christian's information to the English reporters. Meaning they were no closer to determining Spider's identity than they'd been before setting foot on British soil. All the Black Knights were cranky and on edge because of it, stomping around the shop, snarling at each other and every bit of Intel that came in revealing another stinking pile of nada. Which was one of three contributing factors to her headache.

Big alpha males in a pique were taxing, to say the least. Downright *irritating*, to say the most.

Also, they'd discovered the Michelson brothers had been police officers, and that Lawrence, in particular, had suffered from anger issues. Seems he'd had many complaints registered against him concerning the use of excessive force and had been written up more than a time or two for being involved in barroom brawls outside work.

Emily had no doubt that had Christian not stopped Lawrence with a bullet to the skull, Lawrence would have ended up severely hurting or killing someone. So even though there wasn't enough brain bleach in the world to scour away the memory of Lawrence's head bursting like a melon, she couldn't drum up much sympathy for the guy, especially when she added all she knew of him now to the simple fact that he'd shown up at the manor house to, you know, kill them.

The BBC had run with the story of the dead brothers for the first couple of weeks after it happened. Since they were cops, their weapons' ballistics were in the UK database. It hadn't taken long for investigators to discover that Ben's gun had been used to shoot the private jet pilot at Cornwall Airport at Newquay and Lawrence's gun had been the one to off Lawrence himself. But exactly *what* had happened to precipitate either of those events was a giant question mark.

There was some speculation that Lawrence and Ben had gotten involved with shady individuals, and they'd been murdered for the association—Lawrence's reputation didn't do him any favors with some in the press. Others hypothesized that Ben and Lawrence Michelson had stumbled upon a crime scene or some sort of criminal activity and had paid with their lives for being in the wrong place at the wrong time.

However, without any video footage or forensic evidence, the case remained unsolved. Which was good, because there was nothing to point to the Black Knights having been in England. It was also *bad*, because Emily wasn't allowed to call in that anonymous tip about the whereabouts of the farm truck. They'd decided it was too risky to add one more clue to an ongoing investigation.

She couldn't help but worry that the truck's owner was suffering its loss. That was the *second* contributing factor for her headache.

So what's the third? you might ask.

Well, that was easy.

The third was big, tattooed, and named Christian Watson. He had embarked on a campaign of emotional persuasion and physical seduction the likes of which she wouldn't have dreamed possible.

True to his word, he hadn't caused any trouble for her at BKI. In fact, he'd made sure everyone knew that he was in love with her and that she didn't feel the same way about him. He'd announced this at the flippin' *meeting* they'd had after landing in Chicago. He'd gone on to say that everyone needed to understand that him loving Emily and Emily not loving him wouldn't affect their working relationship, and that it was his problem to deal with. Emily was an innocent party, yada yada yada, holy shit!

Then, as if all that wasn't horrible enough—or remarkable enough; she hadn't decided which—he'd gone about his daily grind like nothing had happened between them. He still teased her, still taunted her, still scowled those delicious scowls and twinkled those amazing eyes. Which was all completely head-spinning and conviction-killing. But to make matters worse, he *touched* her. All. The. Time.

A kiss on the cheek and a cheerful *Good morning, darling* when she stumbled into the kitchen at the butt crack of dawn, bleary-eyed and in search of copious

amounts of coffee after a night tossing and turning and
dreaming about him. A pat on the back for making sure
the toner ink was full in the printer or ordering extra
boxes of the sticky notes he liked to write lists on. An
arm thrown around her chair when they sat in their daily
situation report meeting, his callused fingers toying with
the ends of her hair, occasionally giving her shoulder
a squeeze.

She tried to avoid sitting next to him, but everyone
at BKI seemed to be on Christian's side. They inevita-
bly left a space open for him beside her at the conference table.

It was maddening! Infuriating! Totally and undeniably...charming. *Ugh!*

Every kind, teasing word or covert look or gentle
touch increased her bright, sparkly feelings a hundred-
fold. It was getting out of hand. *She* was getting out of
hand, because twice in the last week she'd found herself
standing outside his door in the middle of the night,
hand raised to knock, ready and willing to throw caution to the wind.

Something had to give.

Right then, that something was her headache.

She skidded to a stop in the doorway to the kitchen.
It was located on the bottom floor of the old menthol
cigarette factory that'd been turned into the motorcycle
shop, covert defense firm, and living quarters for many
members of Black Knights Inc. The room was airy and
bright. Big, industrial-size appliances, a long marble
center island, and exposed brick walls gave it a loft-like
feel—much like the apartments on the third floor.

Sitting on the center island was Delilah McMillan.

Her husband, Mac, was standing between her legs, passionately kissing the living shit out of her and reminding Emily that it'd been a long time—four weeks in fact—since anyone had kissed *her* like that.

Clearing her throat, she waited for the pair to realize they had an unwilling audience. Fido, the couple's yellow Labrador retriever—who was never far from Delilah's side and currently lying on the tile floor at Mac's feet—lifted his furry head, blinked at Emily with big, chocolate eyes, and yawned loudly as if to say, *This happens all the time, lady. Don't get your panties in a twist*.

Apparently, Delilah and Mac were too caught up to notice her. In fact, Mac's hand stole up to squeeze Delilah's boob, and Emily decided she better speak up or else find herself a spectator at a real-life, live-action porno.

"Don't you two have an apartment above the bar you can do that in?" she grumbled irritably, referring to Red Delilah's Biker Bar. The Black Knights' favorite hangout and watering hole was owned and operated by, you guessed it, Delilah. "Or if that's too far to go, don't you still have a room upstairs, Mac?"

The couple broke apart, Delilah looking flushed and guilty, Mac looking absurdly pleased with himself. The two of them couldn't be more opposite. Mac hailed from the Lone Star State and had a face as craggy and wide open as Texas. Delilah on the other hand? Well, to put it simply, she was beautiful. Long, dark, auburn hair, amazing green eyes, and an hourglass figure to make Christina Hendrix envious.

Delilah quickly recovered her composure and arched a sleek brow in Emily's direction. "That sounded jealous, if you ask me."

"I didn't ask you." Emily was quick with the comeback, her headache grabbing a jackhammer and going to work on the foundation of her brain.

"Definitely jealous." Mac, the dickweed, concurred with his wife.

Deciding that arguing would get her nowhere, Emily pushed away from the doorjamb, skirted around Fido and his grinning asshole masters, and made her way to the bar cart kept near the back door. The entire journey took no more than five seconds. But during those five seconds, she had time to grumble a whole diatribe under her breath about everyone at Black Knights Inc. rubbing their happily ever afters in her face.

Once she made it to her destination, she grabbed a rocks glass and a bottle of rye whiskey. A quick trip to the refrigerator had her glass half full of ice cubes. Next came the simple syrup, the bitters, a generous pour of whiskey, and two cherries to top it off.

"Who taught you to make an old-fashioned?" Delilah asked.

"My mother." Emily made a face. "One of the few truly useful things I ever learned from her. Cheers." She took a healthy slug of the drink, letting the whiskey burn down her throat as the sugar tingled on her taste buds.

Mac made a show of glancing at his watch. "It's only sixteen hundred." He had a deep Sam Elliott drawl that Emily usually found charming. Not today.

"Oh yeah?" She shot him a look that unequivocally stated, *Mind your own business, or I'll cut off your balls*. "Well, it's five o'clock somewhere."

To prove her point, she gulped down another mouthful.

Mac mock-whispered to Delilah. "Someone's in a mood."

Emily's fingers inched toward the knife on the bar cart that they used to cut fruit for drinks. The man had no idea, but his balls were in serious jeopardy.

"I'm not in a *mood*," she lied. She *was* in a mood. She'd *been* in a mood since England. "I have a headache."

"Most people fight those with aspirin," Delilah said oh-so-helpfully.

"Sure." Emily nodded. "But the trouble with aspirin is it doesn't do a damn thing to take my mind off my long list of woes. But this?" She held up her half-empty rocks glass. "This'll do both."

"And by *woes*"—Delilah made air quotes—"are we talking Christian?" She hopped down from the center island, and Emily saw Mac lick his lips when Delilah's boobs bounced.

Emily wanted to label him an oversexed asshole, but the guy had a marriage certificate that pretty much said he had the right to ogle Delilah at will. Plus, Delilah had a pair of bazoombas that were hard *not* to stare at. Even had Delilah not used the C-word, Emily would have been annoyed at her for that reason alone. Emily's own barely B cups seemed to cave in on themselves in intimidation.

"Ugh." She plunked her drink atop the bar cart, making the liquor bottles and glassware rattle. Fido lifted his head from his front paws again, eyeing her curiously. "Just because *he's* suffering under some insane delusion that he loves me—"

"You reckon it's really a delusion?" Mac interrupted, casually throwing an arm around Delilah's shoulders.

"Because I know the signs of a man in love, and Christian? Well, he seems to show all of 'em."

"*Psshh*." Emily waved a dismissive hand. "I think you're mistaking *love* for *lust*. The man can't love me because he doesn't even *like* me. We argue all the time. He thinks I'm annoying."

"Mmm." Delilah wrapped an arm around Mac's waist. "Isn't it fun arguing and annoying each other? Adds spice, doesn't it?"

Emily assumed Delilah was talking to her, but Mac answered, "*So* much spice."

Mac stared at Delilah with such blatant hunger that Emily was forced to roll her eyes. "Gag me." Deciding the conversation had gone crazily off course, she tried to steer them back on track. "The *woes* I'm talking about have to do with the stalemate in our mission to uncover Spider's true identity and the fact that it's making everyone around this place snarky, short-tempered, and complete pains in my ass. Ever tried to manage an office overrun with a bunch of hardass dudes who possess too much testosterone?"

Delilah's expression turned compassionate. "Can't say that I have. But aren't we supposed to hear back from Samantha's contact soon?"

Samantha Tate was a go-getter journalist for the *Chicago Tribune*, Ozzie's fiancée, and their last hope to nail down Spider's identity. She was friends with a fellow investigative reporter in England. He'd been away, covering the ongoing crisis in Syria for the last month, but he was finally back on British soil. Samantha had tapped him to try to hunt down *who* had given Christian's name to his colleagues.

"Tomorrow at the earliest." Emily nodded. "End of the week at the latest. Plenty of time for the men in this place to drive me completely insane."

"Poor you," Delilah commiserated. "But maybe it'll help take your mind off things if you head out front. I hear there's a show going on."

Emily wrinkled her brow. "Show? What kind of show?"

Before Delilah could answer, BKI's overweight, notch-eared tomcat, Peanut, slunk into the kitchen with the sort of nose-in-the-air arrogance that could only be pulled off by a feline. The cat taunted Fido by strolling past the dog with his crooked tail high in the air. Fido, being a big, dumb mutt, took the bait and sniffed Peanut's butt. In turn, the tomcat hissed and swiped at Fido's nose with a clawed paw.

Then it was on. The pair broke into a chase around the kitchen island, complete with happy barks on Fido's part and irritated yowls on Peanut's part. Emily's headache ratcheted up another notch.

"That's my cue." She grabbed her drink and headed out of the kitchen, leaving Delilah and Mac to deal with the canine-feline catastrophe that was underway.

Exiting the long hall leading from the kitchen into the custom motorcycle shop, Emily noticed that one of the big, rolling garage doors was open. Delilah had piqued her curiosity, so she headed toward it, past the bike lifts, the tool chests, and the line of gleaming custom choppers. The air inside the shop smelled of grease, hot metal, and strong coffee, but the warm spring breeze beckoned her outside.

High in the afternoon sky, the sun cast short shadows across the front expanse of the property. Black

Knights Inc. was set on half a city block, surrounded by a ten-foot brick wall and populated with the old foreman's cottage out front, the large factory building in the center, and a bunch of recently added outbuildings around the back.

It was quite something, actually. The place. The people. All living and working undercover in the heart of the Windy City. Emily felt a sense of home, a sense of *belonging*, and couldn't help but thank Christian for making sure nothing that'd happened between them had jeopardized that for her.

He was a man of his word. A man of honor, courage, loyalty, and strength. She couldn't deny the presence of all those bright, sparkly feelings whenever she thought of him. Whenever she—

Oh, for the love of Frank Thomas!

She was going to kill Delilah.

A show? Seriously?

Emily wasn't seeing a show. She was seeing an ovary-exploding, panty-slicking display the likes of which should be outlawed. She was sorely tempted to call the local police to put an end to it. You know, for the safety of women's reproductive organs and underwear the world over.

Christian was washing his Porsche. A bucket of soap sat on the ground. A big sponge dripped suds in his hand. The lazy yellow sun glinted off his dark hair and bare shoulders.

That's right. *Bare* shoulders.

Christian Watson wasn't just washing his car. Christian Watson was washing his car…shirtless.

The muscles in his tattooed arms flexed and bunched

as he scrubbed at the hood of the Porsche. Tiny droplets of water—or sweat—clung to his pecs. And his six-pack abs accordioned as he stretched across the vehicle to scrub at a recalcitrant spot.

Emily realized two things simultaneously. One, she wasn't alone in enjoying "the show." Two, her mouth was hanging open. Both things became apparent when Becky, BKI's head mechanic and motorcycle designer, and the woman who kept all their covers intact, said, "I think you dropped something, Em. It looks a lot like your jaw."

Emily snapped her teeth shut and turned to see Becky and Penni leaning up against the side of the shop, eyeing Christian with undisguised appreciation. Becky was in her usual coveralls, a grease smudge on her cheek, the ends of her long, blond ponytail dark because she'd inadvertently dragged it through a patch of oil. And Penni, a former Secret Service agent and current wife to BKI badass Dan "The Man" Currington, was bouncing her baby girl on her hip and not attempting to hide her smirk.

Emily mumbled something unkind about both women even as she joined them. Christian didn't bother pretending she wasn't there. When she settled back against the shop's brick exterior, fortifying herself with another swig of old-fashioned, he lifted his head and gave her a wink. The smile that accompanied that wink was slightly mischievous—and completely lecherous. It did naughty things to her, making her tingle in places that had no business tingling now that she'd been forced to put the kibosh on their—

"Is it just me," Penni said conversationally, "or

should that man immediately be inducted into the Hall of Fine?"

"It isn't just you," Becky was quick to concur. "Who knew all that"—she motioned toward Christian with one grease-stained hand—"was hiding under those designer clothes?" Turning to Emily, she took a grape-flavored Dum Dum lollipop from her pocket and pointed the treat at Emily's nose. "So what do you reckon? Are we looking at a case of the body snatchers or is he a replicant?"

"Huh?" Emily frowned, trying—and failing—to rip her eyes away from Christian.

"The guy wouldn't wear short sleeves a month ago, and now he's going shirtless. So what gives?"

A campaign of emotional persuasion and physical seduction, Emily thought, calling Christian every dirty name in the book because, truth was, his plan was *working*.

"Being in love with her has changed him," Penni mused. "He's less repressed. More willing to let his hair down."

"And take his shirt *off*," Becky added with a chuckle.

"Praise Jesus." Penni nodded.

"Amen."

Emily attempted to burn their eyebrows off with her scowl. "Don't you two have husbands you should be ogling instead of Christian?"

Becky grinned. "Why, Emily, that sounded a little jealous."

"Definitely jealous," Penni agreed.

"Ugh!" Emily tossed a hand in the air. "Why does everyone keep *saying* that? Did you all have a meeting or something? Did you get together to come up with ways to drive me bugfucking crazy?"

"Language, please." Penni covered little Cora May's ears.

Emily frowned at the baby, but kept it to herself that Cora May was too young to know a bug from a bunny or a bad word from a battle cry.

"And a word of advice," Penni added, pushing away from the wall. As she passed Emily to head back inside the shop, she leaned close and whispered, "Not for nothing"—her Brooklyn accent made it sound more like *not for nuttin'*—"but it's easier to give in. They always win in the end anyway. Fighting only prolongs the inevitable and makes you miserable in the interim."

Emily scowled at her retreating back before turning to tell Becky that Penni didn't know what the hell she was talking about. Unfortunately, Becky beat her to the punch by saying, "She's right, you know." Then Becky also breezed past Emily and ducked into the shop.

Okay, it was official. This was the day from hell and—

Emily nearly swallowed her tongue when Christian suddenly appeared in front of her. Had he gotten taller? Broader? He blocked out the sun, and the heat of him reached for her like sensual, invisible hands.

Plucking one of the cherries from her glass, he popped it into his mouth. Watching him eat it would have been a huge turn-on if she was allowing herself to think of him in sexual terms. Which she wasn't. She *wasn't*! Case closed.

"What were those two going on about?" he asked, tilting his head toward the open garage door.

The wonder that is your glorious self, she thought sourly. Aloud she said, "Nothing important."

He did that humming thing, and it hit her directly in the uterus. *Damnit!*

"Well, I'm off to make myself another drink." She pushed away from the brick wall.

He glanced down at her glass. "Isn't it quite early to be getting pissed?"

"Two things." She held up one finger. "One, don't judge me." Up went a second finger. "And two, it's medicinal. I have a headache."

"You know…" He leaned in close, putting a hand against the wall beside her head. "I've heard hot, sweaty sex is a miracle cure for headaches. Something about the endorphins it releases."

An image of him tying her to his bed, then looming above her all huge and dominant, had her breath sawing from her lungs. Despite her silent admonishments to them, her nipples tightened.

Christian seemed to know the effect his words had on her because… Yep. There it was. That self-satisfied grin.

He was too close. He smelled too good. She had to get away from him, like, *now*. Five minutes ago.

"For crying out loud." She ducked under his arm. "Get over yourself. And while you're at it, put on a damn shirt!"

His deep chuckle followed Emily into the shop, where she pressed herself against the wall and realized she was shaking with need, with hunger, with the urge to give in to him and all those bright, sparkly feelings.

"Still trying to convince yourself you're not in love with Christian?" Boss asked, coming down the metal stairs from the second floor. He had a face only a mother—and Becky—could love. It was big and square and puckered with scars. Even so, his thick, dark hair and piercing gray eyes somehow combined to make him oddly handsome.

"I'm *not* in love with him." Emily wasn't sure who she was trying to convince. Herself or Boss.

Boss didn't argue, simply shook his head and turned down the hallway that led to the kitchen.

"I'm *not*!" she yelled at his broad back.

All she received in reply was the wave of his hand.

Letting her head fall back against the wall, Emily battled her headache and all the mixed-up, jumbled-up, crazy-making feelings banging around inside her. "I'm not," she whispered to herself, wincing because, even to her own ears, it sounded like a lie.

Chapter 24

THE PITTER-PATTER OF LITTLE FEET...

It wasn't the first night Christian had heard Emily shuffle up to his door. But it was the first night he wasn't going to wait around, heart in his throat, for her to knock.

It'd been hell—but also quite fun—to watch her struggle to resist him these past four weeks. Every teasing remark or quiet conversation only had him wanting more. Every gentle touch or fleeting caress had him fighting the urge to yank her into his arms and kiss her until she begged him never to stop. Every longing, hungry look she shot him—and there were quite a few—had him curling his hands into fists to keep from yelling at her, "You know you want me! You know you love me! Quit fighting and just give in, you daft, dear, damnably infuriating woman!"

But he'd surprised himself by showing the patience of Job. In fact, his restraint up to this point was worthy of a medal. Unfortunately for Emily, tonight he'd reached his wit's end.

Time to press the issue, he thought, a feeling of anticipation tightening his chest. *Time to give her the nudge she needs*.

Quietly, he tossed aside his covers, tugged on a pair of jeans, and walked to his bedroom door. He was still doing up the buttons on his fly when he opened the door and found her standing at his threshold in the dark hallway. When she sucked in a startled breath, he was beyond delighted.

The lamp burning on his bedside table gave off enough light to show her eyes quickly tracing over his naked torso and lingering on the trail of hair that started below his belly button. When she unconsciously licked her lips, his cock—which was always an overeager prat when it came to her—jerked with interest.

"Fancy coming in for a bit?" He held the door wide.

She darted a look into his room, saw his king-size bed with the rumpled sheets, and blushed to the roots of her hair.

Nodding, she then quickly shook her head. "No, I…" She swallowed. "I was just…"

He lifted a brow, loving that she was discombobulated. "You were just…what?"

Her eyebrows slammed into a scowl. "So you're going to spend the rest of your life shirtless, is that it?"

He leaned against the doorjamb, crossing his arms over his chest and not missing the moment her eyes alighted on the bulge of his bicep. It was difficult not to shoot a hand of victory in the air when she gulped and seemed to have trouble meeting his gaze.

"You're lucky I put on trousers, darling." He made sure to thicken his accent. He knew what it did to her. "I sleep in the nude."

Her eyes slipped to the waistband of his jeans. He didn't need to hear her say the word *commando*. It was written all over her face. She gulped again, and he wondered if he'd ever heard a more gratifying sound.

My name on her lips when I make her come, he decided. *That* was definitely more gratifying.

It took everything he had not to pull her into his room. She was adorable in her silk sleep pants, ratty pullover, and hair going every which way. The bruises on her neck and temple had long since faded, and with them had gone his anguish over what had happened in Cornwall.

Not that he didn't still have regrets. He always would. He wished with his whole heart that things had been different. But he'd come to accept that they *hadn't* been different, and given that, he'd taken the only action he could.

"Emily?" He lifted a brow. "This is the third night I've heard you standing outside my door, so is there something you feel you need to tell me?"

Not that he wasn't perfectly pleased standing there, letting her ogle him. And she *was* ogling. *Score one for Christian!* But with each passing second, it was becoming more and more impossible to keep his hands to himself.

"Huh?" She chewed on her bottom lip. "Oh right." She nodded vigorously. "There *is* something I want to tell you. I'm…" She looked around as if she was searching for the answer. "I'm *mad* at you!"

That had his chin jerking back.

"I'm mad that you told everyone you love me and now they're on *your* side. I'm mad that you're being so"—she waved a hand in his direction—"*nice* and accommodating and acting like nothing has changed between us. I'm mad that you keep *touching* me and making me remember all that was and all that *should* have been, had you not gotten all delusional and started thinking you're in love with me."

By the time she got to the end, she was breathing

hard, her small breasts rising and falling against the cotton of her pullover.

A door down the hallway opened, and Ozzie poked his head out. His mad-scientist hair was even crazier than usual. "Hey!" he hissed. "Keep it down out here!"

Never one to pass up an opportunity to cut Ozzie down, Christian said, "You, sir, look like a *before* picture."

Trading insults was one of Ozzie and Christian's favorite pastimes, so Christian wasn't at all surprised when Ozzie came back with, "And *you*, sir, are depriving some poor village of its idiot. But that's neither here nor there, because Samantha and I are trying to get romantic, and it's hard when we have to listen to you two."

Samantha appeared beside Ozzie in the open doorway. She was wearing a robe, but it was obvious by the beard burn on her cheeks and chin that Ozzie wasn't kidding about the "getting romantic" part.

"Yeah!" She scowled at Christian and Emily. "What *he* said!"

Without another word, they ducked back into their room and slammed the door.

When Christian returned his attention to Emily, he found her blinking rapidly. Her blush had deepened to crimson, making the beauty mark on her cheek stand out in sharp relief.

"That's it. In you go." He grabbed her arm and tugged her into his room.

Squeaking her protest, she dug in her heels. Considering he outweighed her by about six stone, the effort was laughable. Closing the door behind her, he marched her over to the chair he kept in the corner.

"Hey!" She slapped at his hands as he pressed her into the seat. "Stop manhandling me, you big bully!"

"Sit!" He pointed a finger at her pert nose. "Stay!"

"And now you're gonna treat me like a dog?" Her South Side accent was back in full effect.

He didn't realize how mad he was that she'd called his love of her delusional until right that minute. "I'm hardly treating you like a dog, Emily. I'm treating you like a woman who insulted the bloody *hell* out of me."

"What?" She wrinkled her nose. "How did *I* insult *you*?"

"Number one"—he held up a finger—"I didn't tell everyone here that I love you so they'd get on my side. I told them because it's impossible to keep secrets in this place. Everyone was bound to find out we'd slept together, and I didn't want anyone to get the wrong idea and give you poppycock about it."

He thrust up a second finger. "Number two, I'm nice and accommodating and acting as if nothing has changed between us because nothing *has*. You're still you, adorable and bossy and altogether infuriating. And I'm still me, single-minded and stubborn and completely barmy about you.

"Number three." Up went a third finger. "If me touching you makes you remember all that we shared and all we could *still* be sharing if you'd only pull your head out of your ass, then that's your problem, not mine. I'm not the one who put a stop to our lovemaking. *You* did that."

By the time he raised his fourth finger, he was shaking with barely repressed fury. "And last but not least, I am not suffering some *delusion* about being in love with you. I *am* in love with you. End of story. And that you would belittle it by brushing it off and saying it's less than it is makes me want to box your ears until your head rattles!"

He hadn't realized he'd been pacing until he came to a stop in front of her. His heart thundered. His chest rose and fell with each livid breath. And seeing her staring up at him with those wide, dark eyes, her mouth open in a shocked *O*, had him fighting the urge to kiss the shit out of her.

Instead, he blew out a calming sigh and said, "You're not mad at me, Emily. You want me, but feel you can't have me. There's a difference."

She stood up. "I *can't* have you! Because if what you say is true and you really do love me—"

"I do."

"Then continuing to sleep with you would make me a horrible person!"

He cocked his head. "Why? Says who?"

"Says me!" She hooked a thumb toward her chest, and he saw her hand was shaking. Brilliant. He didn't want to be the only one having difficulty controlling his emotions. "It wouldn't be right."

He crossed his arms over his chest, smirking when her eyes pinged down to his pecs and then ran over his tattoos before returning to his face. "Why wouldn't it be right? Haven't you ever heard of friends with benefits?"

"You don't just want to be my friend."

"True." He nodded. "I want to be much more than that. But if I can't have it, I'll settle for being your coworker, your lover if you'll have me, and the man who provides a positive male role model for the two children you want to have. Because here's the deal, Emily. For the longest time, I dreaded the thought of BKI going civilian. Like I told you, I tried the Joe Bloggs gig and it didn't work. I thought my soul was too violent, too barbaric. And I thought without the madness that is the spec-ops life keeping me distracted, I'd get sucked back into my past. But loving you has changed me. Made me realize I've no need for an outlet for the intensity inside me. All I need is you. I'm someone else when we're together. Someone more…like my true self. And I would rather be your friend forever, with or without benefits, than a stranger to you for even one day."

A muscle worked in her jaw. Was it him, or were her eyes overly bright?

"Why do you have to be so…so…" She swallowed and shook her head.

"So what?"

"*Wonderful!*" she yelled, then ran from the room, slamming the door behind her.

For a couple of seconds, he blinked at the space she had occupied. Then a slow grin spread across his face. His mind drifted back to the big yellow bed in the manor house and her charming impersonation of the silly sheriff on *The Dukes of Hazzard*. Like Rosco P. Coltrane, Christian was in hot pursuit. But it wasn't a '69 Dodge Charger he was after; it was Emily's admission that she was in love with him.

If he could get her to say the words, she would be his forever.

The next day, Emily looked at the empty chair beside her and then around at the half-full conference table.

She scowled because even if the table had been *completely* full, there still would have been a vacant seat next to her.

It was a conspiracy. She was convinced of it. Trouble was, she wasn't even mad about it anymore. She'd come to *expect* the empty chair.

"So what did you and Christian get up to last night?" Samantha asked from beside Emily.

"Nothing." She was pleased to note her voice sounded smooth and convincing.

Samantha stuck out her bottom lip. "That's too bad. I was certain you and Christian—"

"Stop saying *you and Christian*," Emily interrupted, feeling like a rattlesnake at a petting zoo, poised and ready to strike anyone or anything that came her way.

She'd been ill-tempered and peevish ever since England. But today she was particularly irritable because last night she'd come to the startling conclusion that Christian was right. She *did* want him. But more than that, she *loved* him. There was no other name to give all those bright, sparkly feelings.

Unfortunately, realizing she loved him changed nothing. She was still a Scott and a bad bet when it came to romance, at least the long-lasting kind. Which meant she wouldn't act on her feelings out of kindness to Christian—you know, in case they disappeared some day—and out of fear that if that day ever came, she'd put everything she'd worked so hard for in jeopardy.

"There *is* no me and Christian," she added, perhaps a bit too forcefully.

"Like I said"—Samantha shrugged—"that's too bad. And stop trying to kill me with a look. I'm not that easily intimidated. Besides, if you don't cut it out, your face might get stuck that way."

Emily sighed. As a fellow South Sider, Samantha was immune to Emily's usual 'hood-girl tactics. On the one hand, a pity. On the other, it was nice to have someone with whom to talk White Sox baseball and to share the best places to get deep dish.

Deciding her best bet at self-preservation was to change the subject completely, Emily said, "So what's with the impromptu meeting?"

They'd had their sit-rep at 8:00 a.m. It was now 7:00 p.m. Most of the Black Knights had gone home, at least those who didn't still live on the premises. So the only people sitting around the conference table were Ozzie and Samantha, Ace and Rusty, Angel, Becky, Boss, and...

Right on cue, Christian strolled into the conference area. It was on the second floor, which was open on one side to the bike-building shop below. Wasting no time, Christian snagged the seat beside Emily. A second later, his arm went around her chair, and his fingers began twirling the ends of her hair.

Boom! Pow! That was the sound of all her bright, sparkly feelings, her...*love* exploding all over the place. Christian turned to gift her with a smile that was so sweet it made her heart ache. When she sucked in a startled breath, his sweet smile turned positively wicked.

He was playing her as easily as a musical instrument. And worse, she was *letting* him.

Her narrowed eyes told him to go do something with himself that usually required a party of two.

He leaned over to whisper, "I'm not really into that,

darling. If I were, I'd have saved myself loads of trouble in life. Still, if you fancy volunteering—"

She was about to cut him off—just the thought of what he was suggesting had goose bumps peppering her skin—but Boss beat her to it.

"So, let's do this, shall we?" Boss spun a Ka-Bar knife atop the table. He was a blade man, so the weapon was never far from him. Emily had wondered more than a time or two if he took it to bed with him and then tried to imagine how Becky might feel about that.

Since no one had answered her initial question, she tried again. "Do what exactly? What's with the impromptu meeting?"

"Samantha"—Boss tilted his head toward the brunette to Emily's left—"this is your show."

Samantha nodded and folded her hands atop the conference table. Her eager posture, paired with the oddly timed meeting, piqued Emily's interest. "So I heard back from my contact in London," she said. "He says it took some doing, but he found out that Christian's name was given to the director of current affairs at the BBC, a woman named Layla Sharp."

Emily stilled. Could it be? Was this the lead they'd been waiting for? Her heart rabbited out and started hopping around inside her chest.

She looked around the conference table. "Shouldn't we call in the rest of the team? Everyone will want to hear this."

"We'll brief them in the morning," Boss said. "I don't want to wait one more second to figure out who Spider is."

"Okeydokey then." Emily nodded, turning back to Samantha. "Proceed."

Samantha's eyes were bright with intrigue. As an investigative reporter, she got super excited when she smelled a juicy story. "Supposedly, this source told Layla that he knew Roper Morrison's bodyguard, Steven Surry. According to this source, before Surry died, he'd called to say that besides the agent who'd been sent in to bring Morrison down, he'd recognized another guy, Christian Watson, a fellow former SAS officer."

"Told you Surry was to blame," Rusty said, crossing his big arms over his even bigger chest and leaning back in his chair. His auburn hair was in need of a cut. It curled around his ears and fell over his brow, enhancing his already ridiculous good looks.

"Yes"—Ace nodded—"you were right. Further proof that you're not just a dumb jock, huh?" When Rusty shot him a scathing look, Ace added, "What? Am I annoying you?"

"Only when you're breathing."

The two of them had been trading verbal punches for a month. But it was obvious to everyone at BKI that, despite their outward animosity, they were actually crazy about each other. Trouble was, neither was willing to admit it because neither was willing to bend on his position. Rusty was determined to remain in the closet. Ace was determined never to get involved with anyone who wasn't out. So, just like Emily and Christian had done, Ace and Rusty limited their flirting to flaying each other alive with their tongues any chance they got.

Emily very much wanted to shout at them to work their shit out. Because anyone with eyes in their head could see they were perfect for each other. But considering how all the Black Knights kept trying to convince her to give in to

Christian, and considering she didn't want to be labeled a hypocrite, she decided to keep her mouth shut.

"And let me guess… This Layla broad went to the SAS to try to confirm Surry's claim," Christian said, dragging Emily's mind back to the conversation. And to the fact that his hand was now wrapped around her shoulder, all heavy and warm and reminding her of what it felt like when it was on her breast and—

Ugh!

"According to my contact, that's right." Samantha dipped her chin. "And she must be cozy or sucking the dick of someone there at the SAS"—good ol' Samantha, never one to couch her words—"because she not only confirmed that you were, in fact, former SAS, but that you might have been the soldier involved in the Kirkuk Police Station Incident. Once she found that out, she put a dozen of her finest reporters on your trail."

"And from there they discovered I had an uncle and that my uncle had a house in Port Isaac." The muscle beneath Christian's eye was freaking out.

"That's the long and short of it." Samantha nodded.

Ace blew out a disbelieving breath. "It happened just the way we thought."

"Guess that means we've been in this business too long," Boss said, "when nothing surprises us anymore."

There was a chorus of grumbled agreement around the table.

"Now"—Boss went on, still spinning the blade. It caught the glow of the fluorescent lights overhead and sparkled menacingly—"for the question we've all been waiting for. Who the fuck gave this fucking BBC bird Christian's name?"

Ah, Boss, Emily thought. *A man after my own heart.* He might be the only member of BKI with a dirtier mouth than hers.

Ozzie, who had remained silent up to that point, typed something on the laptop sitting in front of him and then spun the machine around until they could all see the screen. "Let me introduce you to Lord Asad Grafton."

Emily blinked at the photo of the man on the screen. "He doesn't really fit the mold of most English lords."

"From what I can find out, Grafton was the product of a brief dalliance between the prior Lord Grafton and an affluent African princess. He took over his father's business after his father's passing, as well as his father's title and seat in the House of Lords."

Emily took a closer look at the photo. "He has merciless eyes." Glancing around the table, she said, "Is this him? Have we finally identified him?"

The faces staring back at her were tight with emotion. The excitement in the air was palpable.

"I think so." Ozzie nodded, his crazy hair doing a dance atop his head. He was wearing a gray T-shirt that read: Everything I Know I Learned from *Star Trek*. "But the limited amount of digging I've done on him in the last hour hasn't revealed any ties between Grafton and the black-market businesses we know Spider is involved in. Although, there is this…"

Ozzie did some hocus-pocus on the keyboard. For a brief moment, the screen went blank, then a video began playing. It showed Asad Grafton speaking at a podium outside the Palace of Westminster. He was going on about tax reform and bringing production back to Britain.

His highbrow English accent struck Emily. Given the dregs of society that Spider employed and the bottom-feeding nature of his businesses, she'd always assumed the man would look and sound like a thug.

After the video finished playing, the screen froze on a shot of Asad turning from the podium. Across the table, Angel made a noise. Considering the guy was usually as quiet as a church mouse, it caught Emily's attention. For the first time since she'd met him, she saw emotion on his face. *Intense* emotion.

"What?" She turned back to the screen, trying to see what he was seeing. "What am I missing?"

"Sonya Butler," he said in that raspy voice.

"Who?" Emily squinted at the laptop image and the blond woman taking Asad's arm.

"You know Sonya?" Ozzie lifted a brow.

"I worked with her on a case when I was Mossad, before I—" Angel cut himself off. "Yes. I know her."

Ozzie and Samantha both leaned forward eagerly. Boss stopped spinning his knife. Becky had been in the middle of unwrapping a Dum Dum lollipop but stopped. And both Rusty and Ace grew very still. As for Christian? Well, his hand tightened on Emily's shoulder, not helping her pounding heart one little bit.

"So you know she used to work for Interpol?" Ozzie said.

"Used to?" Angel lifted a dark eyebrow, his hell-black eyes fierce.

"She was suspected of aiding and abetting an international fugitive," Ozzie said. "She would have been prosecuted, but her superiors couldn't find indisputable evidence against her. They were forced to simply fire her. Two months later, she went to work for Grafton as his personal assistant."

Angel did the damnedest thing. He popped his jaw. A nervous tick. Something none of them had seen him do before, making it all the more telling.

Obviously, there was more to Angel and Sonya's story than simply working together on a case when Angel had been a Mossad agent. Color Emily intrigued. She might even have asked Angel to fill in the blanks, had Christian not distracted her by sweeping her hair over her shoulder and massaging the tension out of her neck.

She would have swatted his hand away, had it not felt so good.

"Is it possible she's undercover?" Samantha asked.

"No such thing." Angel's raspy voice had gone completely guttural.

"Huh?" Samantha frowned at him.

"Interpol is *not* what the movies show. It is not U.N.C.L.E. It does not have power or jurisdiction over local police agencies. It does not track down or capture suspects. Nor does it send agents undercover for anything."

"It doesn't?" Samantha asked.

"Interpol simply acts as a liaison between police forces," Emily explained. Her time with the CIA had taught her a thing or two about international agencies. "It maintains databases on criminals and facilitates communications between law enforcement from different countries. That's it."

"Huh." Samantha blinked. "Who'd a thunk it?" She shook her head. "But, still, maybe this once they've stepped outside their box and sent this Sonya chick in to—"

Ozzie cut her off. "I considered that, so I made a call to a buddy who works for Interpol. He couldn't find anything to suggest Sonya was undercover for Interpol or anyone else. In fact, he said it's well known within Interpol that she went rogue, turned dirty."

Angel's nostrils flared. Emily wouldn't have thought it possible, but his expression turned even fiercer.

"And we all know how Spider likes to gather disgraced agents and soldiers to his side," Boss rumbled, going back to spinning his knife.

"That we do," Ozzie agreed. "So now the question is, how do we prove that Grafton is Spider?"

"We keep digging," Samantha said. "We follow every lead until we find a connection."

"That could take months," Ace muttered. "Or years. Which we don't have because our funding runs out in December."

Before President Thompson had left office, he and General Pete Fuller, the Head of the Joint Chiefs, had set up an account that continued to pay BKI's salary for one year. They'd done so hoping the Black Knights could identify Spider and gather the evidence needed to bring him and his entire empire down during that time.

"We need to get someone on the inside of Spider's organization." Angel spoke the words quietly, which made them all the more powerful. "I volunteer."

For a while, silence enveloped the conference area. It was eventually broken when Peanut hopped onto one of the chairs before leaping onto the table. The rotund tomcat stalked to the center of the gathered group, flopped down, lifted a leg, and began thoroughly cleaning his balls.

"Becky, your cat has atrocious manners." Christian's accent tickled Emily's ears and made the last word sound more like *mannahs*.

Becky snorted. "Like you wouldn't spend half the day licking your own balls if you could reach them."

Because his arm was still around her, Emily felt Christian's chuckle before she heard it. It rumbled through him and warmed her heart in ways it shouldn't, considering she was trying with all her might to ignore the fact that she was, for the time being anyway, head over heels for him.

"It'll be dangerous," Boss said, getting them all back on track. "Especially if Sonya recognizes you."

Angel leaned back in his chair. "She knew me before I was Angel. Before I looked like this." He flicked a finger toward his gorgeous face. "She will not recognize me."

Boss nodded, then dragged in a deep breath. "It's definitely something to consider then." He slapped the table, indicating the meeting had come to an end. "But I don't want to make any decisions until the whole team has had a chance to weigh in on all the pros and cons. Let's reconvene at the regular time tomorrow morning."

Emily could tell Angel wanted to press his case. But he was smart enough to know that Boss had made a decision, and that once that happened, the man was implacable.

Ozzie and Samantha were the first to rise from the table and disappear upstairs. Rusty and Ace followed, sniping at each other the entire way. Angel, never one to be part of the crowd, headed downstairs. And Becky stood with Boss, pulling a root-beer-flavored Dum Dum from her pocket. "Here, Frank." She passed the treat to her husband. She was the only one of them who dared call Boss by his first name. "Eat this. It'll make you feel better."

"I had something else in mind." Boss snaked a hugely muscular arm around Becky's waist and pulled her forward for a kiss.

Becky giggled, burying her hands in Boss's hair.

"Get a room!" Emily yelled at them. Considering all the times she'd had to holler that very phrase at one BKI couple or another, she considered getting it stamped on her forehead.

"Good idea." Boss grabbed Becky's hand and led her down the stairs, presumably headed outside to the foreman's cottage they called home.

Emily regretted telling Boss and Becky to skedaddle when she realized that meant she and Christian were alone. Suddenly, all she could see was him smiling that smile at her. All she could feel was his warmth pressed along her side. All she could smell was his earthy-sweet cologne.

Gah! Why did he have to be so stinking tempting? So stinking sexy? So stinking…everything wonderful?

Bottom line, the man was the stuff of romance novels. Too bad she wasn't cut from the same cloth. Happily ever afters didn't really exist in the Scott family.

"Come with me." He grabbed her hand and pulled her to a stand.

"What?" She frowned at him. "Where?"

"Downstairs. I want you to make me an old-fashioned and then come sit with me outside. It's a gorgeous night."

Emily glanced through the huge, two-story leaded-glass windows and saw that it did, indeed, look lovely outside. All that remained of the day was a soft pink smudge against the western horizon. To the east, the city lights were twinkling to life.

Everything in her wanted to take him up on his offer, which is why she said, "I've got work to do. Besides, my old-fashioneds aren't that good."

"Come on," he cajoled, giving her hand a tug. "Everyone else has buggered off for the day. You can too. And you know you make the best old-fashioneds north of the Mason-Dixon Line. Don't hide your light under a bushel."

When she searched his eyes, they said all kinds of things she couldn't pin down. But the one thing she *could* read clearly was: *This is nonnegotiable.* Boss wasn't the only one who could be implacable once he'd made a decision.

"Fine. One drink. But then I *have* to get some work done. And wipe that self-satisfied look off your face"—she pointed at his grinning mouth; his *tempting* mouth—"or I might just change my mind."

Chapter 25

CHRISTIAN BREATHED DEEPLY OF THE SPRINGTIME AIR. IT was the city, so the smells of concrete, the Chicago River, and car exhaust were there. But it was overwhelmed by the scents of budding trees, flowering window boxes, and Emily. Her exotic shampoo caught on the breeze and drifted toward him.

He smiled from the Adirondack chair he'd pulled next to her chaise longue. The courtyard behind the big, brick warehouse was covered in gray flagstones, pocked by various outbuildings, and surrounded by a ten-foot-high brick wall. But he could still see the city gleaming on the other side of the river as day turned into night.

Strange that for the first time in his life, and in a place thousands of miles from where he'd been born, he'd finally found somewhere that felt like home. Or rather some*one* who felt like home. And it was time to get her to admit that he wasn't alone in those feelings. He'd spent a month laying the groundwork. Now, he would begin constructing the future, the *forever* he knew was ready and waiting for both of them.

As soon as she admits she loves me, he thought, taking a slow drink of his old-fashioned and letting the whiskey imbue him with liquid courage. She swore she would only say the words to the man she would spend the rest of her life with. He intended for that man to be him.

"So let's revisit the friends-with-benefits subject," he said, pulling a cherry from his drink and popping it into his mouth. The taste was sweet. But it was nothing compared to Emily's candied kisses.

Oh, how he *missed* her kisses.

"Why?" She turned to him. The lights attached to the perimeter wall cast her face in a soft, golden glow. "Like I said last night, given the way you feel about me, it wouldn't be right."

"That might be true except for the fact that *you* feel the same way about *me*."

She sucked in a startled breath, and his heart raced. This was his moment. It was do or die.

"Do you deny it?" he asked, casually swirling the ice in his drink, which was a feat since the last thing he felt was casual.

For a long time, she simply looked at him. Then she swallowed and glanced away. "So what if I do? That doesn't change anything."

Now his heart wasn't racing; it was thumping at light speed. *So close*. He was so bloody close. "How can you say that?"

She swung back to him, anguish contorting her pretty face. "Because even if I feel that way about you *now*, there's no guarantee I'll feel that way about you two months from now or two years from now or two decades from now. I'm a bad bet. Don't you see?" A lone tear trekked down her silky cheek, past that beauty mark that would forever drive him mad. She angrily wiped the droplet away. "And if and when things fall apart between us, where will that leave me? You've been with the Black Knights a lot longer than I have, so which one of us will they choose? *You*, not me. And then I won't just lose my job, I'll lose the people I've come to think of as family."

A second tear leaked from the corner of her eye, and in that moment, his heart bled for her. He considered letting the conversation lie and walking back into the shop. But no. That would be allowing her fear to win against them both.

She might not be able to stand up to it, but he sure as shit could.

"You know as well as I do, Emily," he said, setting his glass aside and pushing up from the Adirondack chair to sit on the end of her chaise longue, "that in life there are no guarantees."

"Exactly." She nodded emphatically. "So why risk it?"

"Because the reward outweighs the risk." He grabbed her drink and set it on the Adirondack's armrest beside his. Then he took her hands and found her fingers cold and shaking. *Poor chit. She really is terrified.* Which meant he needed to be strong, have enough courage for the both of them. Time to swallow his pride and lay it all on the line. "Because we've a chance at the real deal here, the golden ring, a long and happy life together filled with great love and epic sex and—"

"Bickering and squabbles," she interrupted.

"Precisely." A smile tugged at his lips. "Nothing will ever be easy between us. We're both obstinate. We're both bossy. We're both used to having our way, so it'll be a challenge. We will *challenge* each other, Emily. And it will be tough at times. But nothing worth having ever comes easily."

Her chin trembled as she searched his eyes. "But

what if I'm like my parents and grandparents? What if I don't have it in me to stick?"

"You're not like them," he told her emphatically.

"How can you be sure?"

"Because you've spent your whole life holding the words *I love you* dear. If you were anything like your parents or grandparents, those words would have fallen from your lips as easily as *good morning* or *pass the salt*."

She shook her head. He could see she wanted to believe him, but decades of doubt—and a shitty-ass upbringing—were holding her back. "But what about Richard Neely? If I couldn't make it last with him, what makes you so sure I can make it last with you?"

The name alone was enough to make Christian grit his teeth. And it wasn't that Emily had cared for the wanker; it was that Neely had been a stupid, dictatorial prat who'd made Christian's plight harder.

"Because Neely wasn't the man for you. He tried to smother you. But I've no need to control you, Emily." He couldn't help his devilish smirk. "At least not anywhere besides the bedroom. I *fancy* your independence, your grit and courage and fire."

"But will you still like it ten years from now?" She gripped his hands hard, searching his eyes. "What if you're right? What if I let myself do this with you, and then *you* change *your* mind and stop loving *me*?"

"Won't happen." He shook his head. "I'm the forever type of bloke. What's mine stays mine. You need to understand that. The only way out of this for me is a body bag, hopefully sixty-some years from now."

The skin of her face and neck was mottled red. He wanted to follow the tracks of her tears with his lips, kiss away her hurt, show her with his mouth how much he loved her and how he never intended to let her go. But first she had to say the words.

"Emily…" He got down on one knee, still keeping her trembling hands locked inside his. "Love is about choosing a partner and then having their back. Always. Through everything. Even when you don't agree with them. Even when you can't find your love for them, no matter how hard you search. Love is about saying the words, making a pledge, and then sticking to it. I know if you tell me you love me, you'll work your whole life making sure it's true. And I kneel here and pledge to you that I will be by your side for the rest of *my* life, if you'll have me. That it will be the two of us against the world. That I will protect your heart more ferociously than I protect my own."

Suddenly, she wasn't only crying, she was sobbing. Emily did nothing by half measure. One of the million things he loved about her.

"Come here." He sat on the chair and pulled her into his lap, not caring that her tears soaked his shirt when she pressed her face into his neck, not caring that the arms she threw around his neck threatened to cut off his air.

Gently, he rocked her, letting all he'd said, all she'd come to realize, set in. For long moments, he held her close, planting kisses against her crown, rubbing her slender back. Then, when she'd quieted, he pulled back and pinned her with a hard stare.

"Now"—he made sure his voice gave no quarter— "say the words."

—◦◦◦—

Emily swallowed and opened her mouth. *Don't do it!* her brain screamed. But her heart and her vocal cords didn't listen, and a second later, the three simplest, biggest, scariest words of the English language—of *any* language—tumbled from her trembling lips.

"I love you."

Christian shuddered and blew out a wobbly breath as if her words had physical weight behind them. And maybe they did. Because suddenly she felt as light as air. As if by giving them to him, she'd unburdened herself of their gravity.

"I love you," she said it again just because she could, and because it felt so *damn good*! She framed his dear, beloved face in her hands and pressed a kiss to the dimple in his chin.

His hands gripped her shoulders, and his searching eyes pleaded, *Say it again.*

I love you, she swore with her gaze.

"Aloud," he demanded.

"I love you."

His arms came around her and crushed her to him. Burying his face in her neck, he rasped, "Again."

His breath was hot against her skin, his beard stubble tickling her. She giggled—yes, *giggled*; he'd definitely turned her into a giggler—and whispered, "I love you."

No sooner had the last word formed in her mouth than he claimed her lips in a kiss that burned away any lingering doubts. By the time he let her up for air— five minutes later? Ten? She'd lost track of time—she was aching with need and shamelessly rubbing herself against him.

"How about you and I go upstairs and start in on

making the first of those two babies you want?" His voice was rough with passion, low with persuasion.

Once again, Emily imagined a little girl with Christian's bright-green eyes and subtle chin dimple. Every freckle, every eyelash of the child's face was sharp in her mind's eye.

In a piss-poor impersonation of him, she said, "Abso-bloody-lutely."

When he scooped her into his arms, heading for the back door, she threw her head back and laughed with joy, with love, with a wonder that left her teary-eyed and dizzy.

Once inside, he set her on her feet. A second later, he had her hand and was pulling her through the shop toward the stairs. Staring at his broad back, she marveled at his strength, his courage in ripping open his chest and exposing his heart to help her be brave enough to do the same.

It hit her then that loving, *really* loving, was not for the weak.

Thank the good Lord and White Sox baseball that I have a strong man by my side!

*Keep reading for a sneak peek of the next
book in the Black Knights Inc. series*

BUILT TO LAST

Grafton Manor
St. Ives, England
Two weeks ago...

"Everyone calls me Angel."

The stranger's voice was raspy and deep. Quiet. But
backed up by a sharp edge of steel.

When he spoke those four simple words, a feeling of
doom slipped through Sonya Butler's veins. She'd just
met him and yet she could sense the menace that surrounded him. It permeated the air in the office until
her lungs burned with each breath. Mr. Tall, Dark,
and *Dangerous*.

Jamin Agassi, a.k.a. Angel, was not a man to mess with.
Which made the fact that he was sitting across from

Lord Grafton, her boss and the undisputed king of the underworld, that much more terrifying.

"Angel, you say?" Grafton steepled his fingers under his goatee-ed chin. His eyes were beady and black. Sonya sometimes thought they looked dead. But right at that moment, they sparked with excitement.

Grafton had something on Angel.

Her feeling of doom increased tenfold.

Sitting forward in his leather chair, Grafton thumbed on the tablet lying atop his desk. He pretended to read the document on the screen even though Sonya knew he'd already memorized every word. Grafton hadn't built and maintained the largest crime syndicate the planet had ever seen by being slow on the uptake. In fact, in the six months she'd been his Girl Friday, she'd come to realize he was quite possibly the most brilliant man she'd ever known.

And definitely the most ruthless.

Case in point...

"But according to my sources"—Grafton eyed Angel—"your real name is Majid Abass." The spark in Grafton's eyes turned positively incandescent. Next would come the part he loved best. The *gotcha*. "Or maybe you're more accustomed to your nickname? Should I call you the Prince of Shadows?"

To contain her gasp, Sonya bit the inside of her cheek. Her eyes raked over the stranger in disbelief. The name Majid Abass hadn't rung any bells. Prince of Shadows set all of them clanging.

No, she thought. *He can't be. No one has seen or heard from the Prince of Shadows since the explosion in Tehran.*

Standing beside Grafton's desk like the good little lackey she was, she closely watched Angel's reaction. Or should she say *non*-reaction? He was so still he could have been a picture, betraying nothing of what he was thinking, what he was feeling.

"Everyone calls me Angel." His tone was unchanged. His eyes as black as pitch and…not dead-looking. They were simply expressionless.

Grafton laughed at Angel's imitation of a broken record. It was a dry, snapping sound that reminded Sonya of a boots stomping atop brittle bones.

"Come now, Angel," Grafton scolded. "You can drop the ruse. I know all about you."

He swiped through documents on his tablet until he found the one he wanted. Holding the device up, he read in his urbane English accent, "Majid Abass, raised in Tehran. No brothers or sisters. Parents dead. You attended university on scholarship where you studied nuclear engineering. It was there the Iranian government recruited you into their ranks. They wanted your help in their clandestine efforts to build a bomb. *The* bomb." Grafton dropped the tablet. "Does any of this sound familiar?"

For what seemed an eternity, Angel and Grafton had themselves an old-fashioned staring contest. The strain in the air was palpable and it took every ounce of willpower Sonya possessed not to fidget. She linked her hands behind her back, squeezing her fingers together, pushing the tension in her shoulders down into her palms where it could remain hidden.

Five seconds became fifteen.

Fifteen seconds stretched into thirty. Sonya didn't

dare breathe. Or scratch her nose, which, proving the universe was twisted as fuck, suddenly started itching.

To her surprise, Grafton was the first to look away. He glanced at the tablet on his desk and continued to paraphrase the information on the screen. "But instead of helping your motherland become a nuclear power, you fell in with the Israeli Mossad, Iran's sworn enemy."

At mention of Israel's spy organization, Sonya winced. Luckily, neither Grafton nor Angel seemed to notice.

"And during your five years working as a double agent inside Iran," Grafton continued, lifting a finger, "you infected the computers that controlled their centrifuges with the perfidious Stuxnet virus, voiding the viability of their products." Up went a second finger. "You personally assassinated the three Iranian scientists charged with miniaturizing warheads to fit on intercontinental ballistic missiles." A third finger joined the first two. "And you rigged an explosion at a secret missile base in Tehran, killing three dozen Revolutionary Guards and reducing Iran's stockpile of long-range Shebab rockets to a mound of twisted steel and rubble."

Grafton once again steepled his knobby-knuckled fingers under his chin. "But that time your cover was blown. Too many things added up for the Iranians and all of them pointed to you. Now…" Grafton narrowed his eyes. The flames in the fireplace cast dancing shadows across his dark complexion. It was August, but the Cornish coast was cool and damp, and the best way to combat both in the drafty, old manor house was with a constantly crackling fire. "This is the bit where it gets *really* interesting. Somehow, the Mossad was able to spirit you out of Iran. You fled to Europe, where a very talented plastic surgeon took *this* face…" Grafton swiped through documents until he stopped on a photograph. He lifted the tablet and angled it toward Angel. "And turned it into *that* face." He pointed a finger between Angel's hell-black eyes.

Still nothing from Angel. Not a twitch of his lips. Not a flick of his eyelashes. The stranger who had appeared at Grafton Manor like a puff of dark smoke, all intangible and foreboding, was either very, *very* good, or he wasn't who Grafton thought he was.

Sonya would be shocked if it was the latter. Grafton didn't make mistakes.

At least he didn't make them often. *I mean, he hired me, didn't he?* She was determined to make that the biggest mistake of the rat bastard's life.

When Grafton laid the tablet atop the desk, she glanced at the picture on the screen and nearly swallowed her tongue. She must have betrayed herself with a noise because Grafton glanced at her, brow furrowed.

"What?" He saw the direction of her stare and turned back to the photograph. "Haven't you seen a photo of the Prince of Shadows before? Surely, given your previous job, you would have had occasion to come across one."

"No." She shook her head. "As the nickname suggests, he was always cloaked in darkness."

"Ah. Well then, I'm fortunate to have this one, aren't I? Perhaps I should consider giving Benton that raise he's been on about for the last six months." Grafton smiled when he referred to the young computer hacker he kept in his employ.

Sonya barely heard him. She was too engrossed in studying the picture on the tablet.

Grafton looked from her to the tablet and back again. "*Do* you recognize him?"

"No." She shook her head.

The subtle quirk of Grafton's right eyebrow said he wasn't satisfied with that monosyllabic explanation.

Taking a deep breath, she tried not to choke on the smell of Grafton's woodsy cologne, which, by the way, seemed to linger in every damned room in the manor *including* her own. *Gag.* She swallowed her gorge and said, "The man in the photo looks like someone I knew a long time ago."

"Really?" Grafton seemed intrigued. That would never do.

"Someone who died," she clarified.

Someone with the same slashing eyebrows and serious brow, she mused. *Someone I loved.*

Although, the man pictured had a smaller nose and a more prominent jawline. Still...there were enough similarities to have her mind swirling with a hundred beautiful memories, and her heart aching with a loss that even after ten years remained razor-sharp.

"Ah, Sonya..." Grafton's smile turned faintly sardonic. "You are unlucky in love, are you not?"

She blinked, realizing some of what she was feeling was written across her face. Carefully schooling her features, she shrugged a shoulder and resisted the urge to punch Grafton straight in his smug, aristocratic, bitch-ass nose. It was a daily battle.

He chuckled, knowing how much she disliked him and taking great delight in the power he had over her, in the fact that she could say nothing to wipe the smile from his face. If she squeezed her hands any tighter behind her back, her nails would break the skin.

After holding her gaze for a few seconds—both daring her to speak and simultaneously impressing upon her which one of them was in charge—he turned back to Angel.

She breathed a sigh of relief.

She had known Grafton was a bad man before being pressed into his service. But now? Well, now she knew he wasn't just a bad man, he was the *worst* of men. She'd come to wonder if the devil himself had gotten tired of competing with Grafton in hell and had decided to dump the asshole on earth. Which was to say that to be the object of Grafton's intense stare was to look upon the face of true evil. It always left her feeling a little corrupted. As if some of his depravity had wiggled in through her eye sockets and laid poisonous eggs inside her brain.

Grafton tapped the photo, glancing at Angel. "Compliments to your plastic surgeon. Not that you weren't an attractive man to begin with, but…" He let the sentence dangle, waiting for Angel to say something. Anything.

The only thing Angel allowed was the lifting of one dark eyebrow.

Sonya took the opportunity to study his face. Grafton was right. If, indeed, Angel *was* the man in the picture, then his plastic surgeon had been having a *very* good day when he or she carved Angel's new mug.

High cheekbones, broad forehead, solid slab of a jaw. His profile begged to be minted on coins.

In fact, Angel was so gorgeous that Sonya's ovaries rejoiced. But when he turned his unblinking stare on her for the briefest of seconds, it threatened to shrink her uterus and throw her into early menopause.

Again, she was struck by the undeniable certainty that the man sitting across from Grafton was *not* someone to screw around with. Even though Grafton's home library was immense, filled with two-story bookshelves packed with first editions and Sotheby's quality antique furniture, Angel's presence seemed to dwarf the space.

Could he be the Prince of Shadows? The man revered by Western intelligence agencies for single-handedly keeping the Iranians from becoming an atomic power? Not to mention very likely saving the world from nuclear war?

Grafton sighed, an indication he'd become frustrated with Angel's reticence. As he swiped through the documents on his tablet again, Sonya knew he was poised to let loose with his coup de grâce. Hadn't it happened the same way with *her* when he'd summoned her to a meeting at his house in St. Ives?

"Very well," he said. "I guess we'll do this the hard way. How very cliché." His lip curled with distaste, but Sonya knew he was loving every minute of this dangerous dance. Bringing people of quality, people of caliber, to their knees played to his ego and his continual search for power. Ever more power.

Sliding his tablet across his desk, Grafton turned the device around so Angel could see the single line of numbers glowing at the top of the screen.

"Am I supposed to know what that means?" Angel asked in his wrecked voice. The way he spoke was odd. Precise. If he was Iranian, it was impossible to tell. His accent and syntax gave nothing away.

"That is the number to the head of the Revolutionary Guards." Grafton once again donned his sardonic smile. "I'm told they have ways of making men talk. Maybe *they* can get you to confess your true identity."

Angel's impenetrable mask slipped ever so slightly. A muscle in his jaw twitched; hatred blazed to life in his eyes. "Who are you?" His tone was so low, so menacing, it sounded to Sonya like a warning of swift and painful death.

No. Not a warning. A *promise*.

She rethought his earlier title and renamed him Mr. Tall, Dark, and *Deadly*.

"You know who I am. I'm Lord Asad Grafton, Vice Chairman of the Conservative Party and controlling owner of Land Stakes Corporation."

"No. Who are you *really*?"

Sonya was tempted to yell, *Spider! He's the infamous Spider! Run! Run away before he catches you in his sticky web!*

Grafton's smile turned positively venomous. "I'm the man who holds your life in his hands."

For a few ticks of the clock, the stranger who insisted on being called Angel refused to speak. When he finally did, his gruff voice had gone guttural. "What do you want from me?"

"Ah." Grafton sat back, looking altogether pleased with himself. "That's easy. I want you to help me procure the fissile materials needed to build a nuclear weapon."

Sonya's jaw unhinged so quickly she was surprised it didn't hit the ground at her feet.

Chapter 1

Grafton Manor
Present day...

"YOU WERE BORN WITH A DAGGER IN YOUR MOUTH AND A *warrior's heart beating in your chest."*

Those were the words the ramsad—the head of the Mossad—had said to Angel the night he asked him to fake his own death and take over the identity of an Iranian university student. The night he had asked Angel to choose between the woman he loved and the stability of the world at large. The night he had explained to Angel that the mission to Iran would likely end with Angel dead or, if Angel *did* somehow survive, chances were good Angel would never see his homeland's glistening, sundrenched shores again.

Looking out over the expansive back lawn of Grafton's home, ignoring the array of hulking guards Grafton had tasked with making sure he hadn't left the premises since that initial, fateful meeting, Angel settled more snugly into the lush cushions of the deck chair. He took comfort in knowing friendly eyes were on him.

To show those friendly eyes that he was A-okay, he lifted his face toward the weak English sun and studiously turned his thoughts away from the present. Letting them drift back to a happier time. To a time when he wasn't Jamin "Angel" Agassi or Majid Abass, the Prince of Shadows. To a time when he was simply Mark Risa, the name his parents had given him at birth, a wet-behind-the-ears Mossad agent out to make his mark on the world and the spy community by hunting down a Palestinian terrorist responsible for bombing a synagogue in Jerusalem. To a time when an equally wet-behind-the-ears Interpol agent was assigned to help him…

"Excuse me. Are you Mark Risa?"

The voice that met his ears spoke delightfully accented Hebrew and was as smooth and as cultured as the chocolates they sold at Max Brenner back home. He turned his attention from the middle-aged woman walking her dog past the Café Constant on Rue Saint-Dominique and the man with the pencil-thin mustache who watched her from beneath hooded eyes, and looked up at the young woman standing beside his outdoor table. The sun was behind her, haloing her head. Even before he noticed her wide blue eyes, her strawberries-and-cream complexion, and her mischievous half smile, one word flitted through his brain.

Pixie.

Then she moved out of the sun, taking the seat across from him after a polite "May I?" and he realized she was anything but ethereal and spritely. She was a flesh-and-blood woman. Woman as in whoa-man! One good look at her had his libido sitting up and panting like a hungry dog in the summer heat.

Down boy, *he silently admonished, even as she extended her hand to shake.*

"I'm Sonya Butler." The only indication she felt

*the same spine-tingling jolt of attraction that sizzled
through him the instant their fingers touched was the
slight flush that pinkened her cheeks.*

*Glancing at their hands, he noted two things. One,
compared to his oversized man paw, her hand looked
ridiculously delicate. And two, she wore hot-pink fingernail polish.*

Hot-pink fingernail polish? What kind of Interpol
agent does *that*?

Sonya Butler, apparently.

*He decided to like her in that instant. She wasn't
trying to prove how tough she was or how serious she
was. Those hot-pink fingernails said,* I can be young and
vibrant and sexy as hell and *still* catch the bad guys.
Screw you if you don't believe me.

*"Should we go somewhere to talk?" When she glanced
around the busy cafe and the bustling Parisian sidewalk,
he took the opportunity to study her graceful profile and
the cascade of her honey-blond hair. She was, in a word,
stunning. Not beautiful, per se. Her cheeks were a little
too full, her nose a little too thin. But the twin sparks of
intelligence and humor in her eyes, not to mention her
lush mouth, were enough to stop a man in his tracks.*

*Turning back to him, she frowned and asked, still in
Hebrew, "You* are *Mark Risa, yes?"*

*He realized he hadn't said a single word since she'd
arrived.* Hell.

*"Sorry." He shook his head, trying to jangle his way-
ward thoughts into some sort of order. "Yes. I'm Mark
Risa. It's a pleasure to meet you, Sonya."*

*The half smile returned and he felt it like a punch in
the gut.*

How unfortunate.

This was his chance to make the ramsad proud, to prove the man hadn't been wrong to recruit him straight out of the army and train him up to be one of the world's most elite spies. He needed to focus on the mission, not the delicate line of Sonya's neck or the too-fast pulse that beat next to the collar of her creamy blouse.

"We have a few things to talk about." She tapped the file folder under her arm, her blue eyes dilated as if she could read his thoughts.

God, please don't let her be able to read my thoughts.

"Right." He shoved up from the chair and motioned for her to follow him to an alley that arrowed around the side of the building. A set of exterior stairs showed the way to a second floor flat—one of the many safe houses or havens the Mossad kept around the world. He took the lead on the steps, not trusting himself with a view of her ass in those tight-fitting black trousers.

"You have a lovely accent." He fumbled with the lock. Her presence behind him on the narrow landing, not to the mention the smell of her, all fresh and sweet like freesia and apricot blossoms, hit the ignition switch on his lust and now his engine was really revving. "Where did you learn Hebrew?"

"My father was a diplomat in Jerusalem for two years. And languages have always sort of come easy to me. Which, as you can imagine, made the jump from diplomat's kid to working for Interpol a no-brainer."

"How many languages do you speak?" He dragged in a startled breath to find her close behind him when he glanced over his shoulder to pose the question. Close enough to touch if he wanted to.

Oh, I want to!

He didn't believe in love at first sight. But he'd proven lust *at first sight was a scientific certainty. Or at least a* biological *certainty.*

"Six," she said.

"Pardon?"

"Six languages." Again, that knowing look entered her blue eyes. No. Not blue. Up close he could see they were actually some color between blue and gray. A soft, gentle hue that contrasted starkly with those hot-pink fingernails.

"Six, huh?" He shook his head, silently laughing at himself for being such a cliché, for being the guy who couldn't hold a thought in his head for more than a second when an attractive woman waltzed into his sphere. If my ramsad could see me now, he'd shake his head in shame... *"That's two more than I do."*

"You speak four languages?" She canted her head. "Parlez-vous Français?"

"No. No French. Only Hebrew, Arabic, English, and a little Yiddish."

"Hot diggity damn. Three out of four in common ain't bad." She'd switched to English and the slang made him smile. "No chance we'll suffer a failure to communicate."

He spoke in English as well. "Don't tell me you speak Yiddish."

She laughed. It was a low, husky sound that had goose bumps rippling over his skin. "No. Arabic."

Just when he thought it was impossible for her to intrigue him more...

"I lived in Jordan for three years while my father did a stint at the embassy in Amman." Pushing past

him when he finally *managed to unlock the door, her ass—that ass he had earnestly avoided—brushed ever-so-slightly past his happy place.*

He barely stifled a groan.

This is *so* unfortunate, *he thought again, briefly closing his eyes, trying to get his one-track mind on the mission and* off *the woman as he followed her into the sparsely furnished flat.*

Sonya didn't hesitate to make herself at home—he liked that about her too. She pulled out a chair at the tiny bistro table fitted into the corner of the kitchen. The window was open, and the smell of the fresh herbs that grew in a window box next door drifted around them.

Opening the file folder, Sonya slid the top sheet of paper toward him. "Do you prefer English, Hebrew, or Arabic?" She was still speaking English.

"Dealer's choice."

"English it is." She smiled, looking right into his eyes, not trying to hide the spark of interest shining in hers. "Your English accent is a total smexymelt."

"Pardon?"

She laughed. "Smutty and sexy and makes me want to melt."

Acknowledgments

Writing a book is a labor of love. Meaning I labor, and those I love tend to have to fend for themselves while I'm at it. So I have to give a shout-out, as ever, to my husband for having the patience of Job, to my parents and sisters and nieces and nephews for supporting me and understanding when I can't make it to family functions because I have a deadline looming, and to my friends for not taking offense when I say no to dinner dates and get-togethers because I'm off doing publicity. You're all the foundation of my life, and I couldn't do any of this without any of you.

Thanks to all the folks at Sourcebooks—Deb, Beth, Dawn, Rachel, Valerie, Todd, Dominique, and the dozens of others who had a hand in making this book shine and getting it onto the shelves and onto fans' e-readers. Thanks to my agent, Nic, who loves this series as much as I do and is always thinking of ways to make it better and to reach a wider audience. Teamwork makes the dream work! *wink*

And last but certainly not least, hugs to all the fans who keep going on these crazy journeys with me and the Black Knights. Because of you, I get to have the best job in the world.

About the Author

Julie Ann Walker is the *New York Times* and *USA Today* bestselling author of award-winning romantic suspense. A winner of the Book Buyers Best Award, Julie has been nominated for the National Readers' Choice Award, the Australian Romance Reader Awards, and the Romance Writers of America's prestigious RITA award. Her books have been described as "alpha, edgy, and downright hot."

Most days you can find Julie on her bicycle along the lakeshore in Chicago or blasting away at her keyboard, trying to wrangle her capricious imagination into submission.

To stay apprised of Julie's upcoming releases, sign up for her newsletter at julieannwalker.com.

Also by Julie Ann Walker

Black Knights Inc.

Hell on Wheels

In Rides Trouble

Rev It Up

Thrill Ride

Born Wild

Hell for Leather

Full Throttle

Too Hard to Handle

Wild Ride

Fuel for Fire

Hot Pursuit

The Deep Six

Hell or High Water

Devil and the Deep